REDEMPTION
BOOK 1

"I have swept away your offenses like a cloud, your sins like the morning mist. Return to me, for I have redeemed you."
Isaiah 44:22

A Novel By

RONAN JAMES CASSIDY

authorHOUSE®

AuthorHouse™
1663 Liberty Drive
Bloomington, IN 47403
www.authorhouse.com
Phone: 833-262-8899

Published by AuthorHouse   03/31/2023

ISBN: 979-8-8230-0508-1 (sc)
ISBN: 979-8-8230-0507-4 (e)

Library of Congress Control Number: 2023906066

Print information available on the last page.

Any people depicted in stock imagery provided by Getty Images are models, and such images are being used for illustrative purposes only.
Certain stock imagery © Getty Images.

This book is printed on acid-free paper.

CONTENTS

TO: MY GIRLS

"I put these words down to give permanence to our time here, which must and will come to pass. But know that our love is eternally bound and preciously held by the Lord. My greatest hope is that you will find my love in your heart always and that it will be a beacon to guide you home on your darkest days."

TO: MY EDITOR

"Without the eternal gifts of your unbound and gracious love, always dedicated and never wavering guidance, and tender and merciful care never bound by expectation; your unending sacrifice and your ever hopeful eye towards the days ahead and the simple pleasures never to be overlooked in this life, none of this would have been possible. Being able to share this project with you has been an adventure I will always remember as I do your heartfelt smile, the warming embraces that always brought sweet sunshine to even the sourest of days and the proud, loving, and delighted look in your eye whenever we parted ways. There are no words to express the feeling in my heart but I hope that there were times enough when it showed all the same. I love you and miss you lots and lots, forever and always. I thank you from the bottom of my bursting heart!"

TO: MY FAMILY AND FRIENDS

"Without the abundance of your love, compassion and guidance no words written here can be made to properly stand for a thought, a dutiful kindness, a belief held safe by the heart or a lasting memory born of kinships shared that shape the very world of our souls and the world moving about us without boundary or limit. I consider myself so very blessed and honored to share in the laughter, the joy, the sorrows and the tender moments of affirmation that make our hearts sing out to the heavens in union. Somewhere hidden deep within lie little kernels which are the essence of the moments we have shared, so marked by time and the shifting of the wind, thick and eternal like the waking moments of a wonderful and coincident dream. My deepest gratitude and my love go out to you all for the pictures hanging on the wall of this life of mine and the thoughts that will always reaffirm that which is possible and indeed worthwhile. May God shine upon you always."

PROLOGUE.

"There are certain truths manifested in earthly love that are etched into the fabric of our lives, our souls, our spirit. They are indelible pieces of art that tell the very story of who we are. A story made permanent and sung throughout the heavens. These truths are indisputable and beautiful and protected in their innocence and sincerity by the glory of God. This world shall never have them but know they do mark the time we all have shared and are a source of eternal light. We carry the truth of God's love with us always."

BOOK I

Angel Ascending

REVELATIONS & GATHERINGS

Chapter 1

RENDEZVOUS

The tavern of the inn was exceptionally dark and filled with the tang of ancient wood and the dying embers of the great stone hearth. The light allowed to enter through the small windows on the top half of the stout front door died out about halfway into the narrow room and was replaced by the quaint incandescence afforded by the few neon emblems hanging from the wall and those behind the stock wooden bar. At the corner of that centuries-old monolith and monument to the hard-drinking sailors, monks, and vagabonds of a bygone era sat a man awaiting a visitor.

For the sake of preserving the identity of one helplessly, though not hopelessly by any means, drawn into a conflict that was set in motion centuries before his time and to promote the moniker of your faithful raconteur, we shall call this man Ronan Cassidy. Mr. Cassidy was not from the area, and he was dressed in a casual and distinctively American fashion. He would have remained fairly unremarkable to the average local denizen of the island, except that his outerwear was designed for a far colder climate than the one he now visited. Moreover, when his facial features entered an area of better light, it was possible to tell that he possessed a softly handsome and welcoming countenance that the inhabitants of far more hospitable climes would have been drawn to upon noticing the foreign and middle-aged gentleman.

Mr. Cassidy sat patiently and upright while he waited. He also sat perched in a manner that would have led the casual observer to believe that, despite his clearly imported attributes, he was quite comfortable where he took his rest. Ronan had already managed to acclimate to his surroundings, and he drew warmth from his seated position within the quaint shelter on the hillside and its formidable hearth. The inn and its tavern stood alone as shelter from the constant battering of the raw, damp, and unrelenting wind that blew in from the western ocean. The stone structure had been in existence in some form or another since the days when the first Christian monks settled across the angry sea on the island of Inis Mor sometime during the fifth century.

Mr. Cassidy was not a person who stood out to someone at first glance, and while that quality had been both a blessing and a curse in his earlier days, the trait was ideal for his current purpose. He also possessed the unique ability to understand the motivations of most people at a deeper level than those same folks consciously understood their own wants, desires, and creature comforts. Due to these intuitive gifts, Mr. Cassidy had cultivated the rare ability to communicate with people on wavelengths far different than those frequencies of the more traditional social norms. His friendships were nearly absolute and forged in the depths of those slippery emotional realms, which ultimately bond us in an eternal manner to those we endeavor to endear. Furthermore, his conviction for those he loved was unmatched, even if that devotion remained silent at times. The net result of these curious verities was that his tribal footprint existed predominantly in the form of seldom-forgotten obscurities, which were more of the spirit realms than those confined by the limitations of the flesh.

The clouded light outside the shrouded inn of ancient stone had begun to wane but would hold for another hour or two, as the canonical spring season of that year had been welcomed in at midnight. Perfectly alone in the gloaming of what still felt like late winter, Ronan was no longer overwrought by the prospect of confronting his antagonist. A meaningful while would come to pass before the innkeeper began to ready dinner for his few guests and the handful of local seamen who might make their way out of the harrowing weather by venturing up the hillside and into the inn. Ronan was glad to have been gifted the time to reflect on how so much had rapidly transpired to reach this anxiously awaited moment of denouement. As nothing was set to occur at the moment, and because he wasn't much of a drinking man, Mr. Cassidy quietly slipped his backside off his barstool and moved over to one of the large weather-beaten leather chairs stationed in front of the limestone hearth. While walking softly across the old stone floor of the room, Ronan saw that the fuel of the fire had been reduced to burning embers and pulsating coals. He stepped forward to add some wood to the hearth and gently stoke the fire for a brief time while he basked in its radiating warmth.

Beyond appreciating the extra time to reconsider the circumstances leading up to the event of his scheduled rendezvous, Ronan was happy to have had time to carefully study and become familiar with the old inn by the sea. He firmly believed that there was always great comfort and certain advantages to be gained from being acutely aware of one's surroundings. After surveying the murky confines of the room from the vantage point of the old stone hearth for just a short while, Mr. Cassidy convulsed briefly from head to toe and proceeded to shake his limbs to the quick as the strengthening fire drove the last of the remaining chills from the marrow of his bones. He then lowered himself to sit, leaving his legs straightened beneath the end of the old wooden forfeit standing at the center of the four large leather sitting chairs. Once he was settled, Mr. Cassidy rested at ease in a reclined position with his hands folded graciously over the lower half of his winter jacket.

Outside, the cold, harsh, and searing eternal winds that Ronan had endured while making his way up from the docks left the hostile terrain beyond the steadfast and bulking stone walls of the inn just as it had been for the past fifty millennia—and perhaps beyond the known bounds of time itself. Barren rock formations jutted forth from the hillside. Timeless boulders and crags had been subtly but relentlessly worn by the incessant and inhospitable volatility of the climate, such that only lichen and other low-lying flora dared inhabit those foreboding environs of the enchanted island. While he was resting, adequately sheltered from the raw and unrelenting breath of the pale *feothan* and the primordial arrangement of the barren land set between him and the savagery of the sea from which he had been delivered, Ronan came to understand something quite clearly. What it was that he came to understand while basking in the warmth of that ancient stone hearth was that the biggest mistake the devil ever made regarding the future sanctity of the soul of Ronan Cassidy was to let him see and feel utter despair without having the capacity to destroy his God-given essence. He also came to understand that only time would tell if it was the devil he now waited on.

Comforted by the gathering warmth of the blushing hearth and worn down by the tattering lashes of the elements during his travels, Ronan drifted off to sleep. His mind crossed over into the realm of dreams, his mantle a vivid remembrance that he could never feel such emptiness again. He dreamt briefly but brilliantly and curiously, as his dream contained signs and symbols that were immeasurably pertinent to his current station. However, this nearly waking dream lacked any measure of designed messaging that seemed to mesh with his current reality, at least not as far as he had come to understand such things. If given more time to reflect upon the nature of that brief and colorful reverie, Ronan might have said that the dream was somehow concocted from the life-changing visions of his fairly recent past—visions that would soon serve to guide him through this most trying hour of his life. An hour that was nearly at hand.

Ronan saw a rider wearing an ancient cross of gold over his open chest where his blouse split at the unfastened buttons along his dickey. The rider was disembarking from a pale horse that was very much on the muscle and possessed piercing Arabian eyes of crystalline blue. The horse and rider had come to rest after a long and tiring journey in a vast open field of tall whisking grass, which ranged slightly downhill until it met with a forest that shaded the line of the horizon off in the distance. At the center of the field was an ancient oak tree that stood solitary yet obdurate some fifty yards to the rider's south. Once the dashed bottoms of his riding boots had met with the yielding turf of the meadow, the rider pulled the saddle and tack off the horse and let it drop into the long grass. The soft sound of the heavy leather gear hitting the ground traveled only as far in the clear calm of the air as the ears of the two old friends, who were the horse and her rider. The rider gave a long look of appreciation to his companion and then bent his knees and reached downward. He opened the small saddlebag and pulled out the last of the crisp green apples from deep within.

The rider gave the apple a quick dusting with the tail of his shirt. Once it was clean, and with the apple raised in his hand, he walked to the front of the pale horse and gazed intently into her eyes. The weary traveler gently rubbed downward along the long, handsome face of the animal, smoothing out the short hairs of her soft snout. He then fed the pale horse the apple, rubbed the soft, pink warmth of her nose, and smiled.

Quietly, he commanded, "Off you go now, girl," and pointed over to the mountains well off in the distance to the southeast. "I will see you there in three days, Whitney."

At first asking, the pale horse reluctantly disembarked and made her way across the field toward the base of the pass. She galloped willfully and freely, but with a great sense of purpose. When the mare had vanished into the ether beyond a rise in the meadow, the rider picked up the saddle and tack from the grass and slowly walked across the field. He was bent and bowed at the knees and hunched over from fatigue. With the last of his steps taken into the shaded light of the endless, stretching vertical branches of the giant oak, the rider took his rest beneath and against the tree, with his back pressed against the lovely giant's smooth but firm bark.

From his seated position, the rider watched the seeded toppings of the grass sway gently with the breeze blowing across the field as far as the tree line to the south, and he thought about all those that had passed through the sunlight of this fine valley throughout his life. He then smiled wide and joyfully as his heart pulsed with the warmth of the heavens. Shortly thereafter, the rider reached into the saddlebag that lay slumped next to him in the tall shaded grass at the base of the tree. He removed his dispatch from the depths of the saddlebag and opened the folds of the parchment slowly, until he saw the words written in deep black ink upon the light-yellow fibers of the worn and dated vellum, which he held in his left hand. He rubbed the shining cross of gold, which was resting around his neck, with his right hand. After a subtle pause to once again take in the full measure of the beauty of the field, he began to make the eternal words written across the open epistle.

The man arrived at the inn some hours later from somewhere out in the black of the night. He stood over Ronan until the change the long shadow of his wanting and seemingly demented presence made in the room awoke Mr. Cassidy from the rather confounding revelations of that final dream. While he was waking beneath the perfectly still yet seemingly restless presence of the strange man, he recalled that he had seen something else of great importance to the riddle of this secret gathering upon arriving. He had been called to the presence of a verse that was carved into a few of the enjoined ancient stones above the hearth. Without such a divine prompting, he never would have noticed the carved inscription, as the stones that kept the verse were veiled behind an ornate banner of uncommon heft that hung from the ceiling. That ancient standard of a sort, which graced the top of the hearth, was nearly draped over the large, gravid looking upper hearthstones from its tacks bolted into the massive wooden support beams that ran the length of the ceiling from the point where the notched post holders at the ends of the planks had been laid to rest into the smoothly carved slats of the primeval stone.

Upon closer inspection, one could discern that the verse was obscured by a British flag that hung from the ceiling in the opacity of a recondite shadow. A shadow that cast itself backward from the low firelight that flickered in the darkness of the sitting area of the room that Ronan and the man who came in from the night now occupied. The meticulously crafted battle standard was two centuries old and hung down from those two large screw hooks on the ceiling, which were positioned about four inches away from the stone wall that ran down to the hearth. That the fine letters etched into the smoothed and blackened stone of the wall above the hearth and the flag shared the identical birth month of July of the twenty-first year of the nineteenth century was by no means coincidental, nor was it the handy work of the fates. The circumstances behind the verse and the flag were a sad and sordid tale. The tale of a young and murderous Irish revolutionary boy who, cursed by chance and afflicted by the sickness of wrath, took to the sea, never to return. His heartbroken mother remained forever waiting for him to come home to her, until she was laid to rest in that same enchanted sea.

When the trailing vapors of Ronan's dream had fully vanished back into the ether from whence they had arrived, his mind began to quicken as he roused from the shallow depths of his sleep. While the dream he had was tied to the visions he had experienced in the past, he presumed that the symbolic hallucination was more a creation of the recent adaptations of his mind than any divinely given sign. Be that as it may, the foggy-witted Mr. Cassidy quickly realized that he had gleaned something of significance from that swiftly departing reverie. Something that tied back to certain scenes from those visions of the past, which he had yet to decipher in their entirety. In some ways, that recently disrupted dream had delivered a sense of certainty to the execution of his premeditated deeds; deeds that were preordained by his faith alone as of that moment, and deeds that remained the unfinished business of the hour at hand.

In other ways, however, the groggy traveler being watched by a darkly-clad stranger standing over him had been infected by the seeds of doubt. Because of that dream, he did not know if he had failed to process some change that had taken hold beyond the heavens. Moreover, he began to wonder if the waking portions of his mind had, as of yet, failed to process some subtle danger that had significantly altered the course of events to come. Perhaps there was even something of grave consequence that he had overlooked. Something that explained the unease that gripped his conscience and that the tremoring constructs of his sublime, or more instinctive, nature were attempting to make abundantly clear. He feared the latter, but moved on from the disquieting thought. The man he had been waiting on for quite some time loomed ominously over him, and the grave appearance of that man was more than enough to plant those seeds of doubt within the thoughts of even the most steadfast among the faithful.

Ronan lifted his head to have a good look at the man. At first glance, he contemplated the unspent hatred that was burning visibly at the outer edges of the man's light-blue eyes in the low light of the fire. Without hesitation, Mr. Cassidy reached into his jacket pocket and pulled out a small picture of his daughter that was taken when she was five and a folded piece of parchment. He studied the picture carefully for a moment and then handed the man standing over him the small, folded piece of paper. Once the man had accepted his offering, Ronan returned the picture of his little "fleur de lis" to his jacket pocket.

The folded page given over to the man was from a notebook in which Ronan saved the totems of special moments spent with or the milestones achieved by his three girls. The notebook had been a gift from one of Ronan's clients from another professional life, an American commercial bank that traced its roots back to the year 1800. The notebook reminded Ronan of the youthful days of his American homeland and the right to life, liberty, and the pursuit of happiness, which he believed must have been so readily flourishing back in those days following the trials of the Revolutionary War. Furthermore, the notebook reminded Ronan of the freedom of spirit, which set fire to the hearts and minds of the settlers of the vast wildernesses of the western world. That same journal also reminded Mr. Cassidy of just how far the country had drifted from the roots of its founding.

The darkly dressed man unfolded the piece of notebook paper and walked a bit closer to the fire to acquire the light needed to see the words written down on the page. When the man was close enough to the source of the low and mellowly burning flames of orange and blue, he read the words before his searching eyes slowly and evenly. The man's facial expression did not change in the slightest as he came to understand the meaning behind those words. The look on the reader's face remained pensive and stern. He did not read the message a second time. When he was finished considering the few words written down expressly for the purview of his favor, he stepped slowly back towards Mr. Cassidy's chair and stood before Ronan in much the same manner he had before the need to acquire additional light had arisen.

When he was away from the hearth and once again nearly hidden by the shadowy darkness at the center of the room, the man folded up the page until it appeared precisely as it did when delivered to him. He then reached into the inside of his black trench coat and placed the folded parcel carefully against the soft lining at the front of his inner pocket. He was not aware that he had accidentally loosed the top button of his shirt with the outer buttons of his coat's sleeve when he made the deposit. Mr. Cassidy remained staring into the depths of the fire and away from the man while he remained unsure of his fate. He was not scared or remorseful about his choice of words, but he had no foretaste of the path upon which he had just endeavored to tread. Ronan Cassidy had just placed the fate of something far dearer than his own life into the hands of God, and the frightful man standing before him was to be the final earthly arbiter of that fate. As such, Mr. Cassidy did little else beyond silently calling to the Lord above to bring him the strength he needed to finish his task while he gazed longingly into the ambient glow of the hearth.

"Thank you, Mr. Cassidy," responded the man to Ronan's gesture while standing next to Ronan's comfortable leather chair.

The man's expression had changed only slightly in that it now revealed absolutely nothing regarding his intentions, as opposed to the sparingly hopeful catch that had existed at the corners of his otherwise flat and steadied lips prior to reading the missive. His tone was deadly even and possessed an accent that Ronan was vaguely familiar with. In fact, the man's inflection caught Ronan by surprise, as the accent did not belong to what little Ronan knew of the man's more recent history and college of matriculation. Furthermore, the given inflection of his voice was not the one Ronan remembered from the disquieting moments of that chilling flight some three years ago. Though the man had said very little, it seemed to Ronan as if he had decided that he was suddenly at ease in his native tongue. Whereas in the past, the man had taken some form of comfort from concealing the genesis and evolution of this native drawl, it was instantly clear to Ronan that he no longer gave such stern consideration to the more trivial aspects of his presented mannerisms. Either that, or he was simply growing more comfortable in his own skin around Mr. Cassidy. Why that might be true at the present moment caused Ronan to shudder mildly.

At hearing the first of the man's spoken words upon the moment the two men had reached the very edge of some trying and decisive precipice together, Ronan could not place the man's current accent more narrowly than that of someone born into the lowlands of the deep coastal south who now possessed the pretenses of pronunciation and slight air of tone common among the well-educated elites of the Washington beltway. Before this moment, the closest that Ronan had been able to place this man's now-former dialect was that of wholly neutral, outside of some very subtle undercurrents most common in the northwestern regions of the Great Lakes. If Ronan had been forced to offer a guess as to the most significant tribal influences on the man's accent back in April of 2017 or back in Rhode Island just a few weeks earlier, he would have said the man's inflection mirrored the denizens of a region heavily influenced by third- and fourth-generation German and Scandinavian-Americans born and raised in one of the coastal towns of Lake Superior.

Upon further, and wholly unwarranted, consideration of the man's shifting articulation, Ronan was certain his former accent certainly traced back to a Midwestern constituency. One that retained a higher degree of influence from the ancestral inflections and intonations that remained noticeably audible to the naked ear when listening to someone speak the current vernacular specific to that region. Suddenly realizing that he was being subdued by this small but surprising detail, Ronan blinked sharply and cleared his head amidst his somewhat manic bout with an inane attention to detail. He then spoke to the man without turning to face him.

"I presume you have what you need, as was agreed," replied Ronan, while staring blankly into the glowing depths of the lower burning embers and spent coals of the fire.

The man did not operate in that fashion of subtly forced renegotiation. Therefore, he reached into his pocket and retrieved the note. He looked down at the piece of paper and unfolded it once more. He then read the brief contents written upon the page right before Ronan's witnessing eyes, although in actuality, the man merely verified that the first few words read just the same as they did a moment earlier, as it was far too dark to make the letters where he stood. The man did this somewhat superstitiously, and only to confirm that some cruel trick was not being played out at his expense. Yet, even beyond his deep respect for the realms of the supernatural, the man had visibly confirmed the contents of the note to emphasize to Ronan that little, if anything at all, had been delivered as agreed upon. This act, in and of itself, was rather peculiar for one such as the man. A man who, above most other grievances, despised removing the clarity or finality of an act by way of even the slightest check to his previously delivered terms or purposefully revealed mannerisms.

The man looked back down at Ronan without hesitation or any sign of emotion. He responded with a deadly calm laced into his tone. "I do believe that I understand your intent, Mr. Cassidy. Yet, perhaps you do not fully understand the certainty of the response that is required by your reply per the terms of our agreement. An agreement entered into amongst honorable friends. Perhaps, upon being reminded of as much, you may suddenly realize that you have erroneously omitted a detail that you would like to include. Perhaps you have come to realize a pertinent fact that would allow you to forsake the experience of such unnecessary suffering."

The man paused only instantaneously for effect, and added, "There is no shame in disavowing your demented consent to such horrors and the indelible stain that will be forever woven into the fabric of your mortal soul in the aftermath. For I tell you now, and I tell you with certainty, Mr. Cassidy, that such a consideration is far more than I have yet offered under the circumstance of a failure to perform."

"I did not think you would come in person," Ronan said sullenly, attempting to deflect the man's first-of-its-kind second offer into the darkened corner at the far side of the room in tandem with the pitch of his voice.

"I thought you would send the courteous gentleman driving the car, or even the deadly serious man from the back of the car. The fact that you have come here of your own accord only serves to confirm that I have delivered the proper message," added Ronan as he turned slightly in his seat and rotated his head to directly face up to his antagonist. He now wished to address the man, and he wished to do so in a more dignified manner.

When his eyes were locked onto those of the man, Ronan continued to deliberate on a topic that was only indirectly related to what was asked of him. "Thinking back on our first meeting, I wanted to let you know that while few forces in this world are as powerful as the desire to exact retribution for the harm done to him and his family through injustice, disparate measure, dishonesty, and malice, no man who has seen the glory of our God, or what He has prepared for each of us, would waste a minute not employed in the endeavors of bringing his brothers and sisters safely in from the cold."

The man sharpened his eyes in the direction of Mr. Cassidy, yet Ronan continued on with his message, undeterred by that patent show of impatience with his antics. "We are all created to serve our part in God's divine plan, and our good deeds multiply by way of the exponential effect those deeds have on the lives of others. An exponential effect that is driven by God's immeasurable glory and splendor."

The man took the bait for a moment, and asked, "How so, Mr. Cassidy? Have you not looked at the state of the world around you recently?"

Ronan closed his eyes and then lowered his head before saying, "Each one of us is designed by God to be a unique piece that fits perfectly into the divine joy of His perfect and infinite creation. Where we lose one among us to the empty places where the light will not shine, we all lose a beautiful piece of ourselves that has died on the vine."

The man turned away from Ronan to gather his thoughts, but his visible eschewal of Mr. Cassidy did not deter Ronan in the slightest. In fact, Ronan began to gather his strength as he directly rebuked the man's threat. "In response to your earlier insinuation, you should know that I speak with certainty as well, good sir. No decent person who truly believes would choose such a dark path and embrace the feelings of total loss that come with obtaining a personal kingdom of any size through acts of injustice committed against their fellow man. If the truth were believed, all would lament their failure to achieve their poverty that much the sooner, their wealth given over to the very ones who robbed them of their pride, dignity, and possessions if they realized that in not doing so, they had only served to delay, for even a minute, their appointed reception into God's intended graces."

The man stood silent. Ronan paused, took a deep but subtle breath, and then continued. "You see, if one is seeking the truth, all one has to do is obtain the proper vantage point to find it. The truth is always and eternally present. And the truth is this: it would take so little faith in our inheritance from God to turn the world completely upside down, that the devil can never rest."

The man turned back to face Mr. Cassidy and asked, "Given the certainty of your predicament, why do you waste such potent words on someone who is no longer able to hear them?"

Ronan closed his eyes so that he would not be distracted by the man's evocative stare, which gleaned its potency from the unshakable resolve applied to his gelid indifference. Mr. Cassidy did not want to forget the rest of what he intended to say before there would be closure on the matter at hand. His voice trembled some as he spoke further. "If just one tiny seed of pure faith were allowed to take root upon fertile soil, we would clearly see that the truly humble and those of a kind and gentle heart, those who fare so poorly to obtain the wealth and prestige that are so esteemed by mankind, have been granted untold riches, which are valued in multiples of the fortunes of the wealthiest who walk this earth today."

The man halted his measured steps taken in the direction of Ronan and questioned him again. "What makes you think that I seek any of these things you have mentioned as belonging solely to my class of men, Mr. Cassidy?"

Ronan was swiftly baffled by the man's query. Nevertheless, he answered him in the best way he could fathom amidst the confusion of his thoughts. "Though it may be true that the losses your family will experience if I were to relent to your demands would in some way serve to bless them by freeing them from their centuries-old servitude to their possessions, I must, above all else, honor the commands of God. Furthermore, they are my clients, and I cannot be the one to place them helplessly before the whims of your mercy, if such a thing as your mercy does indeed exist."

When Ronan paused again, the man looked at him with profound perplexity. "Surely this one was once the keeper of legend and the standard-bearer of the scales," thought the man standing in the shroud of the long shadows cast off by the warm glow of the low-burning and delicately crackling hearth.

When the man turned his head away from Ronan without any particular impulse guiding his movements and peered languidly across the room, Ronan spoke one last time. "The devil is tireless with you, because you have seen an angel of the Lord ascending who thwarts the dark one's wishes to have you. You have also ventured so close to the fire that your burden is heavy and much of your heart has grown weary and black. You have stood so close to evil incarnate that the damage you could unleash upon the kingdom of the demons is of the magnitude of some savage legend. I understand your fear of failing to resist what he tempts you with after suffering through poverty and neglect as you have. I also know your fear of the devil's incessant promise that just retribution shall be served harshly upon you for what you have done if you forsake the cover of his aegis. He reminds you daily that you are somehow worse than the deeds of your murder, and the cold shadows of terror you once employed to extinguish the hope of so many, only because there was a brief moment when you turned from the face of God."

The man rubbed his chin thoughtfully and replied, "And what if I were to tell you that I am the only devil you need fear now, Mr. Cassidy?"

Ronan shook his head obstinately and called back, "That is not true! You know those subtle whispers in your ear to be false now. The false words of the demons kept you chained to a dark and solitary path for far too long, but only because you were without God and only because you believed you would be left alone in the cold and the darkness to suffer as those now eternally unloved also suffer. But I can assure you that the message delivered on that note is from Him to you! Certainly, I would not be asked to show the way to redemption to the devil itself at such a cost!"

Ronan paused again, turned his head away from the man, and immediately became entranced by the burning embers of the fire. The fullness of his proposition had been spent. There was little left to say. He then closed his eyes and tilted his head back slightly to shift his focus inward. With little of consequence that he might utter in response to such a forthright and wholly unexpected declaration, the man looked down between his perfectly polished black boots at the smooth and ancient stone upon which he stood. It was primordial stone, which had been worn smooth by the effects of both pressure and the passing of the ages.

That unmovable monolith and gibber stone, both one and the same, had been fashioned as the base of the old seaside inn of the island for centuries. For no particular reason, the man found it curious that the stone had been worn smooth by all those who had braved both the angry sea and the inhospitable climes of the island to, at one time or another, grace that haunted sanctuary.

After marveling over how little the place had changed since the beginning of the recorded history of man and sensing the oncoming addendum to Ronan's vital plea, the man closed his eyes to think back upon that instant when the rage of a child was indeed blinded by the light of the angel ascending. He dared not yet consider how it was that Mr. Cassidy had come to know such a thing.

Ronan finished with what he had intended to say to his antagonist by directing his words firmly but quietly into the darkened space beneath the ceiling. He hoped that those words might resound and then echo throughout the seemingly hollow chambers of the man's still vacant yet emergent soul. "While your atrocities of the past have been well documented, and you have been nothing but a man of your word since we met, with the life of my daughter as the price for my obedient faith, I have given you what God above has instructed me to deliver. I have offered you nothing more and nothing less. He walks sorrowfully yet tirelessly at all hours in search of each of His lost sheep. Whether or not you agree, it is clear to me that you are still considered to be among the missing."

Ronan held his tongue for a brief spell before stepping beyond the point of no return, if he hadn't done so already, and said, "Perhaps it only amuses you to know that I fear nothing of what you might do to me or my dear one. Be that as it may, it would be wise of you to conduct a proper accounting of that fact."

The man stood still for a moment, but made no response. He took notice of the emerging slack in Ronan's carriage and perhaps the ease of spirit so clearly revealed by the peaceful abatement of his body resting on the arms and within the contours of that ancient leather chair. For a brief instant, the man's discerning eyes radiated with ire and narrowed with reprobation towards Mr. Cassidy. Yet, he still made no reply to Ronan's faithful and committed pleas. He had faced a similar circumstance where one's faith stood firm in the face of the harsh realities of the waking world once before, and he was not keen on making the same mistake twice.

In accordance with such, the man simply pulled at the front of the brim of his hat in a show of honorable salutation to Mr. Cassidy and turned back towards the front door of the inn. He executed a brief and nearly unnoticeable military pivot in doing as much. While the man turned to depart with only the exclamation of his silence lingering in the slight wake of his precise and efficient motions, Ronan felt a clamoring terror suddenly rise up from within and deftly prod his spent and sedated mind. He impulsively began to doubt that he had called the man's bluff. He began to wonder what might become of his little "fleur-de-lis" if that man walked out the door without so much as saying a word.

Mr. Cassidy moved his hand slowly yet purposefully into the outer pocket of his winter coat until he felt the cold heft of the metal. When his hand was anxiously set upon the object of his agitated need, he pulled the small Luger from his pocket, its shape and weight and purpose being so foreign to the senses of both his hands and heart. Ronan's limbs trembled slightly as he raised and pointed the fitted tack of the pistol's sight at the man while he walked evenly towards the door. There was then the exigent flash of a moment that split the stunted silence existing between one of the man's sharp, echoing steps, in which a black hate wrested itself upon Ronan's thunderously pounding heart. Upon the instant of that broken fraction of time when the furies of hell swept over his intentions, yet before the unmistakable sound of the act, Ronan became convinced that the immediacy of the heinous deed was done. Yet, his hand remained still and the room was nearly silent.

Suddenly, the man halted his steps before reaching the door. He pivoted back to face Ronan in one definitively exercised motion, which was so swift and sharp that the precise yet hasty maneuver caused the heavy pendant he wore to shake free from the confinements of his perfectly tailored button-down shirt. When the man faced up to Ronan from just a short way across the dimly lit room, the gleaming medallion rested openly upon his dark outer vestments.

The man did not notice the sudden shift of his collar or the emergence of the medallion once tucked within his shirt, which was quite a strange occurrence for one so meticulous regarding his outward appearances. Therefore, he stood facing Ronan in the shadowy glow of the firelight with the full gilt of his pendant blazing in the darkness. The spectacle of the moment was not missed by Ronan's instantly bedazzled eyes. The man spoke calmly to Ronan, being that he remained unaware of both the inadvertent revelation of his golden relic and the given sign from above that it mysteriously conveyed to Mr. Cassidy. "You know, Mr. Cassidy, and let me preface what I am about to say by acknowledging that I have not revealed as much about myself in the entirety of my life to someone on the outside. Nevertheless, in light of your recent devotion to your steadfast opinions, I felt the need to tell you something before I depart."

"What might that be?" asked Ronan, in an almost offhand manner, while his eyes somehow managed to grow wider yet still.

The man took a steady step forward and said, "I find it strange that in America, I am thought of by most as a fine solicitor and strategic executive of one of the largest, albeit secretive, family-owned enterprises in the country. Yet, in such a simple place as the jungles of Columbia, where intent is not so cleverly masked by the fineries of corrupted wealth and power, I am known simply as '*El Negro Muerte.*' I wonder which opinion of me is true. You ponder that question very carefully, Mr. Cassidy. So that you may have closure and clarity for your soul."

Ronan was not daunted by the man's thinly veiled threat, and he replied cogently, in accordance with his rising faith. "I give you only this for further consideration, my good man: who is the greater fool, he who passes sound and unwavering judgment in response to spurious provocation, or he who waits to diligently seek out the entirety of the truth at all cost?"

After Ronan spoke, the man initially said nothing in reply. Yet, he made a show of pivoting back towards the door of the inn. Once he had taken a few slow and deliberate steps in the direction of his intended destination, he abruptly turned back towards Ronan and called out, "Good night, Mr. Cassidy. Please, do consider my shame for my low behavior and the momentary lapse of my graces in not addressing you properly upon the initiation of my departure."

With those words spoken, the man walked slowly, silently, and deliberately along the dense and smoothly worn planks of the wooden pilings, which were worn into the very stones upon which they rested and marked the most direct pathway to the exit. When he was standing before the large wooden door to the inn, but still within a reasonable proximity to Ronan, a distance which allowed him to be heard with only the slight elevation of his voice, he delivered the last of his words intended for Mr. Cassidy and, furthermore, accruing to the benefit of their brief gathering amidst the raging Irish Sea.

The man announced plainly to Ronan, "Lastly, Mr. Cassidy, I have now weighed the entirety of the facts and circumstances concerning our matter at hand. For what it's worth, and upon the passing of the hour for such critical determinations to be made, regarding the matter of your honor and your character, I am of the unshakable belief that you have acted courageously and therefore most honorably this evening."

As the man said this, he offered up a sidelong glance in the direction of Mr. Cassidy and a light but noticeable tap on the lower outer pocket of his black overcoat. The tap was plainly in deference to the sheathed instrument once again resting under the cover of Ronan's jacket pocket. "What does remain hanging in the balance, Mr. Cassidy, is for us to learn what redemption truly means."

Ronan looked back at the man still lingering before the steadfast door to the inn, though his tormentor was nearly concealed by the darkness. He did not know if he had acted with cowardice or honor when he stayed his hand that once gripped the cold steel of the pistol. What Mr. Cassidy did know, was that the shrouded man before him had learned a long time ago what defined honor and cowardice in the face of such terrible considerations and the consequences certain to follow, and he knew it better than most men knew the manner of their own hearts. Ronan spoke reflectively in reply. "If it is indeed an honorable thing that I have done, may my deeds here tonight be the first step on the path to redemption for us both."

The man turned sideways so that he could look at Mr. Ronan James Cassidy one last time. He was at a loss to rationalize the inexplicable presence of the boyish innocence that accompanied the pup-like and scruffy-haired smile gracing Ronan's congenial and oddly shaded countenance at that moment. It was as if this utterly lost manchild before him somehow still managed to believe that only good things were ultimately possible in the aftermath of the reckoning still to come. The man stood bewildered and nearly sullen for a short while longer. That child, sitting calmly in the firelight, with its wares of either insanity or unbending faith, vexed him terribly.

Nevertheless, there was something about Mr. Cassidy's expectant guise that seemed to nurture some carefully guarded seed of hope—a seed of hope that had sprouted deep within the man's heart some years ago. In not but the twinkling of an eye, it dawned on the man that both reasons he had considered for the serenely bemused look dressing over Mr. Cassidy's boyish countenance were to blame for such an oddity. The man conceded that Mr. Cassidy may have been in some way touched by God. However, that did not change the fact that most folks living in the shadows of the dark and nearly hopeless realms of the modern world, places where he had lingered for far too long, would have considered Mr. Cassidy's unwavering faith while under such impossible duress to yield nothing short of differing forms of madness.

The man continued to stand before the forcefully hewn conglomeration of massive wooden girders that served as the gateway to the old stone inn. While he paused there to prepare himself to enter the hostile, razing night air, he continued to wonder over the newly given reality of such a seemingly miraculous occurrence. Though he had anticipated the outcome of the affair some time ago, seeing such a presumption shift from that of expectation to actuality in the face of such dour prospects for the one resisting him caused the man to almost vacantly think aloud, "How does one hold so true to the irrational expectation of God and goodness above all else given that the harsh and incessant realities of human loss, sorrow, and greed are so pervasive?" The man then wondered if he had been staring back at Mr. Ronan James Cassidy all this time or some vision of the boy he once was.

There was once a time when the man took at least some sense of fulfillment from his position as final and absolute arbiter over both the explicit and implicit lines crossed by covetous men competing to fulfill their shallow wants. Not on this day. On this day, the look set upon Ronan's face would have robbed him of even that sense of duty had there actually existed a deserved price to be remitted for Mr. Cassidy's deeds. With such unwelcome feelings pulling at a tender chord somewhere deep within, he turned slightly away from Ronan and stiffened. He held his uncertain position for one last moment, as if he might march across the room and join Mr. Cassidy for a drink, and then faced back up to the old wooden portcullis of a sort, which had repelled many a man attempting to gain access to the comforts and protections of the inn throughout the centuries. This time, the man pushed hard against the heavy door holding back the howling wind, and he made his way out into the darkness that was lying fallow beneath the shimmering stars of a moonless night sky.

The meeting was adjourned. So much hung in the balance. Perhaps a triumphant beginning hoped Ronan, though his lingering doubts were still conversely warning, somewhere beneath the surface of those lighter, expectantly driven thoughts, that the whole affair might wind up being nothing more than the close of another fleeting era in the sorrowful tragedy of man. Mr. Cassidy's concurrently racing thoughts, which were swiftly marred by doubt in the man's absence, pined for the easement that only the foundations of his faith, which he had so devoutly revealed through his actions on that night, could provide. Nevertheless, Ronan Cassidy would hold to his pledge before God above all else. He would be praying hard in the days to come for the sanctity of his soul and the safety of his baby girl.

As if the melodious chords were a soothing response to his frenzied prayers for relief, Ronan then heard and felt the timeless vibrations of a violin that began to resonate throughout the worn stone walls of the inn. The sounds of the haunting and lingering chords of the instrument ran deep into the vast caverns of Ronan's soul, which felt as if it were echoing in time to the rhythmic strokes of some slow and unseen hand that played beyond the confines of eternity while aching to unite the forlorn hopes of both the quick and the dead. As the rhythm of the bow vibrating along the perfectly tuned strings of the fiddle slowly gathered energy and increased its tempo, Ronan stepped out into the night air behind the man to check on the state of the very heavens themselves. The sweet and mournful harmony of the ancient and sorrowful tune sounded on through the endless night sky, all the while gathering waves of strength and delivering its eternal dispatch of earthly union and reconciliation throughout the boundless expanses of frequency and rhythm, which enjoined the spatial, the temporal, and the heavenly realms.

As he stepped forward into the night and took cover beneath the shimmering stars, those haunting vibrations seemed to move beyond time, uniting the variously recalled memories of Ronan's life into one scene that reached a glorious climax in the depths of his heart. Tears welled up in his eyes, and those incipient beads of warm, brackish moisture were instantly chilled by the curiously soft breath of the ancient sea. While under the spell of that haunting melody, Ronan didn't seem to find it strange that the normally inhospitable channel just off in the distance was suddenly calmed by that same soul-rending euphony and had, in fact, begun to gently sway with the cadence of a swaddled baby rocking in her mother's arms. To Ronan, those vibrations seemed to pulsate in unison with all of God's creation and exalt the beauty, sorrow, and joy that comprised this strange and wonderful life. Moreover, he suddenly viewed the events of the prior hour as little more than a low note in that soothing tune, which would serve to deepen the ecstasy of some coming crescendo that was well beyond the conjectures of his trifling mind.

The low, immutable chords seemed to cleanse and then steady his raw, untamed emotions as he stared longingly into the sparking heavens above. At that moment, Ronan was certain that the rhythmic melding of the low and high notes was audible to the growing lot of the broken-hearted spanning the ages of that numinous land. The hypnotic wonder of that hymn gave authority and meaning to the ancient secrets of times long since passed in the short run, and returned softly, sweetly, and radiantly to its divine creator, who was eternally calling His children home, in the long run.

"I have no strength but through You, my God," whispered Ronan into the uncommonly childish teeth of the lowly baying wind. "I am little more than Your humble and thankful servant. May Your will be done, and may Your grace shine down upon our often lost but always hopeful countenances. May my sweet girls always know that I love them dearly."

Ronan lowered his eyes from the heavens, turned to face the docks below, and once again stepped courageously forward, ultimately beginning his return to the cold and indignant sea below. That once hostile and angry sea, which had delivered him hence, remained eerily pacified and rocking gently to the reedy, haunting melody reverberating out from the timeless walls of the old stone inn atop the hill and carrying the sorrowful and eternal lamentations born of the heartstrings of the ancients out into the heavens. That deep and resonant song now conveyed the same sorrows, hopes, and fears of a still faithful yet soulfully disquieted man. A solitary man who was such a long way from home and was making his way back down to the sea on foot. A solitary man who now pondered the grand symphony of life, so stunningly visible in the twinkling of the stars against the black watch canvas of the night sky. The beautiful and endless panorama, which stretched out before Ronan Cassidy's eyes from the vantage point of the craggy, barren hillside, openly revealed the delicate smallness of mankind in comparison to that majestic and infinite Creator of the heavens and the earth below the firmament. All had been placed in God's care.

Chapter 2

Winding our way back in time to the late stages of the unending winter of 2012, Ronan Cassidy was getting reacquainted with the underpinnings of the modern global financial system by reading through some curious writings; candidly revealed thoughts, as it were, and thoughts that explained the fundamental principles of and history behind the evolution of our money. The facts revealed within the lines of the text seemed to him to have been lightly misconstrued over the coursings of his extensive education in finance, to say so with a degree of finery, and downright obfuscated when considered more bluntly. As such, and being one born to question the presented nature of nearly all things, Ronan was rather intrigued by these ideas conceived of such beautifully simplistic logic, which served to shed some light on a matter that few, if any, truly understood in its entirety. As many have said, "When it comes to money, it's complicated." While the truth of that catch phrase would continue to hold form in the opinion of Mr. Cassidy, after reading the majority of what had been stated plainly before his ravening eyes, he would come to understand that perhaps the notions of money and wealth remained quite innate to and clearly understood by those in possession of vast quantities of both.

At that time in his life, Ronan had been tracking the disturbances to the flow of money throughout the global economy that had come about in the aftermath of the market crash tied to the housing bust and the corresponding multi-trillion-dollar bailout of Wall Street and the largest financial institutions across the world. Of course, ground zero for this unprecedented financial reckoning of the worst kind remained the failure of the iconic house of Lehman on Monday, September 15th, 2008. The loss of confidence that sparked the historic downfall of the fourth largest investment banking operation in the United States at the time, and one of the largest participants in the subprime mortgage lending boom, devastated financial markets in both the United States and abroad to the point of total systemic failure of the international monetary system. To Ronan, the official narrative around this cataclysmic event, which occurred with such speed and possessed such depth, lacked the inclusion of any rational explanation that accurately reflected the root causes of the devastation to market liquidity and, therefore, asset values the world over.

Like many around the country at the time, Ronan had serious questions about what exactly took place during the sequence of events leading up to and the responses that followed the near implosion of not just the world financial markets but that shining pillar of the American economy itself, the housing market. Ronan trembled in response to the stories of the tens of millions of Americans that went homeless without a voice and the public response, which served primarily to recapitalize the same institutions responsible for the devastation. He was not alone in his abhorrence of the situation. Nevertheless, the cries of so many that suffered through those dark times were eventually silenced in the name of progress and the proliferation of endless propaganda, which so wonderfully contrived the economic "green shoots" of 2011. Ronan's curious mind developed an itch that went well beyond that of a nagging distaste for his lack of a more complete understanding of the situation. Prompted by this overwhelming desire to know more in the aftermath of such a devasting affair, he spent years tirelessly studying the historical evolution of the foundational tenets that served to define and grease the wheels of the international monetary order. Following this probing inspection of the nuts and bolts of our modern money, Ronan began to ask questions that were shaking the very foundations of his conceptual knowledge concerning his professional livelihood.

By that time, Ronan had poured through thousands of essays and publications concerning money and the evolution of the U.S. dollar that appeared to meet his exacting criteria, specifically around source and substantiated accuracy. However, he remained unable to connect those varied data points into the resulting image that would ultimately reveal the fatal constructs of the dollar-centric financial system until he stumbled upon the enlightening thoughts of an anonymous writer, one who claimed to have invaluable insights into those operating within the highest echelons of money and international finance. What that unknown author did reveal worked wonders on Mr. Cassidy's understanding of the historical, socio-economic, and political elements that had conspired to lift the Federal Reserve Note and its offspring, the Wall Street financial machine, to the dizzying heights the American currency and its administrative adjutants had attained more than a score before the first decade of the twenty-first century reached its turbulent end.

The lofty vantage point from which these views on money and finance were expressed, while not entirely foreign to Mr. Cassidy's understanding of the world around him, was certainly not a perch that was even remotely accessible to one inhabiting the carriage class confines ascribed to Ronan's station in life. Still and all, something written within that anonymous collection of thoughts immediately resonated with the avid learner and staunch practitioner of analytics. He quickly understood that the broad truths being laid bare in those publications were the precursors to great change, and that we Americans currently skimming the fat off of the overvalued dollar were standing at the forefront of a seminal turning point in our history.

Mr. Cassidy believed such to be true for the simple reason that the fundamental flaws baked into the world's monetary system nearly a century ago, those flaws which acted as the primary drivers of the market crash of 2008-2009, were still festering beneath the surface. By February of 2012, the powers that be had gone all in to paper over the mess instead of fixing it. They had applied ungodly amounts of lipstick to the proverbial pig by way of an unending propaganda campaign that was run by nearly every facet of the media, which by that time had already been geared to serve the interests of Washington's bought and paid for politicians and the high priests of Wall Street. While Ronan was fervently guided by the fundamental principles of justice and the sovereign rights of liberty and equality as ordained by God, like all Americans now so accustomed to the spoils of government deficits and money creation without tears, he had much to learn about the basic principles of money and wealth. Yet, he now possessed an invaluable understanding of how the game was set to play out in the years ahead.

As Ronan continued to immerse his wits in the deeply layered yet infinitely resolute propositions of those texts, he was initially shocked and then wholly mesmerized by the ideas of that anonymous author. Many of the thoughts offered up by that mysterious financial insider were simple concepts. However, the true genius behind those tenets became quite clear when they were layered onto the complex web of the modern financial matrix, where those thoughts and basic principles tied to the human condition seemed to jar the tumblers of some grand and unsolved mechanical jigsaw puzzle firmly into place. For years, those thoughts continued to prod the intricate configurations working deep within Mr. Cassidy's mind. Those intangible haunts where thoughts are born, which are always so receptive to truth and rational exposition.

At times, Ronan was alight with an unshakable and terrible determination to master the primacy of those tales of the hidden paragons of the evolving monetary order. Each concept that he studied within those texts gave confirmation to the prior fundamental truths that had been revealed through earlier readings, each lesson proving out and supporting the others until the overall message became undeniable yet impossible to time. He let each axiom revealed test the constructs of his inborn and learned principles around money and commerce, until those two paradigms of his formerly divergent belief system were in balance. At some point during his edification, he came to reckon that he had been handed the answer to one of the greatest puzzles known to man, the identity of the sustainable equilibrium point of any durable and mutually beneficial financial system. And perhaps he had been, but only the future was capable of verifying that which Mr. Cassidy came to understand as an inevitability.

Learning to accept the simple beauty of a symbiotic equilibrium born naturally of little more than common sense and, likewise, offset by the evolving political, and many might say, spiritual power structures of the last century and a half, and which balanced Ronan's conceptual understanding of the natural order of humanity in relation to its use of modern money in light of all that is preprogrammed into our waking thoughts on a topic near and dear to the primary concerns of most, and, furthermore, in the case of Mr. Cassidy, veiled by his extensive erudition on the topic of contemporary finance, did not come easy. The truth of the matter was that Ronan had previously ventured into those words, thoughts, and ideas with only small breakthroughs at each sitting in the prior years he spent pouring through those texts as the lost seeker of some buried truth that would explain the financial cataclysm of the recent past. Many times in life, simple truths are obscured so sensationally by lies far too grand and far too complex to be accepted as deceit. These conspiracies, as the pundits would have it, wreak havoc on the bias of our confirmations and, because of this, act to hide simple verities so secretly and so securely that we can spend a lifetime doing little but searching for and circling back to the very same graces of our discernment gifted us at birth. Ronan went through every testing phase of such an endeavor concerning the thoughts of that anonymous author, who wrote such prolific prose and possessed such astute and privileged knowledge of money, wealth, and the world's financial architecture.

The times ascribed to such independent study, as it were, often occurred long after freeing his mind and body from work and the beloved nightly rituals of getting each of his little sweethearts to yield to the soothing whispers of the night. During those secretive hours, upon which the offer of his unwavering attention was requited with the gifts of insight and revelation, Ronan attempted to tame the myriad phantasmal theories that were swirling about in his head. Alone, in the quiet interludes of the small hours of the night, it often seemed to him that these ideas, which were so fundamental yet so cunningly veiled by the examples of the constantly iterated events of his day, were spirit kin to the falling leaves of late autumn. Those spent denizens of the arboreal realms, which had become trapped in some coltish tempest that was teasing them about the crisp fall air in unison just as they were about to make their final statement of settlement upon the earth. Indeed, those tricky and restless ideas did, at times, mirror the transient state of that brilliant foliage drifting in the wind that Ronan had gazed at intently from time to time throughout his life, and with increasing levels of wonder as he reached his middle years.

Ronan took such bittersweet joy in those periods of pensive reflection that belonged to the apex of the season of the autumnal foliage. Those times when the hues of the falling leaves were emblazoned in fiery reds, lush golden raiment, and oranges so deep they looked as if they might set with the radiating glow of the October sun. But alas, many of those thoughts of the small, silent hours, like so many leaves that would soon dedicate themselves to the enrichment of the fertile spring soil before the frozen white glass of the winter months would keep them for a season from their final purpose, would also loose themselves from their branches and twirl rapidly and uncontrollably through the constructs, values, and beliefs tied to the varied conceived orderings of the universe and its loving master that graced Ronan's well-educated mind. Others would remain as dormant buds, patiently waiting to blossom in the new season.

Nearly as elusive as the proximate settling vapors of the lingering mists of first light, such unvarnished wisdom tends to dance in a moving yet artful and ungovernable manner within those abstract ateliers of the supernal mind that foster creative deliberation. Much like the seasonal splendor of those fragile pendent leaves of the diminishing October light, those spent denizens of the ether of our intellect that have been dispatched from above fall away from the source in their present state and run-in circles that reveal the unseen breath and intent of the arbiter of the tempests, who directs them until the last. Yet, the memory of their simple beauty and their former singularity amongst the many leaves a mark on the trail that is unique to a certain time and station of our lives. With each volley of the teasing, impish winds, more of these passing thoughts dance gently back down to the soil in fantastic starts and fits that mark their final earthly ritual. And so it was with Mr. Cassidy as he continued to give shape, reason, direction, and purpose to those shifting thoughts and theories born of the writings of that anonymous author in an attempt to develop a unified understanding of those luminary notions, which were emphatically bending the prior constructs of his mental architecture. After the settling haze of those long and thoughtful seasons of his refinement began to lift, the wisdom gained by Ronan in those months and years spent regarding those writings remained his own indelible marks set upon the great and winding trail of his life.

Such formative thoughts and ideologies are so whimsical and so abstract when measured against the tangible confines of nature, yet so essential to being who it is we were created to be in this changing panorama of life. These often fanciful and always partially contrived ideas are never seen or heard, and they are seldom expressed. Yet, they are always innately understood. They are like foreign words. Words that can be deciphered only by the tone in which they are delivered and through the known circumstances of the speaker of the word. What little meaning is tied to the linguistics of its carried syllables serves only to affirm or deny our initial suppositions. These half-understood ideas and ideals are known instinctively to have high importance at the very instant they are revealed to us. They trigger the release of a once static charge that ignites the soul, but they are not yet able to be captured, put to good use, or fully rationalized by the waking mind.

Nevertheless, for those dreamers who endeavor to chase after these wildly contrived notions until the last, as certain as the day follows the night, there will come a moment of clarity. And so it went for Mr. Cassidy. After some time spent twisting and turning in the wind, he began to take notice of the grand patterns that existed and meshed with those nascent ideas. He was no longer held captive by those individual thoughts that refused to be tamed by the entrenched tendencies of his preconceived notions, which spoke to another reality altogether. In late February of 2012, Ronan James Cassidy saw something very clearly, and that moment of clarity had been a long time in the making.

What Ronan had identified at that moment, the concept that finally lit the light bulb, as it were, was an unnatural conflict that existed between one of the most basic and innate human desires and our modern monetary system. A conflict that would not and could not be resolved under the current financial paradigm. Ronan understood the in-born human desire to trade the fruits of our labor in an effort to better our quality of life in the real world and our need to save our excess capacity for those rainy and less productive days and years certain to come. Moreover, he came to realize that most productive folks wished to save without the risk of loss or having the value of their nest egg diluted by not doing so over the course of their lives. Most importantly, Mr. Cassidy came to understand that the net producers of the world were unable to save without inheriting some form of risk and dilution under the current dollar-centric system, which was debt-based and entirely dependent on an ever-expanding quantity of newly created money.

As the tumblers of his cogitation locked into place around such a newly discovered absurdity, Ronan was presented with an epiphany of simplistic lucidity. An epiphany that had remained hidden among the infinite possible conclusions he imagined he might reach after studying the works of that anonymous author while applying his known experience and the requisite filter of suspicion required for proper discernment. Moreover, the sudden realization of that undeniable epiphany would have had a far greater productive purpose back then, as it does for Mr. Cassidy now, had Ronan even the slightest equivalency of a premise regarding God's true purpose for his life. Understanding the proper coefficients that will bring about great change is one thing. Seeing how that change impacts the foundational propositions behind one's value system and how others may revile the revelation of certainty behind such a cataclysmic upheaval are matters of a differing stripe entirely.

Nevertheless, as time continued to pass beyond that moment of his initial discovery and the corresponding reconciliation of such to his prior understanding of the international monetary order, Ronan began to see the inevitability of such a perfect financial storm forming out on the horizon with rapidly improving resolution. At that time, and as it is with most fresh to the scintillating vapors of a life-altering discovery, he did not fully appreciate how hated the idea of the inevitability of that cleansing financial maelstrom would be treated by those within his social circles. Those who still saw nothing but the advance of a brighter day out along that same vanishing point. Furthermore, Mr. Cassidy had no notion back on that hibernal February day that such a revelation would some years later draw him into the depths of that fateful rendezvous on the island of Inis Mor, and the circumstances surrounding that sordid affair. Yet, let us not jump too far down the path leading up to that fateful moment, which would later be revealed as the hour a storm of an entirely different portent was set to usher in a reckoning more pertinent to the realms of good and evil, and was, perhaps, near to a millennium in the making.

Some months beyond the instant of that initial moment of clarity, on a fine July day filled with pleasant sunshine, Ronan synthesized his fully developed thoughts on the matters of money and wealth. With the sun shining brightly through the patio door windows at the back of the house, he penned a consolidated summary of his emergent beliefs, which were not entirely his own but the summary of his understanding of those who had done far more than he to promote the concepts behind the future direction of the world's financial system. A soft hint of humidity held the lingering warmth like a halo that was ensnaring some angelic radiance captive to the restless air, which continued to calm in the wake of a disquieting summer storm that had passed through Mr. Cassidy's neighborhood in the small hours of the morning.

If pressed on the matter of his source, Ronan would have considered this anonymous teacher one of the few remaining fine men and fine minds dedicated to finance and worldly affairs. Perhaps prompted by some French inhabitant of his soul, who had passed their influences down through his mother's bloodline, or some other ancestor who might have readily understood the meaning behind those written ideas, which would have appeared so foreign to one wholly indoctrinated into the ways of the modern American mindset, Ronan put into words his crystallizing epiphany of that prior winter. In an attempt to capture these newly formed thoughts, which he feared would evaporate back into the heavens as rapidly as they had clarified in his mind, Mr. Cassidy wrote the following in an elegant hand, a hand which he had perfected in his thirteenth year, into a small black journal with a fine leather cover:

Money is a defined promise to deliver an item of real worldly value at a later date and the standardized unit of account of the associated values of the items given in exchange by all parties to a trade. Outside of physical cash on the go, modern money is the book entry behind a universal unit of credit, nothing more, and nothing less.

Wealth is the accumulation of real tangible items that represent the excess production of a person's labor throughout their lifetime. The timeless, innately valuable, recognizable, and tradeable wealth that transcends the barriers of language, political will, and culture is gold.

Dollars are money in the purest sense of the concept and are legal tender by decree. Fiat dollars have worked wonders in the realms of productive economic efficiency and trade. Tragically, our dollar money has been masquerading as both money and wealth for so long that two generations of the world's people have been twisted into believing in the false hopes of an economic model in a state of constant conflict resting on a powder keg. There will be a great reckoning. The fire will be all-consuming as dollar hyperinflation separates the dollar from its wealth reserve function. Tradable wealth will remain.

The path of the world's ancient savers remains open to all.

Ronan James Cassidy – 18 July 2012

h/t The Lord Almighty, The Ring Bearers, all those who taught me the just rewards of keeping after the most difficult tasks in life.

While it can be said of many of the trying times Mr. Cassidy endured before, during, and after the collapse of the American currency, that Ronan struggled with the burden of being the standard-bearer, as it were, in the end, it was with deep and humble gratitude that he accepted the gift of seeing that which could not be unseen well before those events ultimately unfolded. When it comes to currency collapse, identifying that inevitable outcome ten years too early would produce a far better outcome than being one minute late. In truth, having that unshakable understanding of the turbulent migration of the world's money, which would allow national currencies to reach a sustainable equilibrium with an incorruptible wealth reserve, afforded Ronan certain freedoms from many false paradigms born of the dollar's perceived capacity to be all things to everyone. Architypes and corresponding axioms, which, in some instances, had bound themselves to both Mr. Cassidy's heart and his mind.

Ronan was cut from the cloth of those that would rather die knowing the truth than live a life according to the lies of some sweet-speaking yet forked-tongued false prophet. In the aftermath of the robbery in broad daylight that was the Wall Street bailout of 2009, he was also moved by the idea that many seated in positions of considerable power throughout the country, and perhaps the world over, would have deemed such devotion to the truth to be an unfortunate character flaw. Still and all, Mr. Cassidy continued to believe that most others were also created with a deep and innate desire to seek and live by the truth, and that, because of this, the world would be a far better place when the dust kicked up by that calamity certain to come had settled.

The current constructs and real-world distortions caused by the unnatural proliferation of the Federal Reserve Note and its sway over the desires and deeds of those who made their living in accordance with its obscene overvaluation, was a matter that would come to test the very make and gallant framework of Mr. Cassidy's mettle. Such lasting abominations would test his mettle as evenly as they tested the souls of those who contorted the truth to give justification to their ability to prosper materially without risk within the warping paradigms of the dollar-centric financial system. As events progressed beyond that year, Ronan was not exempt from living under the continuing strains of those same compromises of character required to reap the benefits of any predatory system. There were times that he felt no better than some deranged quisling, one trumpeting the imminent demise of the very source of his livelihood in the hopes of benefiting those that might heed such a warning and prepare accordingly.

After Ronan had penned his summary of money and wealth in regard to the current dollar-centric International Monetary Financial System, or what Ronan and others preferred to term the "*$IMFS*" in script, he met a friend named Lewis for a few drinks after their six children were fast asleep for the night. The evening was a fine offering, graced with clear, starlit skies and the cascading half-light of a waxing gibbous moon, which was potent enough to allow someone walking a fair distance from the streetlamps of town to cast a noticeable shadow. The lingering warmth of the daylight hours had begun to cool considerably upon the moment of their rather impromptu get together, which had commenced at around ten o'clock. Lewis and his family lived just a short way up the road from the Cassidy clan. Therefore, the last-minute arrangements required to rendezvous on such short notice were not overbearing.

Lewis MacAleer was a bright, engaging, and oftentimes curiously enigmatic gentleman. In many respects, he was the perfect embodiment of a white-collar American male who hailed from the suburban Midwest. However, Lewis wasn't afraid to deviate from the accepted norms of society from time to time while he kept the nature of even his shallowest of secrets quite close to the vest. He was the sort of person one felt completely comfortable speaking freely around, yet he seemed to live his life in a bit of a detached manner and certainly wasn't the type to mix business with pleasure. That being said regarding Lewis, he and Mr. Cassidy had logged some very interesting conversations over the years while closing down the local tavern, a place where solving the world's problems always seemed to clash with the full reprobation of their spouses the following morning, or even afternoon, depending on the severity of the damage incurred before returning home to retire.

The subject of the American dollar and its financial markets that were designed to promote continuing demand for the world's reserve currency were certainly not new topics for the distinguished Mr. MacAleer. Lewis was a wealth manager for a fantastic company with a super reputation in the trade, and Lewis himself, while not the perfect embodiment of the strait-laced reputation of his firm, was an outstanding individual in his own right, even if he wore the cloth and spoke the vernacular of a more unique parsonage. Lewis and Mr. Cassidy were in philosophical agreement on many of the primary interests in their lives. They could chat for hours about what the kids were into, sports, politics, the ups and downs associated with marriage, and even the oncoming train wrecks and legalized grifting operations that were euphemized within the social narrative as government finances. The latter topic oftentimes went right on up the food chain to the clusterfucks that were the current state of the federal budget and the scam behind the inequitable financial relief measures implemented by the third iteration of the privately owned American central bank during the aforementioned financial crisis. Lewis always had something unique to add to any topic the two gentlemen discussed, and Ronan valued his friend's insight immeasurably. Mr. Cassidy was quite fond of Mr. MacAleer, his wit, and his quirky passion for life.

After Ronan and Lewis had gone through the ritualistic conversations concerning the latest central bank money-printing schemes and regulatory boondoggles that were certain to make any sort of rational analysis of the financial markets near to impossible, life at work, the slight bit of town gossip that the two were privy to, and current events on the home front, their server and casual friend, Isabell, came by to see what might be needed at their table. The hour was approaching midnight, and most of the occupants who had comprised the lively Saturday night crowd, at least as far as that particular quaint, suburban-Chicago, rail-stop town establishment went, were beginning to drift out in small groups and return home for the evening. Isabell was a tall, stunning woman with long, dark hair and evocative hazel eyes. She was built very athletically below the midriff and possessed the finest cosmetic bust to the west or north of the windy city, though neither Ronan nor Lewis had ever ventured as far to prove the point.

When there was a chill in the air at the family-by-day whistle-stop tavern,

Lewis liked to quip quite crassly, yet amusingly all the same, "Those bolt-ons and their raised nubbins are as close to heaven as I can get on my best days." Needless to say, Isabell didn't allow any slack to ride into any of her black, standard-issue tee-tops that she wore nightly for the occasion of earning her keep, and that notable nuance to her ensemble was well-received by the predominately male clientele the tavern espoused during the after-dinner hours.

By the time Isabell had approached Ronan and Lewis at their raised table for two, the pair of almost slaphappy wags had caught a bit of a wild hair. By way of providing justification for their refusal to quit the tavern at that late hour, the gentlemen traded some verbal notes regarding the fact that the last-place Tigers were playing somewhere out in California on the big screen. Truth be told, the momentum of the evening was inexplicably favoring the troublesome duo, and for all of the wrong reasons. They weren't going anywhere anytime soon, and Isabell probably understood that verity better than either of the waggish brutes caught up in the amusement of the moment. When the mildly provocative waitress arrived between her two somewhat glassy-eyed patrons, she leaned into the table and stood on the tips of her toes while excitedly delivering her standard level of energy and in-your-face allure to the ordering process. The tells in response to Isabell's gamesome mischief, which were written all over the faces of the two gushing gentlemen seated at eye-level before her, were quite severe. That didn't stop Lewis from turning his awestruck guise toward Isabell's chest like some Pavlovian lap dog on a distressing biscuit high. His eyes never left the rounded areas marked by the raised, or perhaps even slightly tented, letters displayed prominently across Isabell's screen-printed tee-shirt.

"Shameful," was the thought running through Ronan's mind as he became bewildered by the growing size of Lewis's deviously distorted and grossly enlarged eyeballs, which almost seemed to be making a go at venturing out on their own, and under new management, for the evening. Ronan quickly attempted to take the high road for the team of two that was not displaying any semblance of winning form. To divert Isabell's attention, Mr. Cassidy looked over at her and then began to peruse the large open menu in search of the buxom waitress's input. He signaled his desire for her feedback by pointing aimlessly at the standard array of appetizers from which to choose and asking a few unnecessary questions. The menu hadn't changed in years. Isabell nodded continually and with a bit too much oblivious schoolgirl excitement for Ronan to remain entirely calm. The menu exercise did, however, manage to deflect Isabell's attention away from the embarrassing and almost deformed lineaments of his friend and give at least the pretense of decorum to the laughable scene.

Matters took a turn for the worse when Ronan spotted a small droplet of drool beading up in the corner of Lewis's gaping maw. The previously esteemed Mr. MacAleer was already a bit of a raging dumpster fire at the hands of this seductress, who was so craftily plying her trade, but the situation somehow managed to digress. Boys will be boys, one may surmise, yet perhaps Miss Isabell was simply too naturally and overwhelmingly endowed and too well versed in the postures and expressions of her art for these two gentlemen, who remained rather "repressed" by the more mundane virtues of suburban society. In either regard, the whole affair quickly escalated into just another stunning example of the torrid conflagration of even the pretense of male decency when Miss Isabell had the chattels running at full mast, as she did that night.

Ronan held his menu open to Isabell's left with his right hand in an effort to promptly remove Lewis from her line of sight. He hoped that the covering tactic would provide a moment for his friend to "gather his shit," as it were. This strategic positioning, however, put the giant saucers or gleaming white orbs that were Lewis's eyes, and which were now swirling and crossing at varying tangents, and appeared as if they had been enlarged by the lenses of a set of capable hunting binoculars, straight into Ronan's peripheral field of view. Those engrossed and enlarged caricatures were no more than the length of a schoolhouse yardstick away from Ronan, and they were deftly positioned directly across from Isabell's exquisitely endowed chest. The thin veneer of common decency that had been loosely draped over the already bizarre spectacle of the moment was set to fall away, and Mr. Cassidy feared what might happen as a result of such an unfortunate circumstance.

The entire scene reminded Ronan of the time he and his grade school friend succumbed to a frenzied fit of contagious laughter during their performance of the sixth-grade Christmas pageant. His friend had begun to look back at him while rapidly batting his bug-sized and helpless puppy dog like eyes to convey the look of a happy sheep at the very moment Ronan, while playing the shepherd, was making his grand proclamation to the audience of mostly parents, siblings, students from the other grades waiting to do their bit, and faculty. Fortunately, for everyone involved, that abruptly canceled performance took place during the more sparsely attended daytime rehearsal of the school pageant. Ronan and his grade school friend laughed so hard without stopping right in the middle of the elegant theatrical production that Ronan nearly split his side as his eyes filled with tears of laughter. Their classmates and fellow thespians of the hour were not far behind in expressing similar outpourings of holiday mirth.

The two overwhelmed sixth-graders carried on unabated until the curtains came down rather abruptly in the middle of the act, and they were dragged off the stage simultaneously by their ears by a sorely displeased Mrs. Case. The gasps and cackles coming from the parent-filled gymnasium echoed from behind the curtains for quite some time. That situation was only nearly as scandalous as the look set upon Lewis's handsome yet wonderfully expressive guise, and Ronan had never learned how to whiten his blush or cull his visibly displayed amusement when those subtle comedic nuances of such blissful perfection clicked into place and overtook his wits. With a similar confluence of such excellent comedic peculiarities now rising to govern his emotions, Ronan stiffened to keep from exploding with laughter by lifting his purposefully widening eyes to the ceiling.

With no additional outlet valve that might serve to reroute his bubbling delight available to him, Ronan cackled mildly while staring up at the ceiling, and Isabell directed her eyes over toward Lewis. Worse than both of those unfortunate occurrences, the awkward sound was accompanied by an obscure and unrelated rant. That rant sounded as if Mr. Cassidy had been overcome by the outward manifestations of the latent onset of Turret's syndrome. He yelled something off-color about the umpires calling the baseball game on the big screen television while he attempted to choke down his laughter. However, at that time, the cameras were panning the fans for the singing of *Take Me Out to the Ballgame* during the seventh-inning stretch. Ronan and Lewis were not winning at the moment, and now Ronan was on the verge of having to excuse himself from present company. Had Ronan lost control of his wares right then, the spasmodic eruption would have roused even the derelict ruminations of Lewis's bemused and stunted mind, which perceived naught but the visions of supple and studded dugs somehow set free for all the world to see.

Relying on the resolve granted him by way of what he considered to be a minor miracle, though he only considered such doggedness to remain calm to be miraculous back then due to his nascent understanding of the unending power of God's graces, Ronan quickly settled back down and evened up his posture by once again holding the open menu away from Isabell in a way that suggested he was still seeking her input on what to order. Lewis closed his eyes, bobbed a hair, and then drifted a bit awkwardly back to an upright position, as if he had been overcome by the drink for a spell. When Mr. MacAleer was upright and had reopened his eyes, he fumbled through the condiment basket for his menu with an expression that revealed he was mildly upset. He was irritated not only because he had gone to the trouble of looking for the massive listing catalog in the tiny, squared, and overburdened basket set down in the middle of the small, round table, but also because he didn't have a menu to begin with. That display of readily visible uncertainty brought Isabell back onto her toes, as she prepared to work those boys over just a bit in the interest of maximizing her tip during the evening close-out.

As Isabell leaned in from the tips of her toes with the intention of getting a rise out of the deplorable gentlemen while feigning that she could not hear well enough from the rather cozy distance of her prior stance, Ronan was unable to get past the first choice on the menu before his eyes took a strictly forbidden and sidelong, yet not altogether artful, glance downward. He became transfixed to the point of bewilderment by what he saw. Just beyond the hem of Isabell's short black skirt, the delicately tightened skin of her firm and athletic yet long and perfectly feminine legs, which seemed to run on without end, was clearly on display. Moreover, the effeminately contoured muscles of Isabell's well-defined and smartly raised calves were enough to cause Mr. Cassidy to raise the white flag of his unused table napkin in a show of surrender. From the depths of his near hypnotic state, he believed that he had spied the shapely formations taking place from Isabell's knee down to her slender ankles for just a flashing moment in time. Yet, when she asked him if he had dropped something on the floor, just to tease Ronan a bit without breaking the air of unspoken but certainly improper ceremony, he realized that he was working with the severe handicap of an alcohol-driven time delay.

When Ronan returned to some semblance of his proper senses yet nothing of his decency, he wondered if he was still laughing a bit on the outside while his heart had been taken captive by a sight beyond the capacity for human expression. He then wondered what in the world the perched owl stationed across from him at the table was doing presently. It was all pure and unadulterated monkey business. In the span of thirty seconds, the two lightly esteemed and happily married messieurs had been reduced to nothing more than a couple of misfit adolescents. Awkward schoolboys, ravaged by the onset of incurable hormonal lechery, throbbing uncontrollably within and angling at their table for a better view, or inadvertently given sensation, of what an outsider looking on in awe would be forced to assume were the previously unexplored attributes of womanhood for those two shameless caballeros.

It was no bother of any consequence to Isabell that her chosen customers, whom she had already earmarked for the evening's closing crescendo, had been reduced to a couple of ogre-eyed, wet-mouthed, knuckle-draggers before she even mentioned doing a few shots when the evening came to an end. In fact, the always perky and scintillatingly buxom belle of Northwest-Suburban lore spoke warmly and with a pleasant smile to the two bumbling heathens, who were then smirking devilishly at one another over the puerile behaviors of their inebriety. "I'll just double up the last round, you two. Let me know soon if you want to order anything from the menu. The kitchen closes soon, but I'll put in a good word for you gentlemen."

Then, because Isabell delighted in the game and knew she had the daft pair beyond the point of no return, she made her pretty green eyes widen and once again pursed her lips in that clueless yet seductive manner, as if to say, "Well done boys, shall we be adults and have a drink now?"

Of even greater torment to Ronan, although the aforementioned was Isabell's look that locked him in when he was in the process of being overserved, she half-twirled on the balls of her feet in such a way that the nimble progression gave slight motion to those firm yet nearly bursting balloons tied tightly into her shirt. Yet, that was not the worst of it. What Mr. Cassidy found to be nearly criminal about Isabell's alluring exit was that it gave the full conditioning report on the muscle tone of those long, rangy legs of hers that belonged to a species of prey and not the deadly hunters of the African savannah she clearly espoused with her predatory behavior. Neither of them would be returning home with even a loose dollar in their pockets once everything was said and done.

Whether they were being played to a small degree or not, it mattered little to the tippled miscreants at that moment. They both simply smiled, like twin Cheshire cats that had just swallowed the same canary. After a short while, Ronan looked down at the floor between his feet, which he continued to let dangle beside the elongated legs of the fairly plain wooden barstool. When Isabell had stepped safely away, only then did Ronan raise his head and look over at Lewis, who was waiting like a bobcat in heat to run that scene back down with his friend. Ronan chuckled a bit and smiled at Lewis, yet he didn't give Lewis the all-clear sign to slap his knees and bang his baseball cap firmly on the table because the server of their waking dreams was over at the bar and the remaining crowd had calmed noticeably and thinned out considerably.

Once Isabell had disappeared into the back for a smoke, Ronan hollered, "Sweet Lew!" He had called over to Lewis eagerly and without warning in the hopes of transfusing some sorely needed vigor into the aftermath of the twisted affair. Lewis was still shaking his head in disbelief at Isabell's antics while Ronan steadied his composure and rose from his stool. "I'm going to hit the restroom, Lew. I'll be back in a flash. Why don't you go on up to the bar and see if you can find out what Isabell is doing later?"

Ronan then winked at Lewis and worked his way around his stool with just a slight bit of drunken confusion. When he was poised and pointed in the right direction, he walked off towards the men's room. Once he was halfway down the hall, Lewis called out to him loud enough for anyone still in the tavern to hear, "You're a dirty dog, Ronan Cassidy! I'll let your wife know that the dull throb of that whiplash you'll be feeling in the morning is from slipping on the stairs."

Ronan laughed at Lewis and turned the corner, still thinking about the flawless definition of Isabell's rangy legs. "Men really may never progress beyond the point of manifesting the inbred instincts of a poorly trained dog," Ronan thought silently as he walked on in search of some necessary relief.

While Ronan stared at the professional football schedules set for the fall season that were posted above the urinal, he began to consider the oddities of and the corresponding catalysts for the inexplicable things we do in our lives. He pondered the intricacies of human interaction, the requisite provisions required to survive and prosper, and the vital importance of understanding the relational values of these items we require for varying reasons and the fruits of our labor in a complex world comprised of highly specialized and divisible labor. He then considered the peculiar social indoctrinations of his time and the almost religious fervor for material acquisitions that had come to be. He marveled over the unending desire to placate the preprogrammed fantasies of the mind, now inbred into the American culture and psyche following the proliferation of television and mass media. Ronan was feeling his oats just then, and he had taken a sharp turn towards considerations of a more abstract nature than the cogent forces of nature that were the long and gamesome legs of their server; considerations that would draw him back to the curious notions of his recent epiphany.

As Ronan stood there in solitude, spending a penny or two at the urinal, he realized that he possessed a much clearer understanding of the dollar and wealth, and that this knowledge followed logically in the wake of his understanding of the need to always expand the debt and privilege of the Federal Reserve Note. He began to see how this odd migration of the American denizens away from the country's founding principles, which remained unfortunate in a soon to be catastrophic sense, was, in many ways, innately tied to the flaws inherent in the current financial architecture. For the measure of an evenly passing moment, his savage distaste for the lies embedded in the propaganda of the American media machine softened some beneath the clarifying light of his basic understanding of the money game and the growing machinery needed to maintain the status quo. The reality was that most folks confined to such a predatory system were simply doing the best that they could in light of the current rules of the game.

Beyond all that, Ronan was growing exceptionally hungry. Therefore, he quickly decided that the system, as skewed and distorted as it had become and as toxic, impoverishing, and disarming as it was to the God-given and Constitutionally sovereign rights of the American people in its current form, did possess some benefits yet still. Decent chicken wings were still readily available, the establishment was still accepting the mathematically worthless book entry promises that he was paid for his work, and the pretty lady that was going to make it all happen was no fly in the ointment either.

As the man gracing the hallowed halls of this distinguished watering hole, one not all that far from the last of the outposts on the northwestern commuter rail line running out of Chicago, was a far cry from the man who would venture out on his own to the primeval inn on the island of Inis Mor some years later, and as he was oftentimes nearly manic where it regarded the resolution of an unresolved matter, it wasn't long before Mr. Cassidy was once again fixated upon this quite natural, yet altogether hidden from the eyes of most, relationship between wealth and dollars. He began to see clearly how so many of the economic fractures and financial imbalances the world over had been caused by the artificially suspended break in the equilibrium provided by a stable and freely marketable wealth reserve standard. As he finished his task, his face flushed again with a brief burst of repressed animosity, but he thanked God for the many blessings he and his loved ones were fortunate enough to be granted each day. With a quick shake, which marked the end of the process, a check in the mirror for any fatal flaws in his appearance, and a thorough washing of his hands, Ronan was prepared to return to their table and share his wonderful discovery of the day with his exceptionally bright and equivalently amusing friend, Lewis MacAleer.

Ronan cleared the hall leading into the great room of the tavern, which espoused the bar and the table he shared with Lewis. While glancing over at his friend, he noticed that Mr. MacAleer was locked into a steady progression of intently following Isabell with his eyes while she bounced jauntily across the room between the few remaining occupied tables. Ronan shook his head mischievously while he spied the little lost puppy dog who had entered the bar as his stalwart companion. "This will work perfectly. Lewis likes to have his intellect challenged, and we certainly need to get his mind fixated elsewhere," thought Ronan as he continued on with his approach.

Ronan took his seat and took a quick look at the streaming banners that displayed the scores of each obscure sporting event taking place across the country. The updated scores were slowly progressing across the lower sections of the large television screens mounted throughout the establishment. He even checked the tally, inning, and situational stats of the Tigers game, which was, of course, the reason he and Lewis were locked into staying out at the bar until the lights came on. For the first time since he and his friend had jumped headlong into the grownup pool by ordering two drinks each to open, Ronan realized that watching the Tigers game was probably the flimsiest covering scheme they had ever attempted to employ as an excuse for staying out far too late.

"Nothing to be done about that now," Ronan uttered, almost audibly, as if he had been speaking out loud to his friend regarding the matter for quite some time. He shifted his eyes sarcastically to acknowledge the piss-poor functioning of their logic, though no one was watching him. Upon receiving no response from his friend, Ronan stared blankly at the banners for a bit longer. When he had gathered all of the information he could make use of from the televisions of various sizes that lined the back wall of the great room of the tavern, he called across the muted distance of the raised table to Lewis. Lewis was keenly scouting out a potential skirmish that was now brewing at the corner of the bar. Isabell had gone back out for another cigarette, leaving the two wayward misanthropes to fend for themselves for a moment.

"Lew," Ronan interjected, with enough vim to immediately cajole his friend away from the disagreement he had become so focused on. "What's your take on gold and the end game for all of this outlandish money printing happening right now? I don't recall the class where they were teaching us about all of this back in business school. You are a wealth management professional of the highest order. I'd like to get your thoughts on the matter, and have you consider a few ideas I have been kicking the tires on."

Lew immediately swiveled his chair to the right to have a good look at Mr. Cassidy. When he was eye-to-eye with Ronan, Mr. MacAleer said, "I almost thought we were going to get through one night without you telling me how important it was that I buy a bunch of gold rocks and hide them under my mattress."

Lew shook his head mournfully and added, "Alright. I'll bite, Ronan. The Tigers suck, and I don't feel like stocking up on wheelbarrows at the moment. But not a word from yours truly until you charm Isabell into doing some shots with us. I'm going to get an earful when I get home, and I don't want to recall what hideous aspersions are being used to define my poor character. To top that buggy off, Izzy is looking the best I have ever seen her!"

Ronan laughed and responded to Lew's comment while he checked to see if Isabell had returned from her cigarette break. "Lew, it only seems that way to you now because Isabell has a new boyfriend, and also because you and your old lady are already in a bit of a dust-up over the kids running amuck while you were watching golf, drinking beer, and yacking it up on the phone with your Madison boys last weekend."

"Touché, Mr. Cassidy," replied Lewis in a bit of a drawn-out and deadpanned manner.

Ronan continued on without chuckling, though he wanted to. "Besides, you know darn well that you are going to blame this whole shitshow on me."

Ronan knew he was fibbing a bit. Lewis always stood his ground at home, and tonight was indeed about as good as he had ever seen Isabell look. Those facts aside, Ronan also knew that he had to draw Lewis's attention away from Isabell or the whole endeavor would turn out quite fruitless. Lewis lifted his chest and chin like a proud, posturing peacock and rolled his lower lip slightly, as if to say, "Don't bullshit me, buddy, I can still see straight."

What Lewis actually said was, "Ronan, I'll talk shop with you, but only because if I keep focusing on Izzy, I'm liable to make a complete ass of myself before they have a valid reason for kicking our drunk asses out of here."

Ronan nodded with approval and said, "The Tigers are getting smoked now too, Lew, so just hear me out on this. I'll take care of the drinks and the shots with Isabell until we retire for the evening."

Lewis cheered up noticeably at hearing that news. He straightened his posture and rapidly folded his hands on the table. He did this quite sarcastically, as if feigning that he had been whacked by his mother's strap without warning. At the same time, Lewis widened his eyes three standard deviations beyond eager and bit his lower lip like a reticent child. The look cried out, "Not me, ma'am! I'm all in on learning today!"

Then, in an instant, he unwound the rigid pomp of his demeanor, slammed his fist on the table hard enough to rattle the pint glasses, and said, "Hit me, buddy! I'm super focused on this shit now!"

Ronan laughed hastily and turned his head with a sharp jerk to avoid spitting out his drink. He had taken a leisurely sip while being thoroughly amused watching Lewis posture up like a third-grader who was seated in a bar.

Ronan took a follow-on sip of his stout to clear his throat and placed the pint glass back down on the table before saying, "I know that your undivided attention is always a dangerous proposition. But Lew, I have had a revelation of sorts, perhaps even a life-changing epiphany!"

Lewis offered up a look of visible skepticism in reply, but he remained silent. Ronan expected as much and simply continued on undeterred. "I have been thinking that for the last few centuries there has been a monetary battle raging between the producers of the world and the consumers. Said a bit differently, there is a giant rift in the monetary order. One that places the producers directly at odds with those who overconsume through debt. One camp would prefer a system based upon sound money, and the other is probably happier than a pig in shit with the current mess."

Lewis listened carefully to what Ronan had said. He answered his friend in a rather Socratic or perhaps smart-assed manner, depending on the partialities of the observer. "After all of that excitement, do you mean to sit here with a straight face and tell me that what you have discovered is that the basic premise behind what all of these Marxists and Democratic politicians, and Marxist politicians for that matter, have been hot mouthing about for centuries is, in fact, all wrong? Because I think it's pretty clear that those derelicts have been saying that the problem should be seen as a matter of the haves versus the have-nots. I'll have you know that I paid an exorbitant sum of money for the privilege of knowing as much."

Lewis shook his head in a dubious manner, took a healthy swig of his drink, and exclaimed, "Do you mean to tell me that these icons of philosophy and social justice have gotten the true struggle of humanity all wrong? You are saying that the actual problem is something different entirely and that if I buy some gold rocks and stuff them under my mattress, the tooth fairy is going to swing by later and make it all go away?"

Lewis paused for a moment. He flashed an unintended look of thoughtful awareness of the fact that his friend may have been onto something and capitulated through his dissent. "Okay, fine then, I'll take the bait if you tell me which camp Isabell falls into. If she's a gold bug too, I'll buy every last ounce you got and gladly pay you when we get home."

Ronan expected as much from Lewis as he had "half a snoot full," so he dug in a bit. "That's not exactly what I mean, Lew, but if you're wondering, Izzy loves the shiny and she hates the precious. You wear some Mister T chains in here without tipping over, and you just might come to understand what I mean."

Lewis laughed out loud and exclaimed, "No shit! Now you are speaking my language! I've been working on my game all night over here and I finally know why I'm not getting anywhere. I mean, hot damn, brother! I don't even have a pre-1964 quarter to give her! No wonder you get all the attention."

Ronan angled his eyes upward toward one of the television screens in a show of indecision while he contrived a sufficient response. Lewis put on a low, stealthy smirk, scratched his chin lightly, and needled Ronan a bit more. "That's a big relief, actually, RC. This mollifying point of light of yours means that my nascent game with the ladies is not bush-league stuff. Not only that, my friend, but your grand epiphany also implies that you aren't better looking than me. Your secret is simply all of that gold bullion that is bulging out of your pockets. I mean, sure, carrying like that is great juice for the ladies, as long as you don't fall into a lake."

They both laughed while Lew instantly shifted his focus and cocked his neck to check around the room again for Isabell. He appeared like some babysitter sitting off to the side of the playground who can't spot their charge after fifteen minutes of uninterrupted texting. "Where did she go, RC?" asked Lewis in a slightly disappointed manner.

Ronan ignored Lewis's question because he knew that when the sarcasm came on thick, he had Mr. MacAleer's undivided attention. Ronan continued. "No Lew, not camps with campers separated by political affiliation. Camps that are separated by monetary or financial preference. What I am saying is that you need to think of this as an exercise in human tendencies and broad-based demand when trying to grasp where the monetary order is headed."

Lewis nodded distractedly while stretching his neck a bit further to get a glimpse into the back of the bar. Ronan paid his preoccupied friend no mind. He understood that he was listening. "Now, people within both monetary camps align themselves all over the grand chess board socially. They may have differing political, social, spiritual, and sexual beliefs, and so on. The big point to grasp here, Lewis, is that when it comes to money, there are just two teams on the chessboard. Those that prefer to produce and save their excess production without putting their savings at risk, and those that would rather buy on credit, speculate with other people's money, and happily repay you tomorrow with debased currency. We are in the final innings of a grossly distorted monetary order that caters to the unproductive whims of the latter."

Lewis turned his eyes back toward Ronan, tilted his head slightly, and replied, "Okay, RC. I see where you are coming from. The problem is that ninety percent of all Americans are in the cheap credit camp. The ones that aren't are a different breed, like the Amish or something. But I doubt that is big news to you."

Ronan took another sip of his stout. "Absolutely, Lew. And that makes perfect sense, because our economy has been mutated into something designed to capitalize on speculation and the insane overvaluation of the dollar."

Lewis grew a little annoyed by Ronan's seamless answer to his provocation and asked, "What are you getting at, my friend?"

Ronan loosely focused his eyes on Mr. MacAleer and promptly rejoined him by saying, "I just want you to see that the camps we are talking about now are filled with savers of modest or ample wealth and debtors of modest or ample capacity to incur liabilities, in addition to other gadgets and sundry items sent to us from around the world for what will turn out to be a laughable pile of worthless shit tickets conjured up at will."

Lewis chuckled lightly and stated, "Nothing seems to be stopping that arrangement at the present moment. Shit, Ronan, the whole system was nearly vaporized three years ago, and we seem to be headed right back where we started."

Ronan turned his head slightly sidelong and countered his friend by saying, "That's a timing issue, Lewis. I'm not Nostradamus, but think of the peace of mind you will achieve once you understand this delineation. Once you discern the proper equilibrium values for gold and dollars such that both camps are in balance in the money world and free to do their duty for the sake of the global economy, you don't have to worry about the next financial crisis. If you can see how this equilibrium has swung in favor of one camp or the other during certain periods throughout history, you can understand why the failing dollar and the predatory speculation it is responsible for are the primary culprits behind the recent monetary chaos."

Lewis had drifted into a serene and thoughtful guise. He asked casually of Mr. Cassidy, "Why don't I just go out and buy other currencies instead of gold?"

Ronan was quick to answer the peacefully ruminating Mr. MacAleer. "Everything is tied to the dollar under the current system, and the dollar debtors that have been running the show since Bretton Woods, and who turned it into a three-ring circus following the Nixon shock, have stretched the proverbial rubber band to unimaginable limits. If you can see the truth of that statement through the fog of the dollar propaganda required to maintain confidence in an illusion, you will understand how to properly position yourself for the snap back to equilibrium, which is coming at us like a freight train blitzing through a murky tunnel. No currency that ascribes its value to dollar function is set to survive the fire of dollar hyperinflation. That is, except for the Euro, which was built to transfer its lost currency value into its marked-to-market gold reserves. Unfortunately, we could chat about the nuances layered within all of these fascinating subjects for hours."

Ronan had connected the dots quickly for Lewis, though the subject was one that took Mr. Cassidy years to wrap his arms around. He did this because Lewis was an exceptionally bright guy. Ronan also connected the dots very quickly because he didn't want his theory to get disjointed by a sidebar discussion regarding who knows what before he had laid bare the nuts and bolts of his beaming and beautiful epiphany.

Lewis looked at Ronan for a moment with his poker face so that he might gather his thoughts without conveying any emotion regarding his opinions on Mr. Cassidy's points. Lewis then proceeded to finish his IPA by taking two or three full swigs and said, "That's quite the cause-and-effect chain there, Ronan. I'd still rather do a bunch of shots with Izzy and close this place down with a bang, but I'll hear you out. I'm a curious sort. So, tell me more about this monetary epiphany of yours. Where is the rubber going to meet the road, Mr. Bling Bling?"

Ronan looked down at the table and picked up where he left off while trying to answer Mr. MacAleer's rather direct question. "So, here's the thing, Lew. Allow me to try and tie everything together a little more thoroughly for you while still painting with a fairly broad brush. We could probably discuss the finer points of gold and the inevitable dollar hyperinflation for days on end, but I don't want you to miss this…"

Lew folded his arms over the edge of the round table and quipped, "Me neither, buddy, me neither. Not that it matters a lick, but the Tigers are nearly done receiving their latest beating."

Ronan continued on with his thoughts, though he was a bit flustered by both the unwelcome interruption and the reminder that their time together was drawing to a close just as he approached the more technical aspects of his theory. "We will both agree that specialized production and trade are necessities when it comes to improving real lifestyles in today's world. Make more things better and everyone involved benefits."

Lewis nodded evenly and said, "Sounds reasonable, buddy."

Ronan smiled and nodded lightly to confirm that Lew was on board thus far and went on with it. "The thing is, Lew, over time and to adapt to changes and innovations, you absolutely need credit money to grease the wheels that maximize production and trade. You need currency and lots of it. That means ample access to credit, which is all the dollar is."

Lewis smiled and said, "Amen, my brother. Direct barter is a witch! My kid gave me a snotty napkin for my peach cobbler last night. Who wants to live in that kind of reality? Dollar bills make the world go round."

Lewis paused his response, raised his glass to Ronan, and then announced, "That's my epiphany for you, RC! As good-looking as I am, I highly doubt Isabell would bring over another round if I were just going to write down a bunch of lines for each drink on your cocktail napkin, sign it, and seal it with a hot kiss that made her knees wobble. We are regulars, but this here ain't Cheers, even if practically everyone does know our names."

Ronan perked up instantly once he believed he had effectively delivered his point on money being credit and the need for fungible credit to promote improvement and growth in the global economy. Of course, he knew that was the easy sell. He followed with, "Yes, that is exactly it, Lewis. You need the credibility of the bank to turn the credibility of your future productive efforts into spendable credits or cash on the go."

Lewis scratched his chin for a second. "That's a bit mind-bending, my friend. At half-past midnight, you are telling me my money is nothing more than the bank vouching for my good name and my ability to do something useful before I die? Well, shit, my man, if that's the case, they should be hitting my account with about seven zeros as we speak!"

Lewis scratched his chin slowly again and glanced down at their pint glasses. "That remains true even without a full beer in front of me. Though I can't for the life of me fathom as to why that is the case."

Lewis then proceeded to carry on in a sarcastically incensed manner to get a rise out of his friend. "Where is Isabell, for the love of all things bulging and beautiful? Is she down on our credit now too, in addition to our childish antics? Is she with that thug boyfriend you speak of out back?"

Ronan laughed openly as Isabell walked up behind Lewis and tapped him impishly on the shoulder. When Lewis looked back at her while his eyes crossed clumsily over his nose, she claimed ignorance of the conversation with a lift of her open palms. She then did the big eyes and pouty lips right on cue, and asked, "Need another round, gentlemen?" Immediately afterward, the evocative server winked smartly at the boys and scampered off to her stand at the bar. She did not wait a split second for an actual answer.

Lewis reddened a bit before saying, "Okay, Ronan, keep talking buddy. Generally speaking, it seems best if I keep my mouth shut for a good while. You are not, however," Lewis shook his finger heartily at Ronan, "off the hook for those shots when we hit the last call. Do not forget that, no matter how wrapped around the axel you are over this gold business."

"You know I would never do such a thing, Lew," responded Ronan cattily, as he worked through the last droplets of his stout so that his glass would be properly empty when the next helping arrived.

Ronan laughed a bit more while reflecting upon the scene of the prior moment and then got back into the meat of his thesis. "So, Lew, before we get into the money is credit angle any further, let me back up and give you a little refresher on the primary functions of money. I don't know what they taught you at that socialist hotbed up in Wisconsin, but I can assure you my finance professor skipped the lesson, if it was indeed ever on the syllabus."

Lewis was intrigued by Ronan's topic, but he felt like carrying on a bit and being a pain in the ass after being righteously embarrassed, so he responded as such: "Sounds like the perfect discussion for a Saturday night buddy. Good grief!"

"Sunday morning now, Lew. You are officially in the hot zone with your better half. Congratulations!" Ronan shook his head at Lewis's previously announced indifference as he said that, and moved along without stepping back to address what had just occurred.

"So, Lew, regarding the attributes of money, the survey says … (drumroll, please) … You guessed it. Medium of exchange is the most popular answer on the board of one hundred families supposedly surveyed. Number two on the board is unit of account. And number three is a doozy, Lew. The store of value function of money."

Lew applauded with raucous sarcasm, waved his hands wildly in the air, and then hit the table soundly with the open palm of his right hand, as if it were the game show buzzer. "Steal, please!" He exclaimed with a controlled shout.

Before Ronan could stop laughing at his friend's antics, Lew proceeded to answer the question. "What is a woman's primary measure of male attractiveness as the fourth function of money, Alex? Give it to me, as you must! Bonus round, please! Boom!"

Lew slammed the table firmly with both hands when he had finished hamming it up. The smack resounded forcefully off of the sealed plywood while he cooled his heels from the excitement of his version of the "lightning round." Ronan laughed and continued on in the same vein. "Question two, Lew. Does a balanced financial system use the same medium of exchange, unit of account, and store of value?"

Lew paused for a moment, briefly considered Ronan's question, and then answered. "I would say yes, Ronan. Only so that you can tell me why I'm wrong." Lew then winked at Ronan and turned his head to check on Isabell and her progress with the drinks over by the bar.

Ronan was deep in thought and gave some consideration to how best to proceed. Shortly thereafter, he revealed the answer to the question. "As surprised as you are to hear this, my friend, the answer is actually no, Lewis. The reason why is simple. Using currency as the ultimate store of value creates an unresolvable conflict between the debtor and saver camps we discussed earlier. The resolution of this conflict, which we are currently experiencing to the most extreme degree in recorded human history, is to move the optimal store of standardized value outside of the money system and unchain it from the paper liabilities that dilute its relational price to dollar money printing."

Lewis was actually rather intrigued by that concept. "Wow, I'm floored. How do you go about doing that, Mr. Cassidy?"

Ronan smiled knowingly at Lewis and answered his question directly. "The answer to your question is mind-bogglingly simple, my friend. You remove the best item to serve in the store of value function from the financial system, and you refuse to enforce the myriad paper contracts to acquire gold that have been issued by the bullion banks for decades."

Lewis scratched his head for a minute. He had many questions for his friend, but decided to ask the obvious one. "Yes, but how exactly do you accomplish that in terms of drawing investor interest back to your shiny rocks, Ronan? Gold may be the most despised asset class out there when it comes to the financial preferences of your average, moderately wealthy American."

Ronan was quite ready to deliver the punchline. "I'll skip over the all roads lead to gold discussion for you, Lew. All you do is … wait for it … wait for it …"

Ronan rattled his fingertips rhythmically against the table top as he spoke. "All that remains to be done is to remove the fractionally reserved nature of the world gold market, which is nothing but a holdover from prior iterations of the gold standard. To do that, you just remove the enforcement of all lending and futures contracts to be settled in gold. It can all be done with the stroke of a pen. Gold has been officially outside of the international monetary system since the Jamaica Accords of 1976. Of course, all of that only addresses the structural side of things. In terms of investor interest, the collapse of the dollar and its venomous financial apparatus will take care of the rest. Demand for gold in the non-Anglo-centric regions of the world remains quite robust. Most other countries have lived through a failed currency or two. In some places, and certainly among those with generational wealth, these concepts are understood nearly intuitively."

Ronan wove the look of one rather surprised by his own findings haughtily into the expression beaming from his countenance. He then spoke with direct emphasis. "Lew, I was blown away when I discovered that such a subtle change to the world monetary order would set the world on the path to financial and economic equilibrium. I mean, my jaw hit the floor when everything came together!"

Lewis wasn't yet sold on the existence of such a grand yet simple solution to the world's current monetary dysfunction. As such, he responded with an aggrandized slur, although his actual slur would have been marked had he been speaking to a Puritan, or even someone that had to get up for work in the morning. "Explain yourself, young man. That proposition is just not registering on the screen upstairs. Are you proposing that we hang a cross of gold around the dollar and return to the gold standard?"

Ronan knew that when it came to Mr. Lewis MacAleer, it never took long to shed the appropriate amount of light on a given matter. Therefore, he concluded his thesis by offering up the following statement while remaining prepared to answer the question asked of him: "Here it is, Lew. The world needs credit money and lots of it to keep trucking along with progress. If that statement weren't true, the purely fiat dollar would never have gained the credibility it needed to function without gold in the background. Even if establishing and maintaining that creditability requires the tacit and compelled support of excess producers the world over. However, as we arrive at the end of this ghastly experiment in purely fiat money, we can clearly see that the world also needs an unencumbered wealth reserve that savers can accumulate in exchange for the fruits of their labor without experiencing the ravages of inflation or accepting the undue risks one must take to circumvent the mandatory and exponential expansion of credit money."

Ronan paused to slap a shit-eating grin upon his already smug mien, and then delivered the punchline. "Lew, the simple solution is to value tangible gold in terms of its highest utility. That role for gold is to become the focal point store of value for the producers of the world, or, said a bit differently, the universal standard for wealth reserves. What it boils down to is not a gold standard, which confines the quantity of dollars and takes us back to the same flaw of pitting the debtors against the savers, except with the systemic advantages belonging to the savers, but a free-floating, internationally established market price for gold in the vault. That way, everyone gets what they need. The savers are not forced to become speculators, and the debtors can play all the games they want in the currency arena, though they will be called to task far more quickly than under the current monetary regime."

Lewis thought for a brief moment and interjected a bit of commentary. "That's the smartest shit I've ever heard come out of that gutter dwelling trap of yours. I'm almost impressed. Are you sure they made you wear a helmet to school for all of those years?"

Ronan cracked a sidelong smile, but he didn't want to lose his train of thought. He kept going with the lesson of the evening. "You see, Lew, that way you keep the dollars flowing in the role where they have their best and highest valued use; the settlement of commerce and the accounting entries for the relative values of items bought and sold in an exchange."

Ronan bit his lower lip pensively for a moment, looked up and directly into the eyes of his friend, and finished with the last of his non-collaborative thoughts on the matter. "The real abhorrent cheat in the system, and the single biggest factor in allowing this mess to continue, though there are many mechanisms that support the mirage of continuing dollar value, is the dilutive effect the paper gold market has on the price of actual gold. The creation of the paper gold market is what forces savers to take risks they don't want to inherit or, alternatively, to pay the inflation tax. In either event, they are subsidizing the debtor class by overvaluing the currency and its related financial instruments. It is as simple as that."

When Ronan finished with the last provision of his epiphany, he folded his hands on the table and glanced over his right shoulder to check on Isabell's progress with their order. Though the moment to get his order of wings into the kitchen had long since passed, he felt like he deserved a pint after his brief treatise. Unfortunately, that impishly seductive siren of the parched throats of every hapless family man within a twenty-mile radius of their local watering hole was chatting up a small group of customers still lingering about the tavern as the affairs of the evening began to wind down. Ronan had not even noticed the assemblage of folks seated behind the far turn of the bar earlier. At any rate, he figured Isabell was going to be a minute in doing her thing, so he turned back to Lewis and added a small dose of color commentary to his thesis.

"That is as succinct as I can make it for you, Lewis. I know there are various layers of complexity lurking beneath such a simple theory around something as intricate and sought-after as money, but I promise you, if you spend more time thinking about it, you will reach the same conclusion. The important part for you and your clients is to realize that the value of the dollar is going to drop precipitously at some point, and the value of tangible gold is going to rise proportionally. This see-saw effect will swiftly balance and then maintain the proper equilibrium between currency instruments, physical gold, and other tangible wealth assets in defining the absolute value of the world's demand for savings."

Lewis chuckled for a moment and then straightened his face to reveal a much sterner yet lightly puzzled look. "You are quite serious about this, aren't you, Ronan? Well, shit, my man. How about that! What kind of valuation adjustments are we talking about here?"

Ronan closed his eyes and gave careful consideration to whether or not he should answer the question exactly as he had answered it in response to his own curiosity. After a few seconds of pondering, he responded hesitantly, but only because he owed his friend the courtesy of full and fair disclosure.

"Well, Lew, I'm thinking somewhere along the lines of fifty times for the increase in the relative purchasing power of tangible gold and, of course, a near-total wipeout of the purchasing power of the current dollar."

Lewis said nothing in response to such seemingly outlandish hyperbole. Furthermore, the deadpan expression on his face gave no indication of what he was thinking at the time. He simply got up to use the restroom. He did, however, stop and stand next to Ronan after he had taken a few steps in the right direction. Lewis was a touch wobbly, but his gait was generally serviceable. Then, without warning, he gave Ronan a powerful slap on the back and announced loudly, and with an inflection riddled by audible amusement, "You don't fuck around, do you buddy?"

Lewis shook his head while he chuckled shamelessly. His eyes remained closed. "Playing for all the marbles, it sounds like, RC. Well, hot fucking damn! You bandit, you!"

With that, Lewis's tired eyes popped open, and he began walking forward until he reached the poorly lit hallway that led to the restroom. Ronan was mildly vexed and a bit put off by Lewis's response. He hastily called after his friend, "It's a *fait accompli* with the giant money already, Lew. You need to cover yourself before the gig is up!"

From the moment that night ended, the only discussion between them concerning gold was generally centered around the price movements of paper gold that occurred with some volatility as time marched on. Ronan understood why he had been unable to reach his friend, but he had hoped for a better outcome. However, deeply ingrained confirmation bias is simply a bridge too far to cross before that bridge collapses of its own accord in so many of the significant affairs of our lives.

When Lewis reached the end of the hall and was about to disappear from sight, he called back to Ronan, "And another thing, buddy, I wouldn't go broadcasting that investment thesis around town. You'll get locked up and then divorced. And you'll end up living in a van down by the river."

Lewis began to make the turn at the end of the hall, but promptly stopped before he had finished with that moderately destabilizing exercise. He arched his back slightly in an effort to peer back down the shaded hallway at Ronan, who was immersed in the comparatively ample light of the main barroom. He called back to his friend, and spoke with a far darker bent. "You and I both know that any resolution of the dollar issues hits deep, and has complications you haven't had time to consider, Professor Cassidy. Maybe in the world of financial preferences, your delineation of the debtors and the savers holds some water. But in the real world, where the question is ownership and control, there are also two kinds of people. There are the givers and the takers. And the takers have been running this carnival for quite some time. They ain't going to give up the magic money machine peacefully. They'll blow the whole place sky high before they let you or any of your deep-thinking buddies hang a cross of gold around the printing press. Lackeys, lapdogs, and hopelessly brainwashed idiots might come cheap, but they certainly don't come free."

Having said his bit, Lewis turned back to his left and straightened up his frame. He took a couple of crooked and ill-angled steps forward, managed not to hit the far wall while making the remainder of his wide, ground-losing turn, and then entered the restroom. Only a late and rapid shifting of his arms, which was accompanied by an upward thrust to fling the door violently open, kept the wobbling, late-night toper from breaking his beak on the sign that read, "Gentlemen."

The truth be told, Lewis had offered Ronan some sage advice given all of the facts and circumstances surrounding Mr. Cassidy's life at the time of their little powwow. Such counsel was certainly worthy of consideration and, moreover, inclusive of valuable insight that was well beyond the pay grade of the otherwise inebriated concoctions of Lewis's scurrying mind just then. The wayward Mr. MacAleer's unexpected dispatch of wisdom was a gainful portent to be carefully heeded by Ronan on several levels, yet it wasn't in Mr. Cassidy's nature not to try and sound the alarm if he could help even a few. Therefore, Ronan called back to his friend in the hopes that Lewis might hear him before the slowly closing door of the restroom would thwart his hastily cobbled words, words that were intended to counter such a dire warning before giving proper consideration to Lewis's meaning.

"You're right about the takers, Lewis! And the takers in the debtor camp do love running this game. But that doesn't change the truth of the matter, which is governed by the forces of nature. Sooner or later, this thing is coming back around. But mark my words, my friend. That solitary change to the bullion banking system will turn the world as we know it upside down. When that change occurs, it will have been far better to have been ten years early to the party than even a split second too late!"

The changes to the monetary order that Ronan saw coming back then were indeed inevitable. Yet, as the next eight years of his life unfolded, he would come to ponder those words of advice given by his playful and lightly intoxicated friend quite often. In the years that followed his wonderfully revealing monetary epiphany and his discussion with Lewis that night, Ronan would experience the effects of another inevitable force of nature quite severely. Something that was perhaps viewed more clearly as an unavoidable consequence of human nature and its governance over our singular and collective dealings with the prospects of a coming change set to reorder so much of what had been learned and accepted as truth for so very long. Ronan would come to fully understand that in the real world, people do not search very hard to see things that are not in their immediate interests to see. Unlike the dollar's dilemma of attempting to serve two adversely principled monetary camps, Ronan's dilemma was, for a time, simply that he continued to be the person God had made him to be. He was not capable of looking past a truth that had become as plain as day before the former abeyance of his once blinded eyes. But alas, when it came to money, wealth, and influence, and their unified and congruent specters with regard to guiding even the humblest workings of the human superorganism, it was indeed quite complicated.

At the end of the night, the cab that Ronan and Lewis were traveling in reached Lewis's house first. Mr. MacAleer and his wonderful family lived directly across the oftentimes busy two-lane thoroughfare from Ronan and his family. The quick drive to the northern outskirts of town was rather uneventful, as both Ronan and Lewis spent the majority of the ride uselessly grooming their wares for reentry into their suburban households at an hour during which the best that they could hope for was to remain undetected until morning. They had failed to remove the vast majority of the tattletale signs of their debauchery, but their hair looked nice. Not much was said outside of a few offhand remarks regarding Isabell and the premium state of those famously sculpted appendages belonging to the heavenly collaboration she exhibited as part and parcel of her well-endowed pageantry. Of course, the two of them had fallen for the personalized shot service at the end of the evening and grotesquely overtipped their server, but things of that nature always seemed to even out in the end. There was no harm and no foul in that regard.

The decision to drop Lewis off first was made by Ronan in an effort to get Lewis home and under wraps before Isabelle's flurry of Fireball drams had Mr. MacAleer seeing stars. Ronan was fighting the clock on that issue in his own regard, but he took one on Lewis's behalf since his friend had already been coming in hot to the tavern. When Lewis exited the cab, after a few tries at the door's mysteriously slippery handle, the two barely managed to knock knuckles while attempting a loving fist bump. They said their goodbyes, and Ronan had the cabbie idle his chariot for a moment until Lewis was safely inside, only after wavering and lingering in a state of confused thought out on the driveway for a brief while. Once Ronan had watched Lewis step across the front porch and carefully open the front door, the driver began to allow the vehicle to lurch ever so slowly backward and down Lewis's driveway.

Ronan had one quote on his mind as he prepared to return home that evening. Strangely, the verse was not related to gold or money, or, at least, not directly in the opinion of Mr. Cassidy. The quote reads: *"Just because you do not take an interest in politics doesn't mean politics won't take an interest in you."* – Pericles (430 B.C.). Ronan wondered why those words were on his mind while he made the short walk to the side door of his comfortable, suburban middle-class home, but perhaps the quote was a forethought of what indeed might lie ahead in a time of great change if unsustainable fallacies were to be accepted as the order of the day in the name of self-preservation.

Ronan opened the door and made a bee-line for the sofa. He had previously elected to further stack the case against his errant behavior that evening in favor of postponing the trial to a time when he would be far more fit to provide a reasonable defense on his behalf. The call Ronan had made was a little bit of six in one hand and a half dozen in the other, but his decision easily won the moment due to present expediency. After Ronan had weaved his way cautiously around the dense marble coffee table through the blinding darkness, he dropped back onto the most comfortable spot in the world. The spot where the girls tended to pile up the pillows at the center of the wraparound sofa. While he lay there staring up at the ceiling, yet seeing only the pitch of the small hours before he drifted into the clutches of his alcohol-induced slumber, he could not help but wonder what Lewis had meant when he uttered the words, "Try to hang a cross of gold upon the dollar."

The inferences implied by Lewis's statement were loaded and ran deep into the political and socio-economic roots of the history behind the evolution of America's, and then the world's, dollar. There had been the gold dollar, the gold standard, the gold exchange standard, the internationally convertible dollar, and ultimately, the purely fiat dollar, which followed the Nixon Shock of 1971. Though Ronan suspected that Lewis's reference to a cross of gold being hung around the dollar derived from William Jennings Bryan's speech given at the Democratic National Convention of 1896, a time when the debtor, or easy money, camp was attempting to make money more plentiful by recognizing both gold and silver as monetary standards, the inference also invoked thoughts of God in Ronan's mind, and prodded him to consider the natural order of the world for a short while.

As Mr. Cassidy saw things back then, there was God above all else. Moreover, there was the communal intelligence of the human collective moving in unison with the shared yet individually oscillating rhythms of the mind, body, spirit, and soul. Set against that beautiful creation of the infinitely divine were the grasping and controlling hands of the powerful, the wanting, and the wicked. Those cursed to forever attempt to defile the flawless symmetry of our heavenly creator, and sadly, those fooled into thinking that was just the way of things. At that soulful moment of his tenderly approaching rest, one of those times spent between the shifting boundaries of the earth and the galvanizing ether of his essence, which eternally belonged to the realms beyond, Mr. Cassidy had subliminally understood why the words of Pericles were on his mind. For, it could be said that aside from the Good Lord above and the ones he loved upon this earth, Ronan valued his freedom under God and the freedom he shared with those same loved ones above all else.

But alas, Ronan had drifted off to sleep before he began to sense that the symbolism of the cross of gold ran far deeper within him. He was dreaming long before he would begin to sense that an ancient totem of like description yet tangible form would be irrevocably tied to those defining moments of his life that would draw him across the great ocean to that timeless and enchanted island haunted by the lingering mists and the sorrowful lamentations of the unsettled spirits of the age. That certain cross of gold and its primeval constituency of enduring wealth, which neared exemplifying the full embodiment of where the shine of Mr. Cassidy's mind, body, spirit, and soul intersected, was a matter for another day of God's choosing. In hazarding a guess as to why Ronan had become fixated on such an emblem years prior to even the first of his visions to depict that sacred heirloom, one can only say that perhaps the symbol of the cross, and one of a golden fabrication, were but a few of the eternal representations of true freedom under God.

Chapter 3

THE VISION OF THE GOLDEN CROSS

Some eight years beyond the moment of that rather pivotal epiphany, and at a moment in time that existed within the same annual season as his fateful journey to the island of Inis Mor, Ronan Cassidy imagined that he woke with a start, though he continued to sleep soundly. The date soon to be marked off on his monthly calendar, which was neatly tacked to the kitchen wall, was Wednesday, February 5th, 2020. At the time of that lucid dream of his, a clock on the wall would have revealed that it was the third hour of the morning. According to both the constructs of the waking world and the descending depths of his dream, Ronan had fallen asleep on the wrap-around suede sofa in the same manner. He had been watching his favorite feature film, The Last of the Mohicans. He was unaware that his mind had returned to that identical date in February, some seven years in the past. Mr. Cassidy did, however, remember that he had drifted off to sleep as the movie ended without shutting off the television.

Ronan's dream was initially notable due to the fact that he fondly remembered solving the perplexing riddle behind General Montcalm's release of the surrendering British soldiers at Fort William Henry with the full honors of war. Only then, had he come to recognize that the French general had known that the tattered band of proper redcoats and frontier militia were to be massacred by his Huron allies during their march of retreat back to Fort Edward. That perplexing aenigma had remained one of those nagging curiosities in Mr. Cassidy's life; a nagging curiosity that had plagued him since he fell in love with the writings of James Fennimore Cooper back in high school and the movie some years later. Taking the creative license of both Mr. Cooper and the writer of the adapted screenplay as an aside, what Mr. Cassidy treasured regarding such knowledge was how those candid details of both fact and hyperbole had been woven into that riveting tale of the colonial years of the American experience in such an enigmatic fashion. For him, understanding all that he could in regard to the thoughts, deeds, and societal norms of that period in time was of the utmost importance. Those were the years that the unbound will of the American nation was forged on that boundless and untamed continent in accordance with liberty and under God's law.

Ronan's eyes had adjusted to the pitch of the nightshade, which was given off by this vivid fantasy in such a way that the surrounding darkness was identical to what he would have expected to see upon waking. Yet, he soon realized that he was unable to detect even the slightest trace of those familiar objects that should have belonged in the room during that tricky phantasmal reverie. Shortly thereafter, he sensed that, without moving his feet, he was somehow walking watchfully into an unidentified but strangely familiar doorway, which was also obscured by the scant traces of dusty light present within his uncertain surroundings. At that instant, he became aware, and, in fact, certain, that he was dreaming.

Regardless of the inconsequential details surrounding the flash of his properly aligned awareness with his ethereal environs, everything that Ronan saw and felt seemed so real that he continued to proceed within that dream as if he had returned to the mirrored sensations and consequences of the waking world. Whether he was asleep or awake in the world of sentient things, or he was merely being made aware of some spectral realm that would surely fade into the breaking of the light of day, mattered little to the insecurely entranced Mr. Cassidy. Intuitively, he understood that he was looking for something that existed within the unknown depths of that shadowy realm. There was something lurking within that supernal haven of his mind, which bore such shocking similarities to the cherished places of his past, that he was being prompted to find. He would not deny that urge under any circumstance.

A short while later, Ronan was standing on his feet, or at least he believed as much. After taking a few steps forward, he entered a darkened room, which he soon recognized to be his daughter, Maddie's, but the darling child was not in her bed. A brisk chill came over Mr. Cassidy while a cold and divergent breeze tickled the back of his neck. The large tan blanket that Maddie slept under was pulled back and almost perfectly folded over into the opposite corner of the bed. The unusual arrangement gave the golden-hued comforter, which rested above her fuzzy cotton blanket, the appearance of a somewhat shapely triangle while shaded in that strange and lingering darkness. Maddie's stuffed puppy was lying on the pillow next to the book that Ronan had read to her that evening, yet Ronan could not recall having seen the book before as he studied the outer cover from a short distance away.

He was becoming a bit frightened by the present situation and all the more confused. As such, he approached the bed and flipped through the pages of the story to either confirm or deny his mounting doubts and fears, but the characters portrayed in the few pictures illustrated within the manuscript were entirely foreign to the grown man, who had become so well versed in children's literature as his daughters continued to sprout up. Stranger than the disarming oddity of his unfamiliarity with the work was the fact that the book was suited for a reader far more advanced than Maddie, who was only in her seventh year.

There was a sizable golden bookmark neatly tucked between the eleventh and twelfth pages of the peculiar book. The bookmark possessed a standard rectangular shape and was sized in accordance with most of its ilk. Moreover, it appeared to have been stamped by a library of some sort. The distinct red markings were eerily reminiscent of the date stamps placed on the return cards of the grade school books Mr. Cassidy would take out from his own local library, which was just a few blocks up the street from his childhood home. Though it was initially difficult to read the numbers stamped on the golden insert in the unlit room, Ronan was eventually able to discern what the slightly smeared branding of the thick red ink revealed: a date that was a month, seven days, and seven years in advance of that fifth day of February in 2013.

Speaking in accordance with the proper delineations of waking time, the date stamped onto the bookmark was only one month and a week into the future for the man who had fallen asleep during the ending credits of his favorite movie just a short while ago. Given his subliminal realization of the distortion in time caused by his dream, Ronan began to become disoriented as he continued to stare at the date of the library stamp pressed onto the golden bookmark. A date that can be written down precisely as: 03/12/20. Nothing he was feeling while immersed in the shifting grip of that vivid dream was in sync with the time revealed by that date stamp.

Ronan returned his attention to the book he was holding tightly in his right hand. He closed the grand fairytale and carefully placed the hardbound volume back down next to the indentation in the pillow made by his absent child's once peacefully resting head. Ronan had decided to return to the hallway and see if Maddie had fallen asleep in another room with her sister or her mother. However, when he tried to leave the room, instead of entering the upstairs hallway of his suburban Chicago home, as he reasonably expected that he would, at least while within the confines of that dream, he found himself standing in the upstairs bathroom between the double sink and bathtub.

The humble washroom was also quite dark. Nevertheless, Ronan could make out the marble of the sink and even certain portions of the light and dark shades of the shower curtain. He could not identify the actual colors of the shrouded stripes of that ornamental drapery of a sort, but he knew that it was dressed in the pastel pinks, greens, and yellows of the Easter season. When he looked forward, he noticed that the bathroom window, which was carved into the back wall of the house and overlooked the back porch and the peaceful cul-de-sac below, was wide open.

As if the sight of the open window had finally triggered the appropriate reaction while he remained within the vivid haunts of that shifting and unsteady reality, Ronan was quickly overwhelmed by the arctic air of the outdoors, which rushed in through the gap of the open window and was also blowing faint traces of snow into the quaint and tidy room. He soon took notice of the fact that he was shivering and stepped forward to close the window while he continued to fret over Maddie's absence from her bed. When Ronan reached the open portal, he looked down from the second story onto the back porch below. The nearly ground-level deck was covered in a shallow blanket of dry and flaky snow, which was ancient kin to the arctic air of February. Shortly thereafter, his heart skipped a beat altogether. There was a foreign man standing below him. That man was fully upright and motionless, his black trench coat contrasting deviantly and defiantly against the pristine whites of the untouched flurries that had fallen onto the pine boards beneath his feet.

The man below was tall, or perhaps only presented as such, due to his noticeably slender build, dark raiment, and the position of Ronan's overhead yet somewhat proximate line of sight. Upon further inspection, Mr. Cassidy could surmise that this man was dressed rather ominously, as he was covered from head to toe in what appeared to Ronan's widened eyes to be a color so black that it must belong to the closets of only the soulless. Given the uncommon darkness of that sharp and gelid night air, it was difficult for Ronan to attribute any other prominent or differentiating characteristic to the shadowy ensemble of the man beyond that of his brimmed hat, which was also dusted over in a healthy serving of what must have been that evening's snowfall. That foreign man or entity of the nether regions was standing so very still that he appeared no different than a statue, even as he raised his well-defined chin into the cutting sheers of the icy and biting west wind, which had begun to pound at the back of the house without warning. Ronan was forced to shield his eyes momentarily from the onslaught of the biting gales, yet when he removed his arm from his line of sight, the strange and shadowy figure was still standing directly below him. The brazen, or perhaps lost and confused, intruder hadn't flinched in the slightest.

When the blistering winds paused, though only intermittently, Ronan poked his head out of the window to get a better view of his uninvited guest. However, and not altogether to his advantage, Ronan bumped his head squarely on the wooden frame of the glass because he paid the obstacle no mind once he had focused his eyes on the presence of the stranger below. The clear and unmistakable clamor carried readily out into the bizarre tincture of the almost hollow and echoing air of that dismal evening. The dull yet distinctive sound caused the man below to quickly turn around and look up at Ronan with a sharp yet angling tilt of his neck that locked the shrouded man's eyes precisely onto their intended mark. The stern look that emanated from the man was so black and so empty that the glance alone sent a tremor shooting straight through Ronan's body. The initial shock to his system was so severe that Mr. Cassidy could feel the hairs of his arms and chest stand on end. The sharpened barbs, now at attention on Ronan's skin, remained that way as the soul-piercing wind began to rise again and dart directly into Ronan's flesh through the opening of the small bathroom window.

The man below did not attempt to flee or hide after seeing Ronan looking down at him from the open window. To the contrary, he opened his eyes wide and glared intensely at Ronan from across the void of that strange, almost dreamlike night air. At the moment the shadowy man's eyes had swiftly served to allow him to glean the nature of Mr. Cassidy's drumming heart, the distance between the two men was no more than fifteen feet. Ronan remained frozen at the window. He did not know whether to admonish the foreign man by way of a fierce holler or close his eyes and reopen them in the hope that the ghastly apparition would simply disappear.

Deferring to the latter proposition while given over to the uncertain state of his delicate reckoning, Ronan closed his eyes so tightly that his teeth flashed into the frozen breath of the sudden rise of the sheering wind. Be that as it may, when he had reopened his glassy, wind-lashed orbs, the man below had not vanished at all. Worse than that horrifying, although not altogether unexpected, phenomenon, there was now a fire raging in the unwavering eyes of that dark spirit. That man, or black phantom soul, continued to stare at Ronan with his eyes ablaze, though he made not the slightest motion otherwise. It was as if the only care of those burning corneas was to understand the living pith of Ronan Cassidy's soul.

The rather shocking display, which was surely an omen spawned of the darker order, accompanied a feeling that Ronan had experienced only once in his life. He dreaded even the thought of that horrifying flash in time that had sent him plummeting into the abyss. Feeling terrified, entirely hapless, and unable to invoke any remedies of a more useful nature, Ronan screamed into the frozen glass before his eyes, which was the suddenly tranquil yet still downright brumal night air. His deafening rebuke was directed at the uncertain shape of the terrifying specter below, but the demon simply raised his open palm to Mr. Cassidy before a single octave of Ronan's numinously halted yell split the night. The calmly executed and seamless act of raising his hand had completely silenced Ronan's bootless screams. Ronan heard nothing while the top of his throat drummed on and went raw from the force of his muted yet violently projected cries.

After a half-minute or more of that black subterfuge, which throttled Ronan's attempted squalls of rebuke and accompanying cries for help, the man on the snow-covered deck below suddenly began to pull violently at his throat. He appeared as if he were trying to get free from something so vile to his flesh that he would have severed his neck to remove the object of his torment. As the hollow man drew his attention away from Ronan, his suffocating victim took in a hurried cluster of deep and traumatic breaths. Ronan did this to compensate for the savage and wholly unproductive exhalations that he had intended to be the dins of his alarm. Once his wind had returned after choking down those rapid gasps of frozen air, Mr. Cassidy began to meticulously study that now curiously and frightfully agonized creature below.

As the dark man continued to freakishly pull at his collar with both hands, he inadvertently spun around while consumed by his frenzied struggle and was once again facing Ronan. Then, in what seemed to Mr. Cassidy to be an almost preprogrammed instant of perfect clarity, he beheld what the insufferable object around the dark man's neck was. The man below shifted violently and thrashed uncontrollably one final time until he was doubled over with his knees resting in the thin blanket of snow covering the porch boards. When the man was still, Ronan understood that he had submitted to the unrelenting hold and absolute dominion that the brightly shining object draped around his neck held over him. The once placidly savage and then fitfully wanting creature that had torn at the flesh of his neck until it bled, and in the midst of that passing fit would have been presumed to be either a demon unleashed from the depths of hell or a rabid man, had settled from the futility of its lashing fits in much the same manner as Ronan had settled from the trauma of his muted screams.

The golden object chained around the dark man's neck began to shine radiantly as he rose to his feet. Once he stood at the fullness of his height before Ronan, the object somehow appeared to be shining into the pitch of the darkness of that cold and snowy night from somewhere within that now quite human apparition. It appeared to Ronan at that moment that the strange man was somehow fueling the golden object's dazzling and brilliant luster. The once harrowing transformation, which was now entirely settled and, therefore, able to be understood as the necessary pangs of rebirth that it was, now seemed almost sublime to Mr. Cassidy as he continued to watch on in awe from above.

That strange and foreign being, now clearly more man than the soulless possession of some demon of the night, expelled a harsh breath of hot air, which billowed white and was remarkably stark against the scintillating freeze of the otherwise black and strangely vitreous air. The dark man then coughed so severely that he doubled over once more, that time from the blunt force of the continuous discharge. He continued coughing spasmodically until he went silent, some fifteen seconds or more after the episode had begun. He stood up once again, this time facing away from Ronan's curious eyes, which were tearing up from the razor-sharp shears of the intermittent winter winds that were crossly rifling into the space of the open window. After straightening his overcoat with a firm and almost military-style pull and wiping his chin with an unseen kerchief, the dark man turned and looked upward to face Ronan directly. Ronan remained resolute in the face of the opposing force of the razing winter winds. His focus remained unbroken, and he stared back at the man from the open window positioned above that wholly transformed creature of the night.

The once terrifying apparition of a man dressed in black looked up at Ronan with a meek and childlike, yet somehow knowing, smile adorning his warmly delicate and exposed features, which were dressed in the chilled and pallid flesh of his comely visage. The fire once burning at the heart of his sea-blue eyes had been fully quenched. That suddenly affable and welcoming man now appeared vulnerable to intimacy, at least of a distant nature, and exquisitely human to Ronan as Mr. Cassidy continued to assess the astonishing metamorphosis that had just unfolded before him. There was something tender about the boy-like innocence of the foreign man's almost dumbfounded smile, pinched shoulders, and submissive open palms as he gazed into Ronan's steadfast and discerning eyes.

The childish look worthy of any loving mother gave the impression that the man was silently saying to Ronan, "Here I am. I am revealed to you. Please do not look away. See me as I am and do with me what you will."

The curiously innocent look and timid posture of the man below gave great comfort to Ronan. He felt as if some unknown future peril had been circumvented and, furthermore, was now accruing in his favor. In fact, if asked to explain the almost laughable and perplexing smile on this wholly transmuted and so vulnerably innocent-looking man's face, Ronan would have explained: "His queer yet heart-warming smile belonged to some happy and still playfully meddlesome little boy who no longer wished to hide his shame. Perhaps a boy who was facing up to his mother after having met with success through the act of following her instructions, yet following those directives only after trying every other futile solution that he could conjure up otherwise."

Shortly thereafter, the man below closed his deep blue eyes and lifted his chin and his palms to the heavens in a show of solemn and reverent thanksgiving to God above. At that moment, Ronan turned slightly to shield his tender, frozen eyes from the radiant light shining forth from the four points of the man's medallion. The golden object shone so brightly that Ronan could do little else in the face of such an indescribable radiance. As the wonderfully burning light began to fade, Ronan slowly, and by degree, opened those raw and woefully tested orbs to the returning darkness and the inexplicable and unabashed innocence of the man below. Be that as it may, and against the seemingly rational and hopeful expectations of the younger rendition of Mr. Cassidy, there was nothing present on the deck below.

Ronan blinked, and then there was nothing at all except the utter pitch of night beyond, which was once again muting the sightlines of his wide-open and carefully shifting eyes. Seconds later, there remained nothing but the darkness of the night beyond and the testy ticking of the unlit black clock pricking irksomely at his sensitive ears and keeping time in the room where he lay—the very room where Ronan had been sleeping and was, in truth, physically present during the third hour of that minatory, yet cryptically revealing, February morning in 2020. His Midwestern home and the endearing books he had read with his three little angels were half a world away and once again belonged to the days gone by.

The shifting scope of Ronan's intense and rather evocative dream, or perhaps a vision of a higher order, did not end there. He rubbed his still-watering eyes in the darkness, attempting to press away some excess moisture that had mysteriously gathered around his muddled corneas. He then widened his eyes and batted his eyelids after prodding those mussy orbs to adhere more closely to the limited deliberations that were veiled by the enveloping blackness of his proper time and station within the waking world, a world to which Ronan presumed he had returned once that frightful dream of the prior hour had slipped into the depths of his latent mind. He was soon surprised, however, to find that he was sitting quietly in a room that was nothing like the one he had expected. That quaint and tranquil room was pleasantly lit by the indirect meanderings of the morning sun and held firm to the scents of the countryside and antique furniture. Although Ronan did not recognize the room at first glance, he sensed that the modest quarters were not entirely foreign to him.

Not much time passed before he realized that the strange bedroom was a place he had seen several times in passing but had never dared to enter. The room was small but not insufficient, prosaic but not entirely aseptic, and it was guarded by the pines and hills that surrounded the back of the house, though it remained amiably bright during the daylight hours. Taking further note of the details of his unexpected surroundings, Mr. Cassidy quickly determined that the room was also situated within an interval of time that, while not current, was certainly not beyond the bounds of some early season of his existence.

He began to stare out of the fair-sized bedroom window, which was trimmed by a set of plain white curtains that were fully drawn. The window faced up to a moderately steep, yet pleasantly rounded and grassy hill that was located behind the dwelling. The view obliged by the thinly paned glass divulged little in regard to the broader setting of that dislocated expression of Ronan's fancy, which appeared to him as some peculiar manifestation of the cosmic interplay of the dimensions beyond his waking sensibilities. Though the plain and altogether nondescript room did little to stir his confused yet strangely placated sentiments, he quickly ascertained that the world out of doors was dressed warmly in the pleasantries of a bright summer day. One that had perfectly glossed its magnificent wares over some beautiful but previously forgotten countryside demesne.

After taking in what the windows in the room afforded him of the delightful morning outside, Ronan looked carefully around the room for further intimations that might exist therein concerning his whereabouts. He noticed that the smartly painted walls were of a powder blue so faint that the demure shade was only detectable when contrasted against the white sheets that covered the sleeping man lying in the bed before him. The seasoned gentleman beneath those sheets was quite sick and appeared to be sleeping somewhat uncomfortably, almost as if he had been drawn into the realm of the subconscious by either medication or as the result of some unknown trauma to his head. Ronan did not stare long at the exposed countenance of the otherwise shrouded and altogether infirmed old man, who would have been entirely recognizable to the Mr. Cassidy that belonged to the world of the sentient.

There was a large cross that had been nailed into the wall over the slightly trembling head of the sedentary old man. The cross was created from molded, intricately fashioned, and ornately painted ceramic. The beams of the crucifix were tenderly and carefully enameled in pastels of the softest hues that had come to embody the spring and Easter seasons. The beautiful and exacting detail of the Lord Jesus at the hour of his death quickly captured the full measure of Ronan's theretofore drifting and uncertain attention.

For no reason that Ronan could have explained, he stood up and slowly approached the bed with a watchful eye, as he wished to examine the elderly gentleman who was sleeping so uncomfortably. Mr. Cassidy then looked curiously down at his soft, boyish hands, which appeared to be the sprouting appendages of a much younger entity than he professed to be. Curiously, his boyish hands remained that way for the entirety of the time that he was present in that room. Ronan soon realized that he was also much shorter in stature than his typical six-foot-high frame, and he became uncontrollably sad and confused while he approached the sickly old man with slow, silent, and sidling steps taken on the tip-toes of childlike feet. As these feelings of sorrow grew more pronounced within, Ronan began to fear what he might learn as he timidly drew near to the head of the bed.

Just as the old man's troubled countenance was about to become visible to the small boy, who was creeping his way forward in perfect silence, a blinding burst of white light exploded into the room from the door to the hallway, the hallway leading out to the great veranda windows at the front of the red, A-frame country cottage. Though none of the home's additional details had been made known to Ronan as he inched his way forward, for the simple reason that he had not quite come to remember where he was, those giant veranda windows at the front of the house overlooked a five-acre grass field that ran down a gently graded slope to an uninterrupted gathering of thick and seasoned northern pines, which swayed gently in the offing just beyond the split in the drive. There were a few birch and spruce trees sprinkled into the depths of that wooded terrace for good measure, but those few outliers had to be carefully spotted from the vantage point of that aforementioned veranda or closer.

When the piercing light was fast upon his squinting eyes, Ronan immediately shielded his brow with the warm, soft flesh of his puerile right forearm. He held that forearm in place until the light, without dimming or waning at all from its full-spectrum radiance, suddenly felt warm and gentle and quite pleasing to those once tender sensory receptors. At that moment, Ronan unshielded his eyes and the once blinding light began to fade, until it was reduced to the intensity of perhaps the direct and unchecked sunlight of a cloudless summer day.

In the presence of that purifying light, Ronan once again looked intently at the old man lying on the bed. He could see the details of his face so clearly that he felt as if he could ascribe each perfectly defined wrinkle to the specific series of events in his life that slowly brought those sharp creases into being. Without warning, Ronan began to tear up as he reached his hand judiciously forward to feel for the warmth of the old man's tightly defined cheek. When the skin of Ronan's hand had only lightly glanced the warm but somewhat leathery flesh of the man's slightly writhing lower jaw, the angst that had so vexed the sleeping man gave way to a peaceful repose, which rapidly settled upon his oddly comforted countenance. Not long after the sensation of that first trembling contact from the small boy's hand, the sleeping man's face began to shimmer and glow, as if some great weight and unrelenting rebuke had been taken away from him through little more than the boy's wish that it might be so.

The dying man did not awaken, but he seemed to rest at ease. He rested as if he were at last hopeful that a far better reckoning awaited him in the expanse where the watch was kept over hallowed ground. The light in the room began to intensify again until Ronan could see nothing except for the ceramic crucifix fixed to the wall behind the bed. The artistic emblem had lost the identifying coloring that it possessed when Ronan first came to realize that he was sitting in the room. Then, the cross began to shine brighter than even the blinding white light that had filled the room in the prior minute. In the flash of an instant, the cross began to gleam and radiate like the proximate sun, which Icarus had approached without the proper humility and respect for the divinity and intent of God's creation.

About thirty seconds later, the radiance of the cross posted on the powder blue wall began to cool, until that eternal luminescence resembled the golden light of the twilight hours lingering over and within an unculled Idaho wheat field in the first weeks of October. That stirring aurum shone down not upon the tired and broken body of the old man, but remained an effusive golden luminescence that sparkled gently at the fringes, where the glow of the light seemed to irradiate and give definition to the source of the passing man's soul. The awestruck little boy believed that the very essence of the man was being x-rayed and impossibly measured in the fullness of his conceived glory and grace in the physical realm. Mr. Cassidy was stunned. He could not recall ever seeing such a thing, nor could he have adequately explained the miraculous vision of that purified essence, which was revealed to him during the freeing of the old man's spirit and soul, if so prompted in the days to come.

Ronan could not describe the distinctive shine of the golden reflections and the triumphant refractions of that rich and mollifying light. Nor could he possibly have conceived of how those infinite and absolute streams of radiance seemed to warp and bend the fabric of space and time to their will, as if all that once was and all that will be simply is, and, furthermore, that those sorrows of the past were forever intended to be wiped away in an instant by the grace of God. It was as if those dangling rays of warming light cloaked the old and fallen man exactly as they would have when he was first breathed into the world by his heavenly creator.

Conversely, what Ronan could have explained as the dying man lay there, and remained lying there in stillness as he would, was that the once perfectly vexed and troubled man had been redeemed in whole and in part through God's grace alone. As the remainder of his confusion concerning the nature and circumstances surrounding those events drifted away, Mr. Cassidy recalled thinking that there was an incessant comfort in the revelation of such a possibility, and beyond even the benediction of that soul-warming epiphany, he remembered thinking that there was indeed a great hope that follows us all throughout the entirety of this life. A great hope that patiently bides its time, eternally awaiting the moment of our acceptance and the sublime reckoning of our acquiescence to the will of the divine.

At that moment, Ronan felt a tender softness come over the more delicate cords of his metrically beating heart, a distinctly human contrivance, which had somehow transcended the physical limitations of the supernal realms he now traversed. Ronan bowed his head in response to such majesty, which had been made plain before his eyes and was only given through the purity of divine grace and mercy. As that blessed feeling took hold of Ronan, a great call to be heeded rang out from the kingly voice of someone not visible through the depths of the cascading field of golden light. That perfected voice, which belonged equally to the sentiment of love and the disposition of supreme authority, had called out just as the issuer of the exclamation reached out for Ronan's hand and held it tightly.

The Word had called to Ronan, "Witness, My child! See the world as they do, and in so doing, be redeemed! Only then will you understand how to lead even one among My beloved flock home. My blessings are not such that they are forced upon my children. The work ahead is to thaw their hearts and open their eyes to My presence! The one who calls to you in your dreams will one day show you such things. If only you say yes, all will be made plain to you."

Then, an angel of the heavenly host swathed its giant and resplendent wings, which possessed plumes that felt as if they were made from comforting velvet, around the enrapt and duly startled child to comfort him. The angel whispered in his ear, "See Him, my child, and see His marker before you. Only when your heart is open to His presence in this world, my dearest one, can you rest peacefully through your faith in the Almighty. The road ahead will be long and tiring at times, but in Him alone, you are indeed so fearfully and wonderfully made for the righteous task He has placed before you."

With the thundering echo of those divine words still ringing in his ears and burning in his soul, Ronan lifted his head and opened his eyes into the gathering light. Shining against those rapidly coalescing points of splendid illumination rested a cross of gold on the light blue wall where the ceramic cross had once been tacked.

Ronan's eyes had remained open, or so he believed, yet his field of vision shifted back to the dimming light of the homey and open suburban living room he knew so well. He could make out the blackened screen of the idle television set, and he could feel the suede, wraparound sofa beneath the stillness of his motionless body somewhere beyond the bounds of time. Startled by this unexpected turn of events, which placed him somewhere that he no longer expected to be, he sprang from the sofa and ran up the stairs. He slipped noticeably when clearing the fourth step while his wind pushed forth in quickening bursts of rushing air. When he had reached the top of the stairs, he continued forward for a few steps until he reached the door to Maddie's room. Once there, he hesitated for a brief while, standing completely still in front of his daughter's nearly shuddered door and remitting a silent but steadfast plea to the heavens.

Once he had prepared his vexed mind to discover what lay beyond by way of that brief rite of supplication, Ronan slowly and carefully pushed the cracked door to the little girl's room fully open. He stepped quietly yet hurriedly next to Maddie's bed, and his racing heart began to normalize. She was there. She was fast asleep beneath the layers of warm and comforting blankets. Her stuffed puppy was next to her head, and the book full of animated dinosaurs that the two of them had read earlier that night was opened to the page with the mighty Triceratops and the terrible T-Rex. Ronan released an exasperated sigh of relief and put his hand across his chest to check his wildly beating heart. He then leaned down and kissed his sweet baby girl on her forehead and felt the warmth of her small, softened hand against his fingers. Afterward, he settled down in the bed next to the peacefully sleeping child while rekindling those haunting yet magnificent visions he had just witnessed. He did this while staring blankly at the ceiling and wondering what meaning each of those revelations held for the days to come.

Ronan continued to think through the lingering images that comprised those sharply defined and potent visions that had been branded into the Kodachrome of his mind's eye. He continued to lie still while remaining next to his beloved little girl and pondering the shifting colors, scenery, and sounds that had just twisted his perception of reality. However, at that moment, Mr. Cassidy anchored his thoughts in the warmth of Maddie's undeniable presence. He was just thankful that she was there in her bed, sleeping soundly. Perhaps she was dreaming of that magical place where the mighty T-Rex still claimed dominion over the prehistoric earth.

Once soothed by the presence of his daughter next to him in that comforting bed in the wake of her imagined disappearance and, likewise, placated by some razor-thin tether to the standard constructs of his known reality, Ronan faded off to sleep before he was able to ponder the mysteries of his temporal dislocation any further. Nevertheless, he woke up the next morning still trying to give proper boundary and definition to the reality of the present and the implications of those white-hot and indelible flashes from his past: those imagined, those remembered, and those that were of another nature altogether, and what those given manifestations held for the future. Moreover, he wondered how those images would continue to define whatever it was that mysteriously shaped the delicate spaces that lie in between, those places where all things intersect in the absence of time.

While in the midst of his shifting perceptions of the very essence of life, he wondered, "Is there indeed a difference between the past or the future, or even a difference between those partially and wholly imagined constructs of our mind, which are shaped entirely through experience, and the contorted revelations of our dreams? Is one any more real than the other?"

At that particular moment, Mr. Cassidy doubted that it was possible for any known perception of time, or even the spatial plane, to exist in some defined reality of those primary dimensions made known to us if we are relegated to the use of our fluttering and always distracted senses of the present day. Yet, upon emerging from the shadow of that ubiquitous dream, which was beyond the known delineations of time, Ronan also doubted that the present could indeed exist. At least he doubted that it could exist as he had come to perceive that always nearing yet simultaneously fleeing juncture. There was clearly something that prevailed far beyond the well-understood and even widely accepted limitations of the human condition that Ronan had come to accept as quite real while he slept that night. Mr. Cassidy had finally come to understand the critical nature and identity of his unwavering faith in his omniscient Creator through the soul-rending revelations of that second great vision of his life. Everything beyond love simply became amorphous and subject to the errors and misconceptions certain to accompany human interpretation and, therefore, lacked the capacity to exist in any enduring way.

Although Ronan still loosely embraced the proposition that our human experiences, both past and present, were the universally shared, though individually slanted, and governing events of our lives while wide awake and tarrying by the light of day, and perhaps while at rest, as those experiences of the prior whiles did much to shape the nature of our dreams, he was once again wide awake to the beautiful workings of the most powerful presence that shapes our lives, the presence of God. Drifting somewhere within the profound paradox of that dream that would change his life in all the ways that it needed to be changed, he awakened to the presence of the Almighty and all that had been set against God's creation in the earthly realms. Ronan began to perceive the workings of the world in much the same way that an innocent child remains keen to receive the signs of our God, which are present everywhere yet remain ostensibly hidden from the eyes and ears of those bewitched by the constant and unwavering conditioning schemes of the false prophets that pander to the practice of idolatry.

In the wake of that cogent vision of the golden cross, which revealed the redemption of a broken-hearted man at a moment in his life when he was incapable of any deed that might invoke the tender mercies of humanity and, furthermore, confirmed the safe return of his precious child to his care before she had been placed in harm's way, Mr. Cassidy was no longer able to look beyond those glaring and eternal signposts that were prodding God's children to arise from their slumber. He perceived those blazing emblems of the angelic realms that were once hidden from his tired eyes by the will of hardened and misguided men who had been broken by the ways of the world long ago. He could plainly see the markers that had been lovingly set out for him along the road home. He understood that in the waking world, the thoughts and actions of the present would continue to borrow from the chosen frames that lie upon the fringes of both what has happened and what we, as mere mortals meandering through this fallen place, expect will happen. But, far more important than those insignificant doubts and fears that are the flashpoints and rallying calls of our cherished indoctrination within this flesh-born reality, Ronan now possessed an unshakeable belief that the open gateway to the truth and the promise of the future both passed through the Light and the Word alone.

With his eyes wide open, though useless within the depths of the blanketing darkness of that lonely room, which was fully blinded down and caught within the staid cover of a dismal stretch of early February weather, Ronan sensed where he was and where he had been for the entirety of those visions sent from above. After a short while, his eyes began to adjust to the low afterglow of the few streetlamps below, which appeared to be faintly drifting into the room through the cracks in the blinds. After he had pondered the truth of his temporal collocation to his current physical station during the early hours of the morning of February 5th, 2020, and once he had disposed of a gripping hold he had applied to his racing thoughts, which had caused him to consider all that he once perceived to have been lost from the confines of his fairly recent past, he asked something of the charged ether haunting the room where he lay.

He spoke in the near hush of a solitary and wilting whisper sent into that lingering darkness. "What is it that I am now called to gather from this hallowed cross of gold? Who exactly is this man that has been revealed to me and now haunts the burning marrow of my soul? How is it that I have remained blind to the truth for far too long?"

While pondering the answers to those enigmatic questions that were raised only to the wares of his twisting cogitations, Ronan physically opened his eyes to the world of the present, which was some seven years removed from that first house he shared with his baby girls outside of Chicago. He opened his eyes wide as those tenderly rekindled memories of better days gone by fell back into the recesses of his mind to be called on at another time of his choosing. A time when the promise of his world would be far brighter due to this newly planted seed of hope placed at the center of his soul by the breath of God. Mr. Cassidy then concluded his thoughts while the accompanying images, forever tied to those beautiful days gone by, vanished into the settling ether of the half-light. His mind went blank, and he simply watched intently while the fan on the ceiling circled above him.

He continued to watch in silence as the fan turned rapidly like a rounded blur and then, almost magically, appeared to turn as three separate blades, three separate blades holding firmly to their course as they rounded the overhead fixture's conical hub, which was ornamented in gold and remained unwavering at the focal point of that modified carousel spinning up above. In the seasons of rebirth that followed that fateful rendezvous on the island of Inis Mor, many have asked of me how it was that Mr. Cassidy remained so steadfast in the face of such a daunting trial. The best that I can do to answer a question regarding something far more courageous than I myself might ever dare attain is to begin by inquiring, "Have I ever told you the story of the vision of the golden cross?"

Chapter 4

NEW BEGINNINGS

Nearly a year after meeting with his friend Lewis at the local tavern to discuss the foundational importance of appropriately priced physical gold to a properly functioning monetary system, and sometime during the early phases of what promised to be a harsh winter in the northern provinces of the American Midwest, Ronan Cassidy was preparing to move. He had finalized his contract on a new job just a few weeks prior and was set to begin in about a month's time. Ronan would be moving on ahead of his family so that he could get started on his new professional endeavor while his three daughters and their mother stayed behind until the house was sold and the school year had concluded in the summer of 2013. At times, Ronan had clutched at the decision to uproot all that had been fostered during his family's time in the Northwest suburbs of Chicago. Still and all, given the magnitude and certainty of the event horizon that the world financial order was approaching from well beyond the point of no return, Mr. Cassidy believed that accepting a more stable offer in the Wealth Management department of a sizable commercial banking outfit would be best where it concerned continuing to facilitate the future hopes and dreams of his three daughters. The three smart, loving, and beautiful little girls, who are called by the names given to them at birth: Lauren, the fierce heart; Madailein, the magnificent one; and Cora, the bright one.

At that time in his life, Ronan could feel upheaval coming as innately as some wise and happily worn-down old farmer, nearly at his time in life to make a final peace with the land outstretched before him, would take his signals to act from the changing of the weather. As such was the triggering notion peacefully instigating the myriad thoughts kept within the subconscious depths of his mind, it was not surprising that while he gazed longingly out his kitchen window, Ronan remained half-fixated upon the shadow of a trance coalescing ubiquitously around his overall field of perception, yet not distinctly revealed as an idea by any cohesive point in his mind or, furthermore, projected in the form of a distinct image that was either imagined outright or woven into the unfocused panorama of the landscape visible before his slowing wandering eyes. That changed the moment Ronan exhaled pensively and slowly closed those same eyes to allow those gathering thoughts to form upon the shifting panorama of his mind's eye. Once given over to the gentle flood of that onrushing daydream, which served as a direct metaphor for those nostalgic meanderings of the present moment, he quickly made out the discernable form of an old man walking onto his timeworn wooden porch at daybreak and into the first morning chill of the harvest season.

The old man Ronan had conjured up in his head was still very much upright, as evidenced by his subtle yet potent and confident posture. While he stepped gently forward from the house to find the rail of the porch with an untamed strength of spirit that easily overwhelmed any tiring of his aging body, the old man was clenching his coffee cup between his browned, leathery, and weather-worn forefingers and his faintly twitching thumb. A shy but high-pitched creak of the screen door pierced the silence of the crisp morning air as the door gave way at the threshold and was then gently restrained by the stretching of the tired metal springs fastened to the hinges. Shortly thereafter, the door snapped back into position and was accompanied by a brief rattle of the frame's slightly warped wood as it struck the jamb. That stark reverberation was followed by the farmer's slow, booted steps, which produced a soft, hollow, and echoing discord amongst the decades-old porch boards.

Though this man existed as nothing more than a specter haunting imagined time and ethereal space within Mr. Cassidy's mind, Ronan could sense this old man's thoughts and cares as if they were his own. He is a good and industrious man, formed in the way of the hard experiences that accompany desperately coaxing the earth to yield its annual bounty. As he reaches the rail of the porch, the now thoughtful old man takes notice of the sliding angle of the very sun that is making his eyes sparkle with the radiant illumination of the stunningly translucent blues and lush greens set within. The low position of that rising sun and the cool air give notice of the quickening of the days ahead and the change of the seasons that is at hand.

As the concurrently lingering and interlocking vapors of his steaming cup of black coffee and the warmth of his breath are dissolved by the crystalline clarity of that invigorating morning air, the man looks off of the rising sun. He turns the focus of his careful stare out over the entire depth of the field, copiously filled with stalks of ripened maize bursting at the husk. The silence is broken by the subtly carrying sounds of the soft shuffling of the heavily burdened stalks being gently teased by the soothing breeze. Against the chill of that early autumn morning, the man notices that the sun's warmth is only accruing to the area around his squinting eyes and the firm but creased skin of his cheekbones. His senses prickle gently as a saddening nostalgia for times long since passed meets with a dissipating apprehension shifting to that of a guarded joy regarding his unknown journey ahead.

A loose, curled lock of his whitening hair shifts continually across his prominent and well-tanned brow in the soft breeze, tickling his eyebrow as the wizened skin pulled across his pronounced cheekbones firms up ever so delicately. The man fastens his shining eyes to the furthest point out on the horizon, which is radiantly alight with streams of blue, orange, and pink that paint the sky above the apex of the giant, steadily rising sun that is almost noticeably making its way above the back acres of the field. Taking his cue from the subtle but changing nuances of the opening of the day onto the vast expanse of the prairie, the old farmer points his firm countenance to the red silos capped in silver that stand across the lawn and a few hundred meters to the south. Having properly surveyed the measure of the expanse, the wise farmer gently takes his seat and faces forward in his sturdy old rocker, never letting his eyes lose sight of the wonders of both the heavens and earth on display before him. He then crafts a slight but resolute reckoning for his soul and the myriad tasks of the day that lie ahead. Winter is coming and the silos must be filled for those that will pass through that final season of the year and into the rebirth of spring.

Once Ronan's daydream had faded and the barren trees and windswept leaves tumbling in waves across his neighbor's front yards came into view, he felt the same sweet melancholy come over him that he imagined the old man of his passing reverie had felt. The reality of the financial maelstrom he saw gathering with hurrying momentum, and his duty to position himself to withstand the worst of its destruction for those who were depending on him, affirmed to Ronan that the season of his life in this place, which held so much joy for him and his girls, was coming to pass. Staying on was akin to little more than refusing to take cover before a razing storm, and there were several reasons as to why that was the inescapable truth of the matter.

Looking out to his right through the western partition of the kitchen's bay window, which angled back towards the framework of the rectangular house, Ronan stared at the leafless tree where Lauren had spent countless summer afternoons reading her books. There was a branch where she sat that lurched out over the grass of the backyard and nearly reached the street, which was the cul-de-sac's gateway to the long straight road that traversed the full length of the neighborhood and ran straight in line with the meridian from east to west. Lauren would read in that tree for hours, remaining perfectly balanced while appearing as comfortable as some Caribbean spider monkey napping through the high heat of the day. She could often be seen in the same spot up on that branch when Mr. Cassidy left for a golf outing in the morning, and many times remained stationed up on that arching tree branch while carefully inspecting her open book when he returned home at midday. The darling little girl remained perched up there, enrapt by the closing pages of her paperback and devouring the last of that day's story, which appeared to have thoroughly electrified her vast imagination. Ronan's heart skipped a small beat when he thought about that tree sitting empty in the fullness of its summer vestiges.

And so it went for Mr. Cassidy as he continued to stare longingly out through the window. He did little but track the markers of time left behind by his three little yet growing girls out in the neighborhood. Those fondly remembered moments, visible only by way of the anchored holograms of his memory, which he took comfort in knowing would live on in the adventures they would undertake elsewhere in the days and years ahead. Yet, he found it odd that those memories already seemed to haunt those familiar places, presently before his searching eyes, as if they had all departed long ago.

Now, for the sake of clarity in attempting to determine the underlying reasons behind Mr. Cassidy's decision to move on, it must be understood that while his notions concerning the turmoil to come were resolute, he was certainly no prophet. The great affirming visions of his life were yet to come, and like many of us, he had allowed his soul to dwell in the realms of past sorrows and earthly placations for far too long in his life. He oftentimes pushed the envelope while attempting to reaffirm his freedoms, in search of humor, and in an effort to establish the comradery and excitement that provided a certain spark to his earthly existence. Moreover, there were times when those soulful endeavors caused great harm to his more mundane commitments. Like many born into the ever-shrinking yet still prevalent middle classes of America, Ronan believed in the idea of fairness for all and loathed the times that he was caught out on the business end of inequitable treatment. Those scales of justice, however, have swung widely in both directions for Mr. Cassidy throughout his life, just as they do for so many of us working our way through the imperfections and vagaries of the modern world.

Over time, Ronan begrudgingly grew to accept the fact that fairness was more of a societal ambition than a day-to-day reality in life. There were times that he tempered his drive to compete by learning to graciously accept the many blessings bestowed upon him. At those times, Ronan tended to thrive in the freedom of spirit that came with his devotion to the more natural and divine ambitions that were innate to Ronan's gentle heart. Nevertheless, there were also darker times in which Ronan became overwhelmed by the failings of life that seemed to be manifest all around him. He began to find only disappointment where perfection, or at least a high degree of proficiency, was not to be attained in many of his own endeavors. During those times, Ronan frequently allowed the world's constant imperfections and inequitable stations of sorrow, which his probing and meticulously analytical mind could assess with terrifying and severe acuity, to devastate the very essence of love and compassion that God has endowed upon all of his spiritual creatures.

In those moments, Ronan would reach shallow dead ends, or worse, self-destructive levels so severe that he fell victim to such dark and cold beliefs regarding the depravity of the human condition that his very soul felt shattered and instantly muted. He felt as if he were locked within some endless and inescapable void. While battling through fits of despair, he would isolate his thoughts and cares from the world around him, and he remained locked in the firm grasp of those tormenting seizures, armed only with a frantic desire to unbind his will from those false and deadly passages into the abyss, which were always marked by isolation, confusion, and the imaginary barriers placed everywhere by those sinister principalities seeking power in the absence of light. In those darkened sanctums of the devil's propaganda, only Ronan's love for his three girls could bring him to fully reengage with his brighter hopes for this life and return to his innately auspicious state of mind, such that he began again to deliver a renewed sense of purpose and proper care to his necessary endeavors and, most importantly, to those he loved dearly.

Truthfully, the good Lord, in His unending plenitude of love, patience, and grace, held safe the gentle spirit of His lost child while Ronan wandered through the lingering aftereffects of the choices made by those of the dead and the afflicted. Those who continued to live by turning away from the light. The poor man's soul-shaking bouts of defiance were spent in the darkness and all alone but for the hand of God, which held Ronan up during those times when he most assuredly would have otherwise fallen into the dust of the earth somewhere out along the foundering stone ramparts of his volition and his fury. Once Mr. Cassidy had weathered such storms in the vain effort to shake his fist with rage against the calamitous storms of evil rising all around him like Ahab himself, God steered His child away from the continuing admonishment of those drawn into the shadows.

The Lord simply placed the answers Ronan required to heal his spirit and his soul, and, moreover, to find the goodness forged into his beating heart, in the protective hold of His loving embrace. When Ronan finally gathered up enough sense to seek out those truths from his loving God, they were never withheld, and they were immediately put to the purpose of healing Ronan's wounded but never admonished spirit. Though God showed Ronan only the answers that he was prepared to process, those gentle nudges proved to be enough to end the fits of dread and doubt in Ronan's mind, and Mr. Cassidy carried on again like some bursting seedling of the spring, reaching and wanting little more than to take root in the fertile soil of God's purpose for his life. Most of the time, the Lord revealed something of His plans through certain revelations that involved Ronan's three little girls.

Fortunately for Mr. Cassidy, even in those darker times, he still believed, as deep down he always had, that God has called each one of us to a task uniquely suited to His design. However, Ronan never fully understood or, at least, truly accepted his part to play in God's great plan until much later in his life. In his younger days, and with unintended yet supreme futility, Ronan rushed through his life in cycles of grand achievement coupled with periods dominated by his failings, which were, conversely, nearly as recreant. He tended to run hot and cold at times, like the roused or tired blood pumping through his veins, and Mr. Cassidy came close to reaching the bottom more than a few times while trying to be all of those things that the children of the dollar's distorted influence might admire.

Because he did not fully understand God's truth in the more trying moments of his younger years, he felt as if he was continually being called by two masters: the master of the heavens and the hidden masters that dictated the broadening illusion that too often becomes the perceived practical reality of the world in which we live. Ronan did not yet possess the capacity to faithfully and, therefore, completely see beyond that veil, or the matrix of some shaded illusion of reality, if you will, with its steadily constructed falsehoods and twisted web of primal deceptions that were some centuries in the making, and which so many in the waking world have come to accept and even embrace. As such, Mr. Cassidy did not sufficiently comprehend, or at least demonstratively come to admit, the prevalence of those lies in any observable way beyond what he let slip from the depths of his heart at varying times. Nevertheless, just as he would come to understand the flaws behind and the natural corrections to the conception of the current dollar paradigm, some years later, our man would come to embrace the fact that the true eternal master of all things seen and unseen, known and unknown, possible and impossible, was one in the same. That glorious reckoning to come would change him to the point of being born anew in the eyes of God.

Though our story has crept a bit closer to revealing the will of the man who was staring certain death, or far worse, the death of a beloved, in the eye on that enchanted Irish isle, let us continue on with the tale of the transformation of Mr. Ronan James Cassidy, as there are other lessons to be gleaned. At the time Ronan was preparing for his move, the causes and after-effects of the great recession, which began in 2008 and culminated with the stock market and real estate crashes of 2009, were largely in the process of being rewritten for the consumption of the general public. However, many previously buried skeletons belonging to the dollar construct, which was a lever of control more powerful than anything previously known to man and based on nothing but the illusory confidence of its carefully groomed and then herded adherents, had been revealed. To an instrument such as that, image is everything, and the process undertaken to repair the damage was a sight to behold. That being said, as one who intricately understood the underpinnings of the dollar's ability to function, it seemed plain enough to Ronan that the strength and resiliency of the rebounding economy of late 2012, and its continuing reliance on the dollar to function as a grossly overprinted, and therefore simultaneously devaluing, wealth reserve, only existed on the news and in financial publications touting the prowess of the headline composites of the stock and bond markets, and other accompanying expositions of the Wall Street financial apparatus.

Everywhere Ronan went in the real world of early twenty-first-century America, the ruin and decay of the once dominant American productive function were so glaring that Mr. Cassidy was forced to turn off the propaganda-laden news networks and the talking bobblehead dolls of the financial punditry. He was compelled to do as much lest he vomit all over his shoes in some peculiar hotel, tucked away off the highway in some strange and forgotten corner of America, which was suffering from those same tangible realities attributed to systemic decline that were clearly not fit for print. Ronan believed that the whole affair of the American economic recovery post-2009 was nothing but hocus-pocus accompanied by a series of Roman bread and circus rituals, which were comprised of meaningless yet entertaining contests, and a deluge of broadcasts that were perfectly designed to distract and divide the impoverished masses into believing that everyone but them was doing just fine.

The political and media charade was nothing but a time-tested ploy, something devised to continue to deprive "We the People" of our constitutional authority and our inherent power to change our circumstances in the face of exploitation. At the same time, the uninformed masses continued to be slowly and then rapidly stripped of their God-given right to provide for their families while remaining unmolested by the government or a rigged and predatory financial apparatus. Regardless, Ronan knew that one day the entire house of cards, and the illusions that it fostered, would come crashing down around the elite money changers corrupting the temples of his day. Thankfully, if it accomplished nothing else of a beneficial and lasting effect for the American people, the financial crash of 2009 revealed the certainty of the dollar's spectacular implosion to come to Ronan, and many others, in spades. Beyond that, the true and unseemly colors of America's societally ingrained institutions of commerce and public utility were on display for all to see.

By late 2012, the third iteration of the American central bank was still up to its familiar tricks that were born of necessity following the crisis. Once forced to buy the assets of the debtor class into perpetuity in a Pyrrhic effort to keep the global financial daisy chain from igniting, the central bank executed that strategy with aplomb for the solitary reason of prolonging the apparatus's hold over the financial order. Sadly, however, for money to function, every policy action must have an equal and opposite reaction. The ongoing emergency actions of the American central bank, which were dedicated to a rather arcane, loosely partitioned, and entirely patrician expansion of the money supply, were no different. The big losers in the deal were all those looking to produce real goods and services while being forced to save the surplus of their overproduction in Treasury bonds and other dollar-denominated assets. Yes, that's right, the productive class and prudent savers throughout the world were to be bled dry through unreasonable inflation; inflation of both the immediately realized variety, at least when it came to things funded by debt and the price of financial market products, and then inflation of the price of necessary goods and services that was certain to arrive as a follow-on effect at some point in the offing.

Ronan correctly figured that these economic and financial imbalances, which were the expected result of using a debt-based reserve currency well beyond its useful shelf life, were entirely unsustainable. Given as much, it is reasonable to assume that Mr. Cassidy also understood that, as it goes with all things that cannot be sustained, those false paradigms of wholly imagined confidence and grotesque levels of economic disequilibrium, which truly belonged to some alternate reality by the winter of 2012, would be no different. In Ronan's mind, the whole charade was an unholy endeavor to prolong something that should have been pronounced dead on arrival back in 2009. Without the sheep's clothing of the system, those wolves out prowling the woods in search of their own Little Red Riding Hoods would soon be exposed, and that was perhaps where Ronan had jumped the gun a bit in regard to his expectations for the immediate future. He had no idea how long the people of the world might be duped into continuing to presume that the emperor was actually wearing his Sunday fineries and not marching around naked as a jay bird.

As to whether or not Ronan believed that the unjust proliferation of the dollar debt burden was being driven by people with good intentions, due in part to some past accident that was the result of a few unholy compromises embedded into the core constructs of the dollar-based international financial system, or whether the whole thing was simply a daylight train robbery conducted by dint of the implementation of the Bretton Woods system by those who considered themselves above the just and equitable provisions of the law, and also understood the shelf life of their Frankenstein's monster quite well, Ronan had debated the question quite often. On most days at that time in his life, he leaned heavily toward the latter answer to the tricky question, but he remained open to arguments for the former, and he kept his opinions fairly muted at times because of that fact. Perhaps Ronan kept his spoken opinions on the matter of the dollar dilemma rather detached and in accordance with the considerations of his generally wise judgment regarding the public disclosure of his beliefs purely in the name of self-preservation. Perhaps he simply preferred to keep his options partially open because the "red pill" he would need to swallow concerning his primary thesis was simply too large and too potent for an immediate serving. The most likely answer was a bit of both of the aforementioned explanations.

As with most things in life that concern the interests of so many, Ronan figured that the truth of the matter regarding the dollar financial system and the unending bailouts that followed the crash of 2009 lay somewhere in between. However, it was no secret to those close to him that Ronan's sentient instincts argued otherwise, and there were those times when he chose to be quite vocal about that fact. Whatever the case may be, Ronan could say with absolute certainty that the dollar was going to endure a hyperinflationary flashpoint so hot and so rapid that the heat of the event was going make his hair curl. The transfer of wealth that was coming as a direct result of this dollar hyperinflation would be a monetary event the likes of which the world had yet to witness on such an all-encompassing scale. To make matters worse, the longer the dollar was carried past its natural timeline, the quicker and faster this snapback to a state of monetary equilibrium was going to be. With that as a foundational backdrop, the political saga that would surround Ronan's favorite U.S. President, Donald John Trump, in the years to come was of no surprise to him, but it was of unequivocal and almost unimaginable consequence to both Ronan James Cassidy and the future of the people of the constitutional Republic of the United States of America.

In line with Ronan's thinking on dollar matters as transcribed above, one night during the summer of that same year, on his short but not insignificant drive home from work as a financial consultant to corporate entities, Ronan gave life to a unifying thought. At that moment, Ronan figured that perhaps this global experiment with a debt currency by fiat was simply an ill union of the folly of man and the evil contorts of power that come with the administration of such a system by decree, from which there remained so few difficult-to-identify fissures open in the bottleneck left to make one's escape. In any event, the circumstances of the inevitable outcome were driving Ronan to prepare in earnest for the events he believed would play out on the world stage in grand and transformational fashion.

Irrespective of who and what particular circumstances were behind the coming reckoning for the world's reserve currency, there was no stopping that inevitable reconciliation that would be a few orders of magnitude beyond that of the near-fatal financial cataclysm of 2009. As there was no possible way to time such a monumental dislocation, which no one wanted to assume responsibility for igniting, and with each day appearing as if it might espouse the hour when the rubber band finally snapped, at least to one who understood the true mechanics behind the dollar's function and current system of accounts, Ronan believed that he was quite blessed to be offered a position as a wealth management advisor with expertise in alternative investments with a large financial institution down south. The organization was looking to expand upon their non-traditional wealth management offerings tailored to institutional and high-net-worth clients, or at least do so in name for the sake of appearances if not entirely in practice.

Ronan knew that the next dollar crisis would also be met with direct monetary assistance to support asset prices and the balance sheets of the larger, more impactful financial organizations in the United States and around the world. All of the bigger banks were already directly connected and interdependent upon one another at that point in time, and if one were to fall, such an occurrence would set off the entire daisy chain of cascading defaults, just as the failure of Lehman Brothers had in 2009. At that point in the dollar's lifecycle, the central bankers of the world had no choice but to print ever-increasing amounts of commercial bank reserves to maintain the debts that served as the financial assets and many of the recognized capital assets of the world's complex financial and economic systems, and in so doing, maintain the credibility and, likewise, the required collateral values of those assets.

As Ronan saw things, the most advantageous spot to be when the next monetary earthquake began to tremor was a large financial institution. This was true because, by default, all of those organizations were slated to be on the receiving end of the Federal Reserve's fully cranked up printing press the second trouble arose. Furthermore, following their experiences of the last few years, the operators of that printing press had perfected their craft and were by then quite adept at spitting out dollar reserves in exchange for worthless assets at fully listed market or issuance values. With that in mind, Mr. Cassidy reasoned that a position with just such an organization would see him through to the day when the harder constructs of dollar currency would have to be printed with ink and paper to facilitate the accelerated government spending and direct cash payments to the servicers of all of that debt that would be required to keep the merry-go-round in motion. What happened beyond that point was anyone's guess.

Ronan reckoned that the demise of any large financial institution wouldn't arrive much before that day of rather overt money printing. Furthermore, Ronan figured that if he could hold his seat for a time while helping others to better position their investment portfolios for what was to come, the scenario resulting from this transition had to be considered nothing short of a win-win opportunity. One that he simply could not refuse for the good of his sweet little girls and all that they had to look forward to on the other side of the event horizon.

While Ronan ascribed an almost immeasurable value to his new company's positioning at the business end of the central bank's printing press as the death of the dollar continued to play out over an uncertain amount of time, there were other professional benefits that accrued to Ronan's new role. Having worked through one of the toughest markets for financial deal-making during the years that followed the near-collapse of the financial system in 2009, the professional trade of his former life, as it were, the thought of joining a large team with a more diversified and stable revenue base was rather appealing. In addition to that, Mr. Cassidy could cater to his creative side a bit more by joining an enterprise that was looking to build something that he considered to be of indispensable value for the firm's clients after that organization and its many fine constituents had lived through some of the most heart-breaking after-effects of the financial crisis.

At that point in his life, Ronan had undergone the multiple traumas of two full-on and in-your-face collapses of the dollar-centric financial system. While the bursting of the 2001 technology bubble turned out to be of a far milder variety than what was experienced during the real estate-related debacle of 2009, both events left a lasting imprint on Ronan's psyche and served to shape his understanding of certain patterns that seemed to shadow the world of money and finance. He was a fairly simple man at heart, a saver with a competitive streak for achieving small but noticeable markers of professional success. Therefore, watching the humble amounts of wealth he had managed to accumulate at past markers along the winding trail of his life vanish into the ether at the onset of each prior seismic disruption of the financial markets was partially responsible for igniting his exhaustive search for answers to the faulty mechanics behind the dollar, the wizardry of the Wall Street custodial machine, and the International Monetary System, which the dollar anchored. There were no proper words to describe what Mr. Cassidy eventually unearthed where it concerned our money and the world's financial architecture, and such astonishment was based primarily on those documents that were made available to the public. Far more abhorrent to his inquiring mind were the things that might be lurking just beneath the surface in a world where proper financial reporting was a secondary concern to that of any "national security issue" tied to the proliferation of the overvalued dollar.

Regarding the ongoing paradox associated with Ronan's professional status vis a vis what might have been his true passions in life at the time of his decision to alter his professional designation, he also realized that he did not possess the maniacal drive, indecency of character, or lack of respect for the truth that was required to reach the highest levels of his current station on the sell side of the capital markets carnival, which had been steadily morphing into a predatory weapon by which those of the elite class were able to further subvert the growing masses of the disenfranchised American working class. By late 2012, that carnival, which somehow represented what remained of the free markets and which had driven much of America's unparalleled financial prosperity after 1971, was rapidly transforming into a full-blown three-ring circus with circling clown cars, fiery hoops of death, and stilted giants attempting to walk above the spectacle of it all. And of course, every one of us with a dollar to save was forced to walk the high wire while remaining utterly untrained, or even marginally experienced in such hazardous affairs, in an effort to reach the other side without having our life's savings go up in smoke by way of inflation or market losses.

By the time Ronan had entered his profession in finance on the heels of the tech bust of 2001, it was already beginning to appear that the majority of what remained to be done at the onset of the contraction phase of the dollar credibility cycle equated to legalized looting. By then, the financial world was already a predatory mechanism, which had become so complex that the vast majority of the work concerned laboring through regulation; regulation that was only enforced when the smaller players in the industry bent the rules, and designed to consolidate the industry such that a handful of firms controlled the vast majority of the nation's wealth. Misguided compliance regimes did nothing to fix or curtail the abuses embedded within the system, as the largest banks ran entire business lines that were both grey in nature and responsible for large swaths of their insane profits. Of course, and in reality, obfuscation and misrepresentation were always the ultimate goals of the apex predators sitting atop the world financial order and their rotating carousel of minions seated in Washington, D.C. By the time a youthful Mr. Cassidy's moment to shine in the world of finance had arrived after joining a reputable yet smaller firm, those aforementioned distortions were already prevalent.

To be honest, smaller, more locally oriented financial institutions simply lacked the resources and competitive advantages required to compete in the modern era of finance; competitive advantages such as direct access to central bank largesse; profits large enough to pay their fines, which were nothing more than a cost of doing business for the largest wire houses; and ties to a few key congressmen, or even the Secretary of the Treasury, if the blow-up was extensive enough. It was the small, localized institutions that were slated for the chopping block through the unjust yet orderly evolution of the industry, which would end someday with the controlled demolition of the system, if such a thing could be managed by a few organizations controlling the vast majority of the nation's dollar denominated assets when the time came to pull the rip cord in the name of salvaging some form of control, and thereby establishing those new and far more sinister levers of dominion set to go hand in hand with the next scheme. Most of those small and principled organizations still operating in the space followed every rule until the day they were tapped on the shoulder with the final message of: "Your time is up, friend." While Ronan did not attribute those unfortunate side-effects of an oncoming currency collapse, and the continuing distortions that came with it, to finance alone, finance was the function within the American system that Ronan knew well enough to identify and properly define the symptoms of the rot.

In a country writing hundreds of laws each day, and passing historic legislative bills so complex their congressional "authors" had no idea what they contained, Ronan could have easily lumped in many of the high-level lawyers and the politicians with their lobbyists, in addition to many of the iconic captains of American industry that falsely promoted their organizations as family-oriented staples of society through the morally defunct propaganda witch doctors of the mainstream media, along with the financiers. They were all tied together now, and playing the great game of trying outrun one another to misappropriate, embezzle, and outright steal faster than the dollar was truly depreciating. To finish this grand lift, these parasites of the global order needed you and the producers of the world to continue to save in dollars and dollar-denominated assets. The financial masters rely on the common man continuing to deny their own natural and rational beliefs while they continue to suspend the inevitable hyperinflation of the dollar's real goods purchasing power by keeping the producers of the world locked into the darling asset classes of stocks, bonds, derivatives, and useless financial insurance wares that only perform when they are not called upon to do so. Without that continuing confidence in the dollar to perform in the future, the already crippled purchasing power of the grossly overprinted global reserve currency would have long since returned to the dustbin of history as nothing but a pile of smoldering ash. Beyond that, as the currency goes, so goes the remainder of the greatest con ever perpetrated upon humanity.

These men and women who turned the dollar wheel may or may not have known that the hyperinflationary bear born of our abused currency system was faster than them all, or that this hungry bear was indeed awakening. What they all did know intimately, however, was how to game a system tied to ever-expanding government and financial largesse. To Ronan, the historical context of the deplorable state of affairs was as basic as a Latin proverb he recalled from his preparatory school days spent in upstate New York. The proverb was written by the great Roman historian Tacitus, and it appeared in Tacitus' timeless work, The Annals of Rome. The proverb was written, "*Corruptisima República plurimae leges*" in Latin and was translated as "*The more corrupt the state, the more numerous the laws*" in English.

Ronan understood those unfortunate professional contradictions that conflicted with his values system fairly early on in his professional development process while working within the cogs of the global financial system. That being said, Ronan did work with some outstanding people who mentored his growth and development. He also relished the analytical and problem-solving aspects of understanding the value of an operating enterprise in dollar-denominated terms. He liked the way so many factors and variables came together to arrive at a perceived value for a given business or asset. Part of the young man even enjoyed the order given to the myriad numbers and procedures behind financial transactions and the corresponding bookkeeping. However, if he were being completely honest with himself, it was the reputation and the means afforded by his occupation that drove him to proceed through the long, continuing grind of his chosen profession, even after the purpose and utility of his savvy and sacrifice had become quite murky. Ronan was compensated comfortably in comparison to the middling pay schemes that were offered around the United States at the time, and while he worked long, sleepless hours and for the entirety of many weekends while helping to make the partners and senior executives of his firm very wealthy, he was at least able to afford some lifestyle during the early days of his occupational progression.

Most importantly, where it concerned Ronan's early career progression, like the pretense of the dollar itself, and its accompanying asset investment arena, there was always the promise of much more to come dangling somewhere out there on the horizon. He even worked on several notable transactions in those early days and was around for a few impressive paydays that arrived during the roaring markets that followed the post-September 11, 2001, housing-driven market boom. Such was a boom that was delivered not long after the launch of the first major threat to dollar dominance across the globe, the Euro currency. That particular boom happened to be spawned by way of an ill-begotten lending partnership between good old Uncle Sam and the dollar reserve currency's clever Wall Street offspring, in addition to the emergent support of the prolific goods-producing nation of China.

The result of that particular monetary expansion episode and the corresponding market boom was the financial collapse of 2009, which crippled the pensions of the country's middle-class savers and left tens of millions homeless as a foreclosure wave of unmatched and dubious magnitude swept through the country. The devastating aftereffects of the event were not televised for long. The bursting of the housing bubble and the collapse of the financial markets in the wake of the popping of the "dot com" bubble seven years earlier lit a fire within Ronan to embark upon a tireless and unending quest; a quest that nearly consumed him as he searched for the answers to what was the unifying cause behind this pattern of nearly concurrent financial market disasters when considered through the lens of the long view. The answers he found, over time and at great cost to his prior ambitions, were rather startling, to put it bluntly.

All things being equal, in those aforementioned seasons when Ronan had been completely authentic about his prospects for the future, outside of a few pockets of opportunity in which he was able to assist some honest clients with good intent, he slowly came to realize that the occupational choices he had made were his compromise to adapt to a system that was ultimately run by narcissistic and sociopathic gaslighters in both the financial and political spheres. However, it was not until he had committed to becoming a cog in the wheel of the decaying American capital markets framework that Ronan fully understood the dollar game and the damage it had caused. The overvalued dollar and its perpetual "deficits without tears" had infected the lifeblood running through the veins of the country and continued to threaten what little remained of America's founding ideals, which were still from time to time upheld, at least in principle if not in practice, by the greatest legal document ever written, the Constitution for the United States of America.

Based on what Ronan had learned about the central banks of the world and the dollar-centric international financial system, it should have come as no surprise to him that more than a decade after the global financial crisis, confusing yet transformational and rapacious ideals spearheaded by the ultimate wolves in sheep's clothing, the progressives, were sweeping through the country. The promotion of these ideals was behind the effort to remove the founding American principles of God, family, country, hard work, perseverance, and self-reliance that had slowly and then all at once become nothing short of an absolute anathema to those wishing to push the bounds of their control born of the untethered dollar system ever further. When spoken in the common tongue of our day, those slippery progressives, or perhaps fascists and socialists in disguise, were known as the admirals of "the free shit brigade" and the "get mine now" movements, which were becoming uncontrollably pervasive throughout American culture and were the darlings of the media's always biased and rose-colored lens.

Ronan understood back then that the possibility of a benign extraction of the rot from America's economic and political framework no longer existed. Given where the average person in American society had gravitated both socially and politically, and given what the warped and counter-productive monetary framework, which had placed such a violent strangle hold upon our day-to-day endeavors, had mutated into, there was going to be an inordinate amount of pain that came with the very necessary adjustments to the world financial architecture. There would be hardship and suffering that followed the destruction of their money and the institutions that were built upon that fiat dollar's irredeemable and grossly falsified value for those who continued to meander through the calm before the storm unprepared.

Beyond that, Mr. Cassidy was no longer certain that the cure for what ailed the financial system would not kill the patient at that point in his life. Still and all, and for the sake of his little girls, he did hold out great hope that there would be something wonderful waiting for them on the other side of that reckoning to come. He held out hope that the immutable ideals of human liberty and freedom under God, upon which the American nation was founded, would rise again and manifest the self-evident truths and righteousness of those same ideals when the level-set realities of production and consumption were put under the proper perspectives by the denizens of a nation no longer able to print money without cost. He hoped that those long-cherished beliefs would shine brightest on the day ahead when the producers of the world toiled just as diligently, yet saved their surplus production in other instruments that were more akin to their natural human understanding of both money and tangible wealth, with the value of that wealth predicated upon its intrinsic qualities and not the whims of those who pulled the strings from behind the curtain somewhere in Oz.

While we shall not dwell in the mire by way of providing examples of the country's moral and economic breakdown, the truth should be clear to any person utilizing an honest and unbiased mind in the course of their evaluation of the same. However, it will be said that the shortcomings of the American experience of the modern era, which was underpinned by the dying dollar paradigm, had been laid quite bare before Ronan's eyes in the years leading up to that cold and blustery December of 2012; that uncompromising winter season, which marked the end of a joyful road traveled in Mr. Cassidy's life. Those times of deep thought and dubious reflection carried a high degree of import regarding the choices Ronan believed he was compelled to consider for the sake of his family and for the sake of the principles of freedom under God's law upon which he thrived, and perhaps required, nearly as much as the very air he breathed. For those were extremely important choices that Ronan was forced to make and execute on under his own volition, once he fully understood the dollar's phantasmal value proposition. Nevertheless, he made those decisions without hesitation, although not without remorse, and he made those decisions to move on fully against the aggressively swaying tides of his vast and comforting societal framework.

Regarding his former wife, however, those choices that he made would prove to be irreconcilable friction points, which would continue to grind and fester long past the point of moving on from the standard societal norms of their lives. No one in Ronan's sphere of influence was listening to his thesis and his concerns regarding the chaotic transfer of wealth embedded therein. If they were listening, they failed to find agreement with Ronan's resolute conclusions. Those opinions mattered little to Ronan. He held steadfast to what he believed to be the truth, and he marched on with his plan. On the good days of his ensuing exile, which seemed to commence following his move south, he fancied that his character and determination were akin to those of the undaunted American pioneers of the nineteenth century. On the bad days, he grappled with the many drawbacks experienced by any first mover with an idea that was a decade or more ahead of its time.

While those thoughts regarding his exile were the strange concoctions of a solitary mind, he went as far as conjuring up eccentric and whimsical parallels between his lonely relocation and the legendary migrations of the great frontiersmen of American legend. He reasoned, though such thoughts remained almost inconceivable when measured by the saner graces of those given over to the more harmonious opinions of the day, that like those legends of the past who forged ahead on their own into the great unknown of the untamed wildernesses of the American continent in the hopes of a new beginning, he too was forging ahead into a future that remained hidden from the still sleeping eyes of those around him. For indeed, those were peacefully sleeping eyes—peacefully sleeping eyes that somehow still could not see and, likewise, refused to understand the proclivity for destruction of the soulless men, monsters, and demons lurking all around them.

Mr. Cassidy was also an ardent and, due to his somewhat formidable education, well-trained student of history. That is to say, he understood the dangers of following the collective mentality in times of great change. He saw that the probability of conceived events was rising to the point of becoming a near certainty without divine intervention. Beyond that, he knew that the conceived events set to arrive with the collapse of the world's reserve currency made even the most implausible and horrific outcomes for the country seem tame in comparison to the more daunting scenarios conjured up by his ever-probing mind. The responses Ronan received to his well-crafted and logical arguments were met with nothing more than the tired, old, and always repeated defenses of those living within the entrenched customs of that time and place while grappling with the severe bouts of cognitive dissonance that were so common among the well-to-do and perpetually distracted confidants of his society. He quickly learned that you can't talk someone into believing the truth when their livelihood depends on the truth being otherwise. As such, Mr. Cassidy continued to swim against the inbound tide and wade through the admonishments of his friends and family. Regardless, he stood firm in the beliefs he had espoused over those last few years spent learning, deprogramming his mind, and working through the rigorous back testing of his developing hypotheses.

It was, however, also a fact that Ronan had fully taken to heart the words of a certain sister of the order from his parochial school days. One who firmly believed in the dying principles of corporal punishment when attempting to rehabilitate the more disruptive of her students. There were certain times during his younger days when Ronan shot straight to the top of the list of students under Sister R's purview who required a well-applied dose of her tried and true brand of behavioral conditioning. Though, later in life, Mr. Cassidy preferred to believe that his rebellious outbursts were due to his longing to be a servant only to God, that was only part of the story where it concerned the less than impeccable child he was back then. Unfortunately for our man of the hour, many of Ronan's more deviant occupations in the days of his youth were likely driven by behavioral patterns of an entirely different bent.

The true motivations behind many of the derelict activities that led to Ronan being thoroughly worn out by Sister R. on multiple occasions aside, hearing her say, "Now, Ronan James Cassidy, if your friends all decided to go on ahead and jump off of a cliff, would you join them? If so, we can end this struggle session right here and now!" precisely before she reached the apex in the energy distribution curve of her deceptively well-administered thrashings, had resonated somewhere deep within the soul of the young brigand.

Whatever the ultimate origins of his failings to get in line were back then, Ronan seemed to be born with the qualities of the staunchest contrarians of his time. Much later in life, he often reasoned that all of his puerile refusals to cooperate, and as a matter of further consideration, his more deviant behavior patterns as a whole, were simply a naturally inspired distaste for authority, which was due primarily to his innate calling to heed only the wishes of his heavenly master. With the entirety of those considerations regarding the young Mr. Cassidy's rebellious attitude being truthfully given, perhaps the degree to which Ronan took those words of Sister R. to heart would have been equivalent without the accompanying listings of her staunch paddle or wickedly thick yet lively ruler. Regardless, it was safe to say, under the guise of any presumption regarding Ronan's developing character, that those loving taps of encouragement added an exclamation point to the impact of Sister R.'s forcefully delivered axiom concerning personal accountability and the pitfalls of following the herd.

And so it was that by December 2012, Mr. Cassidy had cobbled together a high-level plan to weather the sweeping tempest he sensed was coming toward the country like a freight train rolling silently through the night. As part of this plan, he was fully prepared to relocate in an effort to find a place that he felt would be best for his family to ride out the storm. He did this even as those closest to him doubted the founding principles that were the lynchpins of his unwavering resolve. In a strange twist of fate, while Ronan was sorting through the contents of the various boxes he had positioned around the middling-sized room he used as an office, and more specifically, rummaging through the souvenirs of some of his most prominent business deals and other assorted keepsakes, he came across a paper that he had worked on in college for his International Law class. As Ronan thought back to that class and the burdensome texts and stringent demands that accompanied the coursework, he became excited by the prospect of reviewing his initial and unrefined thoughts regarding the faulty constructs behind the emergence of the purely fiat dollar and the "Nixon Shock" of 1971.

That Ronan might find such a communiqué while he was packing to move might be easily inferred. However, only because he had become overwhelmed by the discord of the half-packed and scattered state of his belongings, which he was attempting to organize, were his old work and school papers to be considered a pleasant enough distraction from the storm swirling all around him in that once tidy quarter. At that moment, Ronan was attempting to prepare that specific box, which rested on the floor in front of him, for shipment almost as an affront to the fact that he would be leaving behind so much that he held dear in making that move. Most notable among those keepsakes and memories were those he had made with his girls. Therefore, in addition to the hopeless nature of his ultimate goal at that particular juncture, it was a simple and randomly dictated desire to avoid those mementos fueling a brief spell of remorse that had caused Ronan to pay any attention to the contents of that old box at all.

It was an act designed to distract his thoughts from the focal point of his agitation and unease that caused Ronan to actually read that theretofore unremarkable creation of his collegiate handiwork. Yet, before endeavoring to read the text, he took one last look around the room and the chaos it promoted within his thoughts from his Indian-style position on the plush white carpet. Upon confirming the hopelessness of ever corralling that slapdash assortment of half-packed, hastily unpacked, and altogether overpacked boxes, he finally looked back down at the paper he wrote in college.

There were perhaps five hundred relics, tomes, and trinkets from his academic and professional past that remained organized and out of sight. They were all stacked, filed, and boxed, or hidden in some other manner at that moment in time. Ronan could have stumbled across any number of those keepsakes by similar means had he done things just a bit differently. He truly had discovered the proverbial needle in the haystack at just the right moment when he happened upon that old law paper. There were certainly plenty of other loose documents that were haphazardly strewn about the floor of the dimming room that could have captured Mr. Cassidy's frayed attention. Perhaps there was an element of purposeful fate at work, and that was why Ronan took notice of and suddenly became interested in that old treatise of yesteryear.

While the topic of the paper was of tremendous importance to Ronan, his motivation to read on at that particular interval concerned his hopes that those writings would give him some insight into the educational progression he had made throughout his life. Conversely, perhaps he believed that the old dissertation would shed some light on the thoughts running through his head at a time in his life when he believed that money and the dollar were entirely different animals. He began to wonder how those thoughts from his earlier years tied into the formation of his current beliefs regarding money and international finance—beliefs that were being challenged at every turn by all those who knew him, with the exception of his three young daughters. Even so, the indifference of those three lovely ladies stemmed from their inability to understand the depths of those concepts back in those days and their willingness to exhibit unwavering faith in their daddy no matter the circumstances. While those considerations weaved their way through Mr. Cassidy's mind, he slowly shifted the preponderance of his focus to the pages he held loosely in his hand. He began to read silently and deliberately in search of a relevant connection to his views of the past:

A Brief History of International Finance and the Modern U.S. Dollar by Ronan James Cassidy

On Sunday, August 15, 1971, President Richard M. Nixon, who would resign from office in 1974 following the Watergate Scandal, addressed the American people on national television wearing a pale blue suit jacket, white shirt, and pewter tie against the subtle yet well-defined backdrop of a blue curtain. His eyes peered down at his prepared address, and his voice and facial expressions projected a stern and straightforward resolve to his unseen viewers beyond the lens of the camera that he faced. President Nixon did not mince words or spend much time on pretexts in his delivery. The headline subject of his surprise five-minute address was bringing prosperity to America without war. The American economic landscape of 1971 was deteriorating. The president intended to deliver a straightforward plan to change the course of the country through the execution of three primary objectives: 1) to create more and better jobs; 2) to reduce rises in the cost of living; and 3) to protect the dollar from the attacks of international monetary speculators.

By "international monetary speculators," Mr. Nixon meant those nations that were looking to exchange their growing stockpile of U.S. dollars for gold per the terms of the international monetary agreement laid out in Bretton Woods, New Hampshire before the end of the Second World War. This exchangeability of accumulated dollar reserves for gold was a primary tenet of the loose rules governing the International Monetary Financial System ("$IMFS") with the dollar utilized as the primary reserve currency upon ratification of the 1944 agreement. Those rules, which, among other things, allowed for all international trade to be settled in U.S. dollars and exchanged for gold at the discretion of the international holders of those dollars. Mr. Nixon's "surprise" declaration of August 1971 effectively put an end to the fundamental protocol of gold exchangeability under the Bretton Woods monetary system and placed the entire world on the road to a purely fiat monetary system for the first time in recorded history.

At the time of Nixon's speech, the scars of the Vietnam War were still fresh upon the beating heart of the nation. Our warriors had returned home neglected, heartbroken, and cast into the shadows of a lost war that the American people had never fully embraced. Politically speaking, our lost heroes and those who supported the war effort from the factories and production facilities back home were contributing to a growing unemployment problem. The aftercare and support that our soldiers needed were dire costs at a time when the world economic order was hanging in the balance. Following the Vietnam War, the brutal but necessary battle for civil rights, and the war between competing political ideologies that had preceded those watershed moments, the country was at a crossroads economically, culturally, and spiritually.

Post-World War II American economic superiority was waning, the specter of communism was rising in the east, and the financial uncertainty of the times only added to the gathering undertones of political unrest festering within the American psyche. In August of 1971, the very soul of the nation was on fire. For the first time since World War II, Americans were questioning their geopolitical, financial, and military dominance on the global stage. The American people were searching for an identity, and many found themselves wandering through the wilderness and writhing in doubt while the country bled out its formidable stockpile of golden wealth reserves to just a third of what had been accumulated during the peak years following the Great War.

To address the nation's need for "more and better jobs" following the wind-down of the Vietnam War, President Nixon introduced the Job Development Act of 1971. He proposed providing the strongest short-term incentives in American history to invest in industrial capital in the form of new machinery and equipment. To address the rising cost of living that was the direct effect of monetary inflation and waning international confidence in the International Monetary Financial System and its centerpiece for international trade, the U.S. dollar, Nixon called for a temporary freeze on all prices and wages in the United States for 90 days. Lastly, to "preserve the position of the American dollar as a pillar of monetary stability around the world," Nixon ordered former Governor of Texas and then-Treasury Secretary John Connally to temporarily suspend convertibility of the dollar into gold or other reserve assets. Taken as a whole, Nixon's three directives were known as the "Nixon Shock." However, it was the closing of the gold window that would help pave the way forward for the final era of American exceptionalism, the era of the unbacked dollar reserve …

Ronan stopped reading the words on the page. He started blankly through the open doorway to his right and began to ponder how his parents and their generation of post-World War II baby boomers had been molded by the economic backdrop of the period following the Bretton Woods agreement and the end of the Great War. The period in our brief history that many pundits and historians have termed the *"long boom."* The long boom was a twenty-five-year stretch that ended in 1971 with the closing of the gold window and was perhaps the most profound period of American economic expansion in the history of the relatively young country. That period of economic expansion served to define America's place at the head of the global financial and economic order following the worldwide devastation that remained in the wake of that horrific conflict of the age, which claimed some seventy-five million lives worldwide. Ronan wondered how his parents received that shocking announcement of August 15, 1971, which effectively put an end to the perception of American invincibility and ushered in the still loosely defined and casually enforced, if not officially codified, guidelines behind the current purely fiat currency centric international financial architecture.

During those moments that Ronan was failing miserably to get his office boxes packed up for the move, he fully understood the degree to which he had, in many ways, been molded by the rise of the fiat dollar in 1971 and its unending expansion thereafter. Though the dollar and its financial markets had suffered many bumps along the way, the reserve currency's unabated prowess had continued on into the new century right up to the moment of the great financial crisis of Ronan's day. His parents were both raised with high expectations and resilient hopes for the future, which were predicated upon the successes of the generation of Ronan's grandparents following the war. During the long boom, the steadfast memories and stories of the hardships that Ronan's grandparents had overcome during the Great Depression and World War II seemed to all but fade into the ether of passing time. Decades later, the desires of the American people seemed to morph in lockstep with the rise of the paper dollar. More, faster, and easier became the rallying cries tied to that grand experiment with easy money and deficits without end, and Mr. Cassidy was certainly not someone known to be entirely withdrawn from the frenzied buzz of the modern-day American experience.

As with so many of our hopes and dreams in this life, unfortunate circumstances had taken their toll on the families of Ronan's parents. His maternal grandmother, to whom Ronan bore a strong resemblance, depending on whose opinion was carrying the day at the time, died from cancer long before Ronan was born. She had given birth to three boys and three girls before she passed away, and Ronan's mother was the oldest of those six wonderful children. By all accounts that Ronan could recall, though it was likely that he was forced to speculate on the matter some as the topic was not one that was discussed often in his younger days, Ronan's mother, Delia Treacy, was drawn into the role of surrogate mother, though by degree and over time, for her brothers and sisters. This was because her father worked tirelessly at a nearby veterinary clinic to support the family.

Delia's father, Ronan's grandfather, was a witty man with a sharp sense of humor and an even sharper intellect. He was an Irishman through and through, and one certainly wouldn't have missed that fact in looking at the handsome gentleman of a bygone era. The surety of his grandfather's broad smile and his generally thoughtful demeanor were things that Ronan looked forward to seeing each time he was over for a visit. The subtle structure and grace of his grandparents' home during the holidays always filled Ronan with an abundant warmth, which seemed to linger within for the duration of those happy seasons of celebration.

The premature death of Ronan's grandmother was an overwhelming trauma that would forever influence the life of Ronan's mother, though it would never damper her ability to give, even when she had little to give, and to love absolutely. Ronan's grandmother had been supremely demanding of her firstborn daughter, who had always been a bit of a dreamer from the moment of her earliest days. Though her intentions were dutiful and just, and ultimately conceived of the intimate bonds of her unending love for the sprightly child, Delia's mother was of a time and place that were nearly foreign to the age of American exceptionalism, which was taking hold at the time her child was coming into her own. Her oftentimes overbearing stewardship of her free-spirited daughter was, in certain ways, a smothering blanket that was wrapped around the fanciful dreams of her occasionally burning and always passionate little Delia.

Therefore, after her mother had passed, Miss Delia occasionally grappled with the complex paradox of the guilt that accompanied her newly found freedom from the loving but stringent hand of her mother. At the same time, the prodigious responsibilities assigned through divine providence to the young woman, those heavenly obligations that came with caring for her five younger siblings as she approached the years of her delicate blossom and a point in her life that she might experience even a few of those dreams to see the world beyond, seemed to keep a lasting tether around her unbound hopes in the years leading up to her marriage and the subsequent birth of her children. What Ronan, or any of those dear to her, would have said in response to such an insinuation, had it even been spoken aloud, was that she was one of the lucky ones graced with the capacity to love selflessly and without bounds. There was no doubt that, in the end, she understood that to be true, and, likewise, she understood that her family was her true blessing in this life and one that was beyond the scope of the wildest of her adolescent fancies.

In addition to these powerful crosscurrents, the deepening sorrows of the loss of such an endearing and strong-willed force of love in her life had a long-term impact on the warm and heartfelt woman. There were times when Ronan could readily decipher the influences of those traumas that carried out into the later years of her life by way of a few of his mother's more peculiar behavioral traits. Yet, Ronan could also say with unwavering confidence that while these strange manifestations sometimes made the angelic woman difficult to reason with, they were certainly not traits that in any way changed the nature of her noble and loving intentions. There were flashes when Ronan felt a light yet noticeable sorrow for his mother, which lingered in the depths of his slowly shifting empathy and often showed outwardly in the moments of his concern for her. He felt that way, at times, because he always believed the dreams Delia had sacrificed for the sake of the many gifts she gave to others still fluttered out there somewhere, like a yellow spring butterfly fresh from the anguish and warmth of its stifling but nurturing cocoon. Be that as it may, Ronan also knew that his mother would never have changed a thing concerning her family, even if she had not been granted the time to truly find herself until much later on in her life. He always understood in the depths of his heart that she would never have knowingly consented to even one lost moment with any of those she so loved and held eternally dear.

Ronan was always able to sum up the very essence of his mother quite effortlessly and quite naturally. Such was true, because Miss Delia gave of her love wholeheartedly, committing her will to the upbringing of her brothers and sisters following her mother's death and then giving all that she had to the raising of her boys. Ronan thought often about his mother's all-consuming affinity for guilt at times, which, along with her need to nurture her younger siblings, left her wanting for the fulfillment of grand hopes and dreams of the spirit. He firmly believed that if pressed hard enough, not even Delia Treacy Cassidy herself would have denied her hidden desire to experience just a small taste of the carefree moments she had foregone in life due to the unending demands of her circumstances. But for the fleeting moments when those wants and dreams tickled her fancy, Ronan knew that Delia had fulfilled her calling as a loving nurturer who, through the will of a great and unbound love, kept her flock safe through the many great storms and trials of their lives.

Ronan's grandmother was from a long lineage of Irish kin who had lived throughout the plains west of the numinous mountains of Connemara. Her grandparents grew up in a small white cottage situated at the cliff's edge of the known world, or at least the ends of those nearly barren western extremities of the Emerald Isle. The house also marked the end of the western road to Lahinch and did, in fact, rest no more than ten paces from a cliff's edge that overlooked that tempestuous North Atlantic Sea, which had carried many of their people off to the west. Those struggling Irish emigrants sometimes left in little boats that were forced to make their way back to the continent. Fortunately for their progeny, such as Mr. Cassidy, they also departed aboard great ships capable of making that daunting transatlantic passage to the Americas at a time when the pangs of freshly realized independence or famine were the scourges left to fill the power vacuum gifted to them by the British colonizers of the majestic island when those usurpers had finally made their retreat across the Irish Sea.

The white cottage home of the McKerley sect of the ancient MacDiarmid clan stood alone atop a particularly sharp outcropping of those grassy cliffside flats of Connemara as the gatehouse to the breathtakingly beautiful yet rough and eternally inhospitable brine below. The cliff was so sheer and so strident that it kept the great North Atlantic Sea from swallowing the western coast of the island since long before the memories of the heroes of the ancient Celtic tribes lived only in the spoken word of their ancestors. Ronan's grandmother's forebears had survived the harshest scores of the centuries of the British occupation and exploitation of Ireland and its once-proud people. The McKerley family annals, broken legend, and historical lore were rife with abuse and all of the unpleasant banalities of human depravity involved in the subjugation of any colonized, marginalized, mistreated, and fragmented social order. At some point during the great migration of Ireland, a couple of Ronan's grandmother's kin managed to shake free from the thick and haunting shackles of their broken pasts, which cascaded over their meagerly provisioned lives. They broke free and made their way across the sea spanning their front yard to the promise of a new world full of opportunity in America. The brother and his sister are believed to have reached New York Harbor in the early fall of 1888, and eventually settled in the Finger Lakes Region of Upstate New York.

Earlier in his life, some six years prior to that moment of organizational discord, which found Ronan reading an old college paper in his disheveled home office while he prepared to move, Mr. Cassidy had driven by that old white cottage standing sentinel at the edge of the world. As he loosely held that essay on the "Nixon Shock" in his hand, he vividly recalled driving by that enigmatic and solitary Irish homestead standing before the windswept Connemara flats and the mountains beyond. He recalled that as he prodded his rented compact car slowly past the house while dutifully adhering to the demands of the hairpin turn at the edge of the cliff, he had mused over the countenances of an older couple that lived within. The thought of someone from his ancient bloodline inhabiting such desolate yet eternal quarters filled Ronan with an almost voltaic yet nostalgic exhilaration. He imagined that the couple shared matching soft blue eyes and freckled skin, which had been shaded in a light russet tone by the fickle sun and the shearing winds of the barren divide, which set apart the numinous mountains off in the distance from the timeless sea below.

The wholly contrived husband and wife he pictured living inside the storybook cottage are Ronan's distant relatives. They share many of Ronan's more pronounced facial features and bodily dimensions. Their plain yet comely dark-haired daughter is bottle-feeding a newborn baby girl while the father and grandfather of the nursing child read different sections of the newspaper they retrieved while back in town earlier that morning. The two gentlemen are seated beside the mother and her child at the small table that rests against the northern wall of the quaint Milesian kitchen. The kitchen is ornamented with only the necessary cookware and a few token curios that hang subtly from the white wood-paneled walls. The plain curtains and tablecloth are nothing but staid and ascetic tributes to necessity and are emblazoned with markings addressed to the favor of our loving God. Ronan pictures the antiquated man occasionally looking up from his slim newspaper and searching forlornly out the thinly paned kitchen window. His longing eyes are probing out across the endless sea to the fanciful homes of his emigrated kin that this man can imagine with the intricately detailed and richly brilliant contrivances of his mind.

The American houses of those distant and seldom spoken-to blood relatives are surrounded by white picket fences, have double carports, and are surrounded by impeccably manicured yards. Their perfect lawns gleam in beautiful contrast to the elegant white brick of their modern castles, set against the serene backdrop of tall, wispy pines, dwarfing beautiful stone edifices and wide, welcoming wrap-around porches. The older man's wife takes no notice of the dazed and fanciful eyes of her husband. She is elsewhere and busy inscribing the contents of an inherited recipe into her newly bound ledger book.

Once she takes the opportunity to rest her pen, she also gazes out a window that belongs to another room in the cottage. This window before her is in the sitting room and faces the shallow plains and flatlands that lead back to the mountains rising in the east. Before her forlorn and longing eyes are the shifting, wind-bent grasses of those ancient plains that resemble some endless stretch of the Argentinian Puna. She becomes mesmerized by the shadowlands at the foot of the ancient mountains, while the lost souls of her people, who had been scattered with the winds centuries ago, call her back hence. The old Irish couple, as a unified entity, are two kindred spirits that fell in love long ago. They are now both aching for someplace else, but safe in the shared comforts of their provisional no man's land; their shared watchtower to the eastern and western realms of legend just off in the distance, which are home to each of their hearts separately and lethal to the hearts of one or the other jointly.

Ronan, who was now nearly lost in the whirlwind of his formerly imagined paradox of the sacrificial love of his ancestors, once again looked down at the folded pages of white printer paper. While not surprising, though a bit irksome just the same, his reminiscing and other daydreaming had done nothing to promote the advancement of his desired goals. The once-quaint room was still obscenely cluttered by the aftermath of hours of disorderly rummaging through a lifetime of keepsakes and random mementos, which lay strewn about on all sides of the overwhelmed gentleman. He became a bit frazzled until his focus was once again diverted by an object of interest, or at least an object of preferable distraction to all that remained to be done.

The object that caught Mr. Cassidy's eye was a clear, cubed transaction plaque made of a nearly indestructible acrylic resin. This resin was so formidable that it survived the intensity of the fires that melted the steel framework of the Twin Towers with a heat so intense that it sent the pulverized remains of the colossal crowning monuments to the supremacy of American financial dominance cascading down onto Battery Park on that fateful Tuesday morning of September 11th, 2001. Ronan knew that such a tragic event would never be forgotten and, in fact, still haunted the depths of the American psyche while he stared curiously at the translucent cube resting in the palm of his hand. That particular deal memento had not been forced to endure such a harrowing ordeal. Shortly afterwards, his wandering mind returned to the day of that catastrophic event. On that glorious late-summer morning, he was walking to work alongside Baltimore's Inner Harbor when news broke that an airplane had crashed into the North Tower. He was shocked from that moment on, and the worst of the day's horrors were still to come.

Ronan knew many fine people who had perished that morning. He had also lived through the devastating repercussions that those alarming and violent deaths had on the loved ones of the deceased. Mr. Cassidy also worked for a time for a company that lost many of its beautiful friends, brothers, sisters, mothers, and fathers in the moments of that appalling cataclysm that changed America, as she was then known, forever. As he continued staring blankly at the strange, translucent cube, he recalled seeing a picture of the haunting and hallowed remains of the edifice of the towers some weeks later. The picture had been taken after the steel girders of the building, which had given way to the burning jet fuel and the unholy assignments of the compounding loads from each failed beam above, had been hauled off to Staten Island and promptly sent overseas.

In that picture, a photograph dominated by mountains of white dust, the remaining edifice of the building, other crushed debris, and scattered objects that had once been of a useful variety when tucked into a commercial office space high above the vaunted city skyline, there were a few such keepsakes identical to the one Ronan was now studying. He remembered thinking at the time, when the spiritually moving realities of that unspeakable tragedy were still fresh and raw within the human soul, how strange it was that those resin cubes and rectangles scattered throughout the large, high-resolution picture appeared to be in almost perfect condition. He marveled at how such a thing was true when those that would have noted, or perhaps even celebrated, the reason for the existence of those keepsakes were never to be heard from in the manner of a corporal impulse again.

Ronan's mind continued to drift until he could picture the desk that one or more of those resin plaques may have rested on. The desk was higher-end but standard issue and common in the office buildings of the day. It faced a giant pane of thick glass, which offered its occupant a breathtaking view of New Jersey that stretched out to the Watchung Mountains beyond the Oranges, some thirty miles or more off into the western horizon. Next to the plaque rested a characteristically awkward, yet adorable all the same, picture of a young girl with wavy brown hair and braces. She had dressed for school that morning in anticipation of the dreaded event of her class pictures. Next to that annually updated keepsake was a standard eight-by-ten-inch wooden framed collage of six smaller pictures. Each of the equivalently sized photos in that frame revealed some of the most treasured moments that the phantom occupant of that desk had shared with her loved ones throughout her suddenly muted life. The pictures on the desk next to the plaque served as daily and even hourly reminders to the once feverishly busied occupant of that workspace, which rested atop the clouds in such rarified air and loomed over the bustling streets and sidewalks of that great metropolis born of the fundamental principles of free commerce. Those carefully chosen and framed portraits of such seminal moments in time served as continuous reminders of exactly what the purpose of her daily professional dedication indeed was.

Ronan was amazed that the material in his hands was capable of surviving what little else could—an incendiary fire and a fall from the apex of the Manhattan skyline to the concrete poured over the foundational bedrock and glacial till of Battery Park. He was astonished that of the countless objects that had completed the disturbing descent to the earth from the offices of the fallen financiers on the penultimate floors of those colossal buildings, buildings that were at the time the emblematic symbols of the financial underpinnings of the American dream in the era that followed the closing of the gold window in 1971, something so obscure had lived to tell at least something of the tale of what was taken from above.

Though Ronan was now falling well behind schedule concerning his appointed tasks for that afternoon, he continued to give further consideration to the things that remained with us in the aftermath of so much being lost. He looked back at the pages he held in his hand and began to once again read the words written therein, though he remained distracted by those thick and haunting memories from that fateful Tuesday morning more than a decade ago. As Ronan continued to put the words he wrote back in college into the context of the world as he saw it at that intersection of his life, he wondered how many truths had been buried for a time beneath the twisted steel and blankets of white ash on that horrific morning. He wondered at what cost so much had been taken from so many. He then began to speculate as to how much was set to be made known when the blinding haze of the ongoing fog of war had finally lifted from the hearts and minds of those touched by the events of that day. Perhaps a war of previously undisclosed combatants had been raging for far longer than any of us would care to admit, and it was only on that September morning that the reverberations of some hitherto unseen struggle of the age had come home to roost.

For some unknown reason, that final thought concerning the World Trade Center brought Ronan's inwardly searching eyes back to the paper, as if he suddenly believed that by reading further he might make some connection between the events of August 15, 1971, and the tragedy that unfolded in New York some thirty years and two fortnights later. Whether Ronan had acutely or subliminally connected some previously skewed dots in his head or he was simply trying to shift the urges of his motivations by connecting the two events, he continued to read the paper in earnest once he found a section of particular interest to him after skimming over a few pages. While he considered what he had read thus far of his collegiate offering to be somewhat provocative and most certainly accurately graded, the text where Ronan picked back up is transcribed as follows:

*Every period of human history is filled with the unique trials and tribulations of each person living through the singularities and similarities of the events specific to their time. Our innate instinct to apply comparative reasoning and to project the world we see before us today out into the future gives rise to great bouts of worry and anxiety in the very best of times. While the field may be yielding a great harvest, there is always an unquenchable desire exhibited by some to obtain bounties in equal and greater proportion to their neighbors, and there is always uncertainty lurking in tomorrow. The long boom was an American economic boom unlike any other in the generally accepted history of humankind in terms of the speed with which real quality of life improvements were realized by American citizens. The long boom was the post-war party, and the pump had been properly primed for the event. Investments in: **real** productive capital, education, and product innovation; a legal framework built on defending transparency, equal protection under the law, integrity, commerce, and building personal wealth; a vibrant free press rooted in defending the proposition of human rights that had a heritage dating back to the Declaration of Independence, the Constitution, and the Bill of Rights; and a tireless drive to succeed kept the music playing and the dancers dancing as America helped bring the world out of the devastation of the war and raised her own standard of living exponentially.*

However, by the time the Nixon Shock was delivered to the nation, the long boom had the distinct feel of an era of prosperity that had run its course. Accordingly, the baby boomers were at a crossroads ...

Stopping for a moment to ponder those thoughts from his collegiate years, which were probably not too far afield from his then-current beliefs regarding the constructs of the dollar, Ronan was reminded of the old couple who he had imagined in the Irish cottage house, that timeless abode standing defiantly over the sea while lingering between two great epochs of the past. He then proceeded to read on.

... The American long boom was rapidly coming to an end, and with that end, the prevailing belief in a brighter future was becoming marred and confounded by the grey shrouds engulfing the collective sensibilities of the post-war generation. A great doubt had cast its lot upon the once indefatigable land ...

"And I was preparing to be born into the world," Ronan mused wistfully as he briefly paused his reading. Nevertheless, he continued on without giving further consideration to the circumstances of his birth.

In an attempt to provide some much-needed structure to the purely fiat $IMFS following the Nixon Shock, the Smithsonian Agreement was ratified and signed by the predominant finance ministers of the world's foremost economies in December of 1971. The Smithsonian Agreement was the first codification of and corresponding display of critical international support for the purely fiat international reserve currency, the U.S. dollar. The agreement pegged the values of the currencies of the G10 nations to the dollar and symbolically devalued the dollar from a fixed value of 1/35 of a troy ounce of gold to 1/38 of a troy ounce.

In 1973, with the gold window shut and gold removed from the official international definition of the dollar, the United States gold reserves were once again revalued to an amount of $42.22 per troy ounce. They remain recorded on the U.S. Treasury's balance sheet at that dollar value to this very day ...

"And they still are," Ronan quipped offhandedly before adding, "frozen in time and locked away under the infamy of default at $42.22 per ounce while the world market for gold hideously evolved to become nothing more than an additional derivatives-style insurance market designed to help mask dollar value losses."

Ronan shook his head slowly and sighed with a long, continuous, and powerful push of air against his lower lip. He read on while becoming simultaneously relieved and frightened by the very real prospect that the unwinding of the dollar pyramid scheme would occur within his lifetime, barring an untimely end to his perceived and actuarially realistic schedule among the living. Ronan then set his eyes back to task and picked up with his reading where he left off.

The Smithsonian Agreement was intended to promote the dollar as the continuing centerpiece for global trade and as a stable instrument in which to store excess value in the face of the dollar's severed link from gold. By fixing their currencies to the dollar, which would, in turn, set the value of the dollar as the reserve currency for the largest trading nations on the planet, the countries of the G10 effectively committed to the dollar as the continuing exchange and accounting standard for global trade. The dollar had been expanded by the profligate deficit spending of the American government from 1958 to 1971 beyond a credible conversion rate to its golden focal point, a golden focal point that also happened to be limited in amount to the physical constraints of the fixed supply of recoverable gold in the real world. Given the circumstances surrounding the dollar's default, the dollar would need credibility support to continue in its role as the primary reserve currency, helping to lubricate the burgeoning levels of cross-border trade that were shaping the rapidly expanding global economy.

The Smithsonian Agreement was a start when it came to codifying the post-1971 fiat dollar financial system, but the provisions set therein were never meant to be a long-term solution to fostering global trade by way of utilizing the U.S. dollar as the world's first purely fiat reserve currency. More fortuitous for the dollar's prospects than such a loosely cobbled together arrangement was the fact that real economic gains under the global trade regime were surpassing the systemic expansion of the dollar in the early adjustment phases that followed America's permanent gold default. While dollar mismanagement had failed to keep the world's reserve currency anchored to her real-world constraint, gold, the dollar's ability to facilitate global trade as an easily divisible and exchangeable association of values across the fast-growing and increasingly complex global market for goods and services gave the dollar an irreplaceable value at the time of the closing of the gold exchange window. Essentially, it was the dollar's network effect, built up through decades of use as the primary currency for trade; the noticeable benefits of utilizing fungible currency to lubricate global trade; and the natural pull of gold towards its own best and highest valued use that allowed the post-1971 fiat dollar to begin her ascent to complete financial dominance on the world stage.

Ronan's testy knees were beginning to ache, so he got up from the floor and sidestepped his way around the clutter and over to his white wooden work desk. While pulling his red pen from a round container constructed of coated wire, he sat in his chair and put the paper he wrote in college down on the desk. He pressed the page that he was reading to the flat, wooden surface and, with his red pen, inserted the words, *"that peaked some 42 years later"* at the end of the aforementioned paragraph. When he was finished with his annotation and while smiling on the inside, Ronan continued reading. He soon reached the more idealistic and artistic portions of the old term paper.

... Simply put, the world's advanced economies didn't want to lose or severely hinder the economic advancements associated with the continuing expansion of global trade and cheap oil priced in dollars, which were the two major factors driving the world's economic progress in 1971.

Like the earthly soul fastened to the stocks below the guillotine's severe blade and raised heft, and with swift affirmation, the U.S. dollar became free of any earthly shackles and entered the realm of the purely ethereal as it became nothing more than an internationally agreed upon and recorded concept of value. Her sister in monetary servitude during the various phases of the gold exchange standard associated with the $IMFS of 1922 – 1971 was hurried off to an ivory tower to be neglected and rebuked publicly for her simplicity, antiquity, and incorruptible integrity. At the same time, gold remained secretly treasured by the super producers of the world for its beauty, purity, rarity, simplicity, timeless durability, honesty, and historically divined and innately recognized properties as the ultimate earthly representation of intrinsic affluence. Those who understand the history of money await her prudent return as the earthly arbiter of that accumulated wealth. They wait in the hope that some form of sanity can be restored to the diseased financial framework of the world without the forced resolution of war; a war that, if it comes, will surely be the last in the time of men.

Instead of something exchangeable for the real tangible wealth item of the ages par excellence, gold, the dollar became one of the greatest facilitators of trade in human history and a book entry of recorded debt that would multiply beyond the stars in the sky and the grains of sand upon the beaches. The "Nixon Shock" would open up the floodgates to an expansion in world debt, much of it denominated in U.S. dollars, the likes of which would have no proper description in historical context. While the fiat dollar was, for better or for worse, and remains, largely responsible for America's current standing in world affairs, it is also a fact that the laws of mathematics and the politics of man put our dollar firmly on the path to the shocking and unresolvable dilemma it faces today. This catch-22 to come was not, however, entirely lost on the financial architects of Nixon's time.

Ronan stopped reading at that point and began to write with his red pen: "*Today, the dollar is a dying supernova at the end of its useful life. It is nothing more than a monstrous mass of debt, frantically consuming all available energy; its sheer weight has now become a halting impediment to economic progress. The gathering pull of the dollar's gravitational force foretells unbearable burdens and economic ruin to those that continue to approach close enough to fuel its blinding brilliance. The dollar is now forced to devour itself and, in doing so, will deliver, just as rapidly as the stroke of the pen that severed it from gold, an uncontrollable torrent of fire that consumes the illusion of wealth of its current masters in an instant. These lost souls are engulfed by an insanity so severe and so perverse that they are giving their dying energies to saving dollar value by debauching and debasing it. Alas, "There is no torrent like greed." (1) Gautama."*

... The 1970s bore the early scars of these initial traumas of the abrupt transition to the purely confidence-based dollar at the heart of the world monetary order. However, imbalances and financial disruptions to the $IMFS under the gold exchange standard established in 1922 were nothing new. The Great Depression was the direct result of monetary imbalances and excessive credit creation caused by the effective doubling of international banking reserves, which was a key component of the nascent $IMFS protocols put in place in 1922, in addition to the standard over-exuberant optimism in America's rapidly industrializing economy that followed World War I. In the years following 1922, economic expectation and a monetary system geared for far greater credit expansion fueled a gross overextension of lending and the corresponding creation of money that eventually made its way to the financial markets in the form of excessive speculation. By late 1929, the stock market had risen tenfold in value until the speculative bubble finally popped on Thursday, October 24, 1929, when the primary exchange index dropped 11% in a single day.

Sadly, the force of the market decline and instantaneous loss of wealth broke the hearts and souls of many iconic stalwarts on Wall Street. The accompanying destruction of financial capital crippled the lives of men and women engaged in the service of even the nation's most productive industrial and agricultural endeavors. The crash of 1929 was a deflationary bust so powerful that the American economy wouldn't fully recover from this misallocation of both real and financial capital until the end of World War II.

As the story of the dollar continued to unfold throughout the twentieth century, the Nixon Shock and corresponding monetary events of the '70s were part and parcel of the novel and epic transitions to the evolving world monetary system. Specifically, disconnecting the dollar from gold paved the way for limitless and almost mandatory debt expansion facilitated by a government-spending-centric financial architecture. A financial structure described as such because, with gold removed from the system, government spending became the source of the reserves of the nation's commercial banks. While continuing to foster the burgeoning growth in international trade was the primary catalyst behind foreign support and acceptance of the fiat dollar, there was, at the time that the system of necessary dollar assistance was put into place, little political backing to pave the way forward for the unfettered expansion of America's "Exorbitant Privilege."

The term "exorbitant privilege" was coined by the French finance minister, Valéry Giscard d'Estaing, in the early 1960s. The term described the architectural flaw of the double counting of banking reserves of the International Monetary Financial System that had been present since its inception in the 1920s and were, at the time Mr. d'Estaing coined the phrase, accruing to the sole benefit of the United States as the issuer of the world's reserve currency. Stated in simpler terms, since its unofficial founding in 1922, the $IMFS has always allowed for the currencies of primary nations to be used as the banking reserves of other nations participating in international trade. The difference before 1971 was that these primary reserves were freely exchangeable for gold as a way to put a brake on primary nation reserve expansion. This was deemed the preferable solution by the nations attempting to sort out the new financial system following World War I; at least it was preferable to the solution of revaluing gold to a much higher price, which would have reflected the true debasement of the currencies of the countries financing the major war efforts of that day.

As with all things in life, the transgressions of our past that are not brought to light haunt our very souls and corrupt all that we will one day endeavor to create. The foundations of the $IMFS were similarly haunted by an unwillingness to admit to the tragic cost of World War I. Under the old gold standard, gold served as the primary reserve that was redeemable for newly created credit money and thereby limited credit expansion to some credible fraction of the gold reserves a country held. If the credit obligations of a deficit nation became too far out of balance, gold was shipped to settle trade imbalances. Following the birth of the $IMFS at Genoa, dollars, or specifically, at that time, the currencies of "center" countries (specifically, Great Britain and the United States) could be held as reserves by other nations participating in global trade, and those currencies were exchangeable for gold.

The establishment of a gold exchange standard as the primary mechanism for settling global trade accomplished two things. It began the process of settling the majority of trade with a standard currency, which will almost unbelievably be viewed as a net positive through the lens of history, even after the currency fires have burned themselves out, leaving behind nothing of a recognizable quality beyond the char of the violently flashed powder. Secondarily, and perhaps without the transparency necessary to achieve long-term systemic confidence, the gold *exchange standard dampened the need for a steep revaluation of gold by creating a demand for far more fungible reserve currencies to settle international trade. The imperfect equilibrium, or somewhat flawed checks and balances, of that system were anchored in the ability of countries that had amassed large stockpiles of reserve currency debts to exchange those debts and reserve currencies for gold. The idea back in 1922 was to avoid the loss of currency credibility that the world's financial leaders felt would have accompanied a direct revaluation of gold at that time.*

The real flaw, however, as the more astute monetary thinkers of the time had ascertained, was that international banking reserves would be held in the banking accounts of banks in the nation issuing the reserve currency. While in those accounts, the deposited reserves could be used as traditional banking reserves for the expansion of further lending activities. The net result was that debt could pile up in the surplus trading nations, but reserve currency-issuing deficit nations saw no reduction in their banking reserves. This meant that goods could pile up in the deficit nation in exchange for debt, and the deficit nation's banking reserves stayed at the same level due to the fact that net producer nations kept their excess balances on deposit in banks located in countries issuing reserve currencies. The banking institutions of reserve currency nations, unlike their more pedestrian commercial bank counterparts in non-reserve countries, never had to balance their trade deficits to maintain the reserve supplies of their banking systems. Net producers could, before 1971, exchange their excess reserves for gold. This ability to exchange excess dollars for gold ultimately served as the braking mechanism on reserve currency issuer trade imbalances until the exchangeability feature was dissolved by the Nixon Shock in 1971. Not surprisingly, the United States has run a trade deficit with perhaps only a single exception ever since.

In 1944, as it became apparent that World War II was nearing its end, the financial leaders of the victorious nations convened in Bretton Woods, New Hampshire, to establish the post-war protocols of the $IMFS. At the Bretton Woods Monetary Conference, as it was officially named, the United States dollar, due to the country's superior economic position and the post-war condition of the major economies of Europe, became the solitary reserve currency of the $IMFS. From 1944 to 1958, the United States was a pillar of economic production and instrumental in helping Europe recover from the ravages of World War II. Europe recovered much faster than even the Europeans themselves anticipated. During this period, the United States ran a significant trade account surplus. As a result of the aforementioned factors, the ample stockpile of American gold reserves of

20,000 tons allowed for a fairly smooth transition to the Bretton Woods System of the $IMFS.

In time, 1958 to be exact, the United States began running noticeable trade deficits as Europe and Japan regained their productive footings. During the 1960s under Lyndon Johnson's Great Society, the Space Race with the Soviet Union, and the Vietnam War, America's noticeable deficit spending resulted in an increasing number of trade surplus nations exchanging their excess dollars for gold. The evil speculators Nixon was referring to in his August address were simply surplus trade nations attempting to get gold for their dollars before the day arrived that they no longer could. That infamous day arrived on Sunday, August 15, 1971. To give you an idea of how much gold was leaving the United States during the '60s, by the time the Nixon Shock closed the gold window in 1971, the United States Treasury held less than half of its peak level gold reserves, or just 8,133.5 tons.

By late 1973, pressures on the purely fiat international reserve currency began to mount. By way of an oil embargo placed on many western nations, an oligopoly designated as the Organization of the Oil Exporting Countries ("OPEC"), which was led by Saudi Arabia, drove the price of oil from $3 to $12 a barrel on the world market. The official story behind the oil embargo of 1973-74, which was well propagandized in the American press and later historical annals recounting the events, blamed the embargo on the OPEC nations attempting to deter Western support for the Israeli state. The reality of the situation was that the U.S. wanted higher oil prices so that U.S. oil production could help offset a perceived loss in currency value caused by the continuing overexpansion of the dollar through trade and budget deficits. The U.S. also wanted oil production in other parts of the world to become more profitable and weaken OPEC's influence. The root causes of this first bout with inflationary pressure on the dollar were twofold: the Saudis and other OPEC nations still wanted to be paid for their oil in gold, and they had been shut off from their mechanism for redemption by the "Nixon Shock"; and U.S. deficits were expanding the money supply at a rate far faster than the country's productive capacity. The story was simply written by those whose primacy in world affairs would become increasingly dependent on the confidence that supported the dollar as time marched on.

With these events settled piecemeal and in temporary and patchwork fashion by 1975, the world's monetary leaders signed the Jamaica Accords on January 8th, 1976, after a two-day gathering in Kingston, Jamaica. The Accords put an end to the Bretton Woods monetary order established in 1944. The Bretton Woods monetary order had its roots in the birth of the International Monetary Financial System at the Genoa Economic and Financial Conference held in Genoa, Italy from 10 April to 19 May 1922. The Accords officially changed the definition of the U.S. dollar, and all references to gold were removed. Also of note, the Jamaica Accords declared that the price of gold would freely float against the values of all major currencies. This event could have changed the course of the country and the world's financial architecture, but storm clouds were gathering on the financial horizon.

In the spring of 1978, the countries that comprised the European Economic Union stopped their accumulation of U.S. Treasury debt. Additionally, after a brief pause in 1976, the gold price began to rise at an alarming rate while real price goods inflation was taking hold in the United States during this continuing period of economic stagnation. By 1979, the dollar was staring into the abyss. Fearing the severe economic dislocation that would be caused by the implosion of the international reserve currency, which lacked a suitable alternative at that time, the major economic powers of the world established the four-pronged support system for the dollar reserve currency that we still see enabling dollar function to this day.

The four main pillars of that international assistance were: Structural Support, or a return to the stockpiling of U.S. Treasury securities, which removes the dollar overhang caused by perpetual trade deficits by fixing the value of a foreign nation's currency to the dollar; The Network Effect, or additional rules and guidance that further promoted the use of the U.S. dollar to settle international trade; the LBMA Bullion Banking System, or fractionally reserved gold banking, which would synthetically expand the gold supply in an effort to suppress the price of that wealth reserve asset and natural fallback plan to the fiat dollar; and lastly, Financial Product Proliferation, or the gearing of Wall Street to gin the promise of more dollars by taking on investment risk in addition to recycling and managing the unbound expansion of U.S. dollars for the lubrication of international trade ...

While there was quite a bit more to this walk down the international monetary system's memory lane and the fairly comprehensive paper that Ronan had written on the topic, Mr. Cassidy stopped reading there to digest what he had taken in. He found it curious that the truth about the financial system's less than celebrated past remained such an obscure topic to the average American, and especially so in the wake of the near-total collapse of the dollar and the $IMFS in 2009. However, he took some solace from the wisdom that came from understanding that the state of affairs surrounding the rise of the U.S. dollar had caused many of the issues facing the country at that time and, furthermore, that such an outcome was inevitable once the rise of the fiat global reserve currency had begun in earnest. American producers were squeezed out of the international marketplace by the overvalued dollar, and the easy money camp parasites prospered by taking their slice of the dollar pie in return for keeping the dollar system functioning when the natural economic forces of equilibrium would have relegated the grossly overprinted credit instrument to the dustbin of history as far back as 1980.

If the dollar-based financial system was promoted and indeed nurtured by hiding the truth of the dollar's actual purchasing power, then perpetuating this lie relied on the proliferation of big government, the Federal Reserve/ Wall Street financial complex, and a strong enforcement arm that would keep foreign interests in line with dollar-friendly economic and trade policies. As the lie protecting the dollar's true worthlessness grew too big to hide, big tech, a fully consolidated media apparatus, which was woefully immersed in carefully directed propaganda, a progressive higher education system, and the deep-seated corruption of the United States government throughout the legislative, executive, and judicial branches evolved over time to cover up this otherwise blatant reality concerning the dollar's true intrinsic value. Taken as a whole, the coordinated directives of those gradually corrupted pillars of American society were slowly and carefully seeded to defend the ongoing rot as the financial system evolved and became ever more exposed to its inherent fragility, lack of transparency, and, of course, the expanding lies required to keep the clever ruse going.

By the final month of 2012, Ronan wholeheartedly believed that the shadowy depths of that vile corruption were sewn into the marrow of the systems of world government and finance and were the norm rather than the exception. He could believe, though not entirely stomach, that the irrevocably entrenched corruption of the American republic occurred almost naturally at first, as the byproduct of the proliferation of a diseased system founded upon the false pretext that currency was a viable long-term store of value and a reserve asset representing generational wealth. He also knew in the depths of his heart, however, that the dark stain of this illicit corruption was also accomplished through more nefarious means when the lie grew too absurd to be believed by the silent majority of Americans without unending doses of propaganda, slanderous assaults accompanied by the promotion of divisive policies designed to bifurcate the population, and the steady erosion of American liberties. The truth of the aforementioned was self-evident to Ronan simply because he could have counted on the fingers of his right hand the number of people whom he knew who truly understood the underpinnings of the dollar-based financial system, how the legal system actually functioned, and why foreign producers were so keen to stockpile worthless credit obligations of the largest debtor the world has ever known. That stunning reality always amazed Ronan, given that he had studied and worked with so many brilliant minds throughout the realms of both professional finance and academia.

In accordance with Ronan's line of thinking, the crux of the matter rested on a few basic concepts in regard to money, wealth, and the age-old struggle for power. If the evolution of the dollar-centric international financial system proved anything over the last century, or at least since the shadowy founding of the third American central bank in 1913, it was that the functions of money are necessary and beneficial in continuing to improve the human standard of living. What the evolution of the dollar also revealed to Mr. Cassidy was that while currency was the superior monetary instrument to be utilized for commerce and trade, it was always tainted and devalued over time. As such, the intrinsic and incorruptible wealth asset of tangible gold remained the best medium for preserving long-term wealth. With that thought in mind, Ronan held firm to the belief that the financial system of the future was bound to reflect those unavoidable truths concerning the properties of money.

Ronan staunchly believed that the world financial architecture had no choice but to eventually reach its natural equilibrium regarding money and wealth, come the fires of hell or the deluge of high water. He was hoping for high water and a boat, but exactly how the American people reached that point on the monetary trail from where the world financial order was positioned during that dour Midwestern winter of 2012 remained something of a vexing guess to the magnanimous and always hopeful young man. While he searched that old college paper for its conclusion because he had run out of time to do otherwise, he allowed the rushing waves of his gathering consciousness on the matter of money and the dollar dilemma to further coalesce. He could sense the great empires of the world massing their armies, those armies both seen and unseen. Those armies were moving forcefully into position under the cover of darkness throughout the world to station themselves at the ready for this spectacular dislocation of the truly fragile and utterly corrupted U.S. dollar, the global reserve currency that was fast becoming an unending daisy chain of debt and corruption that had been tightly fastened around the throat of the global economy.

Ronan turned his bemused eyes back to the paper as he flipped to the last page. The essay concluded mildly in comparison to the fire embedded within his thoughts on the matters covered throughout the pages of the text at that moment in time in December of 2012. He was surprised by how much he had forgotten about his earlier beliefs and how readily they now converged with the things he had learned from that anonymous author embedded somewhere within the enigmatic ranks of the elite financial order. Although the circumstances that would ultimately compel him to journey to the island of Inis Mor were not entirely attributable to the fate of the dollar in the years to come, his foresight regarding the outcome of that particular dilemma would draw him into the resolution of another conflict, one that was as old as the Western age and one that seemed to be approaching its own intended reckoning on a similar timeline.

… While the closing of the gold window somehow seems like a subtle disruption in the United States' manifest destiny to attain financial superiority in the eyes of the modern American, there was little doubt at the time that Nixon's surprise address of August 15, 1971, launched a whirlwind of social and political change the world over. Thinking deeper on the matter, one could argue that no executive act or edict of the American Century has done more to alter our way of life …

*… **we shall one day know the fleeting pain that cures the horrors of our addiction to the deadly ease and privilege that is born of the Federal Reserve Note. On that day, we will be far better, righteously more humble, and joyfully more thankful men and women under God upon freeing ourselves of that curse** …*

Chapter 5

THE MAN

B eing somewhat better acquainted with our vexed man of the hour, as it were, and, likewise, a little something of the confluence of events driving him toward that unfortunate rendezvous that would in many ways define his given time upon this earth, let us proceed to a pivotal moment that served to unite those two men tied to the "scandalous" legend of little Miss Margaret Anne Basseterre and our increasingly faithful Mr. Cassidy. As it regards what more Ronan had come to learn of the current state of affairs surrounding the dollar and her attendant financial markets, that is a matter we shall leave to the discernment of those kind enough to consider our enchanting tale, though it remains a not entirely insignificant condition to connecting something of those colorful dots yet to be plotted within. With that in mind, we march ahead to those days that were part and parcel of the quickening of events and the time of a long overdue reckoning.

Mr. Cassidy boarded a plane at Chicago O'Hare International Airport at exactly 6:00 AM on Tuesday, April 11, 2017. There remained a lingering chill of winter clinging to the clammy brume of the dusky predawn air of that spring morning. He could feel the chill of that discomforting air in the marrow of his bones just a few hours earlier when he hopped into his black club car, which had been patiently waiting in front of the inner loop hotel where he had spent the night following an intense client meeting the prior afternoon. At that time in his life, Ronan was employed by one of the largest and oldest trust banking institutions in continuous existence in the United States. The organization was founded in the late 1800s and was responsible for administering and managing over $15 trillion in custodial assets for large corporations, prominent financial institutions, and ultra-high net-worth individuals and their families worldwide.

Ronan's specific professional designation was that of Senior Advisor of Alternative Investments. His primary role was to provide counsel and advice to large, sophisticated clients concerning commodities-related investments.

In Ronan's case, "commodities-related investments" was simply a turgid euphemism in the financial parlance for a tangible wealth asset that had come to be much maligned and, in many ways, despised in the financial realms of his day. In fact, due to its simplicity, scarcity, durability, integrity, and, most of all, its inability to gin the interest revenues or large fees that other currency-related financial products of the modern era of finance were able to generate, the financial product Ronan specialized in was seldom ever called by its proper English appellation. The rogue tangible asset class Ronan was specifically concerned with was openly ridiculed by his colleagues, the financial sophists of the ivory towers of academia, and the media alike. Nevertheless, Ronan specialized in gold and gold alone. That fact is not likely to be a surprise to those who have been following along with even a tepid interest in the fate of our man.

While no corner of the world of money and finance was entirely forthright and untainted by the effects of greed, self-interest on far too many levels to count, and obfuscation at that time in human history, or perhaps ever, landing the somewhat obscure but promising role in what Ronan considered to be the final frontier of "honest" money to ring in the new year of 2017 was a notable step in the continuation of his great awakening. Because gold investment was relegated to small subsections of the asset portfolios of the bank's wealthiest clients and never spoken of openly, Mr. Cassidy was often to be found boarding early morning flights, such as that day's offering out of O'Hare, to visit with ultra-high-net-worth clients of the firm. During those visits, he gave what are usually described as discreet presentations regarding the benefits of tightly rationed portfolio allocations to gold and gold-related investments.

While Ronan's firm preferred that he recommend gold-related investments, by the spring of 2017, Ronan had become a staunch proponent of holding physical gold outside of the London-based bullion banking system—or any banking system, for that matter. That preference was squarely due to the chicanery and obscurity associated with such a sorely opaque exchange and the legal fineries that dictated how custodial assets were treated by modern banking institutions "in extremis." That particular morning, Ronan was returning home to Alabama from his old stomping grounds in Chicago after making one of his "discreet" presentations to the advisory committee of a family-owned shipping conglomerate. To the surprise of many within Ronan's firm, and most certainly those who had been repeatedly rebuffed on past attempts to pitch for the firm's client account business, the advisory committee had been aggressively inquiring about diversifying their asset portfolio by making a sizable investment in gold. The company was owned by an old, wealthy family, one that dated the receipt of their rather substantial land grant in the American Colonies back to the reign of King George II of England and specifically to the year 1740.

Upon reviewing the assets of the family that were held in the holding company of the shipping conglomerate in order to make his standard determinations regarding investment suitability and proper asset allocation, Ronan noted that the ownership of most of the assets held within Superior Shipping Lines Holdings, LLC, and its forebears and assigns, predated the First World War and even the establishment of the Federal Reserve Bank in 1913. Ronan found the portfolio review to be quite fascinating. To his dismay, however, he remained unsure as to whether he had broken through the typical confirmation biases that existed around the need to own unencumbered physical gold in the name of wealth preservation. There was a curious older man by the name of Mr. Manley present at the meeting. Mr. Manley appeared to chair that particular committee by way of some transitory political clout that came to him through the direct proxy of another and not in accordance with his proper title or any authority he possessed. That gentleman remained unsettlingly reluctant to accept Ronan's proposition following his flawless presentation of the merits of investing in that purposefully staid and timeless element, which was divinely designed as the perfect embodiment of wealth.

"Irrespective of Mr. Manley's distaste for my proposal, I believe that went well for a first go at things," thought Ronan after leaving the meeting. Those relationship-building pitches of his were always a slow, winding journey. One that tended to commence with the initial stirring of the primal fires of the human spirit but then proceeded to take their natural time to progress as his somewhat radical propositions began to season within the psyche of the traditional client with more of a western financial bent.

The initial presentations and subsequent follow-up conversations always took their time to bear fruit of any kind. That was because to truly understand the wealth reserve function of gold, one had to disavow certain lifelong indoctrinations driven into the depths of the consciousness of those who had been exposed to the supporting pillars and formidable houses of the American establishment. The aforementioned were fine and reputable institutions in the eyes of most, mind you. They include our schools, our media, our banks, our organizations of society and culture, and most notably, the established political order. They all made their hay by hook or by crook due to the seemingly endless supply of overvalued dollars available to almost any holder of an official office. What was required to truly understand the function of gold in the modern world, which, on the surface, appeared to be dominated by fiat currency, was always a test of any new American client's ability to reason on many levels. Ronan found that the basic principles of modern finance and the innate concept of money were usually topics that were more than enough to overcome the initial fears of the unaware and the faint of heart. He understood that yesterday's meeting with the family's advisory committee had merely been the first step down that long and sometimes trying, yet always rewarding, road of new business development.

Ronan moved on from his thoughts concerning the meeting while he cleared the cockpit area of the aircraft. He was prompted to think back to the times following his move when he would board the Monday edition of that same flight every fortnight. He recalled that he would step onto those flights exhausted and already homesick after visiting with his three daughters, his friends, and his wife for the allotted span of just forty-eight hours while his family was still in the process of finishing their move and permanently joining him down south. On that particular morning, those anguishing days of transition had passed some four years earlier. As such, Ronan took his seat on the aisle of the seventh row of the fully booked 737 aircraft with only the anticipations that accompany returning home, though that home was far different than the place he had imagined back in the winter of 2012.

While Ronan worked to get comfortable in the cramped quarters of his seat, the smiles and greetings of the members of the fully engaged and animated crew were almost an affront to the exhausted commuter trying to get settled in for his trip. Whether or not they were aware that their bubbly demeanor was quite vexing at that particular hour, the attendants finished dispatching with the last of their duties to have the commercial jet ready for departure. After standing once again to place his carry-on bag and overcoat in the overhead bin, as he had been undecided on the matter for reasons of convenience, Ronan sat down next to a well-turned-out gentleman. A gentleman who had reached his lifelong goal of accumulating more money and professional prestige than he would have ever dared to imagine back when he was little more than a supremely troubled young boy.

Given that he was assessing the man seated next to him for the first time from the tricky vantage point of an airline seat, and due to Ronan's fatigue and other distractions common to such a moment, he would not have guessed that the casually nondescript gentleman possessed such a lofty degree of societal standing or perceived wealth. Nor would Ronan have known that his neighbor's heart had grown cold and desperately lonely for the second time in his life, and perhaps for a span too long to allow that sometimes knavish and always mercurial organ to feel warmth again. The man had been away for many years and was living in an exile of sorts due to some complex matters that he was working tirelessly to resolve. On that morning, however, as he took meticulous notice of Mr. Cassidy, the man seemed to arrive at the startling realization that the fruits of his inextinguishable drive for earthly attainment had left him as barren and empty as that same envy he had received from those malicious fiends that had once left him an outcast, or in the worst of times, pitiable, wretched, and craven with want in his boyhood. There was no disputing that this fairly nondescript man had, in many ways, attracted the envy of many. Yet he was only beginning to understand why he had failed to garner the admiration, or better yet, the covetous spite, of those wicked few, which he had once prized above all else.

While this man, at one time or another during his young life, likely sought vengeance against the entirety of the human race, tragically, those very wights that numbered among the people deserving blame for his once black and still tinted soul and, moreover, his unquenchable desire for retribution, included his mother. Even when the man was rescued from the utter depravity of his unimaginably impoverished situation sometime during his thirteenth year, his physical reclamation was no good deed that had transpired in accordance with the proper mechanisms of kindness or grace. Instead, the first rebirth of a sort that the man had experienced during his life was almost inexplicably fashioned from greed in conjunction with someone's desire to exploit his immense and unspeakable talents for ill purposes and personal gain. The care and elite schooling he had been granted, and the years of training he received at tremendous monetary cost to his benefactors, had little to do with any love for or emotional connection to the child or young man he was during those times.

The boy was simply the perfect means to an uncertain end for a powerful and evil force lurking in the veiled and vile worlds of the shadowlands. Beyond that, he was the long-overdue storm of the century, sent to settle an ancient score, though, even on that morning, the man possessed little more than an inkling of an understanding as to what that verity would come to mean. Those that controlled him were certain to cast their common enemies, whether or not those enemies were of the darkness or of the light, into their respective supernal realms while claiming a sizable and lasting domain upon the earth. Yet, let us not jump too far ahead in our story, as there is much to discuss regarding this seemingly dubious and insipidly handsome man who was perhaps waiting to engage Mr. Cassidy.

The man possessed a deep intelligence and operated with such comprehensive bandwidth that his potential for achieving material gain was without limit. The fact that such a cold and calculating intellect had been nurtured by hunger, want, loathing, and remorse might have caused the unfortunate story of his younger years to be understood by the casual observer as just another American tragedy of the modern age. One brought about by the continuing neglect of the nation's forgotten. Those that were left behind to rust and rot with the factories and mills; America's founding identity as a land of sovereign statesmen who belonged to a bygone era; and the country's almost rapacious desire for self-reliance that had existed prior to the dollar's Faustian bargain taking hold of the already corrupted heart of the nation. The truth of the matter, however, was something of an entirely different nature.

When the man was enrolled by his adoptive parents in one of the top preparatory academies in the nation, he quickly ascended to the top of his class. He readily perceived and deftly understood the advantages of his new circumstances, yet he made no effort to adapt to the genteel proclivities of the elite echelon of society into which he had been cast after probing the depths of human depravity. He was shrewd enough to see beyond the thin veneer of pageantry and tradition and into the depths of a culture that only superficially masked the infiltration of a centuries-old and inbred desire to do little more than obtain wealth, exploit the unlearned masses of the carriage class, and hold dominion over the meek. What the young man witnessed was a primal and craven desire. One that manifested itself in an oftentimes licentious and always ruthless subculture, which had secretly pervaded even the most esteemed and trusted temples of American society. After just a short time in his new environs, he had come to intricately understand the base traits of this forceful subculture quite well. He had been the victim of those same attributes of primal, and even savage, licentiousness while growing up inside boxes and under porches, and in the dark cellars of abandoned row houses in the Fairfield and Dundalk neighborhoods of Baltimore, Maryland, in the decades of the Seventies and into the Eighties.

While the man seated beside Ronan appeared fairly unremarkable at first glance, that was only true when he was scrutinized with the casual discernment of a disinterested inspection. To the untrained eye, he would not have stood out in the least while standing among an assorted gathering of any size. He was slight of frame and slender, yet not lacking a mildly distinguished level of muscular fortitude within his long, gliding limbs and subtly pronounced chest. His grey jacket, white shirt, and blue-grey tie were unassuming but nearly impeccable in their make and tailoring. His grey hat was slightly more oblong than round in its shape and stood a bit tall on his head, yet the slightness of the circumference of the hat's brim bequeathed a certain fineness to the overall presentation of the man's comely guise.

His facial features were slender yet attractively pronounced, and the rounded and occasionally reddened tip of his nose projected a false inner mirth onto his mannerisms, giving the man a slight air of congeniality and approachability while compensating for his otherwise staid and executive-looking facial lineaments and expressions. The contrast of his light-blue eyes, red lips, and lightly blushed cheeks against his unblemished and slightly tanned skin often projected an almost elfin demeanor that was wholly antithetical to his stern inner disposition. Though the man possessed those nearly concealing and certainly disarming traits, Ronan did not fail to notice the unnerving contrast between the sharpness and then ease of the man's facial expressions, which alluded to a clever intellect, a certain comfort with his surroundings, and a worldly awareness. When taken together as a whole, those corporal traits and mannerisms, in conjunction with his ensemble, projected an aura of refinement and class that, given Ronan's heightened sensitivity to detail, prodded Mr. Cassidy to take particular notice of his new companion for the coming few hours.

The man smiled at Ronan demurely yet artfully. The look seemed to convey that the man knew he had not only piqued Mr. Cassidy's sensitive curiosities but also gained a level of his trust, which would allow him to intercede upon the absolute anonymity that had theretofore established a barrier of courtesy between the two early-morning travelers. While the man's smile was not unwelcoming in the context of the common considerations Ronan gave most folks upon laying eyes on them for the first time, that smile had drawn his attention to the ethereal lack of constraint that allowed the soft blues of the man's eyes to appear endless and eternal within their depths, somewhat wanting, and without boundary to consume. There was a deep and uneasy longing written into the storming shallows of each iris, as if those eyes were trying to confidently confirm some false truth by way of some misappropriated beauty or haunting elegance.

There were times that the tell with that man was his inability to give even the pretense of constraint to those endless raging seas in the moments when they were broadcasting what was otherwise hidden deep within his guarded thoughts. Those moments tended to arise once some wild and unbound desire to acquire something of particular interest to him was set free to find its mark. Beyond those rare flare-ups of intense passion or vengeful rage, there existed a cold starkness embedded within the resolve and acuity of his stare. Once locked within the inauspicious recesses of his more traditional glare, most were likely to presume that the man was intending to convey the unfortunate realities and limitations of this life as something of a soothing gesture, given in the midst of the always unfortunate circumstances that required his presence, regardless of the amount of levity or congenial courtesy he may have employed to disguise the severity of the words that he struck.

Regarding Ronan's opinion on the matter of the man's heart-rending stare, he believed that the refined gentleman had sized him up squarely. In fact, Ronan felt as if someone had handed that ordinary yet chilling stranger the blueprint to his soul before either of them had spoken a word. As such, Mr. Cassidy convulsed with slight twitches of discomfort while the man continued to eye him. Those were, however, almost imperceptible convulsions, which bolted through his limbs from time to time, yet showed only in the manner of a fleeting tension of the muscles of his neck and a slight tightening of his upper arms into the sides of his ribs. Thankfully, both of those places where his reaction to such a dour portent would have been patently obvious to an outside observer were concealed by his blazer. That mattered not. The man sensed Ronan's disguised quivering in response to his piercing stare for exactly what it was: a fearful reckoning of something that Mr. Cassidy did not understand in the least.

While Ronan was only moderately unnerved by the man's penetrating eyes, his breath shortened just a bit due to their intense yet muted interaction. Given the early hour of the day and the harried nature of his arrival at the airport, Ronan lacked the energy and the resolve to further consider the peculiarities of his temporary neighbor, outside of that strange man's unwillingness to move into the empty window seat and open up a little room for the both of them by doing as much. The open seat, a rare gift on that regularly scheduled flight, did agitate Ronan far more persistently than the man's cold and hollow stare frightened him. That authenticity was due to Mr. Cassidy's fatigue and the fortuitous circumstance of being closely surrounded by hundreds of people.

Ronan had arrived late at the gate. As such, he was far more hurried in his efforts to board the plane than he would have preferred. His excellent and normally punctual Polish shuttle driver, Vladimir, had overcome extreme odds to break into his club car after accidentally locking the keys inside the vehicle. Ronan had known Vladimir from his days living in Chicago and had reconnected with the amiable gentleman once he began doing more business back in his former hometown. He did that as a favor to his old friend and sometimes confidant. The story that Vladimir had been holding to that morning was that his wife had gone to retrieve a few items from the trunk of his car after he had concluded his night shift and left the keys behind when she shut the hatch.

Having witnessed Vladimir's disheveled appearance that morning, Ronan presumed that his old friend had stepped out for a few Monday night cocktails with the fellas over at the Post. In any event, Ronan got a much-needed chuckle out of Vladimir's half-assed excuse. An excuse that pinned everything on his wife's lack of common sense, which may or may not have been true given that she had married the old miscreant. Ronan had known Vladimir for quite some time, and while they hadn't missed an early morning flight yet, there were times he had wondered if his man had traveled straight from the tavern to his driveway. Ronan had decided somewhere back on Interstate 90 that the truth of the matter was more likely to have been that Vladimir's wife woke him from a mild stupor with a good bat to the ear. Following that act of divine providence, at least where Mr. Cassidy was concerned on that dreary spring morning, she probably let old Vlad hear about his weakness for the Tullamore Dew loud enough to wake the entire neighborhood and perhaps the dead for good measure. In fact, Ronan thought it likely that she had continued on with her tirade until her husband was three doors down the road in search of his parked car while sprinting away from the scene of the crime.

Irrespective of the exact nature of his driver's tardiness, the fact that Ronan was on board the plane at all was more than a bit difficult for him to believe. To take his mind off of the eerie man soon to be his "bestie" for the next few hours, he retraced the sequence of events tied to his arrival in his head while he ported the last of his items into the overhead bin without leaving an inch to spare. "Packed to a tee," he thought while preparing to take his seat.

Not but a split-second following the firm clasping of the latch of the overhead bin, Ronan's flighty attention span, which had been brought about by the poor habits he had established while rushing through the airport to make this flight when all hope for doing so seemed lost, once again shifted to the fact that the window seat remained open. He played the smart ass to none but his wit in regard to the bothersome open seat for just a bit. He remained silent only because he was not in the mood for any discourse he might stir up by disturbing anyone within earshot at that ungodly hour of the morning. The foremost among the aforementioned being his intriguing travel mate. "Perhaps the announcement that the flight was overbooked was an intentional exaggeration. You know, something to motivate all of the sleepwalking passengers ignoring the completely asinine general directives of the boarding process," he quipped.

Ronan relaxed a little as he gazed upon the weary travelers seated throughout the dim cabin after taking a soothing breath. Those poor devils seated around him wanted nothing more than to interject at least the pretext of comfort into their cramped seating space so that they might reignite their rudely interrupted dreams of the prior hours. Cast into the salt mines of the workday far too early while their loved ones lay enrapt in some perfect state of hibernation within the comforts of their beds, that ragtag group of misfits, masked by outwear and contorted like weeds growing up through tiny cracks in concrete, clutched for comfort in any manner they could find. Ronan smiled inwardly as he felt the warmth of his reassembling composure take hold. He then postured to once again take his seat. When Mr. Cassidy sat down next to the man, he settled in next to him as if he were a feather in an effort to give his neighbor little reason to address him. He also decided against making even a courteous recommendation regarding the open seat, though the oversight continued to gnaw at his mortal soul.

To put up something of an invisible barrier, Ronan kept his focus on his mobile device. He pretended to care about the certainly useless emails that had arrived in his inbox between the hours of midnight and 3:30 a.m. When he was situated, Ronan was thankful that not a word had been spoken by the man so rudely occupying the middle seat. In fact, the unnerving gentleman had remained dutifully quiet and perfectly still. Ronan took further comfort from the fact that nothing needed to be done on the work front until he arrived in Birmingham at a far more respectable hour of the day. As the man remained silent, Ronan straightened his legs and tilted his head back while the plane taxied out onto the tarmac and over to runway 42 for takeoff. Amidst the calming motion of the taxiing aircraft, Mr. Cassidy closed his eyes and thought about his three little girls, tucked so comfortably into their beds, and the stories they used to read until they could not hold their eyes open. In the flash and flicker of a New York minute, he drifted off to sleep once the aircraft ascended to the southeast. The slowly rising sun was finally giving form to the city skyline and the vastness of the great lake just beyond those opaque monoliths.

While Ronan slept, the man, almost inexplicably, remained seated in the middle of the row while his hat rested on the open window seat. He was thinking back to his tenth year while he gave further consideration to Mr. Cassidy as Ronan slept soundly. The man was not clear as to why he was suddenly prodded to remember something of those most troubling episodes from his past. Perhaps it was something about the way Ronan was sleeping so comfortably next to him, or perhaps the unwelcome catalyst was simply the early hour of the day and the almost blinding brightness of the rising sun, which was beginning to pierce through the unshaded window to his left. Whatever the cause, buried within that unholy span of his life was one of the few moments from his childhood that the man of such worldly means and oftentimes dubious, yet always fruitful, endeavors took unconscionable pains not to revisit.

During that time in the man's life, his mother had managed to situate him and his four-year-old sister, who did not share the same father, in the abandoned basement of a two-story row house. The building had last been inhabited by methamphetamine cooks and those addicted to heroin and other illicit drugs. The row house had been condemned, along with half a dozen others on the block, by the Baltimore City Health Department, yet remained standing since no funding for the razing of the dilapidated structures was available at the time. The basement of the particular row house that the man occupied with his sister and mother had no heat, air conditioning, running water, or electricity. A small group of wandering heroin addicts had squatted on the upper floors of the building without impediment from any law enforcement authority, though the group of itinerant junkies made some effort to keep out of sight whenever a sporadic patrolman or government official rolled down the street while making an inspection of the neighborhood. Those creatures of the pangs and deliriums of addiction lived in their filth, and they were generally a harmless sort unless gripped and, therefore, contorted by the dark hells of withdrawal, which certainly happened more often than now and again.

The man and his mother's time spent living in Baltimore had been an uninterrupted spiral into the depths of depravity. On the day that the man was recalling, his mother was spending the majority of her time in the upstairs units trading sexual favors for heroin. As young as the man was back in those days, he clearly understood that fact. His mother got her fix on a stained sofa so fouled by all forms of human excrement that all those years later, the man could still smell the sofa's pungent deposits of waste permeating through the aircraft cabin. The scent was sharp, rank, sour, and unmistakable. In fact, the calcifying odor became so strong at that particular instant that he was certain he had left the room where it once existed only moments ago. That particular aroma, which was traceable to nothing else that was permitted beyond the bounds of hell, had defied 35 years of passing time and hundreds of miles of open air in managing to overwhelm his senses while he gave a passing glance to the latest edition of the Economist magazine. The lingering aroma of those rancid fabrications of another era bluntly reminded him that he could never fully escape his past and that he was only permitted by the limitations of his existence to continually endeavor to reshape his future.

The hours of the day the man was beginning to recall possessed deep and distinct implications for the quicksilver that was his life. He and his sister, Nadiel, had been surviving on rotten scraps he pulled from the garbage with as much discernment as their need for physical sustenance would allow. At the present moment, he believed that they had been living that way for the past two days or so, but he realized that it could have been weeks after giving further consideration to the matter. The young and tormented mind is quite clever in crafting a passable reality when survival, severe trauma, and neglect are involved. As the man thought back on that day for perhaps the first time since he had been exiled to South America, and from the more fortuitous vantage point of having experienced the vast majority of his days not cowering in the darkness in wait, he settled the matter by affirming that he and his sister had been surviving by picking through the trash for a period considerably longer than a couple of days, though certainly not more than a season.

Nadiel, or Nadie, as he had liked to call her, had a subtle and peculiarly innocent inner and outer shine to her. In addition to the natural appeal and draw of those generously bestowed traits, she had large, radiating light-blue and amber eyes, which made her quite the effective tagalong when she was out soliciting money from strangers with her mother. This was true even in the more intense and highly competitive panhandling rackets down by the Inner Harbor and over in Federal Hill. Unfortunately for both the man and Nadie, this was not an occupation that they could have navigated safely for even an hour without their mother present, and even then, only because a few of the local dealers that held some perverse sway in those districts where the legitimate money flowed had taken a liking to their momma.

Those nearly human solicitors of addiction and misery initially took a shine to the man's mother for the striking good looks that the woman still possessed something of beneath the worn-out trappings of her poverty, her malnourished body, and the depraved exhibitions of her heroin addiction. When nearly all of her beauty had been hollowed out by her singular focus on using heroin for her survival, the dealers liked her because she was still sought after by the low-level, degenerate peddlers who injected more of their supply than they sold. Those types were good for business because they always needed more product and were willing to pay almost any price to have it. With such being the case and their mother deep in the throes of a binge that kept her away from home longer than she had ever been gone, the boy was left to scavenge the destitute area for what he could find to feed them both while keeping a close eye on his ailing sister.

Nadie was growing weak. She had taken to her bed a while back and was in and out of consciousness while plagued by fits of angst that followed sweat-ridden spells of delirium. Her rapidly advancing illness and the terrifying hallucinations that gripped the poor girl in her sleep were brought about by her wasting state, broken spirit, and an obsessive fear that something terrible had befallen their mother. The boy he was back then knew their mother was still alive because he could hear her distinctive and forced impulses, which were offered in response to the handful of sexual encounters that took place on the floor above them when she was not in a heroin-induced coma. He wasn't sure if their mother had eaten anything since she last left them to fend for themselves or how she was surviving up there, but he didn't have the heart to tell the truth about any of that to the sickly little blue-eyed girl.

The silence from above extended into longer and longer lapses between the audible signs of life that his mother had delivered on occasion. After a while, the boy found that he was continually listening for her when he wasn't out scavenging for food and water, attending to his sister, or taking the waste buckets down to the harrowing gap that the rail lines passed through. The little boy was beginning to sense that their depraved world and the tattered remains of their family, in as much as the three of them had come to know such a word since they first began to squat in the darkness of that abandoned basement, were doddering before the vanishing point. Overcome with the terrifying need to break the hold of the piercing darkness and the deafening silence, which would surely take his sister at any moment, the boy stepped onto the stool that rested beneath the shrouded slat window at the top of the concrete wall. The window had been painted over with tar of some sort that had hardened long ago.

When the little boy was standing up straight on the chair and at eye level with the sealed window that was letting in just a scant amount of light through a few uncovered cracks at the edges of the makeshift sealant, he peeled off the small patch of rubbery putty that had been carefully adhered to the inside middle of the window where some of the tar had been removed. The boy and his mother had placed the caulking putty over the exposed portion of the window to keep people from looking in and discovering their belongings. Reams of initially blinding daylight burst into the darkness of the room from the suddenly radiating spot on the window. The brilliance of even that small amount of indirect sunlight caused the boy's eyes, which were perfectly acclimated to the infinitesimal drippings of ambient light that pried their way into the pitch of the cellar, to squint severely and ache due to the controlled yet piercing explosion of such natural radiance upon the blackness of their dank and soiled crypt.

After giving his eyes a moment to adjust to the narrow, focused arrow of light that pierced the otherwise sealed window, the boy forced his eyes open and sharpened his focus. He then watchfully looked out through the uncovered hole in the sealant of the window. From a sightline level with the asphalt of the street that ran in front of the bombed-out row house, the small, rectangular slat window of the tenement rested just above some small patches of dirt, burnt-out grass, and rubbish that occupied the tiny patch of front yard. Through the peeled hole of the sealant, which was about the size of a Kennedy half-dollar, the man, as a ten-year-old boy, could spy just the person he was looking to find. That person was a small-time drug dealer who was standing attentively on the cracked sidewalk across the street and near the far corner of the block.

The pusher was a larger-than-average man with long, dark, greasy hair that was quite natty, or perhaps rakish, in its appearance when compared with the mangy pelages of most that roamed the block. He was in the process of making several hole-and-corner sales to the more deplorable and desiccate members of his clientele. After watching the activity for a minute or more, the boy quickly realized that a new shipment of skag, or maybe even thunder, had just arrived in the neighborhood. The opening in the window that the boy was peering through positioned his eyes dead level with the front lot of his building, the street, and the worn-out hand-me-down shoes of the scullions, tramps, and beggars that were shuffling up to the dealer to get their fix. The window was positioned below and next to the chipped and battered set of red brick stairs that ascended to the front door of the dilapidated row house of no particular color or form that could be fixed in the man's waking memory. Someone looking at the front of the house from the street would have noticed only the varying levels of rot and decay that infected the squared and nondescript assembly line-type construction of its windows, frames, and siding; appendages that were quickly thrown together at a time when the neighborhood was a colorful and lively bastion of American industrial production, and almost unbelievably, actually struggling to keep up with an influx of immigrants that were flooding in to man the posts of the city's once-vibrant industrial factories and shipping warehouses.

The boy was standing on a chair that had been discarded from a schoolroom a few blocks up the street. The school had closed a decade ago under the falsely advertised guise of ending its legacy of unintended segregation. In reality, the closing of the elementary level institution had only served to line some crooked politician's pockets, further undermine what little remained of the civic bonds of the old neighborhood, and egregiously overcrowd and overburden the school that served the adjacent neighborhood. A neighborhood that was also struggling amid the darkening economic landscape of the early eighties yet still a functioning corner of society in the broadest sense of the word.

The chair was made with a strong metal frame and yellow plywood for the seat bottom and backrests. The boy was projecting his lanky frame upward and balancing his weight rather adroitly while standing on his fully outstretched toes. He needed to do as much to gain a vantage point of the outside world by peering through the diaphanous specs covering the small opening in the otherwise filmed over and weather-stained glass. While the overall clarity of the sightline the boy was utilizing was clouded at best in certain directions, there were a few angles of precise lucidity that allowed him to make detailed assessments regarding the lower extremities of the circling horde of the undead. Irrespective of his less than perfect vantage point from which to observe the events transpiring across the street, the clever boy could decipher that the dealer was making several sales given the motions of his blurred arms and the number of poorly shod rotters who were approaching him.

While allowing for a wide margin of error in his estimates, the boy guessed that the dealer was pocketing enough money for him to buy at least a few months' worth of food and sundries. Maybe even some apothecary items for Nadie, which could be purchased at the convenience store with the big yellow billboard and barred windows at the other end of the block. The boy had bought a few things from the place before and done so on his own. Therefore, he could price out most of the items he needed. He had only a rough idea of what the people outside were paying for that particular batch of skag, but his calculations were sound enough, given that they were based on his mother's ravening tirades that occurred concurrently with her past searches for some fix money on her bad days. The boy only dared venture down to the convenience store in the middle of the day, and during those rare occasions he had managed to cobble together a few larger coins. He also knew that it was best to go down there when some of the older folks in the neighborhood, those who did garner some respect from the younger two-bits, bought some small necessities or beer for the evening. Those older folks still had a code of ethics that dated back to more civil days, and they kept an eye on things in the disintegrating neighborhood to at least the small degree that they were able.

When the boy was done checking out the weekly neighborhood distribution, he patched the hole in the tar covering the window. That returned the room to the more natural obscurity that the boy had grown used to. Nadie was becoming increasingly nauseous and began to sob inconsolably for her mother to relieve her aching tummy. She needed her mother to hug her and tell her a story. The pathetic angel was pleading from some half-woven state of consciousness for the drug-addled woman to just return to her. The boy, shrinking down from the window to a flat-footed position on the chair, which wobbled only slightly from the loss of one of its foot pegs, began to struggle to cope with his inability to comfort or console little Nadie as her cries grew louder and more disconsolate. For a brief moment, he covered his ears, but the muted halt of her sobs produced a void within him far worse than the grief produced by her palpable anguish.

At least her sobs and miserable cries gave notice that she lived and still hoped for something. Her cries also gave notice that he too lived, even if he no longer dared to hope. The boy knew far better than to expect their mother to answer Nadie's pleas, and for the first time in his life, he began to experience feelings of dark resentment, or perhaps even hatred, for the selfish and seemingly soulless woman for leaving them to suffer and die alone in the darkness of that place. The boy began to hate her for the truth of what she now was. In the end, he was not capable of sorting through feelings so hurtful to his heart. As such, he simply shifted the full burden of the blame for their miserable situation onto his scant and angular shoulders. Once that was accomplished, he began to question only his own derelict care for the innocent and helpless little girl.

"Why is Nadiel so sick? What have I done to her?" he asked of the unseen spirits gathered in wait in the nearly indiscernible shadows of the corner of that underground and nightshade oubliette.

He asked those questions in disturbed, unending, and fruitless iterative overtures. When his rapid and hopelessly cycling mind had settled, the boy reasoned with what remained of his still unbroken awareness. He had been careful to keep little Nadie from consuming anything rotten or spoiled from the rubbish bins close enough for him to pick through. He had dumped their waste cans promptly, carrying them through the hole in the fence out back, which protected the rail lines from the neighborhood that it bisected, and pouring the overused spackling drums into the short gully filled with old car parts, rusted bicycle frames, and discarded furniture pieces. He had boiled the rotten smell from the wastewater on the propane camping stove. He had faithfully and diligently done all of those things, but all that he had to give was simply not enough. The little girl was not of sound mind or body as the hours, days, and nights wore on in their mother's absence.

While beginning to tremble slightly, the boy was once again moved to consider the severity of his sister's health. For the third time since she took to her bed, she was burning with a fever so severe that her skin nearly ignited his hand at receiving even a gentle brush from his cool flesh. He could feel the angel of death hovering over them. He sensed the heavy and insatiable desire that entity possessed to have her from somewhere across the cellar. As for his health, he had been in the grips of a severe case of the trots for several days, which, aside from dealing with the unpleasant after-effects of such a malady in the absence of running water, was causing him to lose what little remained of his strength to hunger and dehydration. As he stood thinking about what to do, he shook violently from a reflexive tremor, one that caused him to relocate his center of gravity to maintain his balance. When that flashing, spasmodic fit had passed, the boy began to consider the consequences for his little sister were he to fall.

Hearing only her pleas and sobs echoing in the darkness against the unseen foulness smeared across the concrete block walls of that underground lair and being rendered incapacitated as much of the mind and soul as he was of the body, the boy felt a seismic shifting taking place within. He sensed a rising awareness of a great strength that was settling upon him as his anger and his rage became the only emotions capable of sustaining him in the midst of those heavy bouts of hopelessness, neglect, and futility, which continued to bear down on him in unrelenting waves. Those dour emotions and feelings left the boy gasping for air, and they all began to reveal the unending depths of the darkness that was now consuming him. The white cotton collar of his dirty tee-shirt began to soak and turn brown with the tears he no longer felt running down his hollow and threadbare cheeks and over his parched and frightfully swollen red lips. All was so near to being lost. Be that as it may, he had always understood that when such a time arrived, he would have one final gift of love to give.

The boy stepped down from the chair. He then went directly to the far corner of the basement by walking away from the window he had been using to track the progress of the drug dealer out on the street corner. From under his ragged pillow, the boy withdrew a small white bear. The bear was matted and dirty, possessed dark expressionless eyes, and wore a blue, tattered, and dirty collared beach shirt. The shirt was emblazoned with raised stitching in the discernible shape and detail of a palmetto tree, in addition to the two words that the boy whispered softly, "South Carolina."

South Carolina had once been home for the boy and his mother, and he had received the small bear when he was around five years old. At the time he accepted the gift, he was gathering his few belongings and preparing to leave the foster home in North Charleston to be reunited with his mother. He had been living there for over a year. The boy's mother, by way of some tragic miracle, a raging expedition of incompetence, or because someone close to her family had leveraged the proper political and legal connections necessary to accomplish her release at the time, had satisfied the demands of the state to get clean and get a job prior to regaining custody of her son. A man by the name of Alford Solomon Ramsey, the boy's primary caregiver and an educator at the foster home, had given the timid boy the bear while telling him about all of the wonderful things his mother had done to be a better parent and provide the two of them with a bright future up north in Baltimore. Alford was quite fond of the boy and wanted his young protégé to remember him and sunny South Carolina fondly in the days ahead. Those happier times to come when the circumstances of the traumatized child's life would surely be much improved.

In truth, Alford had very high hopes for the boy, and some part of him hoped that the somewhat detached child would remember his friend, teacher, and guide in the decades ahead, after he became one of the few to beat that predatory and self-serving system. Alford explained that the bear would be his trusty traveling companion and noble subjugator of any doubts and fears that he might experience while he and his mother were getting settled in their new home. The boy held that same white bear firmly in both of his hands and then squeezed it softly in the darkness of the basement, letting the loose threads on the top of the fuzzy animal's head gently tickle his nose. While he sniffed the unmistakable scent of the careworn bear with a certain longing for those false promises of yesterday, he fondly remembered the soft hug, the gentle yet firm steadying of his shoulders, and the confident smile that would mark Alford's final goodbye.

Alford was a retired teacher who got by on a small pension, a modest annuity from a trust fund, and some poorly designed government benefits that followed a horrifying incentive structure that Alford would never fully understand. The money he received each month afforded Mr. Ramsey a fairly carefree lifestyle, given the basic and unadorned nature of his home and possessions. He worked at the foster home to give those needy children a chance at life through education. He worked long hours at the home and was there each day from the first light of the morning until well past supper. Outside of the time he set aside to read his eclectic collection of books and a few road trips he took during the summer months to follow some of his favorite musicians to places he had not yet been, Alford was at the foster home. He was always engaging the broken children that passed through that waystation of a sort and arrived during varying stages of their otherwise destitute lives. Alford was passionate about his work, and he had a knack for developing nurturing bonds with most of the troubled youth he served. He was a shining star in an otherwise incompetent government institution.

Alford had graduated from Brown University many years before he met the boy. During the Swinging Sixties, he was an important part of the peace movement in the Northeastern United States. His family had ties to the elite members of Rhode Island society dating back to the Revolutionary War. Mr. Ramsay could have readily improved his financial position by engaging in other affairs, but his true calling was to put smiles of hope on the faces of the children he mentored at the facility. He had moved to Charleston to escape the harsh winter weather and the lingering rigidity of his family's looming presence throughout the familiar haunts of his youth that lined the Narragansett Bay.

There were times that the long days at the home left Alford tired and momentarily defeated, but Alford Solomon Ramsey wouldn't have traded even fifteen minutes of his time with just one of his kids for an item of ostentatious material value. His flowered shirts and the long, shaggy hair that he donned while clumsily trying to match the local flavor during his first decade at the foster home had morphed into a more refined style by the onset of the 1970s. Alford's more modern style was crowned by his well-fitted yet bell-bottomed pants, tight polyester button-down shirts with egregious collars, and those dark, squared glasses, which projected the friendly yet scholarly and more contemporary look he was aiming for. The dense lenses of the iconic spectacles somehow served to only slightly magnify the size of Alford's dark, quizzical eyes.

Alford had been amazed by the boy's intellectual capacity from the instant of his arrival at the foster home in the late winter of 1975. The police had found the boy playing peacefully and rather meticulously with a large yellow dump truck in a motel room littered with used heroin needles, scattered clothing, and other sundries the night his mother was arrested. She was to be found in an uncompromising position and without her sensibilities in a car parked near a darkened corner on the far side of that same motel parking lot. Alford took to the boy immediately, and he remembered the first day he laid eyes on the pensive yet handsome-looking child. The boy was diminutive and runtishly put together, but he possessed those stirring blue eyes and other facial features that had certainly come from some mold that had been blessed by remarkable beauty.

The boy was standing in an empty lecture room at the time of their first encounter. He was barefoot and knobby-kneed. His hair was cut straight but unevenly across his forehead, and the wide-eyed yet discerning child looked as if he were studying every detail of Alford that he could process with those large blue eyes of his. The boy possessed a natural ease to his demeanor, and the distinct and beaming yet symmetrical construction of his facial features radiated in such a way that there could be no denying that his inner presence was formed of an unbreakable spirit. Alford could do little more than smile delightedly at the little disheveled paradox standing before him.

The two of them got along famously from the start. That was because the boy had a deep desire to learn and an agreeable nature that was uncommon among his peers in the home. Alford taught the boy reading and math lessons that were far beyond the typical levels of a four- or five-year-old child. Furthermore, he remained in constant awe of the steady control and rigidity the boy held over his emotions, given his age and the unfortunate circumstances in his life.

The man on the plane vividly remembered being alone in the darkness of that basement. He remembered what it felt like to be in the process of being consumed by despair. All those years ago, absent the warm, soft teddy bear in his hands, he remained attached to his mental hinge by only the hairline threads of the darkest promptings of the human impulse. He stood alone in the darkness in the waning frames of that moment of eternal abeyance, which existed before he was to be cauterized or reduced to ash by the fires that burned for the damned, and he recalled receiving the bear from his friend and teacher, Mr. Alford. He could picture the warm smile on Alford's face as his mentor assured him that those big things and happy places were on the horizon for both him and his once-addled and forever addicted but now recovering mother. However, it must have been some alternative spectrum of rainbows that the boy and his mother had feverishly chased from the onset. He had always assumed that to be true, yet only because he firmly believed that Mr. Alford was a wise man of sound judgment.

The boy then thought back to the days beyond the foster home, those days before he and his mother had arrived in Baltimore. He remembered the light-blue and slightly rusted Volkswagen convertible that the two of them traveled in from the Carolina lowcountry to the first motel his mother stopped at to get her to fix. As she had been free of the drug for more than a year, the throes of her addiction were not yet absolute. Her cravings and her highs were about as manageable as he had ever known the side effects of her disease to be. At least when viewed through the imperfect lens that a young and uninformed little boy might look through to develop an understanding of such things. Given as much, the boy and his reformed mother paid the slight lapse in fortitude no mind and continued on with their epic journey while continuing to embrace those wonderful hopes and dreams for a better tomorrow.

A short while after leaving the motel, the contented travelers were driving down a straightened stretch of country road just south of the state line. A large orange sun was setting slowly over his mother's head as she steadied the wheel with a bright smile lighting up her pretty face. When the southern tangent of that fully dilated and radiating sphere met the end of the earth somewhere near the far side of a rolling meadow being languidly crossed by a herd of cattle, his mother turned to face him. She had turned her head quickly and smiled as though she had the most wonderful news to tell him. The look of joy in her eyes at that moment conveyed her belief that she possessed a beautiful revelation worthy of dispatch from the heavenly host. There was such life and energy to her smile that her lips seemed to hold the glimmer of the twilight in place just long enough to give that beautiful face of hers the proper amount of exposure to the natural light of the setting sun.

The boy fondly remembered the whiteness of her teeth and the soft glow of her freckled cheeks, which framed a smile so beautiful it outshone even the colossal sun setting behind her in the distance. His mother continued to hold that smile while she marveled at her little boy in the passenger seat. He appeared ready to take on the world that lovely afternoon. As the car moved patiently down the country road, the wind blew her spritely dark hair across her round sunglasses and then skyward, only to have those playful locks settle back down for just a moment before rushing off directionless to be further teased by the early evening breeze. The boy with the white bear in his hands could not recall another time that the otherwise troubled woman appeared so happy and free. He wondered where that tragically beautiful siren of his heart had gone, and he wondered why she had decided to venture there in his absence.

"The beauty of the wounded bird is fleeting in this hard world," the daydreaming yet always pragmatic man thought while remaining quite complacent in the middle seat of the aircraft. He then carried that thought forward from the depths of his reverie and let the memory of the once infallible beauty of his mother simmer for a while longer. He could do little else but continue to flesh out the abstracts of those tender recollections, which remained tied tightly around his now cold and imprisoned heart like a tense string applied to a prized cut of swollen filet by some strong and over-tarried meat packing plugger.

He soon drifted back to the darker thoughts of his younger days. Specifically, those moments when he was standing scared and alone in the clutches of that foul void set beneath the soil of the earth. The man drifted back to the thoughts that belonged to a time and a place he was incapable of imagining back when he was taken by the beautiful smile of the woman driving happily across the Carolina countryside. As the splendid vision of his mother faded, the man felt the chill of the cold concrete of the basement floor on the bottoms of his bare feet once again. The boy just stood there. He was lost and hoping that it might be possible to hide forever within the configurations of those stirring memories and never again acknowledge the horrors of that dank and accursed hole in the ground.

He remained standing there for a while longer. His unshod feet continued to cool while pressed against the smooth and humid cement. He stood there motionless for all eternity, hoping that what besieged him would simply be swallowed whole by that unending darkness. Nevertheless, the world around the terrified child refused to give way, nor did it offer a sign that might ease his pain in any way. The foul air swirled beneath his nose and drove shame into the burning recesses of his mind. He stroked the bear with his thumbs, pushing gently into the smooth half marbles of glass that were its eyes, and he wondered what Alford would think of the rank smell of their squalor. He wondered how Alford might judge his complete failure to maintain even this bleak and sorrowful station of life for his sister. While Alford was certainly wrong about what was to be found at the end of the rainbow, he was right to give him that bear. The boy had nothing else.

The man on the plane, who was now lost in the swirling fancies of his recall, did not know it. Neither did the boy that he was back then—the boy that the man saw so clearly. Be that as it may, that bear remained the solitary connection between the boy's heart and the love of God at the very instant the staunchest demons of the darkness cried out in ravening and unending overtures of anguish to forever consume his eternal soul; the same moment that the man was now recalling, and the solitary moment of his life that he detested and carried without the hope of reconciliation because he believed it was beyond the bounds of human mercy.

Though the rigor with which he managed his projected character and emotions would never allow him to admit to having such human feelings or readily display the redness of skin tone that might accompany his shame over past matters, the daydreaming man struggled to contain the emotive effects the memories of that day were having on his predominantly gelid heart. When the boy received that bear from Alford and later bore witness to his mother's pretty smile, those would be the last times that he, or the man he had become, would experience any sense of heartfelt joy, or the raw happiness and innocent hope that emanate from true faith in God, or even the good promises of tomorrow. In fact, he would not experience a similar feeling until he reached his 39th year. That bear had gotten the boy through some horrors that the man dared not recall until that very minute. Back then, he believed the bear would get Nadie on through to somewhere else too, but only with his help. The odds the boy had quickly and neatly calculated in his frightened mind were near-certain that wherever the place was, it would be far better than that black, stinking basement.

The boy continued to stand silent and motionless in the dark. He remained that way until the renewed wheezing and whimpering of his sister shook him from the false hope that he had become nothing more than some phantom of the surrounding void. Given the shaping of the blackness of the room upon his equilibrium, Nadie's sobs sounded as if they were whispered directly into his ear. Moreover, those feeble whimpers were accompanied by the wetness and heat of her fevered breath, though the little girl was nearly the full distance of the cellar away from him.

As if he had broken free from the depths of a hypnotic trance, the boy suddenly felt nothing but the raw impulses of that cold, dark dwelling, which was both lonely and infinite, and then suddenly so very immuring while warmed by the slavering breath of the lusting banshees gathering to take hold of her. For some strange reason, he believed his head had been cleared of the ravages of his fear and the despondency that had racked him for the past hour as he stood alone on the cold floor, seeing nothing but conjured images from his past that he suddenly believed were surely lies and false illusions. Perhaps he did exist beyond the grip of fear at the instant something broke loose within him, or perhaps he was simply in tune with the primal forces of evil shifting about in that unknowable pitch. Whether or not those other presumptions were true, he could sense the determination of those demons that lurk in places so few among us are bold enough to acknowledge.

In any event, he was something different once he had passed through that gauntlet of the mind. The boy began to gauge Nadie's weakening sobs in the same way that a callous doctor would gauge a new patient's symptoms. "She is so very sick," he whispered evenly.

He then began to assess their circumstances in cold, calculating, and purely rational terms, although there was nothing sound about his ability to properly assess anything in that place at that particular juncture. The terror tied to his burden had pushed him frightfully beyond his limits to gainfully process the horrifying truth of their condition. The boy became certain that Nadie was dying. He was aware that she was suffering from the loss of her mother's love just as much as she had been ill due to the filth, neglect, and rotten staples of his poorly managed care during the prolonged absence of their designated guardian.

After realizing that her condition was dire, he was shaken from a brief spell of indifference, which must have been caused by his shift to that of an insanely rational, and no longer emotional or hopefully delusional, state of mind. At that point, the continuation of Nadie's weakened cries evinced a certain rage within the trembling boy. That rage was without feeling and precisely focused. Though unintentionally, his dark thoughts invoked the lust of the very demons he was desperately trying to label as illusory while pretending they had vanished into the oblivion from whence they had arrived some time ago. Yet, at that moment, and upon the unwitting summoning of those same demons, the boy became maniacally fixated on his course of remedy. The execution of a plan, as it were. A plan that was rooted from the onset in haste and the fomenting of his psychosis.

It was as if a switch had been flipped and the boy had become something entirely different. His mind was refashioning its wares into those of a sharpened razor—a keen and perfectly crafted instrument set on relieving the source of his unrelenting dread. A perfectly lucid and refined tool that would end his anguish by severing the only pulsating cord that remained as a lifeline to the savage and hell-born rush of those feelings of terror that his innocent heart, once wanting only the impossibility of love and goodness, was incapable of enduring. As such, the boy quickly took that still-sharpening razor to the vibrant pulp of those emotions. He began to sculpt those tender and spirited impulses into the mirror image of his unseen yet wholly known tormentors. Though he understood that his gentle heart was still drawn to the ways of its true Creator and the hope of the Light that had been carefully and lovingly sown into that lively seed of his living and eternal spirit, he also understood that his heart left him vulnerable to the torments of the cold, black void, which held dominion over that place. Furthermore, he understood that such a tricky device must be brought to heel if there was to be any peace from the driving madness and desolation of that unholy hour.

The boy began to breathe slowly and deeply as he set his plan in motion. At the same time, he listened for the soft calls of Nadie's uneven exhalations from across the room. For a brief while, there existed only the silence, the darkness, and the uneven breaths of the two suffering children. Once the boy had been calmed by the simple elegance of his designs to put an end to her suffering, he realized that by committing to such a thing, that fleeting moment in time was all that they had left. He realized that an instant of sorrow and the fury certain to follow were all that remained.

Having come to terms with that awful truth, he picked up a small object from a makeshift end table as he neared Nadie's bed. He began to cry again as his small fingers, suddenly pining for the past, made out the edges of the book he would read to her with the silly pictures that made her smile. The boy touched the raised letters of the book's smooth but firm cardboard cover, and his heart broke. The aftershock released a torrent of sorrow that decimated all hope as far as the heavens once he came to understand that there was nothing but the cold darkness to consume it all. That cold and lonely darkness, which waited patiently to extinguish all that once was and all that might have been theirs in this world. He whispered softly through the salty tears catching at the edges of his swollen lips, "We were a family here, sweet girl."

Shortly thereafter, the boy snapped yet again, severing the last of those human chords that might also dictate the deeds of his hand in the hour to come. While regaining his composure and his nerve, he reproached the grief manifesting in the hollows of his lungs and the bursting glands beneath the corners of his jaw. He soon returned to a mental state that operated almost without feeling and pressed the bear softly to his chest. His fingers delicately retraced the textured features on the bear's face because he knew the shape and the feel of those comforting traits better than he could have recalled his own. The boy then wondered if there was still some magic left in the only true friend he had ever known during those dour years of want and sadness. "She was never here," he whispered to his old confidant.

Though the boy was nearly detached from the emotion of it all, Nadie was beginning to sense the sorrow emanating from her brother's rapidly and then slowly breaking heart amid the deafening silence of the cellar. She awoke from her fitful sleep and began to sob almost indiscernibly while she rolled over and pressed her face determinedly into the compressed hollow of her pillow, which was warm and sullied by the flush of her fever and her tears. The boy heard the sobs after he had contained the last physical representations of the depths of his distress. He stepped forward slowly and carefully towards the sound of the entombed and, therefore, muffled weeping. He remained indifferent to everything except for that of the dying little girl, whom he was forced to consider by way of the errant projections of his imagination alone.

His bare feet pressed flat and firmly against the cold concrete floor, and the hardened skin of his soles rolled heel to toe with each slow and determined step he took closer to her bed. When the boy knew that he was within a few steps of her, he began to blindly feel for the partitions of the makeshift cot to avoid an unfortunate collision with its frame. He whispered his goodbyes to the bear while probing the depths of the darkness for something he might identify with his uncertain hands. He breathed in the familiar scents of old tears and dried sweat like some accidental newlywed, wistfully sniffing the fragrance of a scented letter from a lost and forbidden dalliance of a fine summer that had accrued to his younger years.

Having reached the makeshift cot without incident, he began to triangulate his sister's position by grasping tenderly at the nearest of the effects that kept her warm and feeling safe. The boy then walked around the bed and into the tight space between the far side of her mattress and the chill of the musty concrete wall. He stood in front of her and looked down at the little girl, partially with his eyes but more so by way of the more pleasant fabrications of his mind due to the scarcity of the light being shed upon the weeping little darling. Nadie immediately sensed her brother's presence and removed her face from the heat of the suffocating pillow. In response to her willingness to engage, the boy faithfully reached the childish fingers of his small hand forward, and he gently parted his little sister's matted brown hair from her forehead. He then placed the palm of his right hand squarely on her exposed brow.

She was burning up. The boy had never felt such heat emanating from human flesh. He began to wonder if anything could be done to save her, but that was a matter beyond his purview. All that he might offer her at the moment was the hope that she might be delivered into the care of those who might know what to do. While he fought off the rising impulse to return to a state of despair, Nadiel looked up at her brother. She could not see much of him, yet his presence allowed her to halt her cries except for a few stunted snivels, which caused her to bite down on her mucous-covered and swollen lower lip. Once Nadie had calmed down some, she sat up and turned on the lamplight next to her bed. The head cover of the lamp was in the form of a yellow kitten. The battery-powered appliance as a whole had been procured from some rubbish pile or another so that they might read stories in the darkness while they sheltered beneath Nadie's patchwork blanket. After her tender eyes had adjusted to the soft, yellow light and the washed-out little girl could see the boy clearly, she remained calm just long enough to stare at him with a look of sadness and solitude that belonged to none but the truly forsaken.

The boy, then casting a tight yet slightly angled shadow against the low amber of the light illuminating the brick wall behind him, moved his right hand forward from behind his back and handed Nadie the bear. When Nadiel reached for the inanimate creature with great trepidation, which was revealed plainly enough by her meek, receiving hands, and after taking notice of her sinking countenance, the boy spoke to his sister with a perfected yet appropriately delicate confidence, "Do not be afraid, my little angel. Mr. Bear will protect you. He will love you and never let you feel alone again. He is a magical and fearless bear, and he will not leave you until you are safe."

The boy paused only briefly to consider the familiar oddity that was their dilapidated kitten lamp, and said, "Listen to me closely, Nadie. I have to go now. Mommy isn't coming back."

"No, no, no, Davey! You must not go! I am scared, and I know that Mommy isn't coming for us!" Nadiel begged her brother with the tension of a terror so acute, yet so sweetly broken by her lightly escalating whimpers and stutters, that her pleas alone would have brought the hungry lion to heel and the delicate lamb peacefully to the jackal's watering maw.

As tears welled up in her eyes, the terrified child clutched the bear close to her chest in such a way that it appeared as if she did so out of a desire to immediately possess the creature rather than out of any kind of gracious acceptance. In the dim lamplight, she continued to look at her upright but motionless older brother with her watery and forlorn blue eyes. The boy reached down purposefully and once again delicately parted away the last of the tangled strands of her matted hair that somehow failed to clear her cheeks and forehead when he had tended to the matter earlier. After her brightly burning visage had been absolved of those final troublesome holdovers, he spoke. In doing so, he bestowed upon her the last vestiges of his innocence and the last gift of his unspoiled love that he had to offer his little sister until he might return to her, following his long march of exile through the barren urban wilderness out beyond. "I love you, little Nadie. I will go and take care of something. Things will be better for you, but we will have to go our own way for a while. I will send word to you through Mr. Bear. You are very sick, and you need to rest now."

Nadiel nodded silently in reply to her brother and collapsed back into a deadened posture on her bed. She had fallen limp onto her pillow, quickly overcome by her illness and her worry over not knowing the right words to say. She then gently set the bear to rest next to her head with the last of her waking energy. The boy wrapped his little sister snugly in her knit blanket that came from the Goodwill out past the harbor and draped her patchwork quilt over the top to let its weight comfort her. When he was certain that Nadie was properly guarded against the raw drafts of the dank cellar, the boy tucked the bear inside the blanket next to her arm. Nadiel had watched her brother tend to her in the low, amber light of the battery-powered lamp as her eyelids drifted slowly downward. She understood the words and their meaning as given by her brother in the way that only siblings living through such times of duress would endeavor to presume so much at hearing so little. She tried to hide her expression of growing fear and sorrow while the boy pulled the blanket carefully up under her chin. In response, he accepted the look for what it was, kissed his sister's burning forehead, and for the last time in his life, fought back tears.

The boy stood there over his little sister for just a short while longer and battled that last terrible episode of sadness until he willed his feelings to be nothing more than careless fantasies and useless hopes for something better that had no place in the real world. "If only love existed somewhere beyond the hate and the need of those dirty streets outside," the boy whispered, but alas, he had been entirely transformed into whatever heartless being was required for her deliverance in the world as he understood it at that time.

In the passing fit of that enduring and absolute madness, the boy had precisely calibrated his mind to navigate that very real darkness, which was simply the way of the world. Under the guise of such inauspicious circumstances, he knew better than to consider the possibility of such silly and trivial things as hoping for a better tomorrow. In that forsaken place, hope came from a needle, and the cost of such folly was to perish slowly while lingering aimlessly among the undead. The man daydreaming on the plane gave context to what the little boy knew at that moment. That boy knew then that the absolute arbiters of primal need, addiction, and self-loathing bent their laws for no one and for nothing. Beyond that, the boy was aware that it was money that kept the hideous craven letch spinning on the wheel.

While Nadiel drifted back into the clutches of her fever-ridden sleep, spent from her distress over her mother and then her brother, the boy heard the hurried, muffled stomps of the drug dealer ascending the steps above them. He was going to the room that was furnished by his mother's filthy couch and the large mattress across from it, just as that vile man did every day after selling some product. The ensuing creaking of the settling stairs and the picture in his mind of that foul man going up those steps snapped the boy out of a hasty and irrational appetency to save them both without leaving his sister. Having taken diligent mental notes regarding the goings-on upstairs over the last few months, and with his mind running on parallel tracks to take notice of the sounds from above while whispering his final goodbye to his sister, the boy knew he had about fifteen minutes to prepare. That was all the time that persisted for him in that awful place. He found it strange, at least while staring down upon the little cherub tucked into her bed, that the span of a lifetime was much too sudden to leave and the blink of an eye far too long to remain.

The boy walked over to his makeshift bed and put on his red and woefully worn-out Converse All-Stars. One shoe had a lace that had not yet broken too far down the shoe to be of any use. Therefore, he tied that shoe with care to keep the lace from snapping or unraveling. Shortly thereafter, he threw on his oversized denim jacket to prepare for any stretches of cold on the long and unknown journey ahead of him. From under the rusted-out sink, the boy grabbed the old hammer, which possessed the singular oddity of a grossly oversized head. Holding the hammer tightly in his left hand, he waved it in the air to gauge its heft and his ability to properly wield the unusually formed anvil. The boy then continued thinking through the steps of his premeditated progression. He operated methodically, treating each step as nothing more than a means to his sister's deliverance.

At that time, as bright as the young boy was, he had been overcome by a manic bout of temporary insanity. He no longer fully understood, nor cared about, the sacrifice of his humanity upon the altar of his sister's salvation. He saw the world as an enclosed tunnel. One that required the execution of the unspeakable to pass through to the other side. The boy's thoughts were mechanical, yet they reached dizzying highs and abysmal lows, which were to be the glorious and hellish manifestations of the forthcoming deeds of Nadie's deliverer. He did not comprehend and, therefore, did not consider the evils tied to uniting the authority of judge, jury, and executor under the banner of a traumatized ten-year-old boy.

As he tarried on, the boy began to hear the apex of her quickening guttural moans and girlish screeches coming from upstairs. He hurriedly walked over to his mother's sleeping area, which was largely a collection of old coats molded into the shape of her form and a pillow that was far too soft and musty for the boy to use on the many nights she never returned home. He pressed his nose to her pillow briefly. Somehow, beneath the outer tracings of its encasing, whether in actuality or only in his flashing recollections of those tender nights they fell away from the world together while he held steadfastly to the soft lower lobe of her ear, that mangy pillow still carried the faintest traces of the scent of the beautiful young woman who once upon a time was his world. After allowing those memories to be vanquished by the surrounding darkness, he studied the haphazard condition of her bed for a moment longer, grabbed a rectangular cardboard box from beneath the pillow, and carried the box and the hammer over to his area of the cellar.

Seeing nothing further of note that would serve his future purposes under any probable circumstance, the boy grabbed a dirty pair of underwear from his clothes pile, two oversized flannel shirts that still had some buttons, and a pair of ripped jeans. He then withdrew his stained and moldy pillow from its case and threw the clothing into the makeshift tote. From a small stack at the end of the room, the boy picked up two books of intermediate size and put them in the pillowcase as well. He had probably read both books more than twenty times, yet he managed to find something new embedded within the words each time that he slowly and meticulously went through them. He delighted over every detail that had been missed or a lesson he had not considered with each turn through those worn-out old books. He had decided that those books would keep his mind off of the many dangers lurking out in the streets once it was finished, and they were no longer to be tormented by that dank hovel.

Just as the boy had completed the task of preparing for his departure and exile to come, his time to complete the enterprise of the hour was at hand. The perceived allegiance of his emotionally starved and aberrant mind to effectuate his intended purpose remained solitary and unwavering. While he pictured Nadiel in the comforts of some home filled with warmth and love he had seen on TV years ago, his hope for a dying little girl closed all of his remaining windows to the outside world. He would respond to nothing other than that solitary impulse of her deliverance, that absolute need for her release from the bondage of need, sickness, and sorrow.

He began to confirm the steps of his plan with cold, calibrated, and meticulous ruminations. For a few brief moments in the silent hollow of the darkness without and within, his mind began to race, as it were, triggered by a sally of raw and electrifying adrenaline. Then the boy in waiting heard it happen. He heard the soft sound of the end-to-end rattling of small objects. It sounded as if pens had been dropped on the floor above. The delicate but unmistakable noise set him into motion without the possibility of revocation or even the potential to yield to the phantasmal foreshadowing of some rational yet imaginary advocate for restraint. From that moment on, the boy would be no more than a ghost within those suffocating walls, and the damned were to be consigned to their proper and eternal stations prior to his abandoning that old haunt.

The boy made his way up the stairs and toward the door to the cellar. The rubber soles of his shoes were silent and caused no discord among the worn wooden planks of the staircase. Upon reaching the top of the stairs, he unlocked the bolt and slowly turned the loosely outfitted, old iron doorknob of the portal to their moldering antre. He turned the knob until he heard the sound of release: the light pop of the latch freeing itself from the hold, followed by the sharp and forceful click of the bolt snapping back into place. He was then prompted by the far darker iteration of his nous to open the door slowly and quietly.

The hinges of the cellar door creaked frightfully in response to his gentle prodding while he deliberately pushed the thickset and warped wooden plank forward. When the cellar door had slowly moved away from the frame, the first rays of the piercing light coming in through the broken glass of the front entrance to the building burst through the widening cracks. The bright, luminous beams cut and stung the boy's tender eyes while he braced to face the unknown of what existed beyond the darkness below.

When he had finished opening the door, he stood terrified before the maelstrom of what the man on the plane next to Ronan remembered to be a rushing yet hazy and gray light of day. Such was an overwhelming and revealing light for someone dwelling in the permanence of the nightshade below, and one that quickly exposed the derelict care of the filthy little ragamuffin. The boy stood raw and perfectly exposed in that hanging light of day, and he suddenly felt as if everything he had known about the world below him had ceased to be real at the instant of that blinding flash. He turned back to the stairwell in a desperate panic. He peered down into the depths of that shrouded tunnel, searching and hoping that something of his past might be proven out by that same light, which so effortlessly revealed his squalid presence. He saw nothing of the sort. The soft light of that overcast day dared only to reveal the emptiness of the top half of the stairwell.

Be that as it may, the panic-stricken boy was not immediately deterred. He kept looking down, his gaze never leaving the haunting abyss beyond what had been revealed. A terrifying thought then froze the child cold. In response, he murmured the words again through his stolid, cracked, and unwavering lips, enjoined by sticky threads of saliva, which were swiftly hardening due to his fear that everything he had ever cared for in this life had been instantly erased from the annals of time. He had stepped into the light from the depths of a nightmare, and he knew not where such mysterious projections from days gone by might linger upon waking. There were keepsakes trapped in that horrid place that he desperately wanted to retain. There were moments of love that surely never belonged there.

At a loss for how he might petition for something that had so suddenly never existed, the boy murmured the words to the vanishing spirits that had become what remained of the three of them together as one. The frightfully broken child spoke into the endless void that began beyond the light filtering down some seven steps or more into the stairwell. One final time, he filled that cold emptiness with the vivid contrivances of a loving mother and her two young children huddled together against the damp chill while reading a book by the light of a lantern. They were nestled within the fort of draped blankets, which had safely cordoned off the existence of everything beyond that flickering light. The boy whispered the words as if he were naught but the soft, slight breath of the draft rushing up from beneath his feet. The boy whispered the words, "We were a family there. I know it to be true."

In the presence of that unspeakable darkness below, their gentle hearts had sparkled in unison like the noonday sun to spite that interminable void while being accompanied by a few fleeting yet tender whispers of love. Those whispers were then extinguished, eradicated like so many lost souls who remain unknown to the living denizens of the earth and at rest in some potter's field. The boy had scratched their names into one of the concrete blocks of the wall that was next to his cot. He did as much to leave behind a record of their fleeting moment in time. Following the remembrance of a futile act that none who bore witness to the scattered remains of their lives would ever understand, he quickly turned away from the stairs.

To his dismay, the seemingly blinding incandescence of the hallway had not yet finished inundating the rapidly adjusting sensory receptors of his eyes. To shield those tender orbs from the piercing onslaught of the quickening light, the boy looked down again and desperately tried to recall the aforementioned memory, the memory of the last time they huddled together against the cold, reading books with only a flashlight, and teaching new words to Nadie. He closed his eyes tightly and tried to etch their faces, as they were then, into some indelible chamber of his mind. For the entirety of the time it took him to adjust to that ravenous light, only amplified by the thin haze of the Baltimore sky, he struggled not to lose his hold on those tender images of such an uncertain exposure. He tried to breathe life into the smattering of fond recollections from their past. Yet, when the frightened little boy opened his eyes yet again, the darkness staring back at him from below had swallowed his inner ache to feel, to believe, and to remember. Those things belonging to the past had all vanished. He perceived only the pitch at the bottom of those stairs. As such, he turned swiftly away and stepped into the pervasive, lingering, and timeless light of the wrecked front hall of the battered row house.

The man dreaming on the plane had no memory of the weather during those hours he was recalling. It was as if, in those defining moments of his life, he existed not on earth but within some rapidly moving specter of streaks of light and color, of fearful sounds, and of foul smells that remained with him to that very day. Upon returning to a state in which he was fully immersed in the vivid reproduction of that horrible moment, the man saw the boy ascend the few stairs to the first level of the row house. Though he wished to call the boy back, there was little the man could do as he witnessed that same boy open the white wooden door, which was covered in stray smatterings of rubbish and excrement, to the legally vacant yet not uninhabited apartment. The man's vantage point once again merged with that of the youthful creature, and through the same blue eyes of the boy that were his own, yet belonging to another moment in time, he saw three large windows taped in plastic wrapping to his left; windows that were emitting a blinding burst of perfected white light that once again cut at those still sensitive, and moistened by the pull of emotions he could no longer feel, oceans of the deepest blue.

The light coming in through the front windows swiftly overwhelmed the entire left side of the boy's visual field. In response to the assault, he shaded his head slightly down and to the right in an effort to diminish the effects of the explosive sheens careening off of the billowing translucent plastic at varying angles. Below the boy's shod feet, the floorboards were brown and wooden, in a decaying state, and littered with newspaper, waste, and small containers filled with excrement. He walked across the open floor cautiously but purposefully until he reached the mattress resting on the floor to his right, which was positioned against the smutty back wall of the fetid, white room.

Two people were lying on the mattress, a man and a woman. The two faced the ceiling. The woman was naked and the man was shirtless, and they both had elastic rubber tubes tied around their upper arms. Their eyes were closed, but their eyeballs were beating rapidly against their eyelids, as if their minds were enduring some horrible fit of discomfort. The three syringes with needles that the boy had heard drop from below were lying on the floor. One was empty, one was half full, and the other was nearly ready to burst. They had fallen between the outstretched lower legs and feet of the sedated couple, which were loosely positioned off of the end of the mattress.

The boy did not look at the woman. He picked up one of the needles from the floor and pointed it at the noticeable vein protruding from and pulsating on the man's neck. The skin over the vein had a pair of solitary needle marks. The vibrant nuances, sublime clarity, and richness of detail of each follicle of the drug dealer's grisly black stubble stood in stark contrast to the blinding white light. The boy would not soon forget those striking black slivers of unkempt growth surrounding the point on the skin of the drug dealer's neck where he inserted the needle with uncommon precision. The almost radiant detail of the vulgar man's neck and that particular vein, which were revealed by the cosmic whiteness of the incoming light, caused the boy to pause briefly to consider the peculiarity and coarseness of those features. He found it strange that such finely detailed and garishly human qualities could belong to the same phantasmal monster that had ruined his mother and replaced her with the naked and hollowed-out creature lying next to him.

After studying the position of the needle, the boy decided to push the sharp point further into the tender but somewhat resistant skin of the foul creature's neck. He did this to further secure the tiny, sharpened tip within the chosen entry point to the bulging vein of his victim's throat. The additional push of the sharpened needle caused the drug dealer to flinch in response. He appeared as if he were defying the sharp, surprising bite of an aggressive horsefly. The reflexive movements of the once-fully sedated man startled the boy. It appeared to him that his quarry was beginning to regain some control over his senses and some loose and awkward control over his motor skills. The drug dealer's eyes then popped open hastily while the boy continued to carefully watch over him. The timid boy nearly fell backward and onto the floor from the shock of the dead so suddenly returning to life.

The dealer's eyes were fogged over. Nevertheless, they were projecting something of a sense of recognition and awareness, which intimated that perhaps his body was not responding to the sheer terror that was beginning to electrify his mind. Following his initial seizure of retreat in response to the somewhat false signs of physical capacity that seemed to accompany the cognitive reckoning of his quarry, the boy, while possessing great depths of both practical knowledge concerning the effects of his mother's medicine and an unusual ability to remain calm in the face of extreme duress, as if ice water had suddenly begun coursing through his veins, once again fixed his posture firmly upright and then returned to the task at hand. He remained steadfast and kept after his mark. When he had reassumed the proper leverage to do so, the boy pushed the plunger slowly and steadily with his thumb. He operated like some brutal laboratory technician conducting an offhand experiment. He carefully and methodically watched as the brown liquid in the full syringe emptied into the drug dealer's neck cleanly and evenly.

The injection sent an impulse so severe and so rapid into the drug dealer's shuttling sensory receptors that his body convulsed forcefully yet with an extremely tight range of motion. He appeared as if he were being fried in the electric chair in response to that overwhelming charge of lethal ecstasy. To the drug dealer, it was as if his limbs had been dead asleep and then suddenly awakened by a million or more excruciating tingles of intoxication while at the same time having been rendered limp. The foul creature's body felt as if it were pulsating infinitely, yet without the pretense of motion. The sensation drove him to the brink of insanity or some stark ravening mania, which was brought about by the heavy deluge of an electric current traveling through his body with far too much force.

Once the intense and unabating stimulation had overwhelmed the capacity of his senses, the dealer's rabid burst of energy was instantly spent, and his body was released from the bursting static charges of that convulsion. He fell back on the dirty mattress and went limp, like a settling bag of old laundry. He remained fully prostrate on that mattress with his open mouth facing the graffiti on the ceiling, which was highlighted by the formation of an angel drawn in the thick, black, and unconnected lines and markings of a piece of used charcoal. The image of the angel was stark against the blinding and ethereal nature of the light.

When the drug dealer ceased moving, the boy pulled out his hammer and set it on the bed between that same listless beast and the woman. He then quickly reached back into his pillowcase, removed the cardboard box, and set it down on the floor next to the other two syringes. When everything was positioned according to his wishes, he bent down and opened the box. Inside was a 22-centimeter, sharply-bladed knife that his mother had kept hidden under her pillow to protect them over the years. He quickly picked up the knife, stood upright, and stared at the glimmering blade that ran from the handle to the sharpened point and was about an inch wide. Quite satisfied that his tool was exquisitely crafted for the task at hand, the boy positioned the point of the knife next to the empty needle sagging downward on the drug dealer's neck.

The boy exhaled quickly to clear his mind. He then pressed the point of the knife into the dealer's exposed and delicate skin. Shortly thereafter, he began to coerce the point of the knife blade into his victim's flesh until blood began to run down his neck. After jabbing the knife further into that demon's throat with a terse yet quick and forceful thrust and meeting with the firm and somewhat unexpected resistance of cartilage, muscle, and tendon, the boy gasped as his drive to end that cruel fiend was halted short of his desired goal.

Still and all, the determined little boy did not despair in the slightest. No, he simply picked up the hammer from the mattress and took another deep, calming breath. He then flipped the position of his hand holding the knife handle and closed his fist over its girth, leaving only the nub exposed. He continued to grip the knife firmly by the handle, with the tip of the blade buried about a centimeter into the skin of that stubble-ridden neck. In what appeared to be the blink of an eye, he lifted the hammer with his right hand and swung it firm and true into the butt of the knife's handle. The force of the blow sent the blade of the knife exploding smoothly through the various compressed points of resistance in the senseless man's throat. The boy felt nothing but the exhilaration of a harsh pop and then the soothing release of pressure. The feeling was akin to that of a man digging a well who had just liberated the compression of the fluid chamber not an instant before his drill bit glided fluidly to the bottom without the presence of an opposing force.

Having fallen forward upon delivering the blow with the hammer, the boy was unexpectedly face-to-face with the expiring body. He could smell the flaky, dry, and colorless lips that rested loosely over the yellow-stained teeth and the rich deposits of plaque that infested the gum lines. The air between them was tangy, warm, and sweet with alcohol. The bland, watery, and sterile smell of blood began to overtake the musk of his chest and mouth as the boy pulled his meager frame upright and grabbed the forearm. Once properly standing, he pulled on that arm with some resolve. He soon began to employ the leverage gained from his legs to roll the man over and direct the rushing flow of blood away from the still-insentient woman. After turning the body away from her and regaining some form of his composure by steadying his breathing, the boy looked at the woman with a complete failure of his sensibilities.

Shortly thereafter, the sullen boy looked away from her. He then set to the task of removing the knife from the drug dealer's neck while using the mattress to obtain leverage with his right foot and leg. The small, downward-facing striations lining the knife's sharpened blade made it rather difficult to dislodge. The dismal work reminded the boy of pulling a formidable zipper that was off its tracks back down to the base of one of his old, second-hand winter jackets. He gave a determined effort, one that caused the wound in the dead man's neck to grotesquely rip and rupture further. When the knife was free, the boy placed the handle of the murder weapon in the woman's hand and wrapped her fingers tightly around it. He then callously let her inanimate hand drop back down on the mattress. The methodical boy then picked up a second syringe from the floor—the syringe that was half full of the same thick and sticky brown fluid he had injected into the unwitting candy man.

After brushing the nearly unrecognizable woman's dark hair, which was matted in foulness, over the bruising of her exposed shoulder, the boy began to seek that same vein that had exploded so violently when he crushed the drug dealer's throat and thorax with the striated hunting knife. He found the vessel fairly quickly while pressing along the inside of her neck with the forefingers of his right hand. Then, with great care and watchful deliberation, yet without pause or dutiful consideration, the determined boy slowly delivered half of the contents of the syringe into the woman's vein. Her proximity to her senses at the time he made the injection was of a far greater throw than the peddler's coma had been. Her convulsion was brief, and her body's return to its lifeless state was far more peaceful. And that was as it should be, as he presumed that the woman had injected the preponderance of the consumed skag.

When the boy was about to insert the remaining contents of the syringe into the woman, he became mesmerized by its potency and its simplicity once the brown fluid began to hold the impulses of the radiating light, which was still pouring into the room through the plastic-covered front windows. The heroin encased by the clear plastic tube glistened like some sweet, translucent syrup and possessed the seductive beauty and appeal of a solitary drop of sticky dew resting on the potent pistil of an elegant lily in the soft light of spring. As the boy continued to stare honey-eyed at the shimmering serum, he suddenly hoped for something, and for no particular reason at all. He then looked upon the hideous face of the woman, with its broken teeth and sickly, bruised pallor. Though he could not say with any certainty what that thing was that he had put an end to, he did hope that laced within that last measure of a dream being delivered with the heft and cogency of a freight train running at full glide was the seed of her redemption, which would allow the tormented creature to sleep peacefully and eternally. She would never be cursed to know what became of her children. The boy figured that was the only blessing she might be granted at that hour—or perhaps ever.

The brilliant and seemingly callous boy looked up to the angel on the ceiling, and the man on the plane silently whispered what he could remember of the boy's words: "Maybe something like that would finally free her soul from this rotting thing lying here. Maybe something like that would allow her to rest free of this tricky brown demon boiling in her blood. I will leave it to you to decide, because I can't say what the meaning of redemption truly is. And now, I will never know..."

At that moment, the milky, radiant light in the room surged and blinded the boy's eyes. The disorientation caused by the exploding luster halted the forward thrust of his thumb. Suddenly, the manic child could now see exactly what it was that he was doing. He had been harshly awakened and exposed by the revealing glare, which was coming in through the plastic lining the window with the force of seven suns. As such, he withdrew the needle and its remaining heroin from the woman's neck and reluctantly dropped the cocked syringe into his pillowcase. He then gently covered the beaten woman with the white sheet that had fallen to the floor during her final act of depravity.

When the sheet had been laid across her listless and perhaps already lifeless body, the boy looked at the woman carefully. Her skin, or those portions that were not rotten or bruised, was the pale color of some ancient and foreign sickness that must have plagued humanity centuries ago. There were open sores, scars, and other markings running down the insides of her arms. Beneath those degenerate badges of her honor, the boy could see the discoloration of the deadened veins decaying below the surface of her skin. The beauty of her soft lips and delicate cheekbones, which he would have remembered with such joy from the warm summer days when she taught him to ride his bike, were hollowed out into some demented form suitable only for the maidservants of hell. The boy tried to pity her then, but he could only rationalize that, like his puppy, who had her heart stopped ever so gently to give her rest from the pain of her crippled legs, too much medicine had finally made things better for this currently broken, demented, and heartless creature.

In the next instant, the light withdrew to that of more natural vibrancy. With his eyes now able, or permitted, as it were, to take in the full aftermath of his actions, the boy's mind began to turn meticulously, flawlessly, and with purpose. All the more so given his utter lack of experience with such trying matters, which the vast majority of us are quite graciously never compelled to endure. The boy calmly reached over the turned and slightly twisted mass of the peddler and directed his small hand into the exposed front pocket of his baggy jeans that were covering the lower half of the still warm but stiffening and prostrate remains. After working his hand slowly down and into the warm and capacious hollow, he grabbed hold of the dealer's smooth, plump leather wallet and his money clip, which was tucked beneath. He then pulled the two items free simultaneously and without hesitation.

The boy opened and scanned the wallet for some additional currency. Seeing just a few smaller bills, he closed the wallet back up and dropped the leaden burden of the careworn brown tri-fold into his scantily packed pillowcase. Afterward, he turned his eyes sharply towards the plain but beefy money clip that he continued to hold in his right hand. He then carefully pulled the considerable stack of folded bills out from beneath the clasp of the plain silver clip, opened the fold, and counted the bills just as he might count the number of cards he was dealing out to his mother or sister when they played Crazy Eights. Though he had never laid eyes on such a thing, it did not take the boy long to surmise that there were fourteen bills labeled Federal Reserve Note with pictures of Benjamin Franklin on them and that the value of each bill was equivalent to the number posted in the four corners and on the banner running across the bottom that read: One Hundred Dollars.

The total amount of the bills taken in aggregate was far more than he had hoped to find. He held the unfolded bills in his unusually warm yet nerveless hand while taking some time to think about the relative value of that cadre of currency. The boy then quickly folded the notes into their original stack and firmly tucked the unexpected windfall into the left front pocket of his shorts, which was, not by coincidence, also the pocket that didn't possess a gaping tear running across the end seam. Almost as an afterthought, the hurried boy proceeded to throw the silver money clip into his pillowcase to reduce the likelihood that his proximity to the crime scene would be discovered at a later time. He then collected the two other syringes, the hammer, and the box that had contained the hunting knife and dropped those items into his pillowcase. He was nearly ready to proceed.

Once his manic fit began to subside and his adrenaline had worn through the effects of its stern yet clever coursings, the consequences of his heinous act began to infest the ruminations of the boy's still unnervingly calculating and apathetic mind. Though he did not feel much beyond relief and misguided hope after the deed had been done, he adhered to a deliberate and precisely executed policy of not looking at the woman while he groomed the scene prior to departing. If he had, the boy might have noticed the slight twitching of her bruised and swollen fingers. But alas, singularity of focus and the ability to entirely dismiss the unexpected are things that remain gifts of the youthful mind.

When all was as he had wished it to be, at least where the unfortunate reality of his current circumstances was concerned, the boy became a bit frantic and turned sharply towards the door. He ran back across the old wooden floor of the white room, with the black, charcoal-drawn stick angel watching him from the ceiling. He remained flustered as he glided over the floorboards, but only because he somehow sensed that he had tarried in that place just a moment too long. After the small and gaunt, yet direct and deadly, assassin had moved past the foul couch and its thick and lingering stench to exit the room, he ran back downstairs and into the basement without pausing. He ran down into the darkness, leaving the door at the top of the cellar stairs open in the hopes that some light would be shed upon that abyss of unending sorrow.

The panting boy had reached the bottom of the stairs, but Nadiel did not make a sound from the darkened corner of her sleeping area. He figured that she must have heard him approach, given that her bed was halfway beneath the iron stanchion that supported the planked steps. He had stopped briefly to listen for any sound that would have alerted him to a sudden change in her condition, but hearing nothing, the boy returned to his task by walking over to his mother's cot in the opposite corner of the basement. He began rummaging through the woman's haphazardly piled belongings and continued to do so until he found the specific item that he was looking for beneath some old winter clothing and jackets.

While making no effort to keep the unkempt pile at least reasonably orderly, the boy pulled out a blue coffee can with a red plastic lid. A square, folded piece of white envelope paper was fastened to the front of the tin with clear scotch tape, which was applied generously to each side of the makeshift label. Written on the white square with a thick green marker were the words, "David and Nadiel College Fund." The boy shook the can vigorously and heard the distinctive rattle of just a handful of nickels or pennies. He shook his head briefly to lessen the shock of his anticipated disappointment as he peeled off the plastic lid covering the container. With the lid removed, the boy rummaged through the can with his childish hand only to discover that the total of their mother's earthly provisions for their education totaled thirty-eight cents in the form of three dimes, a nickel, and three pennies.

The boy fastened the lid back to the top of the can and tried to tuck the container into the general area where he had found it. He then stood straight up from his crouched position and walked quickly over to the other corner of the room, where an old television that no longer worked sat on the floor with its back panel facing the concrete wall. The boy slid the technological monstrosity away from the wall and jarred the back panel loose with a perfectly placed strike along the side of the protruding tube. Once it was loose, he was able to easily remove the panel and found, hidden within the circuitry and other curious parts of the ancient electronic staple, some drug paraphernalia, a small packet with just a dusting of brown powder, and four more one-hundred-dollar bills that had been rolled up and tucked into the open tubing of a small plastic syringe. The boy grabbed the bills, replaced the back panel of the television, and slid the otherwise useless beast back into the corner so that it appeared just as it did before he violated the sanctity of the camouflaged vault.

The boy stood up straight once again, pulled the fourteen one-hundred-dollar bills from his pocket, and added three of the four new bills to the perfectly folded stack. He then returned to his mother's cot, fidgeted around some, and placed one of the bills inside the coffee can. Afterwards, he buried the tin in its original hiding place. Having finished with the first part of his rambunctious and somewhat indecisive, yet somehow still clandestine, financial transaction, the boy walked quietly over to where Nadiel was sleeping. He touched her forehead when he arrived and quickly deduced that his sister was still caught in the grips of her raging fever. Afterwards, he reached into the blanket that he had draped over her and temporarily rescued the bear from its hot and smothering resting place.

The boy sniffed deeply at the top of the bear's head one last time until he breathed in that warm, familiar scent of sweat and lingering breath that had lodged itself into the fur and perhaps the very essence of the old teddy bear. He then removed the bear's head from beneath his nose and began to inspect the area between the bear's legs until he found that unstitched gap that he was carefully probing for. Through the opening in the bear's colored and textured but not separate blue shorts, the boy gently pulled out some of the bear's dry, cottony insides. It could easily be said with some degree of certainty that the unfortunate molestation of his inanimate soulmate tore at the boy's already chilling heart more than anything that had taken place in the room up above.

When enough room had been provided by the delicate and ceremonial gutting of the teddy, the boy tightly rolled the seventeen remaining one-hundred-dollar bills into a compact cylinder and slid the roll into the same hole in the bear. He then put the cotton filling he had pulled out earlier back into the bear and shook the stuffed animal back into its former plumped-up shape. That way, the great warrior of the darkness would be ready to serve as sentinel for a brief period over the boy's badly infirmed little sister. After completing the deposit, the boy tucked the bear back inside the blanket with Nadiel, touched her burning cheeks and forehead one last time, and began to make his way back up the stairs to find help for her in the form of a soft-hearted transient named Roscoe, who was very likely to be down by Fell's Point or even as far off as the Inner Harbor, making his panhandling rounds.

The boy found his way back to the top of the stairs and stood in the low, simmering afterglow of that somehow radiant yet also visibly overcast day. Once he was fully illuminated by that strange phantasmal light that was still hovering like a milky haze at the top of the stairs, the suddenly uncertain boy was utterly stunned when he looked down and saw that he was covered in blood. Moreover, and perhaps more damning to his future prospects, he noticed that the familiar and ominous-looking long blue car was moving slowly down the street, its inhabitants already scanning the neighborhood with mild but purposeful curiosity. The vehicle would soon be arriving at the far corner of the block to collect the drug dealer's money for the day. Worse than that, one of the men in the back of the blue car appeared to take notice of the blood-riddled boy standing behind the broken windows of the front door of the blown-out row house.

In the slow time, the boy then witnessed the man in the back seat tap the man in the front seat firmly and irritably on the shoulder, as if he had a pressing revelation to bring to that frightful-looking man's attention. Thankfully, the man in the front of the car was looking away to his left and had not yet seen the imbued boy standing there in the doorway in shock and appearing as if he had just survived a wartime carpet bombing. The terrified boy turned quickly away from the on-looking man in the back of the slowly rolling, long blue car and surveyed the massacre smeared and splattered across his shirt and shorts a second time. He was attempting to assess how noticeable the shocking mess of his prior affairs indeed was, though he had no reason beyond false hope to doubt what his eyes had already plainly revealed to him at first glance.

Quite rattled by the horrid notion that the telltale signs of his heinous act were unmistakable from even the distance of the back seat of the blue car, the boy ran to the back of the trash-littered hallway. When he reached the warped and molded back door, he peeled off his clothes as fast as he could manage and exchanged the soiled dregs for a few of the items he had packed into his pillowcase for the journey to find Roscoe and then on to places unknown. He placed the bloodstained clothes into the pillowcase and returned to the front door to reassess the situation. To the boy's almost manic yet certainly compounding horror, the blue car had stopped at the corner. Two men were exiting the back on separate sides of the vehicle in an apparent effort to question a homeless squatter sitting on the curb about the drug dealer's proximate whereabouts. The man from the back seat, who had noticed the boy just a short while ago, looked back toward the busted-up front door of the row house and spotted the boy ducking down below the unbroken lower partition.

The boy knew at once that he had been all but caught in the act. He closed his eyes and gasped frantically while he squatted on the floor behind the unbroken aegis of the lower half of the front door. While awaiting the moment he would be snatched from his severely deficient refuge, the hapless child gripped the twist of the pillowcase so firmly that his knuckles nearly exploded. He shook in fits of anguish and terror, and he was rendered nearly senseless by the dull throbs that accompanied a haunting awareness that the darkness below refused to set him free.

With nothing left to do, the boy ran back down the hall and out the back door before the imagined hand of the man from the blue car reached into the space below the broken window for his throat. When he was outside, the open air filled his lungs and steadied the throes of his stunted, hyperventilating breaths. The frightened child did not even dare to look back over his shoulder as he took flight. Quickly meeting the challenge of his first obstacle, he squeezed his scant frame through the tear in the back fence. However, his pillowcase caught a barb and was torn open to the point that the items held within fell into the wet, filth-ridden mud of the backyard. In response to that particular episode of his continuing misfortune, the boy quickly released his hold on the unexpectedly empty and utterly unserviceable shred of cloth that he had been clutching so tightly in his hand. He looked down for a quick moment at his fallen belongings that remained on the other side of the fence, made a few split-second decisions, and then picked up the blood-stained hunting knife from the cool, caked mud. With the knife clutched firmly in his right hand, he bounded down the side of the steep, slightly wooded, and absolutely junk-cluttered hill that descended upon the rail lines.

The boy desperately made his way through the nearly unpassable morass of garbage and other obstacles of a more organic nature that lined the steep hillside without the slightest hesitation or care for his physical well-being. He cut his legs several times on broken sticks and deadened thorns as he neared the unencumbered flats of the tracks. Those were rather perilous tracks when occupied by the speeding trains of the northeastern corridor, but they were the only unobstructed passageway the boy could think of that offered at least the hope of concealing the remainder of his uncertain yet altogether necessary advance from the probing eyes of the very bad and very deadly men in the blue car. In that building crescendo of the moment of his failed liberation, which was filled with such horrifying peril, haunting revelation, outright shock, and soul-crushing despair, all seemed lost. Regardless, the trembling child continued onward, completely unprepared for the deadly ghettos that awaited him.

Though a scad of ghastly thoughts continued to terrorize the little boy's sodden and disjointed mind, one chilling realization continued to be broadcast above all others. That singular thought was locked firmly into place. It was not to be overcome or even subjected to the clever rationalizations that might allow the boy to euphemize such a concern while he stumbled onward, fell, got back up, and then stumbled again. That jarring thought continued to repeat over and over in his head until he quietly yet audibly spoke the words intended to define that primal fear. The softly offered lyrics parted his trembling lips while he tussled with the innumerable obstacles before him to remain hidden, yet all the while trying desperately to make his way down to the open pathway of the tracks.

He said, "I should have held on to some of that money, Nadie. It's no good to either of us now, is it then, sweet girl. I thought we could get out. I thought we could get out, but it was all for nothing. There is nothing left of us now but a few scratches on that cold and filthy wall. No one will ever forgive me for what I have done. Don't you dare listen to any of them down there before you go! They speak only lies!"

The man opened his eyes and returned his attention to the sterile surroundings of the commercial aircraft. The plane was traveling smoothly through the lower bounds of the dry air of the stratosphere, some 35 thousand feet above the picturesque bends of the Ohio River Valley, which remained some way off to the south of their current position. With nobody watching him, as the passengers on the plane around him were all in the midst of taking their rest before rushing into the busy morning that awaited them when the wheels of the plane violently reengaged with the asphalt of the next airfield, the man made no effort to check the craven wants of the demon spirits now casting a malevolent shroud over his countenance. He was still wont at times to be given over to those sporadic and shallow, though altogether fewer and less severe, fits of haunting obscurity during that year of his life.

He turned his inadvertently menacing gaze slightly to his right and examined the man seated next to him in an intensely curious manner. He examined him with sharp, unrelenting eyes while that man slept next to him in the aisle seat of their row. His neighbor appeared to be sleeping so peacefully. In fact, it seemed to the man still ominously watching him that somehow the wickedness of the world had yet to even scratch at the rhythmically rushing chambers of Mr. Ronan James Cassidy's so calmly pulsating heart. Though that presumption hadn't been entirely true prior to Mr. Cassidy's rebirth and subsequent awakening, that was about to change.

Chapter 6

R onan Cassidy diligently completed the assigned tasks of his first real, albeit temporary, job some two years after the height of the dollar crisis, in February of 1982. The fury of that year's unrelenting winter season had peaked at the very time Ronan began to dispatch the various tasks and duties of that first noble commission. The streets and parking lots of the inundated uptown neighborhood that Ronan was to devotedly serve were covered in ten to fifteen-foot-high mounds of snow as far as the eye could see. Those tightly packed masses of the incessantly gathering winter precipitation had been built up over the course of the last few months, one late evening at a time, by the never-ending thrusts of the monstrous and indomitable city plows, which managed to push their way through snow drifts that towered over the parked cars lining those nearly impassable thoroughfares. Given the plight of the weather conditions already acknowledged, it should be noted that Ronan performed admirably while committed to properly dispatching those otherwise anonymous and identical gazettes up and down his street each morning, never once depriving a paid customer of their sacred right to read, or at least scan, the headline stories of the day.

Though flawless in his ultimate attempt-to-delivery ratio, it certainly would have been fair to say that Ronan sometimes became distracted during the execution of his assigned tasks. During the mornings, when a foot or more of fresh snow had fallen, he could be seen attempting to score countless imaginary touchdowns by vanquishing his snowbank adversaries and tormentors alike. Those harrowing feats of athletic determination and hibernal skill usually followed some of his more challenging mail slot deposits, which, in all fairness to the young Mr. Cassidy, seemed to defy the laws of geometric appropriation. While the snowbanks normally reach a height of about eight feet that late in the winter, those outsized and nearly unconquerable behemoths of the winter of 1982 required a fair amount of stamina, dexterity, and sheer will to overcome. There were times that Ronan failed to carry his momentum over the crowns of these slippery beasts, and as a result, he was promptly returned in a rolling or sliding heap to the base of each unconquered mound of varying size, shape, and, most importantly, vertical rise. Nevertheless, our fearless hero eventually had his way with each and every one of the Siberian-style embankments of ice and snow while managing to return home and get ready for the mile-or-so walk to school without contracting frostbite.

Ronan was called into service that blustery February by his best friend Stephen. Stephen had the flu or some other lasting malady that kept him from delivering the papers during that most challenging of all weeks. Stephen lived about a half-mile or so and three cross streets up the avenue from Ronan. His standard-sized house for the neighborhood, trimmed out in green wood and accentuated by black detailing, was just about precisely halfway to the Roman Catholic grade school that Stephen and Ronan both attended. Ronan and Stephen met most mornings as Ronan and his brother passed by, sometimes with a few of the other neighborhood kids that attended the same school in tow. During the winter months, such as the 1982 edition of February, there was always a snowball fight or an abbreviated snow football contest that broke out sometime during the walk to school. Every minute before the opening bell was utilized, but because both Ronan and Stephen were also very determined students amongst their small-sized class of eleven boys and fourteen girls, tardiness was a rare occurrence. While Stephen tended to stay out of trouble at all costs, Ronan had a bit of a penchant for pushing the boundaries during school hours. That was a trait of Ronan's that had caused more than a few serious dust-ups with the good sisters in charge of maintaining the firmly disciplined, parochial regimen that the parents of the school's students not only prized but altogether expected.

The street that Stephen and Ronan lived on ran from east to west in a straight line and connected three of the city's major avenues just a few miles uptown from the city center, and it was situated a bit further to the north of the busiest sections of downtown proper. The entire length of the street covered about a mile and a half, or perhaps two miles at most, and began at the avenue that bordered the rough-set east side of town and ended at the gateway to the immigrant-laden west side of town. Stephen and Ronan met on the walk to school most mornings and discussed the results of the prior night's hockey game, or helped each other with any troublesome homework problems when the walk to school gang was of a smaller contingency. They competed for top honors in their class annually but maintained a friendly rivalry that never got in the way of their varied after-school activities.

On the unmanageable weather days, the two creative minds spent hours building endless Lego cities consisting of intricately designed roadways, towering skyscrapers, and detailed stadiums for their favorite sports teams. Stephen's oldest brother, Christopher, had a pinball machine that he let Stephen and his friends use when he wasn't occupied in his room, and in the years following the commencement of his matriculation at the United States Military Academy at West Point. On the Atari video console, Ronan and Stephen conquered the repeating hazards of a video game called Pitfall Harry and took Polaroid pictures of the high score screens to memorialize their record-breaking performances. Down in the half-finished basement, there was nerf soccer and small-stick hockey. On the more organized outdoor days, the gang played street hockey, wiffle ball, and football; did some tree climbing; or ran some manhunt or tag. All of these activities, and the countless others that the neighborhood kids dreamt up, kept Stephen and Ronan very busy when they weren't engaged in organized sports or doing their assigned schoolwork. There was always plenty to do in the bustling neighborhood that intersected with so many different walks of life.

Ronan worked his delivery beat, covering his street from end-to-end while rejoicing in the fact that it snowed plentifully every single day that he had manned the demanding Highland Avenue route. In those days of the infamous winter of 1982, the newspaper had to be delivered without question, and it had to be delivered regardless of the circumstances. The morning paper was the sunrise staple that went along with that very necessary first cup of coffee that so many of the still weary denizens of Ronan's neighborhood, while working to shake off the webbed doldrums of their sleep, relied upon to set themselves in motion for the challenges of the day ahead. Ronan James Cassidy was just the lad to be relied upon to execute such an important task. While Ronan took little joy from completing the inserts or the other preparatory tasks needed to ready the papers for delivery, once those soft and pulpy publications were squared away and ready to be distributed from the depths of his worn-out and newspaper-inked white canvas bag with the blue lettering and thick, puffy orange strap, he quickly set about vanquishing every obstacle in his path. Ronan would bound up the steps of those Victorian-style porches like a gazelle. He would march through the mounting snowdrifts of the untended walkways of late-winter like a strong and steady bison crossing the vast expanse of the snow-covered prairie. He would stare into the blinding squalls laced with stinging snow and ice without batting an eyelid. Whatever obstacle remained mounted before him, Ronan Cassidy would eventually find his proper mark for the conveyance of that prized payload of daily news and other indispensable sundries.

At around seven one Sunday morning, after the final bulging edition of the flagship paper of the week had been neatly placed between the outer doors of the last house at the western end of his street, and while dressed in his puffy light blue jacket, which would not return to the heart of style for some thirty years, Ronan cleared the final five snowbanks on the block without a hitch and began his journey home. After walking a fair distance beneath the cover of the thick and almost blinding clusters of patiently falling snow, he spotted a snow mound in the middle of the block that appeared to reach up to the heavens. He gave the well-packed and steady leviathan a hearty turn. After toiling for a minute or so, he crested the peak in a state of utter exhaustion. He did not linger long at the crown of that urban mountain. He simply flopped his winded body over the top and rolled down this final vanquished peak sideways until he had nearly reached the bottom.

Once his motion had slowly come to a sliding halt, Ronan stretched his body forward as he rolled into an upright position and then leaped to his feet with a glorious bounding motion. He landed at the edge of the street, which was still pristinely steeped in a blanket of snow. Though his feet had landed perfectly, he could not see his shoes beneath the depths of the accumulating powder. Without making any effort to remove the snow that had gathered copiously upon his jeans, hat, and gloves, Ronan walked across the sometimes-busy thoroughfare that had been wrapped in a shroud of comforting and peaceful silence in accordance with the Sunday repose of its normal travelers and the mass of snow that continued to blanket the wares of the world.

The world remained white and untouched on that winter morning. Ronan sunk to his knees with each step he took while walking through that soft and continuous field of snow. A few feet of snow had fallen throughout the course of the preceding day and had accelerated into the evening, whereby those final hours of the storm had encased the traditional markers of the cityscape so suddenly and without warning in the waning hours of the pre-dawn that no human effort had been made to disturb the aftereffects of the wintery deluge. Only a tired ten-year-old boy delivering the Sunday paper dared to leave a mark upon the unbroken blanche as he made his way across the road and into the small churchyard, which was surrounded by a handful of neighboring houses and their fenced-in back yards.

When Ronan reached the center of the churchyard, he fell backward into the soft depths of the pristine snow mass that had settled evenly over that small but wind-shielded field. Ronan stared up into the sky as he felt the soft snow land on the wet and reddened cheeks of his face. The normally bustling city neighborhood was silent and at perfect peace. Not even the bark of a misfit pup could be heard. To Ronan, it seemed as if he were lying there in the depths of a heavenly ordained silence that could have only existed in some other realm that existed within an unknown corner of the universe. He felt so singular, yet so seamlessly connected to some spirited force of the natural order. Beyond that, he felt so alive, as if the expulsion of his every breath mattered dearly to the cold, silent, and penitently settling world around him. He felt as if the discordant maladies that so stained the graces of the waking world had been buried beneath that peaceful quilt of cottony snow. He believed that he was finally in harmony with those spirits of the past that continued to haunt the daily deeds of humanity while that brisk air rested softly yet bracingly on his still warm yet cooling cheeks.

Ronan's knit hat and gloves began to freeze and stick precipitously to the snow that had been briefly tempered by the warmth of his body and, in some cases, the resulting ice that began to form as the extremities of his exhausted limbs continued to cool. Yet, at that moment, time stood still for the motionless boy except for the observable oscillations of each falling snowflake that swirled down in delicately formed circles from the sky above his unwavering eyes. In the resounding silence, Ronan looked over to the branches of the bare elms and chestnut trees and the needled pines that worked their way between the gaps in the houses surrounding the churchyard. He stared carefully at the iced-over branches of the deciduous trees reaching ever upward, though they were burdened by the weight of the frozen elements they bore while yearning for the apex of that hardened steel-gray sky. He was in awe of the wonder of it all.

The snow remained a blanket of tranquility for the silent and watchful boy lying so still at the heart of its depths. The scene was beautiful and uncorrupted. All was quiet, motionless, and perfect. A warming peace filled Ronan with a happiness so pervasive that his tender spirit seemed to awaken in a manner that was so profound that he could not have offered any words to describe that fragile flash in time. One that seemed to be eternally preserved in its stillness by the graces of the divine attendants of the heavens. The moment was so far removed from the anticipated trials of the heart of a given day—those episodes that continually burst through the thin veneer of such peaceful interludes and explode upon the senses with such deafening and immeasurable force, that the tears beginning to freeze as they ran down the sides of young Ronan's whitening cheeks had been pouring out from the essence of his tender and swollen soul.

In the years before that initial awakening of sorts that Ronan experienced in the winter of 1982, and for many of the years that followed, the boy Mr. Cassidy once was often dwelled within the confines of what many considered to be a wild, intense, and all-consuming imagination. At certain times, he was guided by that imagination, while his youthful spirit bucked fiercely against the chains that the deviant overseers of this fallen world use to subdue and subjugate what they might of humanity and shape us in the ways of their deviant and wanton will. Before Ronan went back to sleep for a significant amount of time later in his life, or what was perhaps better described as becoming peacefully sedated by the unending barrage of limitations spoon-fed into his reality, his imagination was delicately interwoven into a part of him that he could not properly separate from those qualities prized for their usefulness to western society. There were even times that this colorful imagination of his dauntingly swung from the tangled vines of his emotions and dared to transform the views he held of the world around him in ways that can only be attributed to an innocent or childlike mind. The best definition Ronan could ever give to this misunderstood connection to some forceful spiritual prompting that seemed to dwell and thrive beyond the bounds of our conjured reality and, furthermore, silently altered his physical and cognitive connection to the world, was that of the Latin word *animus.*

Ronan had learned the word *animus while* studying Latin at his secondary academy in upstate New York. While Mr. Cassidy associated the strength of his inner spirit with the true Latin definition of this word, he liked to think of his animus as more of a broad spiritual energy that was not bound by the confines of some widely accepted or propagandized world view. The animus was a spiritual energy that was shared in exalted places far beyond normal reckoning or the routine and daily affairs of humanity. His animus was a force moving in unison with and wholly connected to the unseen and godly communications of the natural order, and which shaped the makings of the limitless bounds of our cherished lives when individuals worked to fill their needs in accordance with the will of God. Ronan often imagined the joys, fears, differing interpretations, desires, beliefs, needs, and wants of people both past and present who failed to reach some unattainable perfection by wholly exhausting their energy in an unending attempt to bend the world to their will instead of letting the will of God shine into the world through their unique gifts and attributes.

Ronan had a profound connection to his imagination at a young age and foisted those creations from within onto the various manifestations of the world around him. He did not want to let his creative worldview dissipate as it veered sharply away from the broadly defined realities of the collective consciousness and what effect the expectations of such might have on the daily meanderings of an adolescent American boy. Therefore, he kept those obscure renderings of what the world just might be tucked neatly away from the opinions of those who refused to understand that the mind was infinite and subject to something far greater than what even the well-trained eye might discern. He nourished that creative energy by spending countless hours alone in fleeting realms that were elaborately created representations of the surreal, secretly built into towering card houses; makeshift cities crafted of toy buildings, shoeboxes, and assorted knick-knacks; and sandcastle kingdoms fashioned with elaborate moats, fences, towers, and roads constructed of fine pebbles.

The fancies of his imagination were sketched secretly into notebooks or kept as the journals of the imagined sports leagues he brought to life with his brother and his uncle. They were the underground rivers of spring that ran beneath the melting snowbanks lining the roads. They were the countless maps he drew in which he delighted in the geographic oddities built into the cities and towns from the atlas of the states that he pored over for hours. Those creations from the depths of Ronan's imagination were the abstract representations of the life he had come to know and the beautiful worlds that might exist beyond that hardscrabble northern town. Especially when that town was in motion and pulling him along with the forceful yet misguided want of the hungry collective belonging to that time and that place.

Ronan was the designer and final arbiter of all things in his imaginary world, and those talents were transferrable to the real world at times, but more often than not, they seemed to play out far better on his terms. Perhaps he was not alone in experiencing such a phenomenon. He could pitch a tennis ball across the street to the inside corner knee-high on command and hit targets of his choosing from thirty yards out with a snowball, but those talents weren't always transferrable to the more widely regarded athletic endeavors of his day. As an athlete, he strived for certain moments of perfection and had a natural acuity for the perfect pass, catch, throw, hit, shot, or save, even if he lacked that always desired penchant for consistency over varying spans of his meteoric progression in those endeavors. As his dad told him more than a time or two, "You are a legend in your own mind, son." Although Ronan bristled at the comment in the days of his youth, only because he couldn't think of a better place to become a legend, he laughed when he thought about those sage words of his father in his later years.

For Ronan, one "kick save and a beauty," to paraphrase the late Don Cherry of Toronto Maple Leaf's lore, always trumped two or three softies between the wickets as long as the result of the contest wasn't hanging in the balance. To Ronan, the common things of the mundanely passing moment were meant to be forgotten, but that special moment of artistry might live on. During the times when he thought back on those snow-filled days of his youth, the reflection upon such events always made Ronan smile warmly inside. When he was nostalgic and daydreaming about his childhood in his later years, it always made him chuckle to think about how many game-winning plays he left out on some snow-covered field of one.

At the end of the week, Ronan was paid eleven dollars for his efforts from what remained of the customer collections. He could still picture nearly every detail of that first hard-earned ten-dollar bill he was able to keep after he settled things up with Stephen. Ronan's photographic recall was both detailed and vivid. Ten American dollars was an exorbitant sum for a boy of his age early in the third year of the ninth decade of the twentieth century in the Year of Our Lord. Ronan studied the bill carefully, and he made a mental connection between the banknote and what it might procure down at Raleigh and Harlan's corner store, which was just two blocks down the street. He tabulated his haul in terms of real goods as follows: Twenty packs of baseball, hockey, and football cards; four candy bars; three or four sodas; a banner from the hockey game; and perhaps another trinket or two if he was frugal otherwise.

Mr. Cassidy hadn't learned about interest on deposits back in those days, nor did he understand the need to preserve purchasing power from inflation. Therefore, he discreetly tucked the folded bill into a clever hiding place between Connect Four and Checkers in the closet of the room he shared with his younger brother. He kept the eleventh dollar he had been paid in his pocket in case a trip to the store was imminent. Yes, Ronan could still picture that bill perfectly decades later, and he often wondered what it was that he finally received in exchange for the tendering of such a treasure. He guessed that it had been a few of the pennants that formed the growing pinwheel over his brother's bed and any number of the sports memorabilia cards stashed in shoeboxes in the corner of the room, but the case may have been that he had purchased a few extra LPs down at Record Town in those years that he and his brother remained on an endless quest to acquire all of the musical selections within Casey Kasem's Top 40.

At the time he was compensated for delivering newspapers through the cascading drifts of the unending lake effect snow squalls of that week, Ronan did not know, nor did it occur to him to consider such an outlandish event, that just two years prior, the U.S. dollar and the international monetary system, which it denominated, had nearly collapsed. Nevertheless, back in the spring of 1978, the purchasing power of the dollar was declining at an astonishing rate of 50% annually. This period represented the peak of the dollar's waning credibility internationally upon severing its international redemption rights to a fixed and properly defined weight in gold. The dollar inflation of 1978 also coincided with the cessation of dollar reserve accumulation by the nations that comprised the European Economic Union. Few of our current monetary advisors seem to understand, or at least openly admit, that the two events were causally related and not entirely coincidental. Those pundits prefer to suggest that the Federal Reserve somehow saved the day back in 1980, simply by raising interest rates to astronomical levels. They seem to ignore the concept that receiving more of a worthless item seldom installs confidence in those providing tangible and exhaustible resources for something created out of thin air.

While the unbacked dollar as the primary medium of exchange, unit of account, and form of bookkeeping wealth was working wonders for global trade, accounting, and transactional efficiency, countries around the world were losing faith in Uncle Sam's ability to pay his bills. Nations around the world certainly had plenty to question following the United States' default on its gold obligations in 1971 and the soaring deficits that accompanied and followed Vietnam. Plain and simple, global producers needed confidence in the unbacked dollar's ability to maintain value after it was severed from its gold link, and the pillars of the fiat currency's credibility were running dangerously thin in the late-seventies and early-eighties. No amount of interest rate chicanery or dollar supply manipulation could alter that reality.

By 1979, panic was beginning to set in. It became apparent to the central bankers of Europe that the world's primary currency for trade would have to be supported until an alternative currency suitable to handle the current volumes of global trade could be established. Many of the most powerful financial minds at that time believed that losing the function of the dollar's associated values in real world trade, which correlated directly to the dollar's nearly universal acceptance in the settling of such an important function, would have produced a crippling result for the emerging productivity of global trade and hence the global economy.

Ronan barely recalled those dark times for the dollar, and with good reason. In the years when the three-legged stool of international support for the purely fiat dollar was put into place, all appeared reasonably orderly to a little boy who refused to watch the news, stashed any loose change that was able to be saved into a piggy bank, and spent what little available money he or his little brother might come across on a given day on non-essential items. Moreover, there were far more substantial concerns back in those seemingly heady days, or at least concerns that left more of a lasting impression on the young mind of Mr. Cassidy. Things were breaking down at home; he was in a heated battle for top honors in his class with Stephen and a new student from Bolivia; and those baseball cards he and his brother purchased each week were establishing quite a market value as collectibles that might serve as an emergent store of value for the pair of young upstarts. Although a legitimate market value had been established for those keepsakes, both in the neighborhood and places beyond, neither he nor his brother were able to garner anything close to the published blue book prices for some of their better offerings. In any event, neither of them were willing to part ways with the best of their rather comprehensive lot.

Ronan did, however, remember his dad showing him fourteen one-hundred-dollar bills in cash sometime later during that eventful year of 1982. By that time, much of the dollar's turbulence had begun to abate. His dad used the cash to purchase a new station wagon at the car dealership over on the more tempestuous east side of town. The wagon was an excellent vehicle, except for the hole in the floor of one of the back seats, which sucked in its fair share of baseballs, hockey pucks, and a litany of gloves, hats, and other seasonal sundries. When the snow was dense upon the roads, the hole gave back in the form of its fair share of slush and ice, and a bevy of other sullied concoctions that were doused in the elements. The hole was always there with its insatiable appetite, craving to be fed and wet and cold while exposing the road moving beneath, which appeared as rapid, unidentifiable streaks passing below the rusted fracture of the wagon's undercarriage. One can only imagine how such a deformity came to pass, given the otherwise steadfast nature of the formidable and rather functional family vehicle.

To Ronan Cassidy's young and wandering mind, the world of 1982 moved on outwardly and seamlessly. It moved in phases of deep passion, time spent with his brother, relentless competition, freedom, large family gatherings, time spent out in the country, and dogs. There were always sporting events; the occasional recognition of top honors in school; serving as an altar boy at mass and hoping to draw Stephen as his helper; hours upon hours of playing in the outdoors; climbing trees to unimaginable heights without fear; the incurable excitement of the hot breath of the neighborhood girls honoring their dares beneath the mounting piles of the leaves of early October; friends; more family; and the unspoken failings of the past, which, at times, haunted it all. Those unforgiven sins of yesterday were always lurking like an expanding void, pulling like the road beneath that opening in the car floor and moving faster and faster beneath it until the moment of some benign or fateful reckoning would wipe the slate presentably clean.

In 1982, it was our collective lot that the government of the UNITED STATES would continue to squander the wealth of the nation through mismanagement, propaganda, war, corruption, extortion, and theft. The rest of the world went along for the ride, or in many cases, was compelled to oblige, and elected to foist the dollar on its shoulders in the name of achieving some pyrrhic form of continuity without intrinsic stability, which was manifested in the proliferation of an economic system that no longer ebbed or boomed from a sustainable equilibrium point. "Alea iacta est," as the saying goes. The die had indeed been cast, and America gladly crossed her Rubicon.

As such, the story of Ronan's life was crafted while time marched on in the early days of America's unchained exorbitant privilege and the catastrophic distortions caused by her undisputed center of international finance began to take root. Ronan's hopes and dreams, and their closely mirrored demons and fears, were nurtured by a social order that was always one step away from chaos; always out of balance. And somewhere in Baltimore, it was fixing to rain while a small boy, stained in blood and wholly given over to the depravities of some mounting and sinister obscurity set against him, scurried along the tracks of the inner city with only the hope of not being discovered by anyone.

Chapter 7

RETURNING HOME

ocked in the reticence of a dream that took hold of his senses during a season of his life when he was being tried at every turn, Ronan was unable to remember the exact date of that prescient visit to an earlier shine. That day gone by that Mr. Cassidy was reliving from the depths of his nocturnal slumber had accrued to late February of 2010, and the landscape within that pleasant and stirring reverie was blanketed in the aftermath of a sizable snowstorm. Under a cold and settled melancholy sky colored in the customary greys of the winter season, and within the modest suburban home he and a wonderful handyman had taken great pains to remodel in the likeness of something far closer to the preferences of the time and in congruence with his family's prevailing accord, Ronan's middle daughter, Madailein, or Maddie for short, yet under both monikers, the same shy, precious, and beautiful nymph whom Ronan had nicknamed the "magnificent one," summoned her father from across the room. The darling child's sweet yet timid inflections settled warmly upon Mr. Cassidy's welcoming ears, with the tiny evanescent reverberations of her innocent call flitting their way directly into the wellspring of his heart.

"Daddy, is it time to get the donies yet?" the angelic four-year-old child asked of her father.

Ronan stood up from the long, handsomely lacquered wooden bench that ran the entire length of the banquet-hall-sized farmhouse table he liked to work at on Sunday mornings. His seat on the bench on the southward-facing side of the table gave him a view of the fireplace and the ample morning light coming in through the twin sets of double glass doors that bordered the modest hearth. The bench was remolded and finished from its original form as the cross beam of a local barn that had succumbed to the wrath of a bolt of lightning during a violent mid-summer storm. The barn had stood for a century and a half as the notable landmark and storehouse of the grazing meadow of a country farm that was situated some ways to the north and just beyond the suburban developments of Ronan's town. Ronan approached the adjoining room where Maddie was standing on the newly laid brown carpeting in a certain spot, a spot that allowed her to not only accurately monitor her father while he worked at the grand table but also keep tabs on the big screen television, which just so happened to be playing one of the sweet child's favorite movies.

Before Ronan interjected in response to his daughter's query and disrupted Maddie's wide-eyed and enchanted gaze, which was now directly fixated upon her morning movie, he crept silently closer to the mesmerized child. While Maddie's unwavering focus remained firmly upon the animated characters flashing across the television screen, Mr. Cassidy studied his adorable little mess with a certain measure of amazement. The almost unimaginable flow of her opulent, strangely wild, and long brown hair seemed to scatter in every direction. The child's blue and steel-grey eyes were peering so vibrantly yet somehow also pleading so softly for attention while they rested above her slight nose and perfectly rounded yet puffy red lips. The constant redness of her bulbous cheeks gave notice of the enduring length of the cold and blustery winter season in the upper Midwestern realms. Standing there in her pale-blue, two-piece pajama set with the short sleeve top that was ornamented by a yellow flower and the word "fleur," Maddie's curt but plump and pouted lips could have summoned the ancient kings of the lost tribes of the Algonquin; those stalwart former stewards of that land, who passed down the largely untold legends of the antediluvian, and perhaps even primeval, epochs of that fertile stretch of Middle America.

"Yes, sweetie, we can go and get the doughnuts," responded Ronan. A delighted smile came over his face after studying his daughter's endearing curiosities for just a short while longer. "We will leave to go pick them up in five minutes. We need to get you all bundled up first. It's frosty out there, and I don't want you to turn into a Popsicle."

Maddie nodded and smiled in reply, but had yet to pull her mesmerizing eyes away from the magnetic draw of the television screen. Ronan shook his head and added, "I will get my boots on. Then we will get you all squared away and be off, my beloved little jar of peanut butter."

Maddie nodded again and chirped, "Okay, daddy." Her eyes remained unwavering, even as she twirled slightly in unison with a few of the colorful dancing fairies displayed across the length of the television screen.

Before Maddie had beckoned, Ronan had been on his computer reading an article by an unknown author. One who had some perspectives on the

2009 financial crisis that were shaking Ronan's well-educated beliefs on money and finance to their core. The words and concepts were simple and rational, yet so foreign to his fairly extensive financial training that Ronan's mind began racing as he continued to devour the thoughts revealed within the rich texts.

"Were these ideas true?" Ronan wondered, though only partially aloud. He followed that initial query with, "How do I learn more? Why did I not understand any of this sooner? How is it that others are not screaming bloody murder concerning the truth of this financial mirage laid bare for all to witness?"

These, however, were all questions that would have to be answered at a later time. Ronan's little girl was waiting on him, at least in theory if not yet in practice. Feeling a bit stunned by all that had been revealed, Ronan knew that he had seen something powerful and life-altering that winter morning—an obscurely verifiable truth that he would never be able to unsee. Though he was a rather pragmatic and analytical thinker and not one prone to overreacting to just about anything upon initial inspection, he could not recall the last time he had been so violently "red-pilled," and certainly not after reading something of a financial nature that was freely available on the internet for any and all to see.

After setting out a plan with his distracted but hungry child, Ronan walked back over to his computer to turn the machine off and got caught up for a brief moment while reading his email. However, Maddie had unexpectedly followed him into the room shortly after he sat back down in front of his computer. Though three months shy of her fifth birthday, Maddie knew that any persisting state of her father's silence was not accruing to her benefit. In simpler terms, the bright-eyed little girl was on to her dad, and it wasn't long before she was at his side, gently pulling on his sweater and pleading with those eyes, which were sparkling and alight with all of the tenderness and warmth of one belonging to the heavenly host. Ronan quickly took notice of this more direct cue from his daughter, exited the computer program, and powered down the laptop. He then smiled down at her while he purposefully pushed the device closed.

Ronan had a tender heart. He could certainly appreciate that there was nothing on this earth that needed tending to before that little sprite, with her reddened cheeks and eyes the color of a restless ocean meeting the soft grays of a calm but foreboding sky. Maddie tugged at Ronan's sweater one more time and, with what seemed to be the biggest eyes she could muster, pleaded affectionately, "Can we go now, daddy?"

Ronan smiled down at her and replied while in the midst of a soft, cheerful chuckle in response to his daughter's sudden persistence. "Yes, of course we can go now, sweetie. Let's get you ready and go get those doughnuts."

Ronan opened and shut the cover of the laptop to be certain that it had been powered down. He then walked pointedly through the open and adjoining kitchen area until he reached the mudroom. Once there, he adroitly grabbed the articles belonging to Maddie's winter wardrobe from the tangled mess of coats, snow pants, and accessories hanging from each of the hooks that the desired items of the moment were hanging from. He tucked the items under his left arm and then bent down and scooped up Maddie's boots from the rubber shoe tray with his right hand. With all of the necessary articles of clothing assembled, Mr. Cassidy commenced with the task of bundling up his baby girl. Her snow pants went on first and were followed by her boots, scarf, and jacket. Lastly, he put on her knit hat and her large, puffy mittens. Looking out the large unobstructed patio window while he fashioned his little snow brownie for the elements, Ronan could hear the hollow sheers of a brisk western gale lashing out at the windows and rattling the outer screens of the patio doors before whistling sharply along the siding of the house.

Those raw and brutal wind shears blew straight through town as they rushed forcefully across the upper plains of the Midwest, screaming along their eastward coursings while remaining unimpeded from their source in the western mountains of Canada. The feral torrents of frozen air were not buffered in the least when they passed through the flatlands of permanently frozen places like Alberta and Saskatchewan before razing the snow-covered American prairies. The sporadic but violent gusts were spraying snow across the freshly ploughed road from the mounting snowdrifts of late February, and Ronan became acutely aware of what they would be facing as regards the elements once they began their morning journey.

When the startling reverberations began to reduce themselves to low, howling murmurs and the wind gusts, at least when measured by the direction of the blowing snow, began to appear as if they were traveling low across the open fields to the north of the house, Ronan figured he should start the car and allow it time to warm up. He went out to the garage while observing Maddie standing there in waiting. She was bundled from head to toe and more than ready to begin their adventures. Ronan's heart was alight, and he wondered how such signs of grace failed to deliver the hearts of men from mortal ruin and straight into the arms of God.

After clearing the fresh snowpack and exposed firn of the plow's work at the end of the driveway with a quick yet reserved burst of acceleration, Ronan and Maddie made their way out onto the short side road and then out beyond the cul-de-sac. They traveled along the remote connecting road for a short while and then turned right onto the winding roads of the Town Park and Forest Preserve. "There must have been a foot or more of snow last night," Ronan thought silently as Maddie began one of her traditional guessing games while thumbing through one of her books in the back seat.

"What is Rojo, daddy?" Maddie called out from the elevated car seat behind Ronan. She continued flipping through the pages of a rather large book, searching for more questions to ask her father while she awaited his answer.

"Oh, that's red, I believe, sweet girl," Ronan called back to his daughter, whom he could spy as an image in the rear glass, though he could have guessed that she was reading her book about Spanish colors without the visual aid.

"Yes, daddy," said Maddie, while already getting to the task of finding the next testing question for her father. "How about *animalrillo*, daddy? What color is that?"

Ronan paused for a moment to let the suspense build and to let Maddie look over all of the examples of yellow items on the page for her edification. After about fifteen seconds had passed, he responded to the patiently waiting little girl. "Oh yes, I think you mean amarillo, which is, of course, yellow, my little jar of peanut butter."

"Can you find anything outside that is yellow?" he asked, while employing a slightly dramatic tone for effect.

"Everything is white, daddy! The whole world is white!" exclaimed Maddie after she had glanced away from her book and out the window to scan the depths of the snow-covered fields of the forest preserve off in the distance.

"Yes, my love, you are right. Everything is indeed white. It is wonderful," answered Ronan.

Mr. Cassidy looked out over the beautiful snow-covered fields in an attempt to find anything that might defy the purity of the cottony blanket of snow draped over the fields and the muted thickets of the once vibrant chaparral that lined the roads. A calming part had lulled the savage wind into a restive and gentle draft for long enough to allow Ronan's mind to steep in the purity, splendor, and stillness captured within the whole of the beautifully blanched countryside. He found no other color marked against the whiteness filling the picturesque frames of his shifting sightlines. Mr. Cassidy then glanced back at Maddie in the glass and said, "Blanco, perhaps?" as he checked the joyful determination with which Maddie set her eyes upon the world at that moment.

"Yes," replied Maddie's reflection, smiling wide and delighted in the rear imager, "Blanco, daddy."

The car continued to roll onward, progressing guardedly and slowly over the winding, rustic road that was thickly coated in the snowpack of the evening squalls and then dressed in the unending waves of the large, swollen flurries that arrived that morning. The tires of the car, hardened by the bitter chill of the arctic air, dug into the unbroken blanket of snow with a muffled and discordant crunch as the firm rubber compacted the fresh, loosely resting top coat of snow. All else was silent, calm, and uninterrupted in the outside world until the rousing wind began to stir the resting snow that covered the open fields and the branches of the trees that lined the end of the old marsh road. The scurrying shavings of white darted with the swirling tempests in rising, falling, and then circling waves out across the open fields, pathways, and parking lots of the town park as the car passed slowly by that seasonally active venue.

When the snow began to blow in earnest, Maddie put her book down on the seat and delighted in the frenzied blasts of white powder that began to drift across or explode into the windshield. "I love the snow, daddy!" Maddie exclaimed, wide-eyed. "I want to build a snowman and climb the snow hill out front after we get the donies and hot chocolate."

Ronan could think of nothing better to do on that fine winter day, so he responded to his now excited little girl quite happily and in the affirmative. "We will do just that very thing, my little bundled ball of love."

While at the doughnut store, selection was everything. Mr. Cassidy ordered two hot chocolates with extra whipped cream and then joined Maddie at the front of the counter, facing the rows of freshly made doughnuts. Across from them were two very sweet, permanently smiling women who Ronan guessed were about sixty-five years old, though he never bothered to hone his skills in those matters because such things as a woman's age were not to be spoken of openly. At least, not if there was any way to avoid doing so. Whatever their age may have been, the ladies behind the counter were quite fond of Maddie and her sister, and they seemed to enjoy the early Sunday morning visits of the Cassidy girls.

Maddie stared up into the enchanting and almost dizzying promised land of the doughnut rack, which was draped in lush chocolates, the succulent pinks of the summer strawberry, powdered confections, sugary glazes, and the white, creamy middles of some delightful confectioner's pantry. Her mouth was agape. To break the hypnotic spell that had been cast over his child, Ronan queried her. "What kind do you think you want today, sweetie?"

Ronan asked Maddie that most important of all questions while winking at the two ladies still smiling patiently behind the counter. He winked at the proprietors because Maddie always chose the same doughnuts each Sunday morning, no matter how long she agonized over the nearly maddening variety of delectable treats. Pointing with her bulky mitten over the counter to the powdered vanilla crème doughnuts on the third tray of the middle section, Maddie answered firmly, "Those donies please, ma'am." And so it would be, along with the chocolate-frosted doughnuts Lauren would have selected had she been present on that day and a few strawberry companions to round things out.

Ronan stepped over to the far end of the counter and picked up the hot chocolates. He put each small cup into the fasteners of a cardboard pop-up cup holder, grabbed the handle, and turned back to join Maddie over by the doughnut display. When he had made his way back to his little girl, he spoke to the friendly lady behind the counter and her delightful partner working the cash register for good measure. The kind woman behind the counter remained fixated on Maddie. The lady reminded Ronan of pure sweetness, all-rounded in form and wrapped in her brown button-down shirt with its soft and broad white collar. "We'll have the usual, ma'am, if it suits your fancy, to go along with the hot chocolate, of course."

The kind lady behind the counter smiled with wide, rounded eyes and responded while offering a slight nod of her head. "Absolutely, Sir. Your little girl is an absolute angel."

The other woman, knowing Maddie and her sister's standing order, had already picked out and boxed the doughnuts while Ronan and her partner went through the pageantry of properly communicating everything. Meanwhile, Maddie was grinning from ear to ear and had been watching diligently to be sure that proper care was taken as each new treat was added to the box. "Yes, ma'am. She's my little angel," responded Ronan.

In short order, the kind lady had everything ready. She rang up the total at the cash register. Ronan called happily to the wide-eyed woman while handing his card across the counter to pay, "Thank you, ma'am. I hope you two have a wonderful Sunday. Try to keep warm!"

The ladies looked at each other and continued smiling. "No, no, thank you, sir," they responded almost in unison. Then the woman working the cash register added, "Your little girls make our day."

Ronan smiled from across the counter one last time and flattered the lovely ladies with effect, "You two are far too sweet to be believed!"

Ronan then looked down at Maddie, who had the box of doughnuts secured in her big blue mittens, and he was delighted. In spite of the weather, it was a good and cheerful morning filled with blessings of a simpler kind.

Ronan and Maddie made their way out the door and were greeted promptly by the cold wind that was blowing across the storefront. They tucked their chins into their chests to protect their exposed faces from the pelting flurries and tiny ice tendrils caught up in the gusting gales. Ronan kept his hand on Maddie's knit hat while her waddling yet somehow supremely careful steps worked their way over and through the challenges of the mounting contours and rising depths of the accumulating snow. Knowing that Maddie could see very little, given the blinding intensity of the windblown elements, Ronan used the hand that rested on Maddie's hat to help direct the child back to the car. Her nose and cheeks froze instantly in the face of the gusting and precipitous wind shears, but she marched on without pause, determined to shepherd that box of doughnuts safely back home without incident. Ronan took care of the hot chocolate, which he knew Lauren would be excited to receive when they returned.

When they reached the car, Ronan opened the door for Maddie and placed her in the car seat in the back of the sedan as she continued to hold the box firmly in her hands. Her lips trembled something fierce from the cold, but Maddie was unwavering in her commitment to those morning treasures, and she dispatched her guard forcefully over that sacred box. She refused to release her tightening grip, not even to wipe her running nose. Then, Ronan leaned into the back seat and pried the box free from Maddie's hands for just long enough to fasten the exponentially amplified girth of the winterized child into her rather confining and oftentimes confounding car seat. After some effort getting the straps around Maddie's bloated gear, Mr. Cassidy buckled her in and kissed her frozen forehead firmly.

After the safety latch had locked firmly into position with a rewarding click, Ronan straightened Maddie's hat, which was starched through with ice and snow. Once the heavy lifting had been completed, he happily handed the doughnut box, which he had carefully set down in the open seat, back to Maddie and let the zipper on her jacket down a bit so that her frozen face could thaw out some on the short ride home. Ronan then pulled Maddie's scarf down just enough to free her rounded and noticeably dimpled chin. Only after all of that had been accomplished on behalf of his angelic traveling companion did he carefully wipe his daughter's unattended nose and upper lip.

When he was finished with that final maintenance item, Ronan said to her, "You are in charge of the donies, princess. Don't let anything happen to them before we get home."

Maddie shook her head hastily in a show of steadfast negative affirmation. "I won't, daddy," she replied immutably while she held the slightly dented box across her lap and prepared for the brief journey across that magical land of ice and snow.

"You are my number one helper," answered Ronan. "You are my sweet love. I have not a worry in the world with those scrumptious delights being kept so smartly in your care."

There is no disputing that it is sometimes hard to know which of those seemingly innocuous events in our lives will render those burning imprints that are fully emblazoned upon the waking soul. Still and all, Ronan carried the picture of his daughter on that cold and snowy Sunday morning with him like a locket chained around his heart. When the time for the true depths of his necessary trials had come to pass, it was no surprise that when Mr. Cassidy opened his eyes from that glowing and fanciful reincarnation of the better days gone by, he could still see Maddie's puffy red cheeks and her blue eyes peering out in hopeful anticipation from in between her knit hat, her powder-blue ski jacket, and her loosely arrayed, knit scarf. Beyond that, he could still feel the excitement glittering in her pupils and the cold sensation of her frosted cheeks as she rested them against his ear when he carried his little helper into the house. The images, recall, and feelings of it all were so pervasive that, upon such a wistful reckoning, he was certain that the moment existed eternally. Perhaps he was right about that hopeful thought, but right or wrong, he continued to gaze inward as he awoke from that splendid phantasm, refusing to let the heartfelt and timeless image of his daughter go while the tops of the tall shaking pines, some seventy meters off in the distance and directly in his line of sight, made their way back into the periphery of Ronan Cassidy's consciousness.

Losing touch with the remaining silhouettes of his dream as they drifted into the ether, Ronan's focus came upon the shadowy daybreak of the present moment and the unrelenting waves of heavy, cascading rain beyond the swaying balcony doors. Since his dog had been sent away and he needn't worry about her barking at the neighbors and passersby below any longer, he had left the gently swaying balcony doors open throughout the night. That day to come was the fourth and final turn of a dark and unrelenting storm that had overcome him at a moment so contrary to the triumphant lack of vulnerability he had felt when it all began. He was abandoned to the mercies of unrelenting doubt and an inner darkness so intense that he was no longer able to respond to even the most basic external stimuli. There was simply nothing for him in any of it.

He was fighting his way through that indescribable emptiness and despair. His world had turned cold, lonely, and inane. At certain times during the spell, Ronan fought to break free, only to sink further into the mire. A crushing but imaginary weight pressed on his chest and forced his breath outward in quick yet halted motions until he had reached a point where it seemed as if those desperate exhalations would no longer replenish his wind. At that dark moment, he wanted nothing but more sleep, as that was all that was capable of making the unimaginable deprivations of his tormented soul stop. Be that as it may, the despondent Mr. Cassidy began to awaken at miserably quickening intervals as the eternal hours of that incessant depression wore on without reprieve.

Awash in self-disapprobation and disappointment and seemingly bent on self-destruction, Ronan knew that the last of the potpourri of assorted alcohol was gone. That fortunate circumstance was a relief to the wretched man, as it meant he had no immediate reason to attempt to move from his bed. Ronan gave a haphazard thought to the day's demands, which were not overwhelming under normal circumstances but not entirely inconsequential either. In the end, none of that mattered just then as the growing emptiness in his soul continued to play out its own false and hopeless reality, until Mr. Cassidy craved sleep above all else in the face of such mounting despair.

In the brief but ultimately failed moments that Ronan came close to breaking out of his miserable fit, he realized that what he longed for was redemption for his sins and some form of clarity regarding his true God-given purpose in life. In accordance with that revelation, he probed his passing thoughts manically for anything solvent and sustainable that might reveal the truth about who he was designed to be. He believed that the answer to that question would give his soul some form of lasting peace. However, the answer that he was ultimately given some time later was of an entirely different nature and well beyond even the brightest hopes of his admittedly moribund expectations. Upon further reflection and while coming to terms with the horrifying reality that there would be nothing of the sort available in that place where he had become so isolated and almost entombed, Mr. Cassidy attempted to organize his shredded faculties and ready his wares for the day ahead. That was a fruitless endeavor, as there would be no facing reality according to any proper meaning of the term on that day either.

As the dread of his spell had worn on, the pain and guilt of four days in and out of sober consciousness had devastated any and all useful measure of the almost unrecognizable man's resolve. The dross that remained behind was unserviceable and utterly inconsequential to any sort of productive activity. The heavy hold of the quicksand pulled at Ronan relentlessly until, on that final day, he reached some dank, endless, stygian well inhabited only by the rare and echoing cries of the hopeless. "There will be no way out on this go around," Ronan whispered as he entered the realms where all hope seemed to have been abandoned in conjunction with the cessation of time.

He twisted violently in bed to rebuke such a notion. He believed that the angry gesticulations might free him of that curse, but the raging motions only caused him to struggle all the more hopelessly for even a single breath of uninfected air. After his uncontrolled and useless spasms had been halted, the feelings of absolute helplessness began quickening from within. Ronan's soul went black and froze, and his limbs deadened from the burden of the weight of everything that was lost. "Who among us can bear such failure and the loss of love?" Ronan asked. "Do any possess the power to tame such a void?" He would soon discover that there was only One who was indeed infinitely capable of such things.

Sinking and alone, Ronan drifted among the dark hells of his hopeful captor. When he had reached the point that he could bear no more, he called out into the shadows of the night for mercy. To his surprise, God touched the cheek of his dearly beloved child and pulled the blanket up close to his chin. Touching Ronan's forehead briefly, He comforted his lost son and gave him rest. The shallow cold turned to warmth, and the darkness became a soft, sustaining glow of comfort and peace that knew no bounds. An overwhelming sense of love welled up in Ronan's heart. Hope and light and a clear path ahead were in him and so wonderfully visible before him. He then rested peacefully. For a while longer than he remembered, he slept the beautiful sleep of the untroubled mind, knowing that despite being away from home for far too long, he had remained safe and loved the entire time.

He had remained alone in the shadow of perceived failure and the self-reprobation that lurks in such places for a measurable span, yet he had been lifted out of that empty morass by the love and grace of God in an instant. In the aftermath of such a life-altering event, Ronan finally made peace with the fact that he had been walking down the wrong road for so long that he had become a stranger to his own heart. God lifted him up at the very moment Mr. Cassidy needed to be lifted out of that circular, strengthening, and self-reinforcing darkness. That single act of gentle love settled the foundations of his outlook on life, and that alone had made all the difference. On that day, Ronan James Cassidy had reacquainted his beliefs with a simple truth that he had known well in the innocence of his youth: the truth that God is love, and accepting that love, which is kept safe in our hearts, is always and everywhere, no different than returning home.

Some hours after his long-delayed awakening, on February 27th, 2016, Mr. Cassidy boarded a late afternoon plane bound for Philadelphia, Pennsylvania. He was to begin the long journey back to the world as he once knew it, but certainly not as the person the world had once known him to be. He was not yet aware of the earthly cost of his journey to the zenith of the void and his reclamation from that look into the eternal emptiness born of the need to cull the fires of hell raging unchecked upon the earth. Though Ronan, like all of God's creations, was marked by eternal grace through the gift of His offered salvation, he came to realize that such salvation was a miracle of divine grace perfectly suited to the heavens above, not some utopian manifestation that placed Ronan beyond the trials of the temporal and fleeting moments of our corporal existence.

It took some time yet still for Ronan to realize that the knowledge and stalwart devotion he now carried with him as the result of the Lord's having pried him away from the depths of that abyss were not entirely ill-suited for this fallen world. Such understanding did, however, require his immediate and unwavering faith in what had been prepared for us all beyond the material and sensory auspices of the human experience. Ronan was no prophet on that morning when he humbly and contentedly stepped onto that plane. He was simply a man who had been saved from a self-inflicted horror that was once beyond the limits of his belief. Furthermore, he was a man firmly bound to a promise given over to his Maker for the irredeemable gift of that warm and loving hand offered into the infinite pitch of the bottomless void. The day when he would shout such things from the mountain top was still some ways off and would remain the product of some necessary trial by fire; a condition that persisted due to the fact that Ronan had received such grace only due to his stubborn insistence on facing up to the barrel of a loaded gun held by the hand of the devil himself.

Ronan was set to defend his sacred promise not as one who understood the shaded grays of the long, winding, and divinely directed journey of arriving upon the unshakeable ground of his faith but as one who was violently ripped away from the depths of his own futility and placed upon that firmer ground out of a necessity that stemmed from the need for his preservation to tend to other matters. His experience was akin to that of a loving mother remanding her meddlesome toddler to the care of her arms when the effects of the playroom are no longer suitable for one so inclined to find trouble lurking at every turn. Whatever the case may have been, and as with all things, God would put his once rebellious child's caustic determination to good use as someone who would endure even the ultimate test of faith, and do so at any cost. With that in mind, one might begin to understand the actions of Mr. Cassidy while he was forced to appear before, and in turn, deny, a man of such ill repute and a man quite capable of treating the slaying of another as little more than a cost of doing business.

As it turned out, there was one among the Almighty Shepherd's flock who would require nothing short of just such a show of unwavering faith. That man would need to witness the devotion of an act so steadfast that the display of such loyalty to God might keep him from being consumed by his thirst for vengeance. Accordingly, Ronan would be given a specific message to carry with him and then deliver to that man. Moreover, Ronan would be asked to convey that missive with a resoluteness of spirit and aplomb that far exceeded the moral fortitude he possessed while delivering one of those Sunday newspapers he flawlessly dispatched for a short time in his younger days.

The journey Ronan embarked upon on that rainy February morning back in 2016 was not the proper time for that burden. As such, Ronan carried nothing but that song of great hope and rebirth, which resolutely rose from someplace deep within him. After holding dominion over the southern skies for the better part of a week or more, the storm clouds began to break. Ronan looked out the window from his seat on the right side of the plane, and he could see the blur of the runway moving fast below him as the sun suddenly and quite unexpectedly burst through the parting sky. For some strange reason, the running grays of the asphalt passing below the wing reminded Ronan of the road moving beneath the hole in the back seat of his father's old station wagon and all of the memories that accompanied those days of trial and wonder.

In an instant, during takeoff, Ronan recalled a once-forgotten but powerful memory from his childhood. When he was probably ten or eleven years old, or sometime after his father had purchased that station wagon for fourteen hundred dollars in cash back in 1982, he had been riding in the back of that automobile. The seatbacks of the rear passenger row of the car were down, creating a raised but unobstructed space that ran from the back hatch to the front seats. Ronan could not remember why the seats were down, but as he considered that particular oddity all those years later, he figured that perhaps they were down to cover up that hole and keep other travelers from losing a foot, or some other item of irreplaceable value.

Because Ronan had been late returning home from playing an all-day game of manhunt, he was using the added space of the expanded cargo haul to get ready for baseball practice. He didn't notice it at the time, but the long, bulking, yellow, and wood-panel trimmed wagon was probably traveling faster than normal to make up for the lost time. The manhunt contest had spanned the backyards, garage rooftops, and alleyways of about eight city blocks of the neighborhood, and Ronan was a bit sore in his jaw and nose from jumping from the top of a ten-foot-high fence with his younger brother and not accounting for the compression of his upper body and legs upon landing. The oversight resulted in the violent collision of his chin and then his nose with his kneecap. Nothing was broken, and all of his teeth were roughly where they began the day, so it was onward to the next event. Heading to practice with a few loose teeth was a far better outcome than the time he had tried to "fly" his Donald Duck scooter off of the stairs of the front porch years earlier.

As if the memory were being returned to him by way of the imperfect clarity of the plastic glass of the window of the plane, Ronan pictured the tan upholstery of the station wagon seatbacks beneath his bare knees as he scrambled to change his outfit. Rubbing his hand along the open airplane seat next to him, he remembered the warmth of the sun upon the fuzzy nylon fabric and the smooth but firm consistency of the fibers. At the time, he had been drained to near exhaustion from a full day out and about with the neighborhood gang. He was thirsty and working through the proper order of his clothing and equipment to be adequately prepared for practice when they arrived at the ballfields by the lake. Maybe just as important to the young Mr. Cassidy, he knew that he needed to be ready to make a clean getaway following their arrival to postpone the confrontation that was certain to come.

Such a transition would allow the circumstances surrounding his tardiness an appropriate amount of time to simmer down. Ronan was not silly enough to believe that they would blow over entirely. In addition to that benefit of delaying the practically inevitable, there was always the hope of procuring some small token of redemption by delivering a heady performance out on the ballfield.

Directly in front of Ronan's eyes while he contorted to adjust his uniform under the constraints of the short distance between the roof and the raised position of the seatbacks was the back of the tall baseball cap that rested perfectly upon Ronan's father's head. Ronan was so close to that iconic ornament of his father's wardrobe that he could study the minute details of the small plastic fasteners that rested in the circular holes on the band that stretched across the semi-circular void at the back of the mesh cap. Two of the fasteners had broken off at some point during a prior realignment of the tall and unbent cap. His father's thick, dark hair rested beneath the band and puffed out a bit into the semi-circular opening. Ronan guessed that his dad was about two inches taller in that unblemished baseball cap, and most of his other caps for that matter, though he was certainly not the type of man that possessed a natural affinity for getting behind the wheel of a big rig. Ronan couldn't see the brim of the hat, but he was certain that it was as flat as a pancake, just like all of the other baseball caps his dad wore. Such neglect for the appropriate brim curvature of a properly donned baseball cap produced a look that must have passed muster sometime in the fifties or even earlier, but we all have our iconic incongruities.

With that thought in mind, Ronan began taking great care to remold a nice working curve into the brim of his hat. It would have been hard to imagine Ronan's dad ever collecting points for style, but he wrote the book on intensity and dedication to his coaching trade and his players on the baseball diamonds of the Niagara Frontier back in those days. Those tall and unmolested baseball caps with their adamantine brims that he wore to the ballfield each day served as a symbolic reminder, or even a displayed talisman of a sort, of that fact and his overall no-nonsense approach to most things in life. Ronan's dad was quite a good coach and rather knowledgeable about the finer and often overlooked stratagems of the games that he grew up playing during the proliferation of organized sports that accompanied that tangible prosperity linked to the era of the long boom. The other sports his dad coached, yet did not grow up playing, he learned to an impeccable degree as an ardent observer and student of the game. He was a bright man and motivated to win the right way, like few others of his time.

As was in line with his generally agitated demeanor while engaged in the heat of battle, Ronan's dad let the umpires have it a bit more than he should have. He was quite demanding of Ronan and his brother on the field, but he took care of all of his kids out there playing ball, both on and off the fields of play, and precisely when it counted most. Many of the kids Ronan's dad coached throughout the years dealt with tough situations back at home, and he gave a lot to help make those youthful athletes better players and better all-around people, while they tackled the traumas of their burdened adolescent years spent amongst the shrinking ranks of the city's blue-collar working class. He was a hardworking and immensely talented man, and more importantly, a man of high character, even in the moments when his temper got the better of him.

For a brief while, Mr. Cassidy drifted aimlessly through the notions triggered by the rebirth of that memory, which was becoming enmeshed in the ever-expanding fabric of his present knowledge. On that day, he found it ironic that he could do nothing to change the events of the past, given that he knew the absolute outcomes and, conversely, everything to alter, yet certainly not control, the myriad intersecting outcomes of those times lurking just beyond the here and now that remained entirely unknown. He drifted back into the fog of that small, passing segment of his life as it was remembered, while the world of the present remained visible to his inattentively scanning eyes. His gaze remained vacantly directed toward the window of the plane. His eyes were wide and hollow, and his hand continued to feel its way along the side of his standard-issue airline seat as if he were appeasing a sleeping kitten—a sleeping kitten who was only casually interested in the affairs of the waking world.

The plane raced faster, and Ronan's memory quickened. He felt the forces of acceleration and gravity pushing him firmly back into his seat. Then, quite suddenly, the once lumbering and violently shivering aircraft broke free of the earth, bounding skyward, smoothly and seemingly lifted by the air beneath, as if it were little more than the feather of a bird pressed sternly into the wind. The cascading distance that the colossal yet perfectly styled craft made with the rapidly shrinking forms slanted in the February greys and browns of the earth below caused Ronan to realign his perception of the world around him. The deliberate and gentle mechanics of a soft and nostalgically sentimental smile, which were completely indiscernible to the person settled in just a seat over from him on the skyward jetliner, tugged lightly at the muscles of Mr. Cassidy's cheeks and lips.

Continuing through the flitting remnants of that whimsical daydream, Ronan thought about how fortunate it was that the ire he presumed was likely to be infecting his father's stern countenance with a rage that connected to the depths of his own adolescence was not visible. Nor was it revealed in the rearview mirror. At least not once the grand wagon rolled out beyond their neighborhood, a neighborhood that was the last of the safe-haven areas in a city dying the slow death of the loss of its productive industry. Though Ronan certainly could not have appreciated such a thing back then, his hometown was an early casualty of the overvalued dollar, which, under its post-1971 construct, was entirely reliant upon the unending expansion of big government and bigger finance. The resource-destroying creep of those deformed utilities, once born of the intent to serve the public good, had already rapidly mutated into wholly distorted levers of control and dollar proliferation. They had morphed into the institutions primarily responsible for the ungodly misallocation of both real and financial capital, which the world faces in spades to this very day.

Abruptly returning to the sensations of that calamitous moment from his past, which were playing out in his mind as the plane continued to race skyward and towards the unfettered bounds of the firmament above, which was colored in that unmistakably settling tone of an endless and eternal blue, Ronan recalled that he was using the backs of the folded seats in the moving station wagon as his platform to suit up for practice. He had returned to his knees after swapping out his pants and was elevated above the level of the armrests of the front seats. Precisely when he peered forward to take note of how much time they had left on the trip, everything beneath him gave way. It gave way with such force that he was thrown headlong toward the windshield. The lurid resonations of metal repulsing and the breaking of glass were a flash late, yet they gave affirmation to the primal sensations of Ronan's distress as he was hurled toward the front of the car while time stood still. He felt as if a second plane of relativity had opened up and stretched the window of his thoughts by a few orders of magnitude. His mind became disjointed and was simultaneously disconnected from the immediacy of his peril. He was granted the sorely needed interval required to consider so many things in the matter of that instant upon which the fate of his life was to be decided.

Ronan was given an instant that seemed no different than the passing of a lifetime to assess the horrific outcome that had been put in motion with such violent urgency. The young boy staring into the certainty of his demise was no longer bound by the theoretical laws of relativity given his tertiary velocity and relative mass. Just as suddenly as his mind had escaped to some other dimension that operated in the slow time, the terror in his eyes and the certainty of the great suffering he was preparing to endure met the back of the outstretched arm of his father. Pushed to a limit beyond bodily capacity and powered by a drive so swift, strong, and instinctive, the arm of his father halted his beloved little boy before he went careening into the windshield. Ronan believed that he had been sent forward with enough force to pierce the windshield and scatter across the hood of the small silver car that had collided with the front of the hulking station wagon. However, it was more likely that the initial collision within the car would have been enough to produce a rather unfavorable result for the young Mr. Cassidy.

The driver of the silver, 1975 AMC Pacer had run a stop sign placed at the corner of an intersecting side street. His errant haste caused the two cars to collide almost without warning while Ronan and his father were traveling at full speed in the station wagon. When Ronan's forward velocity was abruptly halted, the small, hastily dressed boy fell bunched up into the gap between the armrests that were between the two front seats. Once he landed roughly within that uneven opening, his slightly delayed but powerful scream of terror never left his lungs. The choking off of that ferociously gathered wind had caused Ronan to cough violently and gasp for air for quite some time after he had been granted his unexpected reprieve from maladies of a far more grievous nature.

The young Irishman was certainly stunned by the swift, entirely unexpected, and life-changing shifts in his circumstances but otherwise in good order as he lay bunched up between the front seats. Just a few more bumps and bruises on the day to go along with some mental trauma, which was soon to be forgotten by the mind of an active and always curious little boy. Ronan realized as he thought back on that moment that he certainly had less appreciation back then than he did presently for exactly what had taken place in those brief moments and what he had been spared. The sheer will of his father to halt that once apparently certain catastrophe did not surprise the young boy he was, because his father seemed to be an almost invincible figure. Be that as it may, the superhuman dexterity and strength required to halt his progression in that sudden and horrifying instant surprised Ronan yet again as he watched the aircraft seem to drift through the passing clouds.

He then got to wondering if he would be capable of performing such a feat if a similar occurrence befell one of his beloved little girls. Though it was entirely unknown to Mr. Cassidy at that moment in February of 2016, in some ways, the precursors that would lead to those unforeseen events, those dour proceedings that would compel Ronan James Cassidy to fully understand the answer to that question, had already begun to slowly and meticulously turn. Those catalysts that would send him off to the island of Inis Mor with the fate of his child hanging in the balance had begun to turn like the mechanical wheels of a ticking watch, and they had begun to turn in places that were entirely nameless and altogether foreign to his concerns.

Ronan considered those events of his childhood for a while longer. "How did he do that?" thought Ronan, while still delicately stroking the side of the seat cushion. The memory was so powerful that his smile had slowly given way to a palliative yet blank expression of wonder and amazement. He then wiggled his outer extremities to be certain that the outcome he was remembering had indeed been real, and that he was the manifestation of flesh and bone now present on the smoothly gliding aircraft.

Ronan turned his gaze away from the last of the beautiful scenery of the earth below that had not been swallowed up by the surrounding cloud cover. He began to thoughtfully explore the more intangible realities of the waking world and his unending thankfulness for his Lord and Savior, Jesus Christ. "There is a divine grace that moves forcefully within this world of much suffering," he whispered silently.

Mr. Cassidy had never been able to neatly reconcile the physical limitations of one man that had been offset by the will of the human spirit when those two cars collided without warning. As he raced through the clouds, half a world away and several decades removed from that frightful moment of his childhood, he remained unable to reconcile the phenomenon of his reclamation amidst the fluttering presentiments of that thoughtful interlude absent the presence of God. Although he had grown far more erudite and far cleverer in his older age, he still could not define or accept a different answer to the enigma of the existence of a willful essence beyond the bounds of human comprehension. Ronan understood that no man committed to truly believing in the frailty and doubt so steadfastly drummed into our psyche by the well-tenured teachings of our upbringing would have found the will to do what was done that day. Those life lessons and carefully given examples that result in the abject amalgamations of our repeatedly displayed human futility and, furthermore, those consistently projected demonstrations ingrained into the fabric of our education, which falsely attempt to describe and dictate the delicate balance between our loving wants and the limitations proscribed by our fears, would have rendered a true adherent to those principles impotent in the face of such an unexpected convulsion of the fates.

He continued to sit there, spellbound and silent, yet quite lucid. Ronan soon realized that he hadn't thought back that far in his life in quite some time. At that age, he hadn't the slightest inkling of the power of a parent's love for their child when considering the circumstances of his deliverance from the angry flash of the sudden yet all-consuming metamorphosis of death. When reflecting upon that afternoon in the proximate years that had followed the collision, Ronan never doubted his father's capacity to control a given situation, and he was keenly aware of some terrible resolve to amend all things contrary to that steadfast man's will. Yet, there existed something deeper running beneath all of that, something that caused Mr. Cassidy to wonder, within the confines of the covered breath of a modest whisper, "Do any of us truly understand the divine power of love?"

At that particular moment, Ronan sensed that love continued to flow freely in even the most broken, calcified, and demented souls among us. He spoke once more in the manner of that same soft, almost silent whisper. "Do any of us truly understand the rapture and grace of God when those that are lost are returned to Him? Surely the heavens sing sweetly in all of our hearts in those moments when the Lord's children are returning home."

For the first time in forty years, absolution permeated Ronan's soul, and his eyes closed gently and peacefully for just a short while. The plane continued to smoothly reach its desired cruising altitude. The engines hummed soothingly from below the wing, which was situated just a few rows behind Mr. Cassidy. The restful gentleman took in the subtle warmth of the sunlight above the clouds, listened to that reverberating hum, and simply existed in a state of perfect peace. He had been lost, ensnared, and engulfed by the darkness just hours earlier, but was not the slightest bit afraid of once again coming to terms with the earth below him in any form or manner the anticipated reunion might take. When the sky had cleared some minutes later, the specter of all fear had vanished from within him, and the broad panorama now before his resting eyes included the mountains of Appalachia descending to their myriad endpoints in the highlands and foothills of northern Alabama. With his eyes closed, he understood one thing as he settled back in his seat. He understood that he had been broken down to be rebuilt anew. He was eternally thankful for such a gift.

Ronan was thankful to be found and to be found of faith. Most of all,

Ronan James Cassidy was thankful to be returning home in all the ways that one properly begins such a journey. Once those thoughts gently dropped away from the focus of his mind, sleep took hold as the plane moved smoothly across the cloudless eastern sky with the swollen southern sun at its proudly raised tail. That eternal sun remained, fading into the horizon beyond the western climes, a million miles off in the distance.

Chapter 8

THE VISION OF THE PALE HORSE

S ome dreams dance affably with the twisted constructs of the resting mind. Beyond those pleasant yet seldom remembered incidences of our fruitful repose, there are pictures of life that radiate hot and bright with such impeccable resolution that they burn their indelible forms into the abstractions of the mind in ways not viable to the naked eye. The latter episodes of the aforementioned are quite rare. Nevertheless, they remain with us and are perpetually recognizable. They outlast the moments of our lives when those visions of some unknown future delicately overlay their prescient messages onto the tangibly realized sequential and spatial reckonings of the known world as our life plays out before our seeking eyes. These God-given visions, which are always remembered but only peripherally recalled, color over the myriad abstractions of our subliminal reckoning of the tangible realms like gently or harshly exposed film held up to the light. They help shine the light of God's wisdom upon the more traditional still prints that are the already revealed and copiously gathered memories and recollections that instantly become the forever waning moments of our lives.

Ronan's vision on the plane that afternoon of February 27th, 2016, was not the first visual or instinctual premonition that would become a proven reality in his life. However, given that his vision of the pale horse behaved like the latter phenomenon described above beyond the very moment when the past became preamble and, subsequently, parable, to the present, it was, and forever remained, the first great vision of his life. As there are no coincidences in this richly layered and unbound existence of ours, only the causes and effects of that which we endeavor to identify and stitch into the patchwork patterns, shapes, and colors of the sequentially unveiled tapestry of our enigmatic time set upon God's beautiful earth, we shall say that the timing of the profound revelation coincided precisely with the hour that Ronan finally stopped pissing into the wind of his earthly doubts and desires and gave his life over to the command of our gracious, loving, and almighty God.

Lost within the colorful trappings of that strange and, for a time, inexplicable vision, Mr. Cassidy was walking through a large crowd. No matter how hard he tried, he could not make his way out of this swarming mass of preoccupied humanity. One that faced up to a grand podium and an earthly king of some sort who stood atop that overbearing architectural wonder of a bygone age. As the daydreaming passenger drifted aimlessly through the unending multitude of his fantasies, he witnessed a man ride a pale horse with black underlying flesh directly into a large, strangely angry, and then fomenting segment of the gathering horde without hesitation. The horse and rider split that buzzing mass of humanity directly down the middle. The magnificent beast stepped high-legged and stridently without halting her cadence, while the angry bystanders moved completely away from or fell beside the emergent path of the strong and beautiful white mare.

When the horse and her rider reached the center of that large, irritable group, the king called down from the podium with a thundering voice. He demanded that the angry masses give him one of their own. In an attempt to add some fairness and desirability to the almost deafening proclamation of his initially one-sided bargain, the sonorously throated king added, "If you give me any of your most beloved, I will promise those who remain of your tribe unending prosperity in the day ahead."

In an instant, the suddenly thrashing mob delivered a man into the hands of the king's nearest henchmen. The unlucky gentleman had addressed the people earlier that morning and bid them stop yielding to the daily demands of the dishonest king. His reasoning was sound when he proclaimed, "One day soon you will discover that the king no longer bothers to bargain with the dwindling masses of those among you who remain in the square." Sometime during the exchange, the rider of the pale horse swooped in and quickly took up the man offered to the king in light of his earlier insolence. The rider and the captive then rode off in the direction of the podium.

The next day, Ronan remained lost and working his way through the crowd, though he possessed no knowledge of how he had passed the time prior to that realization. In exact accordance with the affairs of the prior day, the king's unholy offer rang out at high noon and maddened the tender and confused eardrums of the crowd. At that moment, Ronan heard a voice call out to him, "You there, servant of our Heavenly Father, you must return His lost child to Him!"

Ronan looked upward to the heavens quite puzzled, and answered, "Who calls to me from the sky above? How is it that you expect me to find a given man in this unholy morass of angry and deviant humanity? I cannot even untangle my arms from the endless twists of the directionless limbs of this deadened thicket."

To which the angel answered, "God has given over to you the pale horse. The mare that rides in every day at noon to slowly take His people away at the behest of the wicked king. Seated upon the tall and stalwart shoulders of that magnificent beast, you will find your way free of these lost souls and into the field where His lost son awaits. The one you seek will be situated beneath the ancient oak. The mighty tree granted to his gentle and patiently waiting servants to take their rest in times of trouble."

Ronan looked down at the ground upon hearing those words and said, "How is it then, that you expect me to claim my given steed?"

The angel responded to Ronan with a kind and soothing voice. "The rider takes one away from this place every day. All you must do is raise your hand when the king beckons, and affirm your acceptance of the Lord's task. Soon thereafter, you will be on the horse. The rest is not your concern, my courageous and honorable lion of God. Your eyes are now open, and the Heavenly Father requires one who sees Him."

The next day, Ronan had steadfastly raised his hand at noon and most assuredly found his posterior seated high on the back of the white horse. Moreover, he discovered that he could see beyond the maddeningly packed square and out to the beautiful and boundless fields that lay untouched. When he saw the plentiful bounty of the pristine land, he asked of the angel, "Why do these people remain here, collecting scraps from the king, when they could be almost effortlessly reaping the abundance of that unending harvest?"

The angel responded candidly and without hesitation, "These are God's people that remain asleep. They have been asleep for so long that they no longer know how to live without the devil's yoke upon their shoulders. It will take time for them to open their eyes. Just as it took you time, and just as it will continue to take time for you to fully understand the abundance of God's glory that is available to you. You are now awakened to His presence, Ronan James Cassidy! Such has been proclaimed as good news!"

Ronan motioned to speak a bit mulishly in light of his doubts on the matter, but the angel spoke to stem the tide of that unwelcome enmity. "Though it will all seem so very strange for a time, and while it will be difficult for you to walk this path as you begin, know that you were created to travel down this high and oftentimes difficult road. Nevertheless, you will learn the steps as naturally as a newborn child learns to take in the air at the moment of its birth."

Ronan looked around with a watchful eye to be certain he was not being played the fool by someone nearby, and then asked, "What have you done with the rider of the pale horse?"

The angel responded calmly, "You are the rider of the pale horse, my child. You have simply refused to do anything other than what the false king of men has commanded of you up until this very moment."

From the depths of his confusion, Ronan responded, "I don't understand. Certainly, it was not me who rode off with those unfortunate souls each day!"

The angel appeared in all of its glory and placed a comforting hand upon Ronan's shoulder before saying, "No, you did not mean to do such a thing, but each day that you did not answer our Father's call was a day that none were able to advocate for those among the innocent in the face of that fallen presence."

Ronan shook his head defiantly and said, "No, there was a man that rode upon this horse before me. What have you done with him?"

To which the angel replied soothingly, "Wickedness is but a mirage, my child. It is nothing but the tireless work of the devil, who coaxes God's children like a busy bee to turn away from their Creator. As a result, by denying your calling, you unknowingly surrendered one of the sleeping multitudes to the dominion of the wicked man looking down from his podium. But fear not, my precious child. God is in charge, and He makes things right for those who sincerely ask Him to. There is nothing to fear but a lack of vigilance to the call of the Almighty."

There was silence for a moment, and then the angel said, "Doubt not, my child. Our Lord and Savior, Jesus the King, is about to sound the mighty trumpet that will begin to awaken his people in earnest. You must remain awake, and you must remain vigilant too. By morning, those that remain in this place will be those that have given their souls over to the dark angels. You cannot linger here."

"How will I find this man?" asked Ronan, with a slight air of desperation tainting his words.

The angel looked up to the heavens as if questioning the decision that had come from on high regarding Mr. Cassidy, and said, "Your horse is sound. She will carry you until you reach the man that you seek. You will know him by his searing blue eyes that are touched by God, yet remain harnessed by the devil from time to time. This man is awake now, but his once gentle heart remains bound by the sins of his past. He is aware that you are looking for him. He has seen you out of time by the ancient oak that stands sentinel over a field in the Carolinas."

Ronan turned his head for a moment and asked, "Should I fear this man who is still prone to such devilry?"

The angel smiled warmly, yet somewhat speciously, given that she was about to deliver some unwelcome news. Upon future consideration, the look reminded Ronan of a boxer's manager excitedly sending her charge into the ring against a seemingly insuperable foe. Perhaps the endearing smile was tied to some unwavering faith in God above and not Ronan's estimable fate upon engaging with a ravening madman. "He does not know it presently, but he is still a treacherous man to deal with. That is because the devil's lot pines to bear witness to the fruits of the unmerciful wrath they have seeded into his heart."

The angel paused for a brief moment to allow Mr. Cassidy a bit of time to prepare for the words she would speak next. When Ronan's eyes were wide with both anticipation and fear, she delivered the last of her message of great hope and necessary courage, and sent that heavenly dispatch through the tightly bound eye of the needle of blind faith. "The man you seek is also the last person who can protect the children of God's flower by bringing to heel an ancient and wicked sect of worshippers of the false one. Will you graciously accept your duty with the knowledge of all that I have told you, my child?"

Ronan flinched slightly and rolled his head slowly with his eyes directed toward the sky. At that instant, he realized that he had been born to do what had been asked of him. He then looked over to the slowly marching masses of people heading out of the square to bring in the bountiful harvest of the fields beyond. He did not hesitate in accepting his calling, but did ask, "How is it that I, one woven of such fragile and tender fabric, might do what is asked of me?"

The angel replied with a bit more poise than she had earlier, "The same way that any of us do, my child; through our faith in God alone. If you believe that He has called you for a reason, then you need nothing more. You require nothing more than your faith in the goodness and perfection of our loving God. Who but God might transform the weakness of his most humble child into a strength capable of waylaying the armies of the nations?"

Having heard those words reassuringly spoken, Ronan nodded toward the gentle energies of his suddenly unseen companion. Though his faith was only newly born again, he could feel its great strength welling up within him and he could feel its unstoppable nature. He gave the call to his glorious steed, "Take us to find this man, my companion in service to the Almighty." And so the mare and her mount cantered away, having little idea as to where they were going or what they might find along the way.

After Ronan and the white mare had journeyed for six full days and had risen into the morning sun of the seventh day, they came upon a beautiful, downward-sloping meadow that was set before a majestic mountain range. They were traveling in a southeasterly direction when they stepped onto that gorgeous field of subtly shifting, knee-high grass. The gleaming summer sun of that morning was almost directly in their eyes. The seed kernels of the westward bending grass that were proximate to their searching eyes were aglow with the haloed amber sheens of the soft sunlight. Only after the pale horse had stepped a short way through the field beyond the well-worn trail of the high brush did Ronan notice the colossal oak standing boldly on its own at the eastern end of the awe-inspiring clearing. He immediately sought to take his rest under the shade of the sidelong stretching branches of that tree. Nothing appealed to him more.

As the horse and rider approached the ancient giant from a distance of about one hundred yards, Ronan noticed a small boy covered in blood who was being led into the forest after passing beyond the exposed roots at the base of the oak. There was an angelic figure guiding the child by the hand. One that was unmistakably supernal in its luminescence but also oddly marred by smears of almost childishly drawn black chalk. Upon noticing the boy and his heavenly escort, Ronan urged the pale horse forward toward the tree at a rapid gait. When the forcefully blowing steed was within just a few rods of the strange pair, the angel raised a flaming sword to warn Ronan and the mare to halt their progress. While ascending beyond the charcoal lines that had stained her garb, the angel called to the heavens with a resplendent voice. "Is this the one you have chosen, Lord?"

The thundering response from the heavens on that clear morning was, "He is the one. Do you not see that he rides the pale horse?"

The angelic figure then bowed her head while hovering above the ground and replied, "I do indeed see such a wonder, my Lord! All shall be as You have commanded!"

The angel looked down at the boy who was flailing wildly and said, "You have nothing to fear from these. Calm yourself, my child, and scatter that dagger before you pay the price of your soul."

The boy was trembling mightily and let go of the leaden handle of the dagger such that its tip dug into the soft shaded earth beneath the outermost limbs of the tree. The boy then looked up at the angel and asked, "How will I survive that thicket of cutting bramble, the forest beyond, and the demons within without her knife?"

To which the angel responded, "The voice you just heard from above is both your blade and your shield."

The nine-foot-tall angel, shining in white and outlined in black, then said, "Know this man who sits upon the pale horse. You must understand that his actions will be designed to save you from the hostile refuge before us, even if you must remain hidden inside for a time. There are four that seek your soul. You will vanquish the first three. However, the fourth will beguile you with an innocence that is sacred to your heart. That one will only be turned from the darkness by the honor of your love or vanquished due to her covetous and unmerciful heart by the Light of God."

The boy turned from the angel and walked out from beneath the shade of the tree until he was standing defiantly before Ronan and the pale horse. The boy then shook his fist at the sky and said, "I am a curse upon you! Why should I believe that you are the one to deliver me from the torments of those demons and devils?"

Ronan was confused by the boy's words but mesmerized by his trenchant blue eyes. He would never, not even in the passing of two lifetimes, forget those eyes while awake or while once again dreaming. There was an amulet, crafted of gold perhaps, that rested in the hollow of the boy's gaunt chest. The medallion was shining so brightly in the low summer sun that Ronan could not make out the true color or shape of the object. The pale horse neighed and blew out a final time in response to the swift gallop across the meadow and down to the outskirts of the oak. Ronan continued to think about the trembling boy's question while his mare settled. He then spoke gently to the knobby-kneed creature stained in blood. "I do not know what has been set upon you, little boy, but the answer you seek is plain enough. I will always do what God commands me to do."

At that moment, the light burning from the heart of the amulet struck Ronan directly in the eyes, and he was rendered blind to all else. He shifted his head awkwardly to divert the angle of that piercing light, but such endeavors were an exercise in futility. He remained blinded by that brilliant streak of light while the angel moved the thicket's gating branches aside, allowing the child to enter the outer realms of the forest's savage and cutting underbrush. Before the boy ducked into the coppice, he called out, "Look behind you, man! Those that approach are the ones who besiege me! As it has been written, hell surely follows with them!"

With those words spoken, the boy darted forward and was quickly out of sight. The angel who had been charged with his care, who was an entity of such heavenly perfection and Amazonian height, seemed to ascend toward the clouds as some translucent form that did little more than distort the texture of the endless sky. Ronan frantically turned around upon losing sight of the boy and saw the four riders on horses of differing colors. The grass beneath the hooves of those steadfast animals was burning as they approached the pale horse and its rider from the top of the grove. The crust of the earth they had passed beyond became parched and cracked in their wake.

With that troubling scene passing through the restive mind of Mr. Cassidy, the clarion call of the stewardess came over the plane's loudspeaker and gave notice to the passengers that the plane would soon be preparing to land. Ronan awoke with a start and remained disoriented and bemused for a moment while his mind shifted back to acknowledging the trimmings of the temporal world. He looked out the window to gather his bearings and reconfigure his wits in accordance with the shifting reality before his hazy eyes. The earth below was brown and barren, and the events of his strange and vivid dream were still traceable within the projecting constructs of his transitioning thoughts. He remained captive to both worlds for just a short while longer.

Though he was perplexed by what he remembered of that vision, Ronan was rather heartened by the little-understood prospects of such an occurrence. He knew that a message had been delivered. Mr. Cassidy then turned his head away from the window and closed his eyes to think some more and to rest just a bit longer. The days gone by had been trying up until the flash of his reclamation. When his eyes were closed, he saw nothing but the piercing blue irises of the ragged yet defiant little boy from his dream. Those longing eyes and their attendant pleas for mercy remained burning bright and indelible in the depths of Ronan Cassidy's soul. They remained that way until the wheels of the plane colliding with the immovable asphalt of the tarmac shook him from the delicate veil of his delusive ruminations, which were given against the twinkling of the dusk of the eventide. He was nearly home.

Chapter 9

FIRST IMPRESSIONS

Mr. Cassidy was sleeping soundly aboard the plane subsequent to his troubles arriving at the airport under the care of his woefully, though not catastrophically, negligent driver. The day was some fourteen months in the offing from his stirring vision of the pale horse, and nearly three years prior to those revelations of his reverie concerning a dark man and an ancient cross of gold. Twenty minutes had passed by in the blink of an eye since the plane's departure from the tarmac at O'Hare International Airport and wheels up. At precisely 6:45 AM on that morning of April 11th, 2017, the attendant bell rang with two flat but melodious chimes. Shortly thereafter, a woman with an almost modulated sound to her voice announced that the flight had reached its cruising altitude and that it was now safe to move about the cabin.

Since he was seated in the aisle on the left side of the southbound aircraft next to a strange yet exceptionally polished man, one who commanded the respect of diligent adherence to proper posture and appropriate spatial management in such a setting, Mr. Cassidy awoke for the second time that morning with a stiff neck and eyes that were exposed to the direct light of the rising sun. The morning shine of that celestial orb was making its way over the eastern horizon and piercing through the small commercial aircraft window of their row, which also happened to be the only exposed aperture on the plane, as its shade was drawn only slightly. The low and parallel light was immature yet lurid, and severe upon Ronan's slowly opening eyes. To offset the pangs of that initial discomfort, the same luminescence delivered a welcome warmth and a timeless golden glow to the lingering stillness and unbroken serenity within the confines of the smoothly traveling aircraft cabin that existed beyond the proximate area of that uncovered portal to the outside world.

Once he regained his focus and developed an awareness of his surroundings following his short yet sound repose, Ronan took notice of the tiny fiber particles that were alight and lively while dancing in the air on sheets of translucent amber in the space between his resting head and the seat back directly in front of him. For the brief time he was engrossed in that mystical interlude that existed between realms, the world below and all of its complexities seemed quite nonsensical. The space before his correcting eyes remained fixed in time by that low angular light, the comforting tepidity of the air, and the concentration of his senses on that focal proximity—a place with galaxies of dancing constituents suspended in those rapidly mellowing yet richly teeming rays of the first light.

Ronan remained a bit disoriented and slightly out of sync with time while he took in the tranquility of that strangely captivating display before his tired eyes. He confused that morning's flight with the countless other sunrise flights he used to take for work. Those journeys were also of a purely commercial nature and often departed at the same time and from the same place, though the circumstances of his life had been entirely transformed since those years following his move to the South back in 2013. Slowly, his thoughts drifted back to Maddie and the book they fell asleep reading on the night prior to just such a flight some four years ago.

In the tale, a dwarfish creature who lived alone, unloved, and outcast was hiding away in a marvelous castle. Because that creature resented the world so, he built a monstrous machine capable of stealing the dreams of children while they slept. After the gnomish being absconds into the night while in possession of those fanciful dreams, he stores them in glass vacuum tubes and lines them on countless shelves in his magical but otherwise empty castle. Maddie loved the book because the concept of dreams, and being able to contain them, was wonderfully enchanting to her. Maddie and Ronan's favorite part of the fairytale was when the main character undergoes a change of heart and not only returns the dreams he has stolen from each child, but also uses his dream-catching machine to take away their nightmares. "If only such a machine truly existed," thought Ronan while he remained immersed in the magical glow of that captivating light.

While in the midst of that calming rumination, Ronan felt a decidedly unwelcome tap on his shoulder. He turned to his left to confirm the reality of this surprising gesture, which had slightly startled him, and struggled to make out the features of the man seated next to him while he stared into the direct light of the sun still beaming in through the window. The man gazed back at Ronan with what appeared to be a staid look resting upon his calm and frightfully undeclared visage. Without removing his eyes from his quarry, he took his Economist magazine from his lap and placed it face up on the open window seat while he spoke. "Pardon me for the rather crude method of attracting your attention, Mr. Cassidy, but I require a few minutes of your time this morning."

The man spoke in a low and even tone as he studied Ronan with what appeared to be sharpening features, especially at the corners of his eyes and mouth, though his overall expression remained unthreatening. Mr. Cassidy was still gathering his mental wares following his rather brief yet uncommonly intense nap. Nevertheless, he was aware enough of his surroundings to be immediately taken aback by the fact that this strange man knew his name. Prior to takeoff, Ronan had guessed that the man was of some import based upon his observations of his neighbor's wardrobe and mannerisms, and that presumption added a measure of confusion to the surprise of being called by name by a stranger. A look of bemusement ran across Ronan's face as he considered the notions flashing before his suddenly trenchant mind. He wondered exactly who this man, still so abjectly foreign to him, could be. Moreover, Mr. Cassidy wondered how he might respond to such an unexpected request.

"Had the flight attendant spoken my name while I slept?" wondered Ronan silently. He then asked more questions without speaking as he stared back at the man in the seat next to him while trying to frame up a suitable course of action. "Is this someone who has an inside track on a recent or past business endeavor? Has one of my coworkers who likes to live a bit on the edge finally gone down for insider trading? Why is this strangely contrived man here? What does he want from me?" Lastly, Ronan whispered into the fearful depths of his shaken mind, "Am I in danger?"

The man instantly took hold of the pause that occurred while Ronan's mind raced off on those doleful tangents. He did so just as those trepidations had settled on the consideration that would perfectly serve this purpose-driven man's primary objective. "I'm quite sorry to startle you, Mr. Cassidy. I represent …"

The man paused for a second while the glare of the sun kept Mr. Cassidy from zeroing in on his neatly focused blue eyes, and then connected his opening thought. "…Oh, let's just say that I represent the interests of a very old and powerful family. The roots of a few of the more nefarious members date back to some treachery that occurred in the early 1300's, or perhaps even beyond the bounds of time, depending on who and what you choose to believe. Regardless, those of their progeny are involved with, and hold dominion over, several prominent American enterprises and people of significant influence."

The man's initial intention was to wake Ronan up a little bit, make him aware of the true nature of the types of people he was dealing with as part and parcel of his fairly nascent professional endeavors. The man knew the names of each person Ronan had met with while he was in Chicago. He also knew the reason for the meeting, though he did not alert Ronan to those material particulars.

At hearing the rather direct, unexpected, and somewhat startling words of the man, which were delivered under completely unsolicited circumstances, and with his attention now fully devoted to learning much more about his curious neighbor, Ronan responded resolutely enough. There was, however, no mistaking the fact that Mr. Cassidy was more than a bit taken aback. "Good morning to you, Sir. Your artful tact is certainly one way to greet a stranger. There is much to consider in your words, even with so few details being given as to how such a direct approach might be possible in this instance. Before you say anything further, and believe me, I am brimming with curiosity, please do tell me how it is that you have come to know my name."

Ronan was still of the misguided belief that there had been some tell that had revealed his identity. He figured that there had to be a detail that remained unaccounted for, or a prior discussion that the man next to him had overheard, which had allowed his rather cozy neighbor to learn his name, or at least his last name. The man responded openly to the request. "Ronan, you are well known to me and the people I represent. Perhaps not yet directly, as one swallow does not a summer make. However, the people I represent know you in the very real sense that all you hold dear has been revealed to them. They are serious people, Ronan, and they are looking for a reason to trust you."

The man paused for a moment and looked away from Ronan. He glanced into the beautiful warmth of the light shining in through the window to his left. When he was satisfied that Mr. Cassidy had been given enough time to digest what he had told him, the man spoke again in an almost casual and even tone. "Now, I do apologize for calling you by your given name without the formality of an introduction, and more so for startling you, as it were, Mr. Cassidy."

"Think nothing of it," responded Ronan in an offhand manner, which almost disguised his bewilderment and a full-on onset of the crumbles. One that was taking hold deep within him and already mildly shaking the foundations of his equilibrium. Mr. Cassidy then sat upright in his seat and added emphatically, "You certainly have my unwavering attention now, good Sir. Even though you remain nameless."

Ronan peered around the cabin slowly and carefully, checking for other anomalies that might reveal something of use to him. He looked off in the manner of only slightly changing the position of his drifting eyes without altering the straightforward presentation of his chin. While he peered to his right and away from the man, he noticed nothing odd or of substantial enough effect to assist him with sizing up the true nature of his surroundings, or better yet, to help confirm the shocking realities of his present circumstances.

"Yes, Mr. Cassidy," the man continued, as if nothing out of the ordinary had been spoken between them. "Your attention and your understanding are what I require for the benefit of all parties impacted by our currently unfortunate but hopefully promising union. Fate has dealt you the short straw, and we have only the time that has been set aside during this flight. While the matters I need to discuss with you are not exhaustive in their content, absolute clarity regarding your understanding of those items is essential to your well-being."

Ronan swallowed hard in response to the not so thinly veiled threat. "I understand your meaning, rather clearly," he replied while turning to endure the glare of the sunlight and direct the essence of his tremoring gaze into the shifting seas of the man's blue eyes.

"Please continue, my friend," added Ronan, while fretting over having so little to his advantage in terms of establishing a level playing field for the remainder of their discourse. In the end, there was little for Ronan to do but hear the man out, absent running down the aisle and shouting, "Fire!" He saw no benefit in resorting to the latter measure. At least not yet.

The man prepared to speak but allowed Ronan to continue with his response, though Mr. Cassidy's voice nearly cracked as he uttered the last of his shamefully unorganized and nearly pointless banter, which was nothing but a cover for his abject feelings of vulnerability. "In regard to time, I can assure you that we have at least an hour until our flight touches down in Alabama."

"Indeed, Mr. Cassidy," returned the man almost coldly, as if Ronan's observation had no bearing on the actual constraints set upon his future ambitions. "That would be true in the normal course of affairs. Yet, for security reasons, I have only made plans to travel to and from O'Hare this morning. As you may understand, I do not appreciate the exposure that accompanies these unfortunate errands tied to mischance."

Ronan was now entirely perplexed, in addition to startled. He was also thankful that he was flying on a crowded plane. He responded to the man as one gripped by a state of disbelief over this unexpected turn of events, while he let the phrase "for security reasons" simmer in the already boiling cauldron of his befuddled and anxious thoughts. "Well, my nameless friend, that will be some trick, now won't it."

The man allowed a brief smirk, which included a slight and sneaky protrusion of his bottom lip, to convey that, within the confines of Mr. Cassidy's current worldview, such an assumption would be correct. That would most certainly be some trick. Nevertheless, he left the means to achieve that end of his stated terminus to Mr. Cassidy's imagination or problem-solving acumen. Whichever of the two options served the stunned gentleman best was fine by the man.

He thought to speak again, but decided against saying anything further at that moment. He could see that Mr. Cassidy was already deeply unsettled. Instead of commenting in response to Ronan's insinuation concerning the impossibility of his future plans, the man directed his hand toward the overhead console. When his arm was nearly fully raised, he extended his index and pointer fingers and firmly pressed the call attendant button. Once the button was pushed, a fairly loud electronic ding was released into the cabin. Ronan watched carefully to see what the stewardess standing in the aisle just a few rows ahead of him and her caller would do.

The busy and cheerful-looking flight attendant definitely heard the rich, lilting tone of the notification. Strangely enough, she did not approach or even look the short distance over to the row where the two curious middle-aged men sat watching her for a response. The attendant did, however, straighten up promptly after delivering a drink to a passenger in the first-class cabin, turn toward the front of the plane, and walk to the door of the cockpit. Ronan found it a bit odd that while the dutiful woman did seem to react to the call chime, her response was nearly the exact opposite of what he would have expected. For his turn, the man seemed to be following the activities of the flight attendant as if all were precisely as it should be, though he did appear to expect something further from her, judging by the way his neck craned so that his eyes could continue to follow her progress.

When the stewardess was just a step shy of the cabin door, which was secured by an assembly of additional locks and restraints that were added to all commercial aircraft following the infamous hijackings of September 11, 2001, she turned and seemed to knowingly direct a confirming wink and a nod in the direction of the man seated next to Ronan. After completing this peculiar and almost inexplicable gesture, she turned promptly and knocked at the door three times. The attendant delivered the knock on the door very casually. She effortlessly swung her hand sideways and struck the locked portal with three loose, yet adequately audible, and equivalent in tempo and veracity, taps of the top knuckles of her right index and pointer fingers.

The knocks further perplexed Ronan, and, for some reason unbeknownst to him, also agitated him severely. Ronan felt as if the entire world was suddenly conspiring against him. He felt as if some unholy specter was now working to halt his determined advance away from the void of that life-altering journey into the depths of hopelessness, which ended just fourteen months prior to that morning. That void had nearly consumed him, and his extrication from within was entirely dependent upon the grace of God. Moreover, Ronan did not yet understand why, but at the time the attendant knocked on the cockpit door, he was feeling cornered by an unknown, though entirely credible, presence.

The instigation of the man's highly aberrant, unprovoked, and unwelcome engagement had produced a forceful emotional yaw within Mr. Cassidy. For some reason, that heretofore dormant condition was triggered by that carefree knock of the stewardess. His obsessive and, in some instances, manic attention to detail had caused him to recognize that her actions were wholly premeditated and, therefore, tied to the wishes of the odd gentleman seated next to him. That his neighbor was odd only in as much as his appearance was spectacularly nondescript had started the snowball rolling down the hill in Ronan's mind some time ago. At that moment, he had reached a point where further disorientation was impossible within the confines of even the rudderless human mind.

When he glanced back at the man to his left, that man of suddenly pronounced dominion and serious intent, to study his reaction to the events unfolding at the front of the plane, Mr. Cassidy's racing mind began to dart madly between the constructs of the ephemeral realms and the expectations of the common man. Not much time passed before Ronan lost hold of his rational attachment to the workings of any reality tethered to the prior confirmations of his past experiences. The world as he understood it then simply could not be configured to entertain the curious circumstances of his present reality without a seismic realignment of his core beliefs.

Suddenly, Ronan could feel that he was moving at an ungodly rate of speed, high above the earth. He began to float and felt almost as if he were racing through the clouds of his own volition. Shortly thereafter, everything began to spin uncontrollably as his equilibrium snapped free from the fetter of its anchor. Ronan's ears began to feel as if they were filling with water, and he began to suffocate because the cool air was thin, dry, and empty, no matter how voraciously he sucked it into his stammering lungs. His already uneasy paunch became overwhelmed by the immense pressure of some gathering force as he lost all perception of gravity. Spinning faster and faster and losing touch with his senses designed to navigate the physical world, a savage and instinctual panic quickly overran the delicate cohesion of Mr. Cassidy's capacity for rational thought.

Once he was overwhelmed by the rapid movement of the plane, a sensation that he had barely detected just a minute ago, and the crippling onset of an all-consuming bout of vertigo, Ronan Cassidy retched so violently that the horrifying sound of the failed expulsion could easily be heard by the attendant still standing before the cockpit door. In response to Mr. Cassidy's woeful convulsion, the man finally slid into the window seat in an effort to remain out of harm's way. Ronan continued retching until the small dose of orange juice he had consumed from the hotel minibar began to flow copiously from his throat, in addition to about a half-pint of bile. The residual fluid was thick and milky and spewed forth from his open and trembling mouth in the form of a congealed and mucilaginous wave. The discharge erupted like the bursting of a dam onto Ronan's powder blue shirt and oozed its way downward until the rank concoction fell in syrupy riffles and strings onto his pleated work khakis. The event was not a sight suitable for the weak or the queasy. Thankfully, none of the sleeping passengers aboard the aircraft were stirred to the point of waking.

The flight attendant, having heard the vicious and rather sonorous discharge of nothing but air, and then seeing the disturbing twitching of the whites of Ronan's eyes that followed, grabbed a towel from the front service area of the plane and made her way down the aisle to the seventh row. Ronan tilted his head back, and it bobbled slowly to and fro, as if his cranium were rhythmically waxing and waning upon a swivel. Seeing the ceiling of the plane come into view, Ronan's disorientation waned. He soon regained his feeling for the seat beneath him. He then felt his feet planted firmly on the floor of the plane while the last of the vertigo subsided.

When he returned to his senses, Ronan could hear the flight attendant's voice when she asked him, "Are you going to be okay, Sir?" but her words were perceived as only garbled and incoherent echoes.

In attempting to muster a response to what he presumed her question to be, Ronan gasped like he did at the moment of his birth and continued to inhale deeply and desperately while struggling to resuscitate his deadened lungs. He then reached forward with his right hand and grabbed the towel she held out for him. He took hold of the standard issue linen in an agitated and assertive manner, and he reminded the man of a boxer who had been smartly stung by an opponent's jab while grabbing at a similar offering made by his trainer upon returning to his corner. The stewardess that handed Mr. Cassidy the towel appeared unnaturally calm and entirely unfazed by his somewhat aggressive tactics. In fact, she seemed to be entirely disinterested in the altogether dreadful episode.

As if Ronan had been awoken from an awful dream, albeit one that was set to continue for some time, he slowly began to grasp the state of affairs his mind and body had so rudely attempted to vacate while his surroundings came back into proper focus. His first order of business was to wipe his shirt and pants thoroughly with the towel. He scrubbed them to the point that just the darkened discoloration of the saturated bile remained to stain his once impeccably maintained shirt and crisply pressed pants. The attendant, who had stepped away to retrieve a small garbage bag and politely leave Mr. Cassidy to his own devices while he tidied up his ensemble, promptly returned. Ronan confirmed that he was finished with the towel by handing it off somewhat blindly in the general direction of the calm and deliberate woman. The attendant made no overt gesture in response to his callous dispatch of the towel. She simply took hold of an unblemished corner of the soiled rag and dropped it into the airplane rubbish bag.

Ronan straightened up and assured the flight attendant that he was quite alright. "Yes ma'am," he replied, while holding to the assumption that she had asked about his current condition. "Must have been a brief spell brought on by a lack of sleep and a bad bite to eat is all," he confided to the unsettlingly sterile woman leaning towards him to speak quietly and keep from waking any of the surrounding passengers.

When Ronan looked upwards at her right then, she appeared to him to be almost faceless, inhuman, and without feeling. She seemed as if she were wearing a flesh-toned mask designed to conceal her very humanity. In any event, the cold yet handsome woman nodded professionally and without emotion in response to Ronan's assurances. She then went back to the front of the plane to neutralize the pungent odor emanating from the garbage bag and retrieve a clean towel for her ailing passenger. With the preponderance of the emergency passed, Mr. Cassidy sat back in his chair, exhaled deeply, and contemplated the man seated next to him once again. At that moment, he looked upon the charmingly staid gentleman in an entirely new light.

While Ronan continued to recover from his sudden episode, the two men sat there for a brief while, with neither venturing to blatantly look in the direction of their neighbor. They kept their necessary observations clandestine, and they were accomplished through the sidelong shifting of their eyes. The flight announcement speakers rang yet again with the same two steady chimes as before, and foretold of an announcement soon to come. Shortly thereafter, the pilot's voice came over the loudspeaker and broke the awkward silence persisting between the two gentlemen seated in the seventh row. Although the voice of the captain was roughly muffled and slightly masked by the low reverberating sounds of the plane's engines, which had leveled up to gradually change the direction of the aircraft, the words he conveyed over the intercom were still readily discernable to the few that were awake.

The captain released the news as if he were reading from a script that may have been slightly altered. "Ladies and gentlemen, I regret to inform you that we have encountered a mechanical issue that will not allow us to land in Birmingham."

Hollow groans and remarks of disapproval welled up from the few passengers seated in the back who had awoken. Deafened to those unsettling disturbances, the captain continued with his startling announcement as if everything he was saying was nothing more than a common setback. "We will be turning around and landing at Chicago O'Hare. There is no threat to your safety. The service crew has the part we require back in Chicago. On behalf of our flight crew and the entire team at Union Airways, I apologize for any inconvenience that this unfortunate but necessary change to our itinerary will cause you. Our folks on the ground are working on alternative flight plans for you all as I speak, and we will have someone waiting for you at the gate to discuss revised travel options. Again, we sincerely apologize for any inconvenience this change will cause you and appreciate your flying with us here at Union. We should be back on the ground in Chicago in forty-five minutes."

"I certainly hope it's not an important part," Ronan mused silently. He then closed his eyes slowly, lowered his head slightly, and folded his hands in his lap on top of the clean towel given to him by the attendant during the announcement.

Mr. Cassidy did not fully realize it yet, but he had already retreated a long way. He had retreated to the point of accepting a far darker reality for his circumstances based on the known data points of his current predicament. He began searching his thoughts for a reason, or perhaps some logical connection between his current station in life and this bad dream. This nightmare that was unfolding before his eyes, which was seemingly choreographed and directed by the man seated next to him. Though that man was masked by the ensemble of a dignified emissary of reputable business prospects, he certainly seemed capable of wielding the worst of the devil's witchery.

A few ideas ran through Ronan's spent mind. Yet, upon realizing the futility of attaining any sensible perspective regarding the entirely bizarre situation of his own accord, he sat recumbent in spirit and limp throughout his limbs. With little else to do, he looked straight ahead and remained perfectly still while he waited for the man to reveal more. After a short moment of respite, his neighbor obliged.

"Shall I begin, Mr. Cassidy?" the man asked. He delivered his question with no preconceived notion of receiving an objection from his "guest."

"Please do, my friend," Ronan said, reaching shallowly for the only rebuttal he thought was available. Yet, perhaps his dull words were the embodiment of the only response he wished to offer that might remove any opportunity for further conjecture and, moreover, force the man to state his intentions while he borrowed a moment to fully regather his intellectual capacities.

Then, for no reason that he could fathom, Mr. Cassidy refused to leave well enough alone and surprised the both of them by adding bluntly, "Please, Sir, do call me Ronan."

"Yes, of course, Mr. Cassidy," the man answered straight away, and true to his enigmatic fashion. He then paused for a moment to reflect on whether or not he would honor that request moving forward.

After further consideration of Ronan's request for little more than a simple courtesy to be given to someone wedged into an unfortunate predicament, which, in truth, was all that the appeal was, the man quickly shifted the immediate focus of his continuing response by interjecting with, "I do apologize for that level of escalation, Ronan. That was unkind. However, you must understand that I hadn't planned on being bound by any courtesies that extend beyond the due course of the professional matters that need to be addressed."

Ronan was struck nearly limp by the fearful feelings that follow being browbeaten like a wounded dog. Yet, his anger caused him to break free from the refined protocol of the engagement up to that point. He sounded as if he were lashing out in vain against the deplorable state of his helplessness, and his profanity was entirely unbecoming. "The fuck you do, Sir!"

"Indeed, Ronan, but such pleasantries are unfortunate requirements of the trade. Disarming displays of control and adhering to proper manners will suffice in regard to my intentions here today. I do believe that your unfortunate episode would have been far more severe had I simply told you what I have been up to these last six years." The man said these things while taking no offense to Mr. Cassidy's crude outburst. In fact, the richly experienced dignitary of a sort expected as much.

As Mr. Cassidy's charming guise had drawn starkly blank, the man simply continued on in an almost monotone voice. "Those unfortunate things are akin to punching a man in the gut while you are staring into his eyes. If you have not experienced the pleasure of as much, you should know that the blow weakens a man and knocks him off balance. More importantly, it also raises his level of attentiveness and his ability to give proper consideration to matters that are a few orders of magnitude more severe than our typical day-to-day concerns."

Although the whole front third of the plane was populated with company men and women with some type of corporate security clearance, those useful "volunteers" on their way to a conference that would never take place hadn't been told much. Ronan would certainly have complicated matters for that man of rather dubious and duplicitous intent if he had gone completely off the rails. In response to that risk, the man had meticulously done his homework regarding Mr. Cassidy. He did not believe that Ronan would behave in such a childish manner, even though he was not used to that level of peril. The man sensed that he had delivered a blow of appropriate force with the stick, as it were, and he believed that all would be manageable with just a small taste of the carrot soon to come.

In accordance with the aforementioned, when the man spoke to Ronan once more, he did so without darkening his tone or demeanor in an effort to set the stage to deliver that carrot and make the affair much more cordial and measured going forward. "You see, Ronan, there are only three types of beings that truly belong to the dark mirage of this misshapen world: the rich; the poor who covet; and the demons. In the far more expansive reality that includes those places where the spirit and the soul dwell, there are the good; there are the wicked; and there is God above all else. Since our matters at hand concern the realities of this temporal mirage of the fallen and dismal world that has been blanketed over our eyes, let us consider those among the rich and poor who are not demons and, therefore, continue to struggle with the righteous burdens of God."

Ronan was not yet completely following the man's curiously divergent yet captivating line of thought. Nevertheless, he warmly welcomed the change of pace and nodded to the man to continue on with his present designs. The man obliged, and did press on with a slight air of enthusiasm, at least as far as his formal, tightly guarded, and very particular mannerisms were concerned. "For the rich, their burdens are those of a guilty spirit. They are continually justifying their gains while they are, at the same time, called to steward the resources of this world and satisfy the needs of the lost and those of insufficient means. For the poor, their burden is their requirement to deal with the harsh realities of a life without the earthly blessings of the rich. Or so we are led to believe."

The man paused and looked over at Ronan, who returned the casual glance with a questioning look. While following Ronan's eyes, the man spoke further. "I know that I said we should not consider the demons just yet, but let us do that in the event you are uncertain as to the existence of such presumably mythical entities. The burden of the demons is their unwilling accession to the ultimate authority of God and the curse of only being able to experience the immediate pleasures of the flesh or the darkened soul. That is why they lust after things in ways that a good man cannot fathom."

Ronan nodded again as his once quizzical mien drifted downward until it revealed feelings that were approaching outright concern. He then asked of the man with an almost childlike innocence, "Are you of the opinion that these demons are indeed real?"

The man closed his eyes and replied solemnly. "Looking into your eyes, Mr. Cassidy, I am able to discern that you know the truthful answer to your question. Be that as it may, let me add to what you do know by saying that these demons are so real that when their deeds are brought into the fullness of the light, your episode of a moment ago will seem to have passed as if it were little more than a walk in the park on a pleasant spring day."

Ronan's mouth went agape, and his eyes grew wide. He nodded again in reply, but said not a word. The man turned toward the window and looked out upon the rich and uninterrupted blue sky that was visible due to the fact that the angle of the sun was less severe. He spoke while he became entranced by the beauty of that April morning sky, which was bound by nothing but the horizon. "Let us not veer too far off course, Ronan. As you have heard me say, our time together runs short and there is much to discuss."

Ronan nodded curtly and answered simply by saying, "Of course. I am eager to learn what has brought about this unexpected encounter."

The man returned to the point of his message, which had been his initial focus. "Of the rich in this world of bastardized money and wealth, there are those with gold and those without. Though I cannot give you an exact date, the time draws near when that fact will become brutally apparent. Of the poor, some are lost and defile their brethren to obtain what they need or want, and others are quite happy with the graces and divine provisions of the righteous providence of God. Of the demons, some adhere to the devil's commands on earth, while the rest do little more than suffer the eternal torments of the scourges of hell. For the fallen among those I have mentioned, the idolatry of the rich is vanity. Therefore, they perceive wealth as a right of birth meant to glorify their image instead of a gift attached to the responsibilities of God. The idol of the poor is earthly wealth because it feeds their own meagerly provisioned vanity and makes them covetous above all else. The idol of the demons is the one who fell to earth from the heavens."

Ronan gave careful consideration to what the man had said. His words were broad in scope and apt to be considered somewhat stereotypical in a general sense, yet Ronan believed those words carried the weight of truth on varying levels. Many questions began to arise and drift across the cascading inflections of Mr. Cassidy's mind. He was not, however, in any position to press the man for additional clarity or prod him for the reasons he believed those simple yet richly layered tenets were to be known as the truth. Furthermore, Ronan dared not ask why the man was focused on the importance of these rather general human verities or how they related to his situation as he sat there before the man upon the instant. No, he was not prepared to untrack or even sidetrack the progression of the man's carefully couched thoughts. Therefore, Mr. Cassidy responded quite innoxiously by asking, "And what manner of man are you, my friend?"

The man closed his eyes and kept them closed while he considered Ronan's question and prepared to respond. He possessed the gentle look of someone meditating on a difficult reality as he faced forward, straightened up his posture a bit, and added a bit of depth to his breathing. The man then gently interlocked the ends of his fingers just above his lap and finished the soothing motion by straightening out his thumbs and index fingers until the opposing tips of each were connected in the formation of a slightly downward-facing triangle. When his forearms and hands were completely at rest, he answered Ronan in a straightforward manner and without altering his heretofore dispassionate and pragmatic tone. The man's eyes did not open, and he did not turn his head to face Ronan while he spoke. However, he did not answer the question altogether truthfully, though the slightly altered version of his current status among the living was given for effect at that crucial juncture of their discussion.

Just the same, when taken under the purview of what the judgments of most would have been if the entire body of his life's work and other deeds had been revealed to any critical being assigned with the task of properly labeling him, the man did not altogether lie either. He said, "I am now a servant to the demon class, and one who hopes that what I have told you is true. My only wish is that, in time, I will truly perish from this earth and all other realms that may be inhabitable by my hopelessly darkened soul. In this coming age of great wrath to be served upon the wicked, I now search for my pound of flesh from those who made me what I am, but I follow my commands so as not to attract undesirable attention. I follow my commands precisely. I follow them without question or hesitation. Lastly, dear Ronan, I execute those commands with faultless precision and exacting diligence."

While Ronan managed to keep some measure of his poise after the man had finished speaking, he was becoming frightfully careworn. His determinations were again fraying so rapidly that he did not know which fibers of his cord to this shifting world were still connected or what the remaining bounds of their resiliency were. He watched the man as his neighbor breathed quietly and motionless for a moment while he attempted to gather his withering proclivities. Ronan could not understand how this man, or perhaps demon, though the man did not yet appear to Ronan as such, rested so calmly, as if nothing were capable of altering his dismal intentions of the hour. The calm and stillness with which the man cloaked the lethal venom of his tongue was a trait the likes of which Mr. Cassidy had never come close to witnessing throughout his moderately tenured life.

"That is truly pitiable and most unfortunate," Ronan gasped, a bit more impetuously than he had intended. In spite of the better attributes of his compassionate character, he even took a small sliver of vindictive contentment from the man's circumstances, given his own tender condition. Nevertheless, Ronan did attempt to keep the fire of his core spiritual values lit.

Before Ronan could say a word more, the man interjected and quickly put a halt to the small positive bursts of energy that Mr. Cassidy was attempting to gather by continuing to turn his fear and confusion into anger. "Make no endeavor whatsoever regarding my circumstances, dear Ronan. Yet, do make a full determination to grasp the things I tell you now. I cannot properly underscore the importance of your doing as much."

Upon hearing the man reaffirm his solemn intentions, Ronan paused to check the haphazard flush of his cheeks with the palm of his hand. He then closed his eyes and rubbed the bridge of his nose on both sides with a slow downward pinching motion of his thumb and forefinger. When his extended fingers reached the well-defined tip of his nose, Ronan slowly withdrew his hand from his face. That twitchy hand soon came to rest on his upper thigh, which was still covered by the unsoiled towel. The completion of that nearly ritualistic motion had provided Mr. Cassidy with the slightest of cover to repurpose his thoughts. Those small and inconsequential movements were all that remained to shelter him from the oncoming storm. Just as the man had intended when he had that in-flight meeting arranged at the request of one of John Edward Calhoun's top adjutants, a man he had never laid eyes on but one who was rumored to possess eyes of an ominously ruddy hue, there was nowhere for Ronan to hide even his unspoken thoughts; thoughts that were plainly revealed in the depths of his eyes and written broadly across the disquieted contours of his face.

After a brief moment, when Ronan had settled out some, he opened his eyes again. When he did that, his vision was blurry, so he cleared the mild smattering of film that was causing the obstruction by opening his eyes wider and rolling them in a moderately frenetic yet upwardly biased motion. When his focus was clear and he had returned his sightline to the center, Ronan responded to the man's dour remark. "Understood," was all that he uttered in a clear and direct tone. In truth, he possessed no reference point that stemmed from the actual affairs and past experiences of his life to reply otherwise.

Ronan was not entirely certain how to deal with someone admittedly accustomed to dwelling in realms that were veiled by eternal nightfall. He had never known anyone of that man's ilk and, furthermore, lacked the capacity to understand someone who functioned under the joyless paradigm of a world without love, or perhaps a world governed first and foremost by mortal want and depravity. Therefore, Mr. Cassidy was left purely to the devices of his imagination where it concerned trying to fathom who or what this self-described demon still lurking in his human form was, and what mischief he was capable of dispatching.

With those considerations in mind, and knowing so little about the man or the reasons behind his intentions, Ronan dared not cross the exquisitely mannered fiend at that juncture. Furthermore, he was effectively hemmed in while onboard an aircraft that was attended to by a crew who appeared attentive to the wishes of his adversary. Although the man assuredly knew the truth of the matter as it regarded Mr. Cassidy's limited options to respond in an unsavory manner, Ronan did not want the indiscriminate henchman seated next to him to see that his hackles were raised because he was effectively cornered. Those tiny hairs standing on end at the base of his neck were raised in the way that a muddled pup might broadcast ferocity in response to some undefinable fear; for those were the same emotions that were manifesting themselves in that tattletale electric crimp beneath Ronan Cassidy's well-starched collar, though his anger and fear were also readily visible in the heated blood of that ardent blush making its way down his burning cheeks.

The man had positioned Ronan precisely as he desired. Therefore, he continued with his one-sided deliberations before the fear of not knowing set off the wild Irishman lurking somewhere inside Mr. Cassidy, an inner numen certain to be hell-bent on screaming through hills and bringing down some insidious maelstrom from the heavens. Though he had nothing to fear as things were then situated, the man could sense that Ronan's inner beast was finally making its way to the surface. The red-faced yet still pensive and altogether frightened-looking gentleman sitting next to him was not so far removed from doing something entirely irrational.

The man spoke to calm Mr. Cassidy as much as anything else. "Let us further consider the abundantly wealthy, Ronan. Though I know that your typical clients have wealth to protect, when I say abundantly wealthy, I mean those that belong to maybe the top four to five hundred families in the world. Families with proper title to unimaginable possessions and the corresponding capacity to influence the way things work."

The man broke from the hold of his stillness and turned his face toward Mr. Cassidy with the slight yet joyful smile of a friend engaging another to talk through the remarkable and curious moments of the day. "That detail will keep our definition very simplistic and not lead us away from the proper motivations of the people I seek to describe. Since my definition may differ from your standardized industry jargon of high-net-worth client and so forth, does my description make the type of person I am looking to describe clear enough?"

Ronan nodded his head slowly and steadily in reply. He kept his lips pensively pursed after responding to the man's query. At that moment, he possessed the long and wide-eyed gaze of someone whose thoughts had drifted elsewhere. That his lush, dark hair had gone askew in scattered directions across the top of his head did not assist in portraying the look of a thoughtful man who had his "shit" still held together. Regardless, the man did not prod Ronan to deliver a given sign that revealed the certainty of his attention. He continued to speak as if they had reached the more pleasurable side of their gathering aboard the airliner, cruising along at about 500 knots through the clear blue skies while nearing the apex of its rise.

"Those that I represent are from such a family, Mr. Cassidy. Believe it or not, those of the more unsavory bloodlines believe that they acquired the beginnings of their wealth after the fall of Rome. From there, their ancestors amassed an even greater fortune from their contributions to the dispatch and liquidation of a certain knight of the Templar order in the early fourteenth century. To their dismay, that righteous knight left behind a certain relic that dates back to the Crusades. One that continues to haunt those responsible for his demise to this very day. In many ways, that medallion lies at the heart of the conflict you were so carelessly drawn into, but that is a story that must remain idle for another day. That is, assuming everything finishes up orderly between you and I on this fine morning."

When the man spoke of the ancient medallion, Ronan finally realized what it was that had continued to confound him as strikingly familiar about this bizarre gentleman who seemed to belong to another era. He possessed the same eyes as the blood-stained boy being guided by the angel ascending in his vision. Connecting those dubiously uncertain dots did little to answer the myriad questions Mr. Cassidy continued to harbor, but it did grant him a sorely needed measure of serenity. He decided to remain silent on that oddity and merely responded to the man's earlier suggestion with the intention of learning more. "I am certain that all will end well between us, my friend. I feel entirely more hopeful about our prospects."

The man took a second look at Mr. Cassidy after hearing such an unexpected comment. He then turned abruptly to face the window and finished telling his tale. "Those of that ancient family that became enmeshed with a clan of distinctively American bloodlines have been successful in many productive endeavors since those ancient times. They have been good stewards of their inherited capital and also captains of industry throughout the generations, in addition to implementing any and all methods of political and industrial sorcery, blackmail, and even warfare to increase their wealth, power, and prestige throughout the millennium."

"Of course, lineage gets complicated with the passage of time. Nevertheless, I can assure you that many members of this family's bloodline have prospered for centuries and still do according to almost any measure that some of the richest people in the world would apply during these distinctively "modern" times. They wield immense influence and have generally settled in and around the areas of Washington, D.C., New England, and the Saint Lawrence Seaway. The members of the family whom I serve directly hail from a branch with a more southern bent, if you will permit my slang. I have not lived among any of them for some time, but I took up residence with my adoptive parents while I matriculated adeptly through secondary school and college. After college, I ventured out to live on my own and joined one of the preeminent family businesses, though I was but a bastardized and disconnected heir of a sort."

The man took a brief rest to regather his thoughts and then continued as if he were truly interested in telling his story. "Mr. Cassidy, the branch of that family that I represent, at least as the world appears to be stationed today, is currently enjoying what many who do not know any better would define as an era of prosperity not exceeded at any point in their rich and also dubious history."

"Well then," interjected Ronan softly. He was looking upward to center his thoughts as he contemplated what must have been the one constant among the family's wealth holdings throughout the ages. "I should think that your benefactors do not have much to worry about given what you have just said."

"Ah, if only such a thing were true, Ronan. If only such a thing as having nothing to worry about were indeed true for your own sake as well, my friend," responded the man solemnly.

Ronan was beginning to connect the dots, but as the man was finally telling his story, he said nothing about those things he was beginning to suspect. The man shifted to a decidedly thoughtful tone and said, "What you must also understand, Ronan, is that there are two types of rich people. Some have gold stored away in places that are safe, while others do not. Simple is as simple does. The family that I represent does not currently have gold in an amount that is, by any measure, even close to proportionately representing the stated dollar value of their net worth. That is to say, they are nearly rich on paper only. I am sure that is a concept that you are uniquely familiar with, given the rather specific nature of your line of work, Mr. Cassidy."

The man caught his mistake the moment the word left his tongue and spoke to make amends for his brutishness. "Do forgive me. I, of course, did mean to address you as you have asked, Ronan. Speaking with people on a first-name basis has only occurred on rare occasions these past six years."

Ronan took in what his currently far more affable neighbor was saying. Although he had a fairly good idea where the man's discourse might be heading, he wanted to learn more about the importance of having versus not having gold for those wealthy families of the world. He was certainly not of the highest castes of American society, and his wholly Western-influenced finance training would have led the laymen of his profession to believe that gold was simply a commodity, or worse, a forgotten and barbarous artifact of a monetary system that had long since passed into the annals of history. The concept of gold being true wealth was one that Ronan had spent a long time deliberating over, and it was the primary reason he had chosen to migrate over to his current professional role after reaching the abyss of his near-breakdown a little over a year ago.

Ronan paused his reaction for a moment to consider a few of the ancillary details embedded within the man's message while he stroked his chin in a thoughtful manner. When he had deliberated long enough on the matter of money and wealth, he thoughtfully questioned the man. "How can it be that your benefactors were in possession of that much money and power for so long, yet they have no gold? Certainly, gold was the singular constant that marked their wealth over the centuries. No fiat currency has survived for that long."

The man smiled at Ronan for only the second time that morning. His assenting grin was not artfully given this time. In fact, Ronan believed that the bizarre, self-declared man of the demon's realms was genuinely smiling at him. He wondered what other pleasantries lay in wait as the conversation progressed. While Ronan pondered the significance of the sincerity behind that smile, the man answered him in rather animated fashion. "That is a terrific question, Ronan!"

After he had replied with such vigor, the man became amused by the paradox of the underlying circumstances of their encounter when enmeshed with the fact that it would now have appeared to the outside observer that the two were in the midst of performing a rolling comedy skit for a late-night television production. Ronan's snarky disdain for unjust and improper authority, a trait of Ronan's that the man was well aware of from his quarry's file, and aware of long before he had ever laid eyes on Mr. Cassidy, was now providing a form of comedic balance to what had heretofore been an intense exchange between the two men. "I am glad you did not ask me why having no gold was of such importance to the family, Ronan," said the man.

He then turned his eyes back to Mr. Cassidy and clarified his position. "Your understanding of these matters will spare us the inefficiency of redundancy and, moreover, offer me the grace of precious additional time that will allow me to explain to you how it is that you have come to play such an integral role in the family's story. While perhaps you are simply the one who has been chosen as arbiter of this ungodly quarrel of the Western age, I see no reason why your proper understanding of the facts and circumstances should serve as an impediment to your "calling," as it were."

The man paused for a short breath and then completed his second thought. A thought expressed solely for the purpose of establishing a bond of trust with the very person he had worked so hard to instill fear of God in just a short while earlier. "Though I suspect that talk of such things will only serve to frighten you more before you have had a chance to summon that inner spirit warrior of yours, you should also know that this long-awaited reckoning, or final settlement, as the case may be, may, for better or worse, turn out to be the concluding chapter of my own colorful story as well."

The man continued speaking at a pace that left no opportunity for Ronan to interject. "As I mentioned earlier, the family made the first part of their fortune as part of the unfortunate liquidation of the Templars in the early 14th century, as they, the Templars, that is, missed some major changes in the social and political climate of that day following the last of the holy pilgrimages to Jerusalem. While the knights of that ancient order righteously upheld their values and traditions, it cost them dearly when the struggle for power shifted from Constantinople and the Holy Lands to Western Europe. One of the old family patriarchs, of decidedly German descent, capitalized on this shifting of the winds, so to speak, and built a lasting legacy of agriculture and industrial concerns throughout Northern Italy and France, in addition to the German Saarland."

"Today, that legacy is an industrial empire of sorts that the Sinclair and Morgenthau families control from Canada and parts of northern New England, with a few of them scattered throughout South Carolina. Now, few, if any, not ordained into the highest orders of that sect might properly trace how that bloodline evolved over the centuries. Their progenitors seemed to possess an affinity for outliving the given generational term of a mere mortal and all manner of incestuous inbreeding. At least, that was the case until the late 1800s. Although I have been made aware that a far more selective propensity for inbreeding didn't end there, I am almost certain that none of those spawned from the fourth child of my maternal matriarch have lived longer than a century."

Ronan's eyes grew wide, but the man only offered a sporting wink in response to that show of dismay before moving on with his tale. "Not to make those wide-eyes of yours go crossed, but where things tend to get exceptionally complicated is how those rather spurious bloodlines intersect with those of my direct employers, who are also my maternal kin. Because you are dealing with my current employer, which is a Calhoun entity that I suspect is nearly controlled by someone of the Morgenthau ilk, I am trying my best to connect the dots for you in the short time we have been granted."

Ronan's notions were a bit mislaid, but he was not far from developing a working understanding of what the man was driving at. Therefore, he simply nodded and offered up a look of contemplation to his suddenly gracious host. The man accepted Mr. Cassidy's gesture as a motion to proceed, and he acted in accordance with such. "The Calhouns are a predominantly American phenomenon with a bloodline that has been tainted in notable ways by those of the Morgenthau line. In any event, though their methods of surviving the aftermath of the Civil War might seem confusing, or their deeds therewith ascribed to a clan of the fallen order, if only to those who understand just the preponderance of their story and not the subtle nuances laced within, I am able to say that the Calhoun family managed to hold on to just enough following the Civil War. Furthermore, they survived that episode with their souls intact, though not without future vulnerabilities to those of a darker order and not without a very damning skeleton still lurking in their closet."

Ronan nodded in acceptance once again, and the man picked up where he left off. "In the years following the Reconstruction, their patriarch at that time began branching off, as one might have it. He took on several and separate responsibilities for a host of primarily American ventures that flourished in the late 1800s. That, however, is also a story for another day—and at this juncture, perhaps another lifetime altogether. To add some context to your pertinent comment earlier, the very origins of the Calhoun family's wealth were kept in gold and land. However, following the Civil War, most of their rights to gold might only be claimed through a disjointed relationship with those of the Pinkney Trust, or in a severely disjointed manner, a treasure that belonged to the lore of ancient legend."

"The first method would be accomplished through a marriage that repaired an old rift. However, that gift was then squandered by my current employer. That is the mistake that you are set to rectify before time gets away from us, Ronan."

To which Ronan interjected with a bit of enthusiasm by asking, "And what of the treasure?"

The man answered somewhat coyly. "Although part of the reason why you and I are gathered together at this ungodly hour, the second method, or boondoggle, whichever you prefer to call something so rigidly adhered to yet opaque and shrouded in mystery, shall remain a hidden concern for quite some time."

The man turned to face Mr. Cassidy, smiled as wide as he had in years, and asked, "Have I captured your imagination yet, Ronan?"

Ronan grinned somewhat begrudgingly at the man and replied in the professional manner of a true advocate for his product. "That you have, my friend. I was certain of their past gold holdings, but I am still in doubt as to how such an ancient legacy of wealth escaped the deep-seeded traditions and financial practices of your direct sponsors."

The man raised his open palm to Mr. Cassidy to slow his suddenly eager attendant down some, and said, "Let me explain that very phenomenon to you, Ronan."

Ronan nodded in acceptance of the man's proposal, and the man went on with it. "The gold wealth belonging to the darker side of the family survived the age of alchemy, the vast advances in science and mathematics of the Renaissance, and continued to lie very still into the colonial era, when even more gold arrived in their American strongholds from Europe, the African continent, and the mines of the West Indies and South America. Their gold wealth survived countless popes and kings, myriad renditions of fiat paper money and scrip, innumerable wars, and even the tumultuous, and in some cases, ongoing, upheavals of culture and political will that span the globe. That side of the family and the Pinckney clan tied to the Calhouns adhered to two valuable lessons throughout history, Ronan: the first of which was to amass wealth in gold, and the second of which was to keep the amount of that wealth to themselves. However, many among the planter class of the Western Age, such as the blue-bloods within the Calhoun clan, were enamored with land and were notoriously short on tradeable wealth items or currency at various times throughout history."

Ronan smiled openly in reply this time. The welcome distractions of a conversation near and dear to his heart and the visible humanity of his antagonist had done much to calm him. He rejoined the man with a newly found sense of surety. One that was not entirely well-founded but amenable to his belief that, deep down, most folks were formed with an innate goodness that still lurked somewhere within their hearts. "Those sound like excellent and entirely un-American strategies. Perhaps if I'm still upright after our flight lands, you will join me out on the road. The families tied to newer money seem to doubt that the richest among us recognize that gold, and not stock or bond portfolios, is the standard measure of timeless wealth."

The man looked at Ronan curiously in response to his unexpected quip. He had not come across someone who became so informal so quickly after receiving such strident threats. He was not worried about the development just then, as it was easily rectifiable and because he ascribed such pluck to Mr. Cassidy's expected naivete. Instead, the man grew curious and began to wonder if this Mr. Cassidy was perhaps the person he had been seeking for far different reasons, though he had always believed the one who might lead him down the path of the forgiveness of his sins would be someone of the cloth. The man did not remain stuck on the thought for long. There were enough balls to juggle with this exercise. He merely filed it away for subsequent consideration and returned his eyes to Ronan before saying, "If I am ever permitted a second line of work, I will gladly join you, Ronan. I am not worried for your safety because I know that in your heart you want to do what is right for those dear to you."

The friendly but still pointed reminder hit Ronan like a sledgehammer to the forehead, and the look on his once hopeful guise immediately became vacant. The man looked down at his well-made and rather expensive shoes to inspect them for blemishes and carried on as if all remained just as it should be.

"But alas, eventually, greed and vanity will usurp all virtue where those vices are allowed to fester and infect our souls. The family did well for many years to escape the alluring mirage of value that is the dollar and her accompanying cornucopia of get-rich-quick schemes. Old Charles Calhoun even shunned the long-term bond as a suitable store of value worthy of offering a counterbalance to the ravages of credit-money inflation. Nevertheless, as Will Rogers once said, "There are three kinds of men. The ones that learn by readin'. The few who learn by observation. The rest of them have to pee on the electric fence for themselves." Mr. John Edward Calhoun is far more agreeable than his father was, and far closer to human, but also apt to see what happens when you make it rain on just such a fence."

"That is an interesting analogy," responded Ronan, while continuing to once again steady his wits. "Are you going to give me the back story on how the family patriarch managed to be talked into dishoarding their true wealth? I can guess, but I would imagine that in this case, some of that gold had to be in the form of nearly priceless artifacts from long ago."

"Once again, great question and a superb initial observation, Ronan," responded the man. He then winked confidently at Ronan. He did so with the indifference of one in possession of leverage-giving wisdom and seated at the downwardly slanted end of the table. "Since you will be held to a standard of silence on matters of far greater import, one which will directly govern the promised safety of you and your family, I will indulge you in the instance of the event that will have caused you to enter into such an unfortunate agreement on this eleventh day of April."

"Of course," replied Mr. Cassidy, "I wouldn't conduct business with a client without the expectation of appropriate discretion."

"Yes, most certainly," answered the man before saying, "I'll allow for your liberal, or perhaps urbane, application of the term discretion, but do keep a far more potent term handy in the event push comes to shove somewhere down the road."

The man then shook his hand to keep Ronan from clarifying his meaning and returned to his prior intention of explaining John Edward Calhoun's financial gaffe. "First off, it would be wise for you to remember that the ancient gold I believe you are referencing belongs to the Morgenthau and Sinclair families. They are nearly extinct, as luck would have it, and ran into some financial problems of their own sometime during the Great Depression, but the few who remain are partners in all of the Calhoun ventures by way of an ancient agreement and some rather unsavory familial entanglements."

"I certainly appreciate your leniency on the matter," replied Ronan, a bit smugly. He had been pining to swear, but ultimately restrained his lips from producing another vulgar response. He deplored the use of poor language. More importantly, he was infinitely curious to know more about how such a wealth-destroying transaction had come to pass. Especially after centuries of tradition preserving the family's wealth through physical gold ownership prior to that unfortunate mishap.

"As I presume you are aware, Ronan, and I say as much based upon my readings of some of your recent work, the dollar had entered a period of severe turbulence by 1979. As I am sure you are also aware, it took some negotiating of the highest order to see the world's first unbacked reserve currency through to 1980 and beyond. After the gold window was closed, there were several options for the dollar. The goal of the "better-natured" financial types was to establish the dollar as the primary currency for trade and float the other major currencies against the dollar. Gold was to be removed from the financial system and traded as a free-floating wealth reserve asset."

The man paused and took notice of Ronan, who appeared ready to finish this historical segment of the story for him. He then interjected a question into his storyline. "Did you wish to say something, Ronan?"

Ronan nodded at the man and filled in the next segment of the story behind the metamorphosis of the modern U.S. dollar, at least as he understood the historical course of events to have transpired. "The fly in the ointment was that the oil nations wanted their share of the gold pile in exchange for their presumably nonrenewable oil reserves. The oil-producing nations were already thinking in big player terms. While their nonrenewable assets were invaluable to the progress of international commerce, so too were the benefits of a flexible book-entry unit of account and medium of exchange to lubricate this burgeoning market for global trade. There was an impasse."

"The European bankers were willing to agree to fix their currencies to the dollar for a time. Or, in layman's terms, they would soak up the dollars over and above what the U.S. could offer in the form of real trade production from their economy by purchasing U.S. Treasury bonds. At the same time, Federal Reserve Chairman Paul Volcker raised interest rates to astronomical levels to entice other trade surplus nations and global dollar users to do the same. The missing link at that time was how to prevent gold prices from blowing out when big oil wanted real value in exchange for their very real and quite indispensable oil assets."

"Right, you are, Ronan," responded the man, quite impressed by Ronan's dollar-related acumen. "Allow me to take us a bit further down the dollar road if you don't mind. That way, you will understand the circumstances leading up to John Edward's unfortunate gamble with his family's wealth."

To Ronan's surprise, his host's mood had brightened marginally, though the average observer would never have picked up on the subtle shift. While considering any improvement in the man's demeanor to be a win given his current predicament, Mr. Cassidy attempted to keep the focus of the conversation squarely on the demise of the dollar. "How do you see the future denouement of the world's reserve currency playing out? If you don't mind my asking such a loaded question, that is."

The man nodded his head rather deliberately and gathered his thoughts. After just a brief respite, he answered Ronan's question as directly as he was able. "While I have come to learn much about the more unsavory elements in this world, I have also learned that God works in mysterious ways. He does things on His time and in a manner we would never imagine, let alone expect. As such, I would be speaking far beyond my purview in endeavoring to predict when and how such a cataclysmic yet liberating event for humanity might transpire. Were you to ask me what I have learned from my time spent captive to these serpents of the earth, I would respond simply by saying that they are fashioning a mirage that is designed to enslave you by controlling every facet of your life. Those who pull the strings make it appear as if you must not only bow before the princes and princesses of their system to survive, but also work like a slave in the name of its proliferation."

The man paused for a moment to look out the window and then said, "Perhaps that is where you and I are in agreement, Ronan. We both know that such a thing is simply not true. We also know that once you have been tricked into taking a sweet bite of their deadly fruit, it becomes very difficult to return to the light. Perhaps that is the real reason why we have been brought together under such extenuating circumstances this morning."

Ronan's mouth dropped slightly open yet his eyes remained frozen in place. He spoke not a word in response to such an unexpected, though not entirely unwelcome, presumption. The man closed his eyes and considered a dreadful moment from his past, but pushed his thoughts beyond that dour recollection so that he might answer the question a bit more directly. "Ronan, you must first understand that nothing these people feign as the truth makes a bit of sense when considered in its proper context. Still and all, when taken as a whole, the lie is so big that few can wrap their minds around what it is that these wicked people have accomplished in their attempt to usurp what belongs to God."

The man looked away from the window and back towards Ronan. He spoke with a bit more passion than was usual in the normal course of conducting his affairs. "They are so close to having it all that their flesh shines and their eyes sparkle. Yet they must be constantly nourished by more. Their greed and their insatiable lusts of the flesh will be their undoing. In my humble opinion, the fact that their fatally flawed dollar instrument, which serves as the primary means to their desired ends, reaches the event horizon, has begun to draw them into the open, where they are far weaker and far more vulnerable. We shall see how this battle for our souls plays out, but I am hopeful for the first time since I was driven into exile to dig up some gold at a fraction of the cost you all will be forced to endure in the market for players of size. Perhaps such words are welcome news to your patiently listening and readily tested ears, Ronan. Even if those words may be no more than worthless drivel spoken by a compromised man desperately hoping for better things ahead."

The man paused his story and rested his voice while giving many things careful consideration during the brief interlude. Ronan remained silent in response to those deeper-level opinions on money and the dismal state of affairs in the world. The man then turned his head and looked back out the window with longing eyes that searched the depths of the morning horizon out to the west. He noted that some weather was heading in to dampen what remained of the day ahead. Given the other clues that were revealed to him from beyond the window, he surmised that they had about twenty minutes left in their conversation. At that point, they would begin their final descent and, soon thereafter, land back at O'Hare. Following that stark realization, the man took a moment to reflect on the benefits of having the proper vantage points in life while he considered those down below, those who were beginning their working days in and around the awakening fields of Indiana in the early spring.

Ronan paid watchful attention to the man while the dapper squire looked away and out beyond the small, rounded portico of the seventh row. Mr. Cassidy was reminded at that moment that the man was still something he dared not think about further in real terms, and that his deeds were contrivances best kept hidden from even the wonders of his imagination. With that thought in mind, Ronan casually shifted his eyes to the seatback in front of him and interjected a harmless query into the silence of the man's westward-leaning stare. "What you have said about structural support for the dollar as the world's unbacked reserve currency seems to match the accounts I have pulled together from various sources, old notes, and otherwise. What was the catch in putting this deal together that you mentioned earlier?"

Ronan asked the question somewhat rhetorically. He wished to bring the man's attention back from the edge of some abyss beyond the window, which seemed to connect directly with the darkened corners of his neighbor's soul. For that reason, the man's extended silence scared the living shit out of Mr. Cassidy. There was something about having the stranger's sea-blue eyes focused on his humanity that provided a necessary comfort to Ronan at that moment of some frightful reckoning that he had yet to fully grasp. That the man would likely speak in his sometimes cold and perpetually detached voice was another matter altogether.

Ronan was not prepared to hop down that rabbit hole with a man capable of such wide-ranging and altogether antithetical remedies for the certain trespasses that displeased his employers. Thus, while he knew full well that, as with most of the attempts of the international monetary order to organize in a manner that was balanced and fair, the hang-up was always nature's money. The hang-up in establishing a balanced monetary system for the last century had always been the true value of unencumbered physical gold. What Ronan didn't entirely understand was how the deal regarding gold and the establishment of the current international monetary system played out behind the scenes. He had always fantasized about shady backroom deals and the like, but the fact that he was perhaps going to hear a true second or third-hand account of the dollar deal excited him to the point that he found the state of his turbulent emotions had shifted from emotions of total fear to those of balanced anticipation. After a second or two spent staring out and onto the raw, post-winter fields of the American breadbasket, the man turned back to Ronan and answered his question straight away.

"Well, Mr. Cassidy, the catch was complicated from a modern monetary standpoint, as the case always seems to be for those of us raised on the fiat dollar. However, the solution was quite simple when viewed through the lens of exchanging items of equivalent real-world value to facilitate trade. From a monetary standpoint, I think that we are both able to, and do, wholeheartedly agree that money serves three primary functions in a world where we exchange real things for other tangible things that are useful to us, yet also have an absolute need to save for a rainy day and those days when our capacity to produce begins to wane."

"The first two of those functions are the unit of account and the medium of exchange. Those intrinsic traits of money are the strong suits of infinitely expandable and fungible fiat, or ledger entry, currencies. In that regard, we also both agree that having dollars around to value everything from a unit of labor to a widget has allowed for great strides to be made in the human capacity to produce. What was taken from us on the day that the dollar severed the last of its golden links, Ronan, was our ability to save without taking on risk or being subjected to theft through inflation. The oil producing nations and those with a more expansive understanding of money throughout history understood that truth innately."

Ronan nodded amiably and said, "I couldn't agree with you more, nor could I have delivered the punchline better myself."

"As you probably also know, Ronan, specialization of labor and the removal of the double incidence of wants are two of the biggest success stories of using fungible and easily issuable fiat money in the roles of unit of account and as the universal medium of exchange. Where things get messy, and always have in the world of fiat money, is the attempt to burden that fungible money with the primary store of the value function. Likewise, given its proven track record as the ultimate store of value, things tend to end in tears when we use fixed amounts of gold as the unit of account and medium of exchange, given the need to lend and invest in projects for future production as things change and evolve. The old bird in the hand analogy comes to mind in that regard."

"You see, Ronan, the attempt to unnaturally force our fiat money, or gold in past practice, to serve in all three of the primary roles of money has created a natural friction between those who prefer to utilize debt in the endeavors of stockpiling the things they need and want in life and those who choose to overproduce and save their excess capacity in this wealth reserve par excellence that we call gold. Gold is a tangible wealth reserve that can't be diluted and tends to expand naturally in line with the real things we need each day and work diligently to produce."

When his host paused for consideration, Ronan nodded and responded to the man in a similar manner. "Again, I couldn't agree with you more. It's refreshing to hear those thoughts coming from the mouth of another. The ardent parishioners of the church of the almighty dollar are so very asleep to the critical importance to humanity of what you have just revealed."

The man nodded in affirmation and asked, "Do you have further thoughts on the matter, Ronan? This continually evolving conundrum regarding money and wealth runs deep and can be considered on many levels."

Ronan looked over to the man and regarded the abruptly troubled look that showed noticeably on his normally guarded countenance. It was as if the man was considering an evolving struggle that went beyond the axioms of money and wealth and into the realms of the human spirit and the soul. Ronan had no basis in fact or even a conceptual framework to hold such an opinion, but he was quite adept at reading the look on any man's face. What little he knew of this strange and presumably deadly attendant to some faction of the family he had hoped would become his largest client was not enough to ask a personal question of him, or even briefly change the subject. Accordingly, Ronan simply answered the question that he was asked.

"What most people fail to understand is that fiat money, in and of itself, is an extension of credit in the form of a promise to pay in the future, whereas acquiring gold is payment in full. Most folks that I know also fail to grasp that the interest they are paid to save in fiat money locks them into a system that must grow exponentially to avoid failure. They do not understand that, by definition, there will come a day when those running such a system will be unable to make good on those promises to deliver more in the future. In the world of real things, we simply cannot grow our standard of living exponentially for extended periods of human existence. What we have seen time and again with fiat money is that late-cycle credit contracts lose their stated basis in value as those contracts are no longer able to maintain a viable connection to real economic output in the present or what is perceived to arrive in the future. At that point, folks tend to know that they have been had, and rapidly lose confidence in those infinitely expanding promises to pay."

The man spoke up in agreement with Ronan's thesis and added some further context. "Well said, Ronan. Add to that the moral hazard baked into the ungodly measure of control handed over to the banking system and our government stooges, and you will see quite clearly that the current system possesses a finite timeline. Many who understand these things would argue that the dollar began to outlive its useful life some time ago, but the power to do anything about it had already been transferred to those eternally committed to fighting a lost war. Utilizing a system that lends gold to serve as the credit money for trade can be even worse since the losses are far harder to mask and socialize than the systemic overextension of credit. The end of gold-only money standards usually results in war, as someone has to go get the gold they were promised upon default."

"At any rate, I could cover volumes on this topic alone, but suffice it to say that any cursory review of the history of money, and especially money since the rise of the industrial revolution, will more than adequately prove out the theories we have put forth here today. The dollar will become worthless and gold infinitely more valuable. There is nothing to be done about that now."

The man paused again, and neither hearing nor seeing any objectionable sign, facial gesture, or utterance from Ronan, who sat still and was devoutly listening while facing the seatback in front of him, he continued. "Our time together shortens yet still, Ronan. As such, allow me to hurry us along some, so that we may get to the point of the matter before the hour we have been given passes us by."

The man looked over to the cover of his Economist magazine, sitting face up in the open aisle seat. The headline read, '*Why computers will never be safe.*' "Yet another reason to own some physical gold," he thought silently.

After that thought had dissipated, he worked his way back into the story of the establishment of the fiat dollar at the heart of the global financial system.

"Even with the support of the European and other Western central banks and Dr. Volker's stern policies on using high-interest rates to combat inflation, the odds remained stacked against the purely fiat dollar. Though it may seem like child's play today, overriding thousands of years of innate and learned human behavior regarding preserving wealth was no easy task. Innovation, cheap labor, and oil were the keys to the fiat dollar kingdom when accompanied by brute force and unending propaganda. Nevertheless, without cheap oil, the boom in global trade of the late '70s and early '80s would have been stopped dead in its tracks."

The man then gently pulled at his chin with his thumb and forefinger and added a certain manner of insouciance to his bland and casual tone. "And wouldn't you know it, Ronan, the Arabian princes, who had stumbled upon endless reserves of portable energy in the middle of a sand-covered wasteland, wanted a real and tangible store of value in exchange for their consumable wealth. Like most of the world's giant oil producers of that era, the Arabians had a rough idea of what the value of all oil was in terms of all gold. Truly, they may have undershot the intrinsic value of gold using those elementary estimations, but let's just say that the number would have blown the lid off of the dollar price of gold and sent us back to a world where gold was performing all three of the functions of money. Oil was that important to all things economic, and the sheiks were far too shrewd to be handed untested monopoly scrip in exchange for their one-time only windfall."

The man paused briefly and offered Ronan a packet of airline peanuts from his coat pocket in the event his compatriot needed some sustenance for his settling stomach. Ronan declined with a subtle wave of his open palm and a slight shake of his head. The man nodded in a genteel manner in reply and put the package back into the inner pocket of his fine, grey blazer. He then continued on with his story.

"Nobody with a sound understanding of money who had lived through the deflationary impacts of gold as the primary form of exchangeable money in the late 1800s and the Great Depression wanted to head back in time for another helping of that. Therefore, the deal was cut to pay the Saudis and a few of the world's other oil-producing nations under the table with a fixed amount of gold per barrel of oil and a nominal number of dollars in plain view. In exchange, the Saudis would lend penultimate credibility and network effect value to the dollar by ensuring that all oil transactions completed through

OPEC would be settled in dollars. And there you have the setup, my good man. Do you have any questions about the dollar's deal of the century?"

Ronan again shook his head, partly out of deference to the curiosities running through his head regarding just who this man who possessed such knowledge was and partly because he was enthralled by this segment of the story. "No, please, continue," he answered.

"Indeed," said the man, and continue on he did. "By 1980, the purely fiat reserve currency known as the dollar was supported internationally on three major fronts. The excess dollars created through the continuing U.S. trade deficit were being mopped up by the central banks of the trade surplus nations in the form of Treasury purchases that pegged the value of their currencies to the dollar and sent all of that dollar liquidity back to Washington and the banks on Wall Street. Once Saudi Arabia agreed to settle all oil trade in dollars, the rest of the OPEC nations quickly followed suit, and dollars became highly sought after for their unique ability to procure oil in the world energy markets. The failure of the Jamaica Accords of 1976, which attempted to establish a free-floating price for the gold wealth reserves at the center of a network of freely floating global currencies, meant that the fly in the ointment of the fiat dollar monetary regime was the true price of unencumbered physical gold in terms of oil. That is where the fractionally reserved gold banks of the London Bullion Market Association, in conjunction with the world's central banks, kicked it into overdrive to dampen the gold price by magically expanding the "quantity" of gold available for sale on the open market through a system of unallocated paper gold liabilities and futures contracts."

The man paused once more to assess his companion's mental state. At seeing the man's captivating eyes once again, Ronan was initially inclined to remain silent, but felt a slight urging to confirm his full understanding of the profound knowledge the man had imparted upon him regarding the beginnings of the gold for oil deal. He conveyed the words of his question slowly and deliberately. "Are you saying that the tenuous situation with the nascent fiat dollar required the perception of "cheap" gold in relation to oil?"

"Yes, you are directionally correct, Ronan," the man responded. "The real gambit was to make the dollar appear more attractive than gold to the big producers of foreign oil and, furthermore, to make the central bankers' promises to deliver real gold in accordance with their multiplying paper promises seem credible. The fact that no one would learn the true price of gold in oil terms or the non-fractionally reserved price of the gold in the vaults of the bullion banks was where the real sleight of hand occurred. Those heady deals of the late-seventies and early-eighties were ground zero for the upcoming main event of the dollar's denouement. Over time, the system we see crumbling before our eyes grew up on what appeared to be cheap gold and cheap oil in dollar terms. That was how enduring dollar credibility was established. The big players have always known the true price of gold, and even paid close to that second-tier market price to acquire enduring wealth reserves of market-disrupting size."

Ronan's was bristling with curiosity at that moment. He had heard many theories thrown around concerning the unlevered price of gold. He generally held to the presumed values he had conveyed to Lewis nearly five years ago in the summer of 2012, though he had learned a great deal more due to his first-hand experience with the trade. Still and all, he was no insider, and he had no way of confirming the revaluation numbers he liked to casually mention for the benefit of his potential clients. Those numbers were generally conservative and came to him as the result of an ardent process of elimination. The presumed bullion values Mr. Cassidy used to convey what would happen in the event that a physical-only gold market came to pass in the wake of the dollar being ravaged by hyperinflation were never directly confirmed by a credible source.

Ronan had no idea if the man could answer such a loaded question in accordance with his direct knowledge, but he couldn't hold his tongue. "Are you one of the few who knows the true off-market price of gold?"

The man smiled cattily in reply to Mr. Cassidy and said, "Sadly, the only verified account I can give you dates back to before the turn of the century. The number then was somewhere around $10,000. If you were to put me on the spot concerning what that number might be today, I would say somewhere near $50,000 per troy ounce."

Ronan slapped the side of his knee cheekily with his right hand and whispered aloud, "I knew it!"

The man tried not to indulge someone who might yet remain in a rather precarious position by laughing even mildly at such childish antics. Though he was amused and strangely heartened by Mr. Cassidy's behavior, he tightened up his guise and steered the conversation back to his primary point. "Regardless of the actual dollar price, or relative purchasing power of unencumbered physical gold, the amount by which dollar value will drop commensurately is a tragedy of almost biblical proportions for the venerable family I represent. Therefore, your star-crossed path with them may end just as tragically if we are not able to work together to resolve the issue. I hope that my loose banter and casual tone have not softened the initial impression I have tried to convey upon you this morning, Mr. Cassidy."

Ronan swallowed hard but did not utter a sound otherwise. The man decided to go on a short rant to draw that potent inner demon a bit closer to the surface for effect. "Their subtle ruse is also a grave tragedy for the once-great American nation and the world at large. One little detail hidden in an effort to get the stars to align forty years ago, and here we all sit with a giant and irrevocable mess to sort through today. Beyond that, up is now down, black is now white, and you have sociopaths running the world's largest financial institutions with carte blanche given to them by the petty criminals, larcenists, and those of a far darker bent in Washington."

The man directed his sharpened blue eyes toward Ronan and spoke in a far more foreboding manner. "An ill wind blows, Mr. Cassidy, and you and I are now ensnared in the same web. An ill wind blows as these global cartels feed the socialists what little remains in the coffers of the productive class while robbing everything that isn't nailed down under cover of propaganda, lies, and graft. There is no refuge for those of us caught in the middle of the seismic shift set to occur between the power brokers of the world. Let us keep that in mind while we discuss the gold deal that contributed to the dire circumstances we face this morning, my friend."

Neither man spoke for a brief while. They simply considered the strange twists and turns that life takes as the airplane raced across the sky, though it appeared to the man from the vantage point of the window that they were barely moving at all. He looked away from the ground below and back towards Ronan as he began to speak. Time was running short, and the look of concern that was mounting deep within the man's suddenly soft and wistfully pleading eyes spoke of the growing need for expediency. The true intentions of the man were far more intricate than Ronan might have guessed, and the man did not want to leave the importance of Mr. Cassidy's role in the affairs set to transpire in the coming months, and perhaps years, opaque in any way.

While he never would have been so bold as to explain the true motives lurking behind his need for Ronan's ventures with the Calhoun family to succeed, he needed his quarry to understand that failure was not an option. In that vein, the man continued with the story of the final separation of the dollar from its golden anchor. "The gold for oil deal was simple in concept but fairly complex to manage. This was due to the second-hand reverberations the under the table deal would have on the world's financial system. The scheme was not much different than the countless other important policy decisions that are kept from the public eye. I will not hold us up on the details, but suffice it to say that gold needed to flow to the oil-producing countries of the Middle East for their oil. Moreover, and of equivalent importance, the value of this gold in oil terms had to be kept from those eagerly participating in the evolving dollar financial markets and world currency trading arenas. There would be no confidence in the fiat dollar of the 1970s if that cat ever got out of the bag."

Ronan allowed an exasperated smile to peter out before the probing eyes of his neighbor. He was becoming quite fatigued. The hopeful energy tied to his curiosity and what had been the far more agreeable nature of his keeper were fading into the harsh realities tied to his ongoing and entirely unexpected ordeal. The gathering of two had been full of life-altering surprises, and the tagline had yet to be spoken. In fact, the sudden turn of events was something that was completely unimaginable when Mr. Cassidy began his day in the darkened hours of the morning. In many ways, the affair remained entirely surreal to the rather pragmatic man of such a traditional American upbringing, and that was true even as he was in the midst of a soul-rending reawakening at that time of life.

After releasing a deep and calming breath, Ronan asked half-heartedly of the man, "What caused this gold for oil deal to be such a challenge to the wizards and warlocks of the unholy triumvirate of London, Washington, and New York? Were there limits to the unbound capacity of their sorcery back in those days?"

The man covered his mouth and chin with his cupped right hand while he considered Ronan's question for a moment. He then answered Mr. Cassidy rather thoughtfully. "There is a line from a movie that I am quite fond of, Ronan. The line goes something like this: "The greatest trick the devil ever pulled was convincing the world that he didn't exist."

Ronan knew the film was titled The Usual Suspects. He liked the movie as well, but he tucked the notion away as something to think further on at a later time. The man didn't seem all that concerned about Ronan's opinion while he carried on. "You will have to pardon me if I misquoted the film, but I view the attempt to hide gold's true value from those who overproduce and save in the same light. How do you convince the people of the world that something they understand so naturally no longer exists? How do you throw a rug over an elephant standing in the middle of a room? That is what our benevolent masters of finance were up against in 1982, and perhaps much earlier than that, Ronan."

Ronan shook his head in a dejected manner, as one who found such a thing hard to fathom, but the man paid him no mind and said, "The biggest obstacle to their plan was that no government treasury wanted to pony up the gold reserves required to pay for the oil. The central banks did eventually deliver some gold to the oil producers while the bankers worked out a plan to coax some of the gold held in the large private hoards back out into the open. The whole deal was a masterful stroke in constructing a false reality for those that weren't part of the club. The general public bought into the easy money plan hook, line, and sinker once the cheap credit started flowing. For the wealthy who were not subject to the gold confiscation of 1934, the transition took a bit more time. Nevertheless, when the Dow began to skyrocket in response to all of the excess reserves pouring into the New York banks, many well-heeled entities eagerly took the bait. The same is true for the chairman of the company that will hopefully be your newest client. That is, if you stand to pass muster with me here today."

The man had finally revealed at least the official reason for his unconventional parley with Mr. Cassidy that morning. The grace of such a gesture was not missed by his counterpart. Ronan's face lit up in the splendid way that only someone sensing the passing of a grave and incalculable danger might respond to such welcome news. The man saw that Ronan was taking a great deal of comfort from the revelation that he was simply being vetted by a very powerful client. He would have preferred a more tepid measure of relief. However, since the lion's share of the danger accruing to Mr. Cassidy was tied to his divergent needs, which most certainly were not to be revealed at that juncture, the man went on with his story concerning the gold for oil deal. He did so without making any effort to temper Ronan's rashly hopeful expectations. For his turn, Ronan did not interject to ask the dozen or more questions that were swirling around in his somewhat relieved yet still unsettled and deeply confused mind.

"Sometime in or around 1980, the powers that be devised a scheme that involved gold to be mined at a future date. That future gold would be backed by the balance of national reserves held in central bank custody should anything unfortunate arise with those planned mining operations. Now, someone as bright and knowledgeable as you are, might ask, "Was their intent malicious?"

"I will simply respond to my hypothetical proposition by saying that, knowing many of those types of people in the intimate way that I do, most of their plans that involve as much patience and obscurity as the plan to establish the unbacked dollar reserve currency did, usually serve to benefit the wants of the few over the needs of the many. Nevertheless, allow me to educate you on the financial logic behind the scheme. You may form your own opinions about the intentions of the global elite as it regards our presently failing currency system. Time does yet reveal all things, Ronan."

The man offered a quick wink sent in Ronan's direction before speaking. "At this point, the European central banks were in a bit of a pickle. They were keenly aware of the pitfalls of using gold as transactional money. They were also keenly aware of the fragilities associated with and the finite lifespans that accompanied purely fiat monetary systems. Bear in mind that every fiat money system implemented throughout history has failed. You should also consider the fact that explicitly hard money systems frequently lead to other problems, such as war and depression. The general preference of the European financiers would have been to let unencumbered physical gold float freely as a wealth reserve asset, working alongside the dollar and other national currencies. Or so the story given by a few insiders goes."

"This idea regarding a free-floating physical gold market, born of the creators of the Euro, is a groundbreaking monetary concept. One that we are likely to see play out over time. Such a system would keep monetary expansion in check and allow realignments in the fiat monetary system to occur without a complete annihilation of the currency. It would also remove the inherent debtor/saver conflict that is caused by wrapping all three properties of money into one instrument. That is the direction physical gold is taking, Ronan. It will serve in its natural role as a long-term store of value once it is released from the fractional reserved monstrosities of London and New York. Currency may go digital to a large degree, but I think paper dollars are here to stay for a while. At least until they kill all of the trees while printing those dollars through this oncoming hyperinflation. Balance sheet dollars simply will not function in such an environment."

For a while longer, the two gentlemen exchanged some additional banter about the catastrophic nuances of the current monetary order. The man then directed the conversation back to Ronan and the importance of his uniquely positioned ability to provide some measure of relief to his current benefactors. "Outside of my limited first-hand exposure to a few of the notable people that were directly involved with the facilitation of these unfortunate financial half-measures, I know that most of what I am saying is nothing you haven't read about before, Ronan. My hope is that the context will prove useful to you; that my testimony will give you a bit more confidence, as it were, while you work to win the business of my employer. Only you might save them from the unfortunate circumstances of their current financial position before we enter into the storm of the dollar's trial by fire."

"Your unique vantage point is quite helpful," responded Ronan. "I appreciate your confirming my thoughts on the developments of the international monetary system. The invaluable detail that you have just provided certainly supports the thesis I had always presumed to be true."

"You are most welcome, Ronan. And again, my apologies for the trauma to your smartly attired ensemble. Unfortunately, these stories of relevance to your business endeavors are the best I can do in terms of providing some measure of restitution at the moment. However, our journey together is just beginning."

Ronan looked down at his shirt and at the towel still covering his lap. The mess was not entirely unworkable if he were given a little time and a few housekeeping essentials. Thankfully, Ronan Cassidy was never much for breakfast, except on Sundays with his girls, and this morning had been no different. He was not sure how to respond to this suddenly friendly and altogether caring man who had usurped the deadly demon that had greeted him less than an hour ago. Therefore, Ronan simply nodded with his eyes closed in a reticent show of acceptance.

Following that halfhearted nod of acquiescence to his will, the man spoke further. "I am certain that you have questions and, moreover, that you would be thrilled to learn more about the dollar story as I understand it. This topic must remain near and dear to your heart as you move forward with your prospective client and my current employer. However, we have reached the time to clarify certain matters. There are things that you need to know regarding the current state of affairs that surrounds you and the family that has called me to represent them here this morning. Precisely as I alluded to when we began our discourse just a short while ago, the time has come to discuss the unfortunate business that we do have at hand, Ronan."

The man stopped speaking with the intention of removing his hat and setting it down on the open window seat. He drew the fine cap downward and slowly across his face and chest until the back of his hand rested on his right knee, which was crossed over his left leg. He then stared briefly at the inside of the hat, taking particular notice of the somewhat obscure markings printed on the silken cloth that served as the rather comfortable lining of the high-end bowler. There was an object strapped within the hold of the inner band. While the man had become temporarily distracted by the elegant craftsmanship within, Ronan spied his neighbor with a darting glance that was stolen without notice by moving only the apples of his eyes slightly to the left. He noticed the top edge of what appeared to be a wallet-sized photo. Though the man made no effort to conceal the presence of the object, there was no way for Mr. Cassidy to glean who or even what the image was.

The man appeared to Ronan to be contemplating a burning thought that was perhaps a bit emotional in its origins. Neither of the gentlemen broke the silence between them while the hat remained in its owner's hand. After about ten seconds had passed, the man turned the hat back over and rested it on top of his magazine in one purposeful and efficient motion. He then folded his hands loosely above his lap. The tips of the man's fingers lightly gripped the knuckles of each opposing hand. The man then proceeded to rub his left thumb delicately with his right thumb. He seemed to be feeling for the slightly protruding scar that ran from one knuckle to the other. He had torn that thumb something fierce in his youth while making his escape to nowhere in particular through a small opening in a rusty fence. While he delicately rubbed that ancient scar, he looked out the window and again took notice of the vast plots of thawing farmland miles below. They were nearing Chicago, and those perfectly demarcated tracts of open terrain were not quite as far along in waking from their winter dormancy.

The man ended the brief interlude by speaking calmly and clearly. "For the sake of conserving our remaining moments together, we will skip the remainder of the establishment of the dollar's international support system. I hope that you will forgive me for the sleight, but I must address my employer's current situation so that I may help you along in your quest to engage such a noteworthy client."

"We will trade more comprehensive notes on the dollar and gold at a later date," answered Ronan, as if the omission was no skin off of his back.

The man nodded smartly and said, "Before you think poorly of John Edward Calhoun, you must remember that the bankers were willing to offer up quite a windfall to those who were willing to pitch in reserves that might support the paper gold markets when they nearly collapsed in 2001 and 2009. The central bankers were never willing to offer up much more of their gold if push came to shove, but they could offer plenty of dollars and dollar-denominated assets to someone like Mr. Calhoun; someone who was quite captivated by the bells and whistles and the idolatry of the American age, and someone who had little to no practical knowledge of the underpinnings of modern currency."

"To be balanced in our considerations of Mr. Calhoun, he might have bothered to learn something from the family's struggles during the Civil War. Moreover, he was well aware that his miserable father would never have fallen for such a dubious and ultimately luckless proposition. Nevertheless, like most Americans of the 21ˢᵗ century, he had no understanding of how this Frankenstein's monster of a monetary system had become so fragile and distorted. He had no way of knowing that the truth, in any form, was like kryptonite to this beast of global enslavement. Given his limited education in finance, telling him that a free-floating price of unencumbered physical gold traded outside of the financial system was somehow representative of an instantaneous hyperinflation of the reserve currency would have been as productive as teaching a dog how to mow the lawn."

The man then turned to face Ronan and finished with his thoughts. "You have seen the truth and, therefore, that golden truth has become obvious and undeniable to you. Mr. Calhoun will never arrive at such a useful reckoning. The good news is, there are those within the family that already understand at least the merits of some form of gold ownership, if little else. Our job is to make certain that those bright few select you to complete the task of diversifying the Calhoun family's portfolio. And, to make certain it is done the right way."

Ronan didn't know it at the time, as he was unable to conceive of the man operating in a manner that was unfavorable to the Calhoun family, but that last sentence was the only hint that would be given regarding his ulterior motives. As such, Mr. Cassidy responded in a purely professional manner. "You certainly do not have to worry about receiving my best efforts on both fronts. I hope that moves us past some of the unseemly outcomes that you wished to infer were entirely possible a bit earlier."

The man remained unresponsive to Ronan's closing presumption. Instead of fretting over the lack of affirmation that he remained in good standing at that juncture, Mr. Cassidy interposed with a bit of color concerning his beliefs about the fatally flawed international monetary order. "It is truly amazing what having the right vantage point will do for the betterment of your understanding. Your insights further clarify that our problems related to money and credit are systemic and that they were baked into the cake from the onset. While one might make the argument that those responsible for the mess we face didn't know any better, I find that hard to believe. I am sure there were some that yielded in the hopes that reason might overcome those glaring flaws in the system at a later time, but it seems to me that the proposition was already scripted before World War II came to an end. As far as the Nixon Shock is concerned, "Tricky Dick" was simply the one to announce the inevitable when the time had come. They certainly couldn't have kept the fiat dollar in the driver's seat if he had waited until the Treasury had exhausted all of its gold reserves defending a continually debased currency."

The man nodded at Ronan and provided a statement of acknowledgement for his insightful commentary. "There truly were some honorable intentions involved in the gold for oil deal. What happened as time marched on was certainly to be expected, though impossible to openly establish contingencies for. And yes, Ronan, perhaps that was precisely how those with a darker agenda wished for things to be. Whatever the case may have been back then, you and I are left to consider how we might spare my employer the worst of its aftermath."

Though the man's tone had darkened considerably as he closed out that notion, Ronan chuckled politely into the lingering silence that followed his neighbor's less than amiable proclamation. He was a bit too frayed of the mind to conceal his frenetic disposition, and he lacked the energy to behave in a startled manner when his instincts were telling him he had nothing to fear, at least not presently. Furthermore, Mr. Cassidy was of the belief that the only thing left for Mother Nature to do was to withdraw the phantasmal value of the mighty dollar and let the world sort out the origins of a new currency that was to be governed by an honest, free-floating, physical gold market. At that moment, he clearly understood that only God could have devised such a simple and just solution to the wildly complex entanglements of greed and power that had evolved since 1971, if not 1913, and which now plagued our great country and the rest of the world.

The man, sensing Ronan's amusement and the pleasure he was taking from the existence of such raw irony, was willing to continue on with a bit of levity. He reasoned that establishing a bond of trust with Mr. Cassidy was going to be far more effective than trying to threaten someone overcome by a delirium that was nearly beyond the scope of fear. He would save his dry powder in that regard for another day—a day when Mr. Cassidy would be forced to make the hard choices that had become the burden of his unique and woefully unfortunate position. "I do truly believe that the advancements that came with fiat currency needed to shine of their own accord before flaming out for all to see. The unbacked dollar needed to prosper for a time so that we might finally understand the evolution of a balanced financial system. Unfortunately, two generations of hard-working American savers, farmers, teachers, and laborers will have to endure the severe misfortune of watching their dollar purchasing power and, therefore, the value of their investments in dollar-denominated assets, eradicated as we, those among the global collective, continue to learn our way through the complexities of money."

Ronan nodded in agreement and responded to the man almost cheerfully, though the delusional qualities of his mental state were not so well hidden. "Well said, my anonymous friend!"

The man remained rather moved by their discussion concerning the rise and fall of the dollar. Some frightfully maligned part of his essence had survived the seedier elements of the almighty dollar's destructive capacity, and what remained of him was now the direct beneficiary of its continuing largesse to those in positions of power. In many ways, the unfortunate turns of his life had been the byproduct of the gross deformations of society caused by the dollar's unnatural proliferation. He spoke further of the promise of tomorrow. "Likewise, Ronan, the poor laborers of the third world, those who have been effectively enslaved to keep up the proper appearances of this mirage of dollar value, have lost much while the fruits of their labor were squandered in the name of dollar debt purchase support. Yet, on a less dour note, it is also true that some of those "emerging market" laborers have gained some lifestyle due to the progression of the global economy, which was arguably helped along by trade being conducted in fungible fiat currency."

The man turned his head to look out the window and gauge their proximity to Chicago before saying, "Hopefully, America will succeed when the playing field is level, and workers and savers the world over are once again able to retain the fruits of their excess production without undue risk and the burden of inflation. On the day that gold is set free, the ivory towers of Wall Street and Washington will have seen their dour influence rendered limp as a eunuch. Perhaps, those foundational keystones of our profane society will be reduced to the vessels of public service they were always intended to be."

"I hope that you are correct," responded Ronan. "It would be quite a sight to see a monetary system that does not rely on an ever-increasing transfer of paper wealth from those forced to save their modest wages in dollars to the dollar-based asset holders who already prosper. I would certainly be in support of such an arrangement. I also understand the pain that will be inflicted upon those who refuse to see the stark nature of the truth that is being unveiled before their eyes a bit more with each passing day."

"Indeed," said the man while shifting his focus elsewhere. "If only your future client had the good sense to maintain such a vantage point before pledging what there was of the family's gold for paper wealth. Even with the benefit of hindsight, and at the time John Edward's father, Charles, had committed to a far less grandiose version of a dollar asset for dusty gold in the vault deal, it would have appeared as quite an opportunity to expand the family's net worth and influence. The bull equity and debt markets of the early eighties commenced as expected once the mirage of cheap oil priced in dollars got the ball rolling and those overprinted dollars being spent the world over began to return home to Wall Street. Furthermore, their friends, family, and business partners in Washington continued right on spending until our corrupted government was the lifeblood of the American economy."

The man paused to consider those of the time when the honorable constituents of his bloodline had become entangled with the Calhoun tribe and added, "Though his great-great grandfather, Edward Calhoun, who sacrificed much to salvage the family business in the aftermath of the Civil War, might still be turning over in his grave, John Edward's decision to go "all in" after Charles died was looking quite prescient for a time. Those dollars kept flowing into Wall Street and Washington once the twin disruptions of the Euro's introduction and the bursting of the tech bubble had passed. Although just about everything that drove the markets higher after 2001 was paper shuffling to mask inflation and bubbles being blown in every sector to accommodate the necessary expansion of the world's reserve currency, the temporary surge in the Calhoun family's stated paper wealth was quite impressive."

The man paused to take a breath and deaden his mildly enamored tone. "Some of the rapid increases in the value of the dollar-denominated assets received in exchange for Charles Calhoun's "small-scale" divestiture of the family wealth reserves had to do with the growth in real productive output of those company shares he owned, or at least it appeared that way. As we both know, "productive" is a slippery and relative term at this late stage of the dollar's life-cycle. Perhaps that is why John Edward felt emboldened to take things a bit too far."

The man looked up to gather his thoughts for a brief while. He was reaching the heart of the matter, and his selective disclosure at that moment was paramount to setting Mr. Cassidy on his proper course that morning. Once he was satisfied with his tact, he added, "However, I suspect that someone within the organization is looking to make good on an ancient pledge to those that belong to the demon class that I spoke of earlier. They are looking to take control of the aging Calhoun imperium as payment on an eternal contract that they view to be spuriously vitiated, though I doubt their beliefs are based on anything more than spite. Be that as it may, the deviant seed of that old hobgoblin was not eradicated, and those of its line seek to once again consolidate their power precisely as the stars align for some form of permanent settlement."

Ronan was catching on quickly. His eyes grew wide with surprise. At that point in his life, he understood that those belonging to the demonic principalities were quite real, and that meant things were hurriedly taking a second turn into those realms that would be deemed delusive by the common observer. The man, seeing that he had hit his mark, spoke to conclude that sticky moment of the informal yet meticulously planned gathering. "These are old, knotty, and unsettled affairs, my friend. Nevertheless, it would appear that you are the one appointed to preside over what promises to be the concluding episode in an ancient drama approaching its climax. That is why the future success of your endeavors has become so critical and so fraught with danger."

After his rather stark warning, the man smiled warmly at Ronan. He smiled with the knowing look of someone who realized he had captured the implied trust and coerced loyalty of his adherent. Ronan felt a strange kind of appreciation for the care and detail with which the man had revealed such trusted secrets of the financial world and his powerful employer, despite being once again apprehensive and rather tired of both his body and mind. After all, that employer possessed enough influence to arrange for a commercial airliner to be turned around in mid-flight, which in and of itself was a frightening proposition. Though Mr. Cassidy still believed that he would depart the aircraft in good order, he also understood that this man's neat little trick was only the beginning as it concerned his ability to confine and control Ronan's actions in the seasons, and perhaps years, to come. Beyond that, the unfathomable ramifications of his failure to win the Calhoun mandate seemed to be lurking just beneath the thin veneer of the man's refined and sometimes affable mannerisms.

The man looked over at the cover of his magazine, which remained resting on the window seat, and began again. He wished to bring things to a satisfactory conclusion. "In the opinion of many amongst the wealthiest class, and certainly those of the long-established pedigrees, there is no longer any sport in obtaining more dollars than what is needed to manage their extravagant lifestyles. To those folks, the fact that dollars are being readily printed to cover any and all obligations signals the end of their functional timeline."

"What do you suppose that means for our task at hand?" Ronan asked with a rather blank stare pinned to his guise. His question was not entirely well-considered, but the oversight was forgivable given what he had endured.

The man was a bit surprised by the dullness tied to the inquiry, given Mr. Cassidy's previously displayed capacity for wit. However, he understood that his guest was reaching the outer bounds of his ability to be tested during that hour. Though Ronan's inexperience in his trade had always been a concern, and while that naivete was showing out a bit as he tired, the man answered with an air of diplomacy rather than calling Mr. Cassidy's slight mental lapse to task.

"That means we are lingering in that strange interlude that lies between the end of determination and the moment of realization. As you can imagine, Ronan, that leaves my employer in a rather precarious position as gold liquidity continues to evaporate with steadily increasing velocity. I point that out to you only because I understand that you have not yet ventured into the gold market with such sizable demands. It is a rather opaque forum and riddled with devilry. I do not envy your position in that regard. However, I will leave it to you to get creative when the time comes to settle that long-overdue trade tied to this unfortunate and enduring affair. After all, there is a reason that you are here."

Ronan had not yet tied the eyes of the man to those of the boy in his vision. He was, however, beginning to sense that the reason he was cast into the middle of this apparently sordid matter had more to do with the strange man now prodding him than filling a sizeable order for gold; an order that would presumably allow those of some miscreant family to carry on in the wake of the most disruptive financial realignment the world has ever known. While he considered that forceful notion, Mr. Cassidy nodded silently in reply to the man's latter supposition.

Though he was curious in regard to his guest's suddenly guarded nature, the man continued speaking. There was little time to spare. "While you have only seen the old and more eccentric assets of Superior, I can assure you that John Edward fared quite well from the period after his father passed until the financial system came apart at the seams in 2009. Mr. Calhoun has also fared well from 2010 until today because the Federal Reserve has bought up every asset it could get its hands on in the open market at grotesquely overvalued prices. Nevertheless, he understands that he was not truly made whole and that many of the valuations applied to his holdings are little more than window dressing designed to keep bank balance sheets afloat. He can watch CNN all he wants to fill his head with conjured reports on the robust nature of the economy, but a man like John Edward Calhoun sees what is happening at the bottom line."

Mr. Cassidy made no motion to acknowledge the man's useful revelation, and his host never thought to scan Ronan's insipid, though nearly thoughtful, guise before saying, "The problem that the Calhoun family faces today, even before the dollar goes into the dustbin of history, is that there is little liquidity for their private enterprises in a down economy. New loans to keep the enterprises running at loss are in abundance, but no reasonable value will be paid for the equity ownership without ungodly and certainly catastrophic amounts of leverage. Those once-formidable enterprises, such as Superior, and other more traditional financial investments are much of what remains of that once-invincible and multi-generational Calhoun wealth. To say that John Edward's lack of leadership and understanding of the financial marketplace has been a drain on the family enterprise would be an understatement."

"The good news for you, Ronan, is that there are others within the organization who sense that they are exposed, though they lack the totality of your own discernment to fully understand the reasons why. It scares them all to death to think that if another seismic event occurred within our foundering financial system, they would be left to turn a hoe to feed the family, so to speak. Given these diverging political wills within the clan, there is an opening for you to step into. There is a way that you might help them see just how precarious their "unbacked" financial position truly is. The biggest challenge you face is that the amount of unencumbered physical gold they can procure now, at least when compared to what they once owned, will truly be a religious experience for them."

The man paused for another brief respite, reached over to his left, and put his grey hat back over the dark hair that covered his perfectly rounded head. When the hat was situated as the man wished, he concluded his summary of the current state of the Calhoun family finances. "Again, you must understand that the dollar world is all that John Edward Calhoun will currently acknowledge, Ronan. He still believes in the paper illusion of wealth. Even after the events of 2009 shook his faith in the system to the core. John Edward was not alive the last time Americans were allowed to use gold as money within our borders. Though he no longer believes that the dollar is invincible somewhere deep within those only partially functioning recesses of his blunted mind, he sees no other way to recoup what was so suddenly realized to have been lost than to keep playing the same game."

The man turned to study Mr. Cassidy so that he might gauge his response before saying, "Unfortunately for our benevolent patriarch, the real money coming into the Calhoun dynasty these days comes from their enterprises of a more dubious nature. Those illicit operations are beyond his control. While that fact may or may not stand to one day save his mortal soul, that is the only reason John Edward has allowed you to speak to the board of the company that protects the oldest and most prized of the family's legacy assets. He doesn't want you there, but the others near to seizing control of things desperately wish to hire someone capable of swaying his opinion on the matter of "portfolio diversification," lest they seize a worthless conglomeration in the years to come."

The man paused to think back on his walk through a quaint and timeless churchyard back in those more pleasant days before he was driven into exile; those days before he had fallen into the wicked man's trap, and allowed his thirst for vengeance to get the better of him. There was a moment in the aftermath of that event when he believed he was a dead man. A dead man with an empty soul, who was only waiting for the world to go dark when he least expected his end to arrive. Something wicked had been festering deep within those secretive yet vaunted conclaves of the Calhoun family back then. He knew that the presence was of the dark Morgenthau line, his maternal kin, but he hadn't yet stared into those foul crimson eyes of both unspoken legend and heinous portent.

Though his only saving grace in the fall of 2011 was his connection to the very thing that those of the loins of that ancient demon had failed to possess for the last century or more, he was no longer certain that those protections of yesterday still held. Something had shifted behind the scenes while he was off digging for gold and cleansing the brutal heart of darkness that governed those savage yet beautiful jungles deep in the mountains of Columbia. That he had been called home from his exile to supervise the affairs involving Mr. Cassidy most certainly meant that someone deep within the organization had played a pivotal card for his benefit, or perhaps the benefit of those that remained standing in opposition to the Calhouns of the modern era and those other unsavory ghosts from the past that exerted their will within the family.

The man had no intention of speaking about any of that just then, if ever. He shook his head in a disapproving manner for emphasis, and intoned something designed to help Mr. Cassidy continue to understand the political will that governed his whale of a prospect. "Losing money, or even losing the perception of money, is something that these nearly heartless people cannot accept. In truth, the Calhouns and their inner circle would rather lose a child than even a penny that they remember once finding and claiming as their own. Such a thing sounds horrific to you or me, but expectations of wealth and power are a sickness that is bred into their blood at birth and taught to them as innately as a common man might learn to breathe in the air. Most of them are caught up in the throes of your typical dollar neurosis. Your only hope is to convince them that they will be left with nothing if they do not hold some gold to ride out the coming currency storm."

The man then shook his head again and somberly added, "Sadly, they may prefer nothing at all to anything less than what the currently contrived dollar values of their assets tell them they are worth today."

To which Ronan answered, "I have noticed that to be a strange trait that persists among several of the families and organizations I speak with as part of my business development efforts. Unfortunately, I have not had any luck overcoming the stubborn tendency. I believe you when you suggest that it might be inborn."

The man closed his eyes and replied mindfully. He had reached the end of an already oversold pitch. "I know your past well, Mr. Cassidy. Therefore, I also understand that, with my assistance, you alone are the one to ensure that the right thing gets done regarding this extremely delicate matter. I am counting on you, and that should be more than enough to persuade you to find a way to get things done. Furthermore, as inhospitable as I have been prodded to become at times, those of the darker bents within the family are likely to make a show of your demise if they wind up as commoners."

The man laughed softly and reminiscently at the thought of a few of those elegant yet nasty noblemen showing up for an honest day of work. For his part, Ronan choked down the sudden need to cough rather violently. The man chuckled a bit more while he signaled with his hand for the flight attendant to bring the stifled gentleman some water.

What the man failed to disclose to Mr. Cassidy at that moment was that a man by the name of Lucius Manley, while under the direction of another, had already won the war with John Edward Calhoun regarding the purchase of at least enough gold to keep the family reputable. Since reputable included the substantial lifestyle expenses the family simply must incur in order to appear in public, in addition to the escalating costs of keeping their many dubious skeletons from the past buried in the event the dollar did indeed flame out, the amount was not insignificant. Nor would it be easily acquired in an allocated and unencumbered form. There was already a dearth of physically transferable bullion reserves housed within the vaults belonging to any of the major players that were active in a market that had become largely a paper trading arena by the early-spring of 2017.

Beyond that purposeful oversight, the man did not tell Mr. Cassidy that the primary objective of their partnership was actually to expose the Calhouns and their handlers of the Morgenthau line for their sins of the past and, most certainly, those heinous deeds that involved his immediate family. That he had been called home from exile in Columbia, where he was already attempting to extricate raw ore from the ground, by John Edward's sister, Talia, to oversee the matter of vetting those pitching for the business of assisting with a large gold purchase, spoke volumes concerning the tumultuous state of affairs behind the scenes. Someone in the know had said something to someone about where things might be headed financially. As such, the man was the one to initially arm Talia's son, Lucius Manley, with enough credibility to achieve some small measure of success with John Edward, or at least frighten John Edward into accepting Mr. Cassidy's invitation to present the capabilities of his firm where it concerned asset diversification. All the while, Ronan was led to believe that a little birdie had dropped the lead of his career magically into his lap. He was still that green.

The veiling of the aforementioned essential actualities was precisely as the man wished for things to remain that morning. They were all things that would be brought to light in due time and as necessary. The man did not require Mr. Cassidy to sell John Edward on the idea of buying gold. That difficult task was already in the process of being accomplished quite naturally and due to obvious necessity by the red-eyed Morgenthau man, who pulled many of the strings from behind the scenes. In fact, the man's work regarding his Columbian mining ventures and bringing the house of Calhoun to its knees would have been far easier if he believed John Edward would be allowed to carry on without rectifying the issue of the dishoarded family wealth reserves. Given as much, what the man had planned did require that Mr. Cassidy become the custodian of record for the gold purchases and several of the older Superior-related accounts. The two primary reasons he required such a thing to come to fruition would not be disclosed until the end came to this clever game upon which he had staked what he perceived to be the very deliverance of his own redemption.

Though the man did feel a bit guilty about shading the truth in regard to his communications with Mr. Cassidy, he presumed that his revelations on the inner workings of the financial system were at least a sporting measure of recompence offered in response to his purposeful omission. No one would argue the point that the truthful gold for oil tale was primarily told to assist Mr. Cassidy with his quest to win the Calhoun's business, which was a feat that the man absolutely required to execute his still tenuous plans. Be that as it may, the dapper gentleman did sincerely hope that the stunning information would prove exceedingly useful to Mr. Cassidy in his very specialized and still developing professional endeavors. That is, assuming the point did not become moot due to Mr. Cassidy's obstinance somewhere down the road.

Now, Ronan had been worked over quite thoroughly over the course of the last half-hour or more. Furthermore, he had been caught off guard, his equilibrium had been thrown into a foreign intelligence agency-grade blender, and he had been rudely ordered to take on an assignment that he would have willingly begged for only an hour before; before being elucidated on the presumably dubious inner workings of the Calhoun family fiefdom. That being said, Mr. Cassidy was exceedingly cautious as it concerned any matter that he did not fully understand. Though the man had tried to knock him squarely off of his foundation, he remained watchful and not yet inclined to consider how he might leap headlong into the act of meeting this strange man's expectations.

Though he did feel quite threatened in this instance, Mr. Cassidy's intuition continued to signal that he needed to gather as much information as he could before he revealed anything of his dismally drawn hand. In regard to the man sitting next to him, Ronan had correctly figured on three things: The first was that the man was well educated and clearly understood the mindset of Ronan's typical client; the second was that the man was capable of acting with lethal consequence, though Ronan believed that his comely neighbor preferred to avoid violence at all costs; the third bit of information, which Ronan had surmised on that diabolical morning, was that the relationship existing between this strange and knowledgeable man and his employer was not quite right. The latter of those nuggets of acquired wisdom was the one causing Ronan to fret the most, simply because he believed that he might be caught up in the middle and useless to both sides at some point during the settlement of that ancient entanglement.

Ronan took a deep breath with his eyes closed. When he exhaled, he decided that the best course of action was to play along. Arriving at such a conclusion was not rocket science, mind you. It is worth noting, however, that Mr. Cassidy believed his decision was optimal despite the fact that he had never approached, let alone interacted with, someone who had previously acted with such presumably lethal abandon in the course of their commercial affairs. As such, and with careful consideration given to all of his troubling thoughts concerning the shocking events of that morning, he posed the safest question he could muster. In so doing, he had hoped to learn something more without triggering the man's penchant for using unnerving words and oddly delivered impulses that were designed to clarify his ability to enforce his will upon Mr. Cassidy. Ronan doubted that he would react to receiving another passive threat with as much diplomacy as he had employed during the man's prior instigations. He was at his wits end.

With little to no forethought of expectation and in the manner of someone looking to pass the time, Mr. Cassidy calmly asked, "The information you have provided to me today is invaluable to my career ambitions. Where did you hear of such high-level, second-hand accounts of those rarely discussed deliberations and under-the-table agreements concerning the historical constructs underlying the dollar and gold? Of course, I am presuming that you did not witness those events directly. Though you are certainly wiser, you do not appear any older than I am."

The man smiled at Ronan. He did not hesitate to reveal his source. "One of my only true friends at the secondary academy I attended back in Virginia was from very old money. One night, when his father was just a few brandies shy of actually finding some religion in his life, he told me all about his work at the U.S. Treasury and the Federal Reserve during those days. He even allowed me to partake in a few cold beers while he divulged those scintillating secrets of the world monetary order. My apologies if I had led you to believe that the people I represent might interact with that sort of statesman. Those hidden demons pulling at the good man's strings perhaps, but in that instance, I would have divulged that I was speaking from the vantage point of probable hearsay. I never thought much of what he told me back then, but it began to make more sense some years later, after I had reclaimed a dear gift that was taken from me in my childhood."

The man laughed graciously and added, "I am glad that I had the foresight to pay attention. I suspect that had I let him drink a bit more, he would have eventually spilled some of the spicier details, but I didn't know any better in those days, and I never had a dollar to my name to fret over."

Ronan laughed a bit in a gracious yet mentally spent manner, and asked, "Even armed with such indispensable knowledge, what makes you think that

I can convince the men entrusted by your employer, or even your employer for that matter, to reacquire significant amounts of gold for the Superior Freight portfolio? It has been my experience thus far that those fully given over to a false paradigm will choose to remain in that milieu rather than experience the sting of real-world consequence. These days, most prefer the sugary suppressants and not the stuff that actually works."

The man sent a hard yet discerning look in Ronan's direction. Mr. Cassidy noticed little beyond the intense narrowing of his scathing eyes. The man did this only to reinforce the necessity of baiting John Edward and his men to buy specifically into what Ronan was selling. Without providing verbal notice of that starkly displayed thought, he shifted gears a hair by softening his expression, and then replied in a calming yet mildly devious tone. "It is good to see that your facial color has softened much from the aposematic burn of our rather bumpy beginning. That is a welcome sign, Ronan. It is a sign that you possess the capacity to overcome your fears when you have been pushed well beyond your comfort zone."

The man turned his eyes away from Ronan so that he might think a bit more expressively before adding, "John Edward is not a man of stout mind or formidable character. Yet, I feel the need to warn you about dealing with him. Unlike most of his ilk, he is not a wicked man by way of his natural demeanor. Moreover, he does not tend to be assertive because he spent the prime years of his life being overwhelmed and overshadowed by his vile old man. I can also tell you that Mr. Calhoun is a fearful and cowardly man at heart. Those verities might tempt you to breathe a false sigh of relief when the opposite is true. What you must never forget is that John Edward is a dull and deadly man when provoked by fear, and he is a man who was taught his particular brand of ruthlessness by that same father, who was perhaps the cruelest man I have known."

Ronan choked down a gasp, and the man said, "You must force him to become dull and deadly, and, therefore, resentfully in agreement with your proposal, only after your knowledge of gold and wealth preservation has won the day with the others present in that boardroom. Sadly, however, you must provoke him to secure the mandate because he does not want to admit to what he has done while he still believes the dollar markets might save him. The rub there, my friend, is that if you provoke him before the red-eyed man, or his assigns, are in your corner, you will need to return home with your head on a swivel."

The man laughed openly while Ronan grew wide-eyed yet again, and concluded by saying, "If you survive the provocation, the blunt hammer will be handed to you once John Edward realizes that he cannot wield the tool he needs to make the matter disappear."

The man chuckled rather joyfully once again, and then added an addendum to his description of the woeful predicament in an effort to lift the spirits of one with such a stark expression lighting up his naturally welcoming guise. "What an elementary assignment for one as astute as you are, my friend! But fear not. I will be with you in spirit the entire time, and never far from your side if I sense that you or those you love are in imminent danger."

Ronan giggled outright at the man's response because he was too far gone to do otherwise at that point. The reaction was part nervous tic and part madness. The madness was instigated by the surreal situation that had ensnared him without warning. Once the laughter came to an abrupt and awkward halt, he responded dutifully to his resurgent antagonist. "Better me than you, I suppose."

The man laughed heartily at Ronan's tricky quip and rejoined with, "If it makes you feel any better, Ronan, please know that if I was still in the position to evince John Edward's unfailing trust, as I once was, I would never have lured you into such a sticky predicament. Furthermore, I would never have exposed myself simply to meet you, as I have done this morning. Not even in the manner of our fully controlled little goat rodeo here."

Ronan laughed again. This time he sniggered childishly at the man's choice of words while he asked a far bolder question of his host. "Does John Edward know that you are visiting with me in person this morning, or are you working for your own benefit?"

As Ronan had struck something of a nerve, the man was not as cordial with his somewhat plucky guest. "John Edward knows that I am vetting you. My job is to provide him with feedback on your suitability to become a business partner to the family in the event he decides to pursue your agenda. He knows that, as part of my current assignment, I have learned quite a bit about gold and its rather opaque marketplace. Nothing this extravagant will remain a secret from him. What he will never know, however, is the nature of our conversation, Mr. Cassidy. That fact will remain an inviolable truth. Otherwise, John Edward might think that I am trying to trick him into doing something solely for my benefit. That is how his childlike mind works. Giving him such knowledge will have disastrous consequences for us both, as you will simply become a potential accessory to my contumacy and a thorny matter that he will prefer to make go away. Do know that we are bound by one another's confidences on this fine morning, my friend and future colleague. There is no changing that now."

Ronan grimaced slightly, nodded, and then responded rather dully, knowing that he had been not only sternly warned but also reminded that his predicament was quite real. "Fair enough. I have little choice but to side with the devil I know."

The man looked upward for a quick moment. He had a quizzical expression of anticipation frozen on his comely mien. He appeared as if he was listening for something that he was expecting to sound off at any moment. At hearing what he awaited off in the distance, or upon deciding that the time was not right, the man affirmed Ronan's statement with a genuinely encouraging and upbeat rhythm to his hopeful voice. "Unfortunately, Ronan, you and I are now unlikely but faithful partners in circumstance. I will do my best to ensure that everything works out quite favorably for you if you will endeavor to extend me the same courtesy."

"Of course," responded Ronan in a bit of a disheartened fashion, "what choice do I have?"

The man seemed to disregard Mr. Cassidy's implied grievance, and said, "Your assignment will take some time, but it is not accepted without its justly due rewards. You will hear from me if such correspondence is required. Otherwise, know that I am working on your behalf behind the scenes. When you have achieved your goal concerning John Edward, I will see you again."

To which Ronan replied, "And what if I fail to achieve my goal regarding Mr. Calhoun or Superior, Sir? What then?"

The man looked down at his shoes. Seeing nothing to wipe free from their impeccable shine, he closed out the conversation while the returning aircraft fell into line for a westward approaching landing at Chicago O'Hare. "Spending your time thinking about such unfortunate and unproductive alternatives is a disservice to us both, Ronan. I am fully behind you. That will be more than enough. Although I suspect that you are beginning to understand that there is a greater power at work within you, one that shares a common enemy with the timid and hopeful boy I once was."

Suddenly, something clicked into place for Ronan. He finally understood who the blue-eyed man was, or at least that he somehow fit into the progression of his awakening and rebirth. He nodded swiftly in reply to conceal his rising hopes. The man received the response as acceptable and looked out into the aisle when the stewardess came over the loudspeaker to announce that the plane was about to land. Following the announcement, and in direct opposition to proper airline protocol, the man stood up to depart. Ronan quickly wiped down his shirt and pants a final time with the clean towel resting in his lap while the man gathered his few items and straightened his shirt and pants.

Once Mr. Cassidy appeared nearly fit to return to the outside world, the man offered his hand. When Ronan shook that hand with a curious look set upon his otherwise restive guise, the man spoke firmly. "Have a safe journey home, Ronan. A second flight will be ready for you in thirty minutes or so. It was a pleasure to meet you, and I truly enjoyed speaking with you today. I understand that our encounter will require some soul searching to seem altogether real once I have departed. Take your time with everything and do your job to the best of your ability. The rest will fall into place."

Ronan nodded and attempted to respond by uttering, "Likewise," but he didn't feel like being insincere just then. The man understood as much, and said, "If it makes you feel any better, I will tell you that I do believe God is calling you to do great things. Although I am certainly not someone to be viewed as having the proper credentials to convey the intentions of the divine, I have seen as much in my dreams, and I hope for the sake of my soul that what I have seen is true. You are seeking something in earnest, as you awaken to the truth of your imprisonment. While I can't say if I shall ever be forgiven for the terrible things that I have done, my credibility in regard to such a seemingly outlandish statement derives from the fact that I am well versed in that particular phenomenon. Perhaps one day, you will return the favor of delivering such a hopeful message."

Ronan nodded yet again, though half-heartedly, in the hopes that his disinterested silence would bring things to an end just a bit sooner. The man sensed Ronan's will at that moment, but proceeded to expound upon his prior statement. "I will also tell you that you are close to finding what you seek. Stay the course. The true possibilities of the world are in the process of being revealed to the faithful. The meek shall one day inherit the earth. The truth of that statement lies at the heart of my bitter existence. Who else might drive these demons from the face of the earth in preparation for such a lovely occasion?"

Ronan released his fading grip on the man's hand and spoke to him almost indirectly, as if he had suddenly become somewhat addled. "I believe that I have seen you someplace before. Exactly where that was will come to me in time. It is quite comforting to hear that God is asking something of me here today and not the devil himself, though I hope you will pardon my initial hesitance in believing such a thing."

The man stepped cleverly past Ronan and out into the aisle. Before he made his way up to the empty first row in the first-class cabin to prepare for arrival, he spoke one final time in the manner of formally parting ways. "All I ask is that you follow your heart, my friend. I was once given over to the ways of the darker order when it came to compelling men to my will. Not today, however. I believe that you and I have chosen to walk in intersecting directions. I hope that we are able to stay true to our intended purpose until we reach the end of this shared endeavor. If we do, I am certain that all will be well. I believe that to be true for reasons that neither you nor I conceive to be possible, Mr. Ronan James Cassidy. For the second time in my life, I am truly hopeful. I will worry about the reasons behind the need for a third occurrence of such an expectant shine when that moment arrives."

The man returned his hat to the top of his head, winked encouragingly at Ronan, and added, "Your task with Mr. Calhoun is not as daunting as I led you to believe, but do proceed with an abundance of caution."

Ronan nodded in return to the man's closing benediction of sorts. He appeared as if he were somewhat dazed and certainly lost in the thoughts and dreams of another time and another place altogether. This final and rapid change of direction was almost too much for Mr. Cassidy to wrap his mind around.

The man took notice of the blank, or even troubled, look on Ronan's face. He offered up the last of the words of encouragement that he knew to give to someone who was struggling to find a useful focal point or center of gravity, as it were. "If you doubt your ability to persevere as you move forward, Mr. Cassidy, I can tell you from my own experience that the strongest among us are not those who arm themselves to wield power over others, but those who allow God to reveal His strength through them. Those of enduring faith are the truly unstoppable forces of this world. A beautiful woman and a distant ancestor of mine taught me that not so long ago. You have nothing to fear because you are in good hands."

The man winked at Ronan one last time and quickly disappeared up the aisle and into a seat in the first row. Ronan closed his eyes to rest for the short time that he remained suspended above the clouds and the worries certain to follow that life-changing affair. He thought back to a singular moment in time that seemed to soothe his tremoring heart. It had been a long and trying morning. The world below would be a far different place when the aircraft returned to the scarred asphalt of the awaiting runway. Much had been revealed in the preceding hour, things that somehow fit into the grand and quickly evolving patchwork quilt of Mr. Cassidy's once deliberately and now rapidly blooming metamorphosis. The door that he might walk through to leave behind all of those dismal missteps that once troubled him had been opened, and he was never so afraid. He was left to question nearly everything he had ever known.

Chapter 10

ON THE ROAD HOME

After quickly departing the plane once they had landed and making his way through the busy airport, the man exited Terminal Three at the lower level. He had passed beyond a few of the baggage claim areas before making his way into the dampening air of mid-April. He carried only a small leather brief with two straps that fastened into loop and buckle mechanisms at each end of the case. The leather that comprised the body of the brief was smooth, slightly worn, and of a rich and dark reddish-brown tone. The shoulder strap was of a much lighter hue, a sandy blond perhaps, but also crafted of fine leather. Once he was outside, the man walked a hundred yards or so across the access roads beneath the raised thoroughfares of the upper level of the bustling terminal. He never once steadied his stride for the few vehicles that approached while he completed the crossing.

There was a cold and steady rain coming down at that hour. The poor weather had moved in quickly from the west and settled into the once clear and promising blue skies that accompanied first light. Those pretty skies that the man had looked out upon from the vantage point of the swiftly cruising airplane had become little more than a fleeting memory. Based on what he had seen out the window toward the end of the flight, the wet and foul weather he was experiencing on the ground was not an entirely unexpected turn, though it was certainly one that was unwelcome. Nothing present in the texture of the damp, low-lying air matched the confines of the cloudless, sunny skies he had witnessed from above less than an hour earlier. Furthermore, at the time the man was notified of his pressing errand to isolate and speak with Mr. Cassidy, none of the pleasant ladies covering the weather down in Chicago had mentioned that such a dreary day lay in wait.

Although the same expectations of warmth and sunshine, which might move the enduring winter closer to its long-awaited end, were also true for those walking the same pathways and crosswalks as the man not thirty minutes ago, so went the throes of the early spring season in the great Midwestern metropolis. Though it was April, the cold air now coursing in from the northwest and the rain that had savaged the once fine and hopeful spring morning still belonged more to the winter months than to those of spring. When the man walked out from beneath the final overpass, he zipped his overcoat to the top of its track and tucked his chin and mouth into the top of that jacket to preserve something of his warmth as he stepped into the raw, wet weather, which seemed to seep into the very marrow of his bones. He checked rapidly for any oncoming traffic approaching from the hotel parking lot as he crossed that final thoroughfare. Seeing nothing moving in his direction, he quickened the tempo of his purposeful steps by increasing both the speed and length of his strides. The echoing thunder of the larger trucks and buses passing by on the raised road above masked the cascading pitter-patter of the light rain falling intermittently upon the concrete and asphalt that the man traversed as he smartly made his way to his destination below.

After walking a short way in the open, he lifted his chin from the top of his coat to scan the hotel parking lot. He soon spotted his black car waiting at the other end of that narrow car park in front of the Hilton. Precisely as the man had expected, the black club car was idling beneath the glass awning of the check-in station. He lowered his moistened face back down to the ground to shield his countenance from the rain and continued walking in a defined direction and with purpose. As he pressed on, he watched the water from the gathering rain run speedily across the rectangular sidewalk slats beneath his well-made shoes. He followed the motion of the running water until it settled into and poured over the fine shallow grooves of the long since dried cement blocks.

There were explosive pops where the largest of the raindrops struck the grooves of the concrete directly. Those forceful disruptions were quickly erased and overrun by the reemergence of the gently streaming flows of the lightly viscous and partially settled running water. The rain that had already fallen immediately reestablished its intended course along the entirety of the pathway after each intermittent blowout of the concave and circular collisions of the larger raindrops falling from the low-hanging clouds drifting ominously across the skies above. The grooves in the sidewalk had been left by some purposeful brush strokes taken in recurrent motions to smooth the drying concrete. Those deliberate, defining strokes were made a decade ago by a long-forgotten Guatemalan refugee. One who did what he could to exploit the dollar's overvalued exchange rate in an effort to feed his extended family and their twelve children on six dollars per hour taken off the books.

When the man reached the glass front awning of the hotel, which extended across the façade of the square building adorned in black, tinted glass, he raised his eyes from the sidewalk. A large, round man, with neither the look of someone happy in their present circumstances nor the mannerisms of someone who appeared to take much care in administering to their given responsibilities, was standing to his left. He was smoking a cigarette next to the lean, waist-high, plastic receptacle designed to accommodate the remains of that generally frowned upon habit.

The man noted that the smoking fellow had a lightly salted black mustache and beard. He also donned a grey windbreaker, which rested squarely on his gargantuan belly before hanging down over the uncomfortable and quite indeterminable situation taking place in the area where his jeans met with his Chicago Bears tee-shirt. His formerly white tennis shoes with blue trim and wide laces were worn and had been molded under duress to expand well past their rubber bottoms and, therefore, distended with a rounded fullness beyond the conceivable bounds of their manufactured condition. As the exhalation of his smoke visibly diffused into the cold, wet air, the man stepped a bit quicker as he passed this smoking man. He wished to avoid the onslaught of the thick, pungent, and gripping tentacles of the tobacco-laden vapors sifting outward in the form of an escalating plume.

The man reached the bell stand shortly thereafter. While nodding to the almost indiscernible form behind the wheel of the black car, he reached into his coat pocket and handed the bellman a twenty-dollar bill. He then thanked the youthful porter for allowing his driver to wait for his arrival while parked in the hotel check-in area. He would have given the bellman more, as money in those amounts was no object to him, but he preferred not to draw undue attention to his activities during those rare moments he was exposed to the public view at that stage of his life. In any event, the man figured that the young gentleman could certainly cover his lunch with the tip. He smiled warmly and hurriedly responded, "of course," when the bellman thanked him for the generous gesture.

The man then proceeded to walk over to the black car until he reached the vehicle. He opened the back passenger side door, as it was closest to the sidewalk. Once the car door had been pulled open, he placed his brief on the far seat, turned to his right while placing his left foot inside the car, and sat down on the rich leather of the interior. While pausing for a brief moment before he firmly shut his door, he reflected upon the fact that his brief period of exposure out in the open had come to an end without incident. He then closed the door with its deeply tinted windows and remained hidden from the outside world for quite some time.

When the car was rolling out past the airport grounds and onto interstate 195, the driver, who was named Daniel, rolled down the thick, black partition glass between the front and back compartments of the car. He wished to address the man. Daniel was an interesting character, to say the least. He was very slim and appeared slightly skeletal in the face and extremities. Daniel was also the kind of driver who liked to philosophize fairly deeply on matters when given the opportunity to do so. Such a "needy" trait was not always welcomed by the man, yet Daniel's inquisitive nature was never wholly rebuffed by his employer at that point in their enduring relationship. In many ways, they were friends, and the man was woefully short on those most delicate and fruitful of life's blessings.

Irrespective of his colorful personal quirks, Daniel did know how to do three things very well. Those traits, which were dearly esteemed by the man, did not, however, fully explain Daniel's current station behind the wheel, as his employer's only relied upon driver. Daniel could drive for long hours without a break, and Daniel could drive nearly undeterred by external stimuli under even the most extreme situations of duress. Still and all, the most important of those three aforementioned traits was the fact that Daniel could communicate with the man in a way that did not irritate or offend his younger boss. Though he was a chatty older gent, Daniel knew how to keep his thoughts to himself when due provision called for silence, and he also knew how to be very pragmatic and resourceful in the rare moments that he was called upon to provide advice.

Daniel had not been made aware of the reasons for his employer's rare venture into such an exposed place as a commercial airport. Nevertheless, he decided not to press the matter just then. He simply greeted the man warmly by saying, "Hello, Sir. It is nice to have you back. I trust that everything is in good order."

At seeing Daniel's nearly pandering open-mouthed smile, which had no business adorning the face of an almost frail man with sixty-five years of experience on this earth, the man looked up at his driver and returned a glance of subtle wonderment. The look efficiently concealed his inner mirth, even as he responded by saying, "It is good to see you as well, Daniel. Yes, all is quite fine. Let us see if we can make it home before dark. I have to deal with a few unfortunate situations pertaining to our Columbian enterprises."

The man paused for a second to look down at a scuff, or a lingering watermark from the rain, that had remained on his otherwise perfectly polished shoe. He made his careful inspection while he repositioned his feet on the black, shag floor mat and pointed his toes slightly inward for additional comfort. After casting aside his irritation over the unwanted blemish, the man raised his eyes to Daniel's image in the reflector and added, "We will chat for a short while later, Daniel. Thank you for all that you do."

"Very good, Sir!" exclaimed Daniel, with a particular joviality that was not inherent to his overall demeanor but did arise from time to time.

The man smirked back at Daniel with a light and sarcastic inuendo of suspicion attached to that initial look of levity and then spoke by the bye. "I'll ask you just exactly how the cat managed to finally swallow the canary somewhere down the road as well, Daniel."

The man then sealed his remark with a wink toward his driver, who was still carefully looking at him in the rear imager. Daniel directed his wide-eyed smile fully into the mirror, specifically for the man's purview. "Yes, Sir," he responded, while he rolled up the back partition with the press of a two-sided button, which locked into place like a seesaw favoring one of its riders.

The dark, heavy glass began to slowly rise and relegate Daniel and the man to worlds unto themselves. While the glass went up, the man continued looking forward. The highway, once visible in front of the rapidly moving black car, appeared to become slowly engulfed by the man's steadily rising but shallow and opaque reflection in the dark glass of the divider. The man stared into the depths of the shadowy hologram of his visage rising steadily before his fixated eyes. When the glass had nearly risen to its full height, it seemed to the man that he had become locked into the false depths of the partition. Once the glass had settled into its holding frame, with a gentle compression upon entering the cushioned liner that was followed by a discernable bump, the man thought it odd that he appeared as if he were encased in some dim world within the glass. While he carefully noted his reflected posture, he did not alter his position in the slightest. After a few seconds pondering his simultaneous existence within two starkly contrasted dimensions, he looked away from this dour apparition of sorts, opened up his brief, and pulled out his phone. There were matters that required his attention.

The man quickly touched and illuminated the screen of his mobile device. When the menu prompt flashed, he hit the home button and very adroitly entered his password. When he had gained access, he quickly connected to the telephone interface by selecting another icon. The man then proceeded to push a fair number of the buttons now visible on the screen in a firm and deliberate manner until a ring sounded out from the speaker. After three waves of rolling and monotone yet pulsating beeps, a voice came across while he held the phone facing upward in his left hand. The contact identification tag displayed across the top of the man's phone read simply: Falcon. Once the connection was established, the man began leisurely looking out the window of the back door that he was resting against with his outside shoulder. He was taking notice of the first signs of spring that had appeared with the arrival of the earliest of the vibrant clusters of effervescent green out among the passing fields in the distance and the popping buds of the low shrubbery that lined the highway.

"Hello," said the swift voice with the sugary foreign accent of a young man. The voice was neither hurried nor harboring notes of concern, yet it did possess an inflection that expected expediency.

"Hello Giorgio, I hope you are well," responded the man. "I have a request for you."

"Ah, boss," said Giorgio. "What's the matter at hand?"

"There are two pressing matters for you, actually, Giorgio. First off, we have some unpleasant business on the horizon with one of our operations down in Columbia. I need you to travel to Buritica, Antioquia, first thing tomorrow. We are running into some issues concerning our mining prospects there. There are a few notables that need an absolute realignment of their beliefs."

The man lifted his eyes torpidly to the roof of the car as he finished speaking. He was calculating something and wished to relegate his visible reflection in the partition to the background of his focus.

"Okay, boss, no problem. What's the sheet?" responded Giorgio promptly.

The man answered Giorgio's question as he continued to simulate the outcome of some unrelated event in his head. "You will receive your standard package on the matter once you arrive in Buritica. It is bad business but highly profitable for you, I'm afraid, Giorgio."

The paradox of the man's reference to the job being highly profitable while using the term "afraid" was not lost upon Giorgio in the least. The young and handsome Italian was a rational actor for profit in the purest and most cold-blooded degree. Still and all, there were unfortunate tasks that were sometime requirements of his trade that Giorgio preferred to avoid.

The man spoke further. "This will not be a warning, Giorgio. There is no appetite for leniency, and that is inclusive of all ties that may lead to future retribution. That ore mine must be confirmed as copious by way of its provable reserves come fall. There are political winds of the highest order that are once again shifting. Once the immediate matter is settled, you should be clear to have Henry remain for a few months, get the right people paid or compromised, and interject a renewed sense of urgency into the project."

"Okay, boss," answered Giorgio tersely. "But you know the faces of the little ones give me nightmares until I get back to the boat."

"I know," said the man. "Make sure the young children are taken good care of. The cost of this business lies heavy on the untrained conscience. If the fact soothes your conscience any, Giorgio, you should know that these people, in particular, are all very sick. Their sickness is part of what has made them entirely impossible to reason with."

"Fair enough, boss man," Giorgio retorted.

"My advice to you is not to linger," said the man while shifting to a more business-like tone. "The atmosphere down there is always highly complex, and our political ties are not as firm as I would prefer. There is a man from the company in place down there that will direct the flow of funds. You pay who you need to pay, but honor that company man's assessment of the social and political hierarchy. Run everything through the municipality."

Giorgio was already losing interest. He shortened up just a bit on his already direct cadence, yet he did not disrespect the man in any way. "I got it, boss. Not my first rodeo down there. What is the second matter?"

The man closed his eyes and rubbed his temple gently with the primary fingers of his right hand. He contemplated discussing additional matters with Giorgio for a brief moment, but simply went on with the business of closing out the items at hand. "Thank you, Giorgio. As always, I do appreciate the certainty of execution and professionalism that you bring to your work. I am convinced that the Columbia matter will be dealt with precisely as it needs to be. It has been some weeks since I have been down there. The second matter is far less demanding at the moment, but must be managed with care just the same."

The man continued. "I spoke with a man on an airplane this morning about a curious, and in some ways for him, unfortunate, crossing of paths with one of our patriarchs. You will receive some additional information on this man. It's a low-threat situation presently. However, I fear things may escalate down the road due more to the personal agitation of our patriarch than to any of the business matters he is involved with. Please put one of our private investigative partners on his tail. They can track him and run some non-invasive psychological impact events on him. See what he believes in and how he reacts. To be clear," the man now spoke emphatically, "There is no need for anything drastic to be done at this moment. Such is far better if there is nothing that this man can directly trace. I do not want him threatened, nor do I wish for him to know that he is in imminent danger. Do you understand me, Giorgio?"

While the man began to reconsider Mr. Cassidy, his loss of visual focus was producing a blurred rush and a running together of the low-lying objects proximate to the highway that the black car was passing at a high rate of speed. Giorgio's voice came over the phone again. "The matter will be dealt with precisely as you have requested, boss."

The man closed his eyes to offset the imbalance in his equilibrium caused by the blurring flashes of the objects being passed on the road. However, he reopened those piercing blue orbs at once to scatter the uninvited images conjured by his subliminal mind, as they were far more upsetting. "Thank you, Giorgio," he replied, with a slight detachment to his air. "Take care of yourself before and after your trip. Confirm your effects and submit your anticipated remittances through Lucy." The phone then disconnected and went silent.

While once again looking at his faint reflection in the false depths of the black glass, the man touched the red "end call" button on the screen of his phone with his right index finger. He paused while he remained undecided for a brief moment, and then leaned back into the comfortable, tan leather seat back of his chair. As he reclined, his hands fell to his sides, though his left hand remained loosely grasping his phone with just enough tension to keep it from falling onto the seat. The man simultaneously closed his eyes and tilted his head back. The slow movement of the motion gently stretched the muscles at the back of his neck that ran into the base of his skull. As he inhaled deeply and slowly, he began to gently roll his neck and head in a semi-circular motion from left to right while he saw nothing. Soon thereafter, he exhaled purposefully to expel some stressful thought he could not pinpoint. He then repeated the process of rolling his neck but in reverse motion, from his right back to his left. When he had calmed considerably, he opened his eyes as his chin came to rest languidly above his chest.

Looking toward his brief with some manner of intensity, the man released the feeble hold of his left hand and dropped his phone onto the seat. The rectangular device landed flat on the back of its protective casing. When it rested still, the man turned the palm of his freed hand face up. He then made a fist with that hand and flexed the muscles of his forearm tightly as his thumb stringently closed the grip and formation of his fist. When his arm was as tense as he could muster, he reached across his body with his right hand and stroked the firm muscles of his left forearm with his cupped right hand, rubbing the tightened skin beneath his soft cotton dress shirt from the nook of his elbow to his wrist.

After a few strokes spent feeling at the potency of his lower arm, the man's right hand came to rest over the notched vein that ran down his left forearm. He could feel the trauma marks that dotted the vein beneath the fine fabric of his white dress shirt. He caressed the firm points of the scars with the tender, smooth, and circular motions of his index finger. He did this until the sensations of the raised marks tickling the papillary ridges of his index finger began to fuel an unquenchable fire that hadn't burned within him for quite some time. He had picked up the seldom entertained habit, which he despised for obvious reasons, after being exiled to Columbia under rather uncertain circumstances some years ago. He had seen and experienced things deep in the heart of that feral jungle while beginning the clean-up operations for the mine; things that left him vulnerable to experimenting with anything that might dull the searing pain that followed his exposure to such banal atrocities.

Once given over to the potent spark of those primitive urges, which came upon him rarely, he managed those moments of weakness with a refined decency, precisely as he conducted the entirety of his worldly affairs. He would never behave like those shameless addicts he witnessed in his youth. In fact, he was more likely to entertain an assignment tied to a lethal turn on behalf of the employers he loathed than he was to be seen openly in need of his mother's medication. At least there was some measure of dignity in honoring his commitments to wicked men. With that in mind, the man gently squeezed the tab at the center of the dividing console between the two back seats with the grace of a nobleman looking to procure a breath mint. The top of the console opened slowly and revealed a small storage area that contained three items.

The first item was an old black notebook with the outside covers rebound in black leather and marked by the initials "BMS." The notebook was a childish reproduction of a certain journal which was purportedly kept by the man's father back in 1977. Though the awkwardly photocopied ledger entries were somewhat legible in their own right, the man was of the belief that a few key entries had been accidentally, or perhaps even willfully, omitted. Such was hard for him to know since the journal had been sent by an older gentleman that he was not familiar with at the time. That man's family was connected to the Calhouns in some presumably indecent way, and he would have been around the same age as his father if his father were still alive. He was also a man who was clearly still living out the high times of the sixties and seventies somewhere down in South Carolina.

The fleeting recollections of the addled mind of that gentleman upon speaking to him a while back caused the man to only marginally second guess his want for the ecstasy of his temporary escape. He had already fully submitted to experiencing the numbing effects of his anticipated dose. Though he had remembered just then that the rather eccentric man by the name of Mr. Jemison had told him that he kept hold of the original journal for safekeeping, and in the name of his own self-preservation, the man possessed no desire to hop down that rabbit hole. Nevertheless, such a curious intimation born of seeing the journal had also directed him, though foregoing the benefit of any needless deep thinking on the matter, to believe that not only were there pages missing from the reproduction of the original journal, but also that those pages were of particular importance to someone out there somewhere.

In any event, the man picked up the notebook and put it carefully into his brief. He did not want to forget that he intended to send copies of certain pages contained within the ledger on to someone when he returned home. The second item hidden in the console was an emergency phone of anonymous ownership, which he left as it lay. The third item was a small, black felt bag, tightly noosed by a yellow satin drawstring, and which contained a syringe that was capped in plastic around the point of the needle. The syringe was filled about a third of the way with a syrupy, brown liquid that the man presumed was some of the finest heroin on the market. Time would tell regarding that supposition.

The man took a little time to mentally prepare for the injection. Once he was ready, he wasted no time rolling up his sleeve and steadily feeding the brown rhine within the syringe into the marked vein that ran visibly through the upper section of his left forearm. When the heroin hit his bloodstream with fiery, pulsating torrents, the man convulsed slightly and then tensed his body to control the onslaught of the euphoric discharge upon his senses. He continued to absorb the violent trauma of the invasive mini-bursts, which were boiling his blood and galvanizing his mind with a heavy and damply charged electric current, like a man who had crossed the desert gorging on water for the first time in days. After a short while, he was perfectly sedated.

As the rush of the drug continued while the heroin diffused throughout the entirety of his bloodstream, the man was transported away from the shallow concerns and emptiness of his solitary life. He was spared those anxieties that ran latently and in tandem with the subdued will of his subconscious, except in the rare moments that he disconnected from his professional considerations. The infusion's violent start soon gave way to the euphoric pleasures of his riddled endorphins. Shortly thereafter, the calming effects of the drug had taken hold, and the man nodded off to sleep with his soul unbound by earthly restraint but wholly exposed to the wants of the darker realms. He was swiftly met by an apparition that still haunted the remote corners of his heart, though he had falsely presumed to have buried the last of those feelings long ago.

Following the harsh shock of the nostrum to his system, the man slumped gently to the right until the side of his head and right shoulder came to rest at an awkward angle where the back passenger side door met the edge of his leather seat. As his sudden euphoria gave way to the extreme calm he was so desperately seeking, his thoughts began to rise in slow and distorted turns amidst the fading vapors of the brume of his induced delirium. Forms began to take shape within the grey mist of the sallow miasma of his mind and upon the settling plains of the unending havens of his essence. At that moment, the man saw his mother stitching the final buttons onto a shirt she had made for his father.

The buttons on the shirt were a bright blue and artfully accentuated. The soft, almost silky, cotton was of a golden hue, and the shirt's very fine material had been blended and woven to produce a slight sheen, which gave an ornate look and subtle elegance to the heavy threads of the shirt's alluring presence. The man's mother had spent months making the shirt while overcoming a lack of expertise in her chosen craft with love, care, and a heartfelt devotion to her task; a devotion that only those gifted with overriding compassion for the nurturing of those in their care can administer. The colors were carefully selected because they reminded her of the midsummer sun rising over the beach. Not just any beach, however, but the Carolina beach where she first clearly remembered converging with the boy's father, and the beach where the two had spent the night together in the hopes of resurrecting one another from the hollow wants of those from whom so much has been taken.

The bright blue buttons of the shirt perfectly highlighted that magical soft, sleek cotton of a lilting golden tincture, which comprised the majority of the shirt's fine material. No detail was missed by the neophyte seamstress. The oversized poet's collar was even double-stitched with fine and visible yet perfectly matching threads for emphasis. In the man's dream, which was overrun by the haunting vibrancy of the moving pictures emanating from those few remaining hollows of his heart that were still in possession of those raw and tender recollections; loving memories as it were, which had refused to be suffocated by his blinding drive to forget the horrors of his past by way of achieving his desired acquisition of worldly status and control, he continued to watch this woman of such simple yet elegant and delicate beauty, with no possessions of this world of any significance that were then given over to her care, translate and transcribe her greatest gift; the gift of the absolute wonder of her love and dedication, into her finest material creation yet. She had, in many ways, been reborn while crafting that shirt and while she awaited the arrival of her boy's handsome father, but she would be set free so easily.

When the last stitch to be made on the shirt was completed, the still beautiful woman called her son into the room to show him the finished product. The man came directly to the warming sound of her call. Although the shirt was far too big for the boy, he put it on with great excitement, which was currying the favor of his very essence. The smiling woman helped him work the buttons through the catches, her strong but delicate and lengthy fingers easily guiding the bright blue knobs into their set positions along the soft, sturdily crafted placket. The shirt draped down well past the boy's noticeably knobby knees. Nevertheless, with a total indifference given to the seemingly gargantuan size of the fine evening blouse, the boy rejoiced over the soft, heavy feel and the beauty of its shiny coloring.

The patiently handcrafted item was by far the nicest article of clothing that the boy had ever worn in his life. The enthralled child ran in celebratory circles around the room, letting the shirt flow over him like a satin robe catching a fine summer breeze. He relished the feel of the cool shifts of the fabric against his soft, warm skin. When the boy changed directions, the shirt caressed the length of his back and shifted along his outsized ribs. The heavy softness of the fine, weighty shirt was a pure delight to the enamored little boy's innocent sensibilities. After a few circular turns with his arms held out straight, turns that resembled the coursings of his imaginary airplane that flew about the house, the boy stopped in front of his brightly smiling mother and raised his hands in the air to exclaim, "This is the best shirt there ever was momma! I would wear it everywhere!"

The boy began circling the room again, moving on the tips of his toes and swaying his body from side to side to fully size up and experience the weight and feel of the fabric. "Maybe you can make one for me too, mommy. Then we won't look too poor to go to church anymore."

The boy said these words to his mother as he continued circling the room while waving his arms and flapping the sleeves of the shirt along the drawer fronts of the dresser, the end table, and the sides and corners of the bed. The boy's mother was still resting on her knees in the middle of the floor. Her feet were positioned directly under her so that she was approximately eye level with her beloved boy when she helped him button the shirt. She watched him smile and continue to run and take delight in the splendid creation that was the golden shirt with the blue buttons. Tears of sorrow welled up in her eyes while the boy darted behind her, but she kept all but one of those droplets from making its way onto the sides of her soft, perfectly sculpted cheeks. "I have so little to give him," the woman thought. "Surely, such a tender, smart, and loving creature deserves so much more in this life."

The woman calmed her emotions after a time. She once again plied her hopes against the mounting sorrows of her reality that the arrival of the boy's father would somehow fix their poverty and their isolation. Furthermore, and perhaps keenest to the sufferings of her heart, the woman hoped, almost beyond reason, that the boy's father would somehow rid her of that self-destructive and devouring sensation of guilt and loss that oftentimes ruled her every waking thought. Once again, she began to believe that there would be good and proper things in their future, maybe even gifts similar to a few of the finer things she possessed as a little girl. "Maybe, just maybe," the woman whispered aloud, "the three of us will one day watch the sunrise together on the very beach that the boy's father and I brought him into the world."

"Maybe, just maybe," she whispered a bit more forcefully in conjunction with her rising spirits, "they could watch that sunrise every day for all time." For but a brief respite within the cascading light that revealed her sweet boy's dancing happiness, it suddenly felt okay for the deeply troubled woman to dream again.

The boy's mother and father first remembered meeting in the way that lovers do on the night the boy was conceived. To say that their union on that lovely evening was star-crossed would depend on the convictions of the person evaluating the entirety of their brief but deep and feverish liaison. It could certainly be said that the meteoric affair flourished during the tender moments when the passions of those two young people, who had lost so much in such short amounts of time, reached out for and into each other with the intensified longing that was then present in the depths of their souls.

The two were certainly both wayward and rebelliously leaning by that point in their young lives. Their pasts had been riddled with the torrid maelstroms of misfortune and the intentional acts of an unknown but dark and foreboding presence. Yet, at that time, neither of them had been entirely consumed by the darker depravities of their circumstances. The once emergent young man and his spectacularly beautiful attaché still held out fledgling strands of hope for the future. The hope that some great love would rise from the depths of the ashes littering their bleak existence was the singular virtue shared between them that remained as a light flickering in the darkness.

On that night, they were just two saddened, broken, and completely mortal creatures looking for anything to fill the void of the overwhelming emptiness they felt deep within. Neither of them was capable of sustaining love in all of the ways that love must be nurtured, or perhaps even any of the ways that cause love to be real. On that night, the man and the woman were merely casting the dying embers of what remained alight in their hearts into the unknown souls of each other in the hopes that a spark might exist there. Their shared needs to somehow be made whole again were consumed in a united, untamed, and lustful energy. One that blazed brightly in an unavailing manner and then flamed out, like dying celestial bodies with an ill-conceived desire to become one with something else by discharging what little remained of their hotly burning sustenance.

When the shifting realities and the yoke of the basic and perceived needs of life were set upon the handsome pair once again, in the form of the sun rising into another day in this instance, their fears and weaknesses proved too much to allow them to hold together, but for a momentary final flicker of their already wind-bent flames. When they paused during the night, they marveled in awe at the multitude of stars above them, shining brightly in the night sky. They watched the sun break over the horizon with a sense of amazement. When that brilliant light of morning first broke, they wondered in unison and amidst a perfect silence, which was broken only by the soft lull of the sea and the intermittent calls of the ducking seabirds, how such beauty was given over to each new day, and that, given this truth, how the horrors they had experienced could be and would continue to be quite real. They stared out at the glory of that perfect morning as two wounded birds stuck on the sand, realizing that they no longer carried the courage for love upon their broken wings. They sat there in silence until the tide came into the place on the beach where they rested shoulder to shoulder, yet still very much alone, penitent, and spent.

Their toes curled in the soft coolness of the sand. The bottom of her right foot smoothed and pushed the firmer sand beneath the dry layers into cupped ridges as the friction of her motions tickled her heel. With the water continuing to rise to meet them at the spot where they lingered as naught but two of Charleston's lost children trying only to forget, the boy's father took his mother's hand as he rose from his spot at her side. He had a business proposition that required his attention; a prospect that just might change his circumstances permanently for the better if he played his hand well.

When the man's soon-to-be father turned to head up the beach, he squeezed the tips of her fingers gently. He then let her hand drop as he stepped backwards towards his destination. He said not a word to her, for one word was too many and a thousand words were not enough. He looked upon her face one last time, and he thought right then that she must be an angel.

While he watched her at the last, the amber of her eyes took hold of the low light of the sun. The disarming beauty of the phenomenon added a golden clarion to the simple elegance of her well-defined cheeks; her angular and pointed nose that was so perfectly rounded at the tip; the light freckles below the rounded hollows of her eyes; and the straightness and fortitude of her exquisitely sculpted lips. Moreover, her gentle brow and the stridency of her chin, in conjunction with the gleaming of those eyes, gave notice of a will and a rising fortitude that shone with such promise for just that short while on that perfect morning.

The man's father smiled brightly at her, and he smiled brightly within while he turned to continue toward his destination on that newly gifted day. As his steps continued up the soft, cool sand of the beach, he felt a great unease rise within him, and he stopped. When he looked back at her again, he pitied her deeply while she continued to sit motionless and fixated upon the rising sun. Her thick, handsomely cropped, black hair was resting wildly in wet, salted musters along the perfect smoothness of her well-tanned neck and the strong and supple dimple of her cowl. The man knew at that moment that she expected nothing further from him, but he also understood that she hoped for so much.

It was indeed a fact that most men in the area would have attributed the direction of his choppy ambulation along and over the miniature cascading dunes of sand of the high beach to some temporary form of insanity raging deep within him. It was also true that this same sampling of men would have been accurate. She was indeed that beautiful. While she may have been lost and without her proper scion amongst those of the high caste of her native haunts, she still possessed a deep, athletic, and intelligently wild beauty. To those who were unaware of her somewhat twisted and unsavory legend, hers was a beauty that most men would have paid dearly for if they had been granted the benefaction of having laid eyes on her for any length of time and the grace of having watched her navigate the world for only the burning flash of an instant, desiring nothing more for days on end than the attention of her smile and some small taste of the sweet richness of her lips.

The woman continued to stare into the colorful depths of the horizon. She stared out where the ocean met the sky along the vanishing line, a trick played on her eyes and subtly highlighted across the expanse of the panorama by the glow of the large, low-hanging sphere that pierced the distant clouds and radiated brightly along the gently chopping water. She wondered how long it had been since that terrible night when she lost everything and was set upon the wilderness. She wondered why she had given her mind so wholeheartedly to the plagues of remorse and addiction and the accompanying prostitution of her body, which at most times occurred in trade for little more than shallow, fleeting comforts.

Though she was alone, she asked the questions that continued to haunt her without end. "What would my baby look like if it were alive? Did my parents forgive me before my anger and recklessness killed them all? Do they forgive me now? Was there any form of endearing love to be had in this world gone mad?"

Not but a moment later, the woman's thoughts shifted to a more positive bent as she became briefly but fervently inspired by the beauty of God's canvas now painted in the sky and on the endless sea chopping before her eyes. She whispered to the heavens, "Surely the beauty of this new day set so splendidly before me bears witness to a tender yet enduring thing such as love. Will the one who left my side not feel anything of the glory of this new shine?"

Sadly, the remaining qualities of her inner strength that the tragedies of her life had not yet taken when she was staring into that majestic sunrise, the demons always lurking in the shadows were preparing to have. They were preparing to have all of her, and they were only to be held at bay for a moment upon the biding of their time. Once the boy's father had made the top of the beachhead, she was again alone and ill-prepared to outlast them for long while locked within the impenetrable confines of her solitude.

The man sent to her had missed his prompting and the immediate appointment to restore this broken angel of the Heavenly Father. He had been called to restore her inner beauty and her solemn strength to their rightful place while she still dared to dance on the sands of those beaches. Be that as it may, he was still moving inland amidst the chaparral and the waves of bending beach grass. He was vanishing before her eyes. At the distance she marked him, his recognizable features were nearly lost to her sight well before the rising sun transformed from that of its giant, lambent state and produced the full and absolute illumination that would take its proper hold of the coastline until the day's end. To her, that man was swiftly becoming a vanishing illusion. Each of his steps were taken together in one solitary moment in time with a predetermined destination; away.

He was present still. He could have heard her voice had she compelled her words with urgency and an invigorated inflection to travel along the soft, steady breeze and up to the long, bending grasses of the last of the shallow dunes. Yet, she had not yet learned the words that could transcend the broken hollows of their two hearts. Therefore, she was silent.

In a moment marked by the first pushes for life of a neophyte known to only God, the full light of day was then pronounced. It was pronounced suddenly and without a defining moment in time that noticeably marked the final stages of the ambient glow of the pre-dawn, which she hoped would continue forever, and the clarifying illumination of the entire measure of the sun's white and gracious shine. With the fullness of the aurora, the radiant orange and pink glow of the sky and the golden sheen running across the water to the ends of the earth were replaced by the clear light of day and pristine light blues, which now claimed the entire panorama above the illusory depths of the horizon. As the visions put forth from the sky normalized, she began to cast a long shadow backward along the sand; a shadow that, like her man of the soft, tender moments of the preceding darkness and the brume, now pointed directly westward and inland. Then he was gone, and the sounds of the small pulsating waves caught between the receding tide and their initial drive to the beach took hold of her attention.

There was an eternal peace tied to the unbroken pattern of sound and the continuum of the gentle, rolling undulations of the repeating waves. The subtle and rhythmic urgings of that endless sea fit her desire at the moment of his departure to just be. For a brief moment, the peaceful lulls and easy starts of the water dulled her constant search for answers she would never find without some newly formed and proper context. In precisely the manner of a downward drifting spark sent from the heavens to cross the clear night sky, the reality of his diminishing presence faded into the ether of her thoughts, though the marks of his feet were still being made upon the drying sand of the shallow dunes up at the beachhead.

To her, he was already a distant memory. One that was but a tangential glimmer of that once radiant golden sheen angling off of the water directly upon the soft amber of her shining eyes; those haunting orbs that rested above the catching firmness of her tanned and freckled cheeks. He was a beautiful glimmer that for a fleeting moment had punctuated her fixed yet sorrowful resplendence, which now faced the rising approach of the morning sun and the revelations of the day to come. For no matter what direction that man traversed from there, she would be with child.

The confused young man off in the distance, taking heed of nothing but his shattered and feeble command of the affairs of the mortal world, which were readying to once again be flung in discordant and rapid convulsions at that same new day, he continued walking down the beachhead hand in hand with the devil. He was off to do that one's bidding in the hopes of better prospects for the future. Such was the sad reality of just one man in a world groomed to understand expectation, always at the expense of the priceless treasures hidden in the present moment of the very hour at hand.

ABOUT THE AUTHOR

Ronan James Cassidy has spent time living in various regions throughout the United States. His primary field of interest is colonial literature from the Americas, Ireland, Africa, and India. Mr. Cassidy also possesses a graduate degree in finance and spent several years studying the evolution of the current monetary order.

Ronan was inspired to write Margaret Anne and the Redemption series that follows as a loose yet captivating metaphor for his journey towards devoted faithfulness to God and the tearing down of the veils of deceit so rampant in the modern age. His website is https://ronanjamescassidy.com.

In addition to his three beautiful daughters, his father, his four brothers, and his stepmother, all of Mr. Cassidy's writings are dedicated to the tireless hours his devoted mother spent living her life as an eternal example of the joys of enduring love and assisting her son with the creation of his published works.

Printed in the United States
by Baker & Taylor Publisher Services